PENGU[...]

The Wi[...]

Praise for Nicci Gerrard's novels:

'Beguiling, poignant, wonderful' *Sunday Express*

'Acutely observed, this is modern relationship territory with a twist' *Elle*

'Unpretentious and page-turning' *Independent*

'Truthful and wise . . . this is a fine anti-romance' *Daily Mail*

'A quietly impressive novel that isn't afraid to take on the big themes of life, love and the inescapable influences of families' *Guardian*

'A skilfully observed book about grief, sibling relations and first love' *Company*

'A thoughtful tale of love, sibling rivalry and family secrets' *Vogue*

'A moving and perceptive insight into deception and renewal' *Sunday Mirror*

'A heartening story of a woman betrayed by her husband who slowly realizes she has her own passions and dreams to follow' *Good Housekeeping*

The Winter House

NICCI GERRARD

PENGUIN BOOKS

PENGUIN BOOKS

Published by the Penguin Group
Penguin Books Ltd, 80 Strand, London WC2R ORL, England
Penguin Group (USA) Inc., 375 Hudson Street, New York, New York 10014, USA
Penguin Group (Canada), 90 Eglinton Avenue East, Suite 700, Toronto, Ontario, Canada M4P 2Y3
(a division of Pearson Penguin Canada Inc.)
Penguin Ireland, 25 St Stephen's Green, Dublin 2, Ireland
(a division of Penguin Books Ltd)
Penguin Group (Australia), 250 Camberwell Road, Camberwell, Victoria 3124, Australia
(a division of Pearson Australia Group Pty Ltd)
Penguin Books India Pvt Ltd, 11 Community Centre, Panchsheel Park, New Delhi – 110 017, India
Penguin Group (NZ), 67 Apollo Drive, Rosedale, North Shore 0632, New Zealand
(a division of Pearson New Zealand Ltd)
Penguin Books (South Africa) (Pty) Ltd, 24 Sturdee Avenue, Rosebank, Johannesburg 2196, South Africa

Penguin Books Ltd, Registered Offices: 80 Strand, London WC2R ORL, England

www.penguin.com

First published 2009
7

Copyright © Joined-up Writing, 2009
All rights reserved

The moral right of the author has been asserted

Set in 12.5/14.75 pt Monotype Garamond
Typeset by Rowland Phototypesetting Ltd, Bury St Edmunds, Suffolk
Printed in England by Clays Ltd, St Ives plc

ISBN: 978-0-141-02407-3

www.greenpenguin.co.uk

Penguin Books is committed to a sustainable future
for our business, our readers and our planet.
The book in your hands is made from paper
certified by the Forest Stewardship Council.

To Jackie, Tim and Kate

Chapter One

The phone call came at a quarter to eight, when it still wasn't fully light outside; a chilly drizzle spattered the window-panes and spread a fine gauze over the skyline, so that nothing was entirely clear and rooftops and trees acquired a blurred, mysterious air. Marnie hesitated. Her slice of bread was under the grill and already done on one side; her coffee was brewing in the cafetière; a newspaper lay open on the table beside the plate and the jar of marmalade. This was her peaceful time of the day. She had already been out for a run and taken a shower. Now she was wearing her dressing-gown, scrubbed and virtuous, the pleasurable ache of exercise in her limbs, in a kitchen that smelt of toast, detergent and the basil that grew in a pot on the window-sill, which she watered every morning. Eva and her boyfriend would be asleep for hours, the door shut on the unimaginable squalor of their room. The unblemished day lay ahead of her. Reluctantly, she picked up the phone.

'Hello? Marnie here.'

'Marnie?' The voice, overlaid by a static crackle, was not one she immediately placed, though it was oddly familiar and, as certain smells can, awoke a powerful but elusive memory.

'Yes, speaking.'

'This is Oliver. Oliver Fenton.'

'Oliver?' She frowned, and her grip tightened on the phone. The morning tipped into strangeness. 'But – I mean, what –?'

'I know this is unexpected. I'm calling about Ralph.'

'Wait,' said Marnie. 'Please hold on for just one moment.' She put the phone down carefully, noticing that her hands were shaking slightly, and went to turn off the grill. The toast was just beginning to burn, its crust singeing. She poured herself half a cup of coffee and picked up the phone again, turning her back on the ordered morning she had prepared for herself and looking instead out of the window. In the flats opposite, a man in boxer shorts was eating cereal straight out of the packet. 'Sorry,' she said. 'I had to – Ralph, you said?'

'You need to come and see him.' The voice bounced, losing syllables. It sounded as though Oliver was shouting through a high wind.

'I need to come and see him,' she repeated stupidly. 'I don't understand.'

'He's dying.' A young woman in combat trousers carrying a polystyrene cup of coffee was passing beneath the window now; Marnie gazed down at the straight white parting in her sleek black ponytail. She walked very gracefully, like a dancer. 'Marnie?'

'I'm still here.'

'I'm sorry.'

'I can't hear you very well.'

'I said, he's dying. And he wants to see you.'

'But I –'

'He's in his cottage in Scotland. I've booked you on a flight to the nearest airport. It's about sixty miles from here.'

'Hang on. I can't simply – as if –'

'The plane leaves at three twenty this afternoon. From Stansted. You just need to show your passport.'

'I have to go to work today.'

'Someone will meet you there,' continued Oliver, as if she hadn't spoken.

'You're breaking up.'

'I said, someone will meet you there. OK?'

'Oliver, wait! You have to tell me – I mean, *why*?'

'I can't do it alone,' he said. Or she thought he said, through the crackle.

'Wait!' The wind blew down the line at her and she shuddered, imagining she could feel its cold breath against her skin. 'How long for?' she shouted against it. 'Hello? Oliver? Are you still there? Can you hear me? Damn.'

Frowning, she returned the phone to its cradle. Her hands were no longer trembling, but she felt cold and oddly heavy. She took a gulp of coffee, but it was tepid and bitter, so she poured it down the sink. She threw the toast into the bin. Put the marmalade back on the shelf. Folded the paper so the headline ('Family die in fire') was no longer showing, and sat at the table, shutting her eyes and resting her head in her hands. She wanted to think but for a while no thoughts came, no images, even, just a voice in the darkness repeating words that made little sense. 'It's Ralph . . . He's dying . . .'

When she lifted her head again, the room seemed suddenly unfamiliar to her, as if she had already left it, and it had receded into her past, like a story that was over: a small, well-lit space; four chairs pushed against the wooden table she had rescued from a skip and restored;

well-stocked cupboards; shelves lined with herbs; the calendar on the wall turned to December – a bare tree spreading its boughs across an empty winter landscape. There was a small whiteboard on the door, items to remember written on it in red felt-tip. 'Milk', 'Bin bags', 'Phone council', 'B'day cards to Claire, Martin and Anna'. It was snug and functional, like a cabin on a great liner. Returning from work in the evening, she would look up at her illuminated window, and it would seem to her that her flat was bobbing in the buoyant darkness above.

Perhaps she would simply ignore the phone call, pretend that it had never happened. Then her life could continue on the same tack, a steady course that over the last months had consoled her. But even as she thought this, imagining herself going smoothly through her unchanged day, she was making plans. She heated up a second cup of coffee in the microwave and made a list in her head of all the things she needed to do, her mind skittering across the icy surface of the news and trying not to break through into scary waters. Pack a few clothes – it would be cold in the north of Scotland in December. Walking boots and thick sweaters, gloves, thermal socks. Layers: that was what her mother had always counselled whenever Marnie was packing, and she seemed to have been packing for most of her life. Ralph was dying – at least, Oliver had said so, but it didn't feel true or even possible. Passport, although it was only a domestic flight. A couple of books. Her notebook. Travel light – how long would she be gone, anyway? A day? Two? More? For a moment, Ralph's face flashed into view, vivid with life, youthful with time unaccounted for, smiling at her as she sat befuddled in her kitchen. She felt a vicious pinch of panic. He couldn't die. He couldn't leave yet. Tampons, toothbrush, makeup, migraine tablets. She hadn't asked how he was dying. Had he been hit by a car? Or perhaps a stroke, so now his mobile face was slack and lopsided. Would she even recognize him?

Eight o'clock: only fifteen minutes had passed since Oliver's phone call. She needed to tell Elaine that she wouldn't be at work for the next day or so, and she knew Elaine would not be best pleased. Marnie worked in a puppet museum in Soho, just a few minutes from her flat, and Elaine was the owner. She was a short, fat, squashy American woman of indeterminate age who lived in Chichester with her cats, wore mustard-coloured leggings and prickly woollen jerseys, carried her purse (often containing great wads of cash) in a plastic bag, talked in bursts of furious speed, and was as sharp as a tack. She was also, it seemed, very rich, although Marnie had never discovered how, and the museum – which was really too small, dark, dusty and strange to deserve such a name – was one of her hobbies on which she occasionally, fiercely, lavished her attention and money until she forgot about it once more. She never expected it to make a profit and it never did.

Indeed, unpublicized and hidden down an obscure side-street, few people seemed to know of its existence. There were entire days when Marnie would receive not a single visitor; she would spend her time rearranging the items that were for sale, dusting exhibits, cleaning windows, making cups of coffee. Sometimes, turning the handmade 'Open' sign to 'Closed', she would play truant for half an hour or so and wander round Soho, speeding past shops where leather corsets and alarming sex aids stood in the windows, but lingering in places that sold Indian wedding shawls or battered second-hand books of engravings.

Nevertheless, Elaine liked her to be at the museum from nine thirty until six, except on Wednesday and Sunday when it was closed to the public. You could hire it then for parties, apparently, although nobody had done so in Marnie's time: the rooms were too small, the stairway too narrow, there was no kitchen and only one tiny lavatory, which was squeezed into the space between the Sicilian marionettes and the shelves of tiny finger puppets.

Marnie dialled the number.

Elaine answered on the first ring. 'Hello.'

'Elaine, it's me, Marnie – I hope I didn't wake you.'

'Nonsense – it's past eight. What time do you think I get up?'

'It's just . . . I have a problem. I've got to take a few days off work.'

'Are you ill?'

'No, not me. A friend.' She hesitated. 'A good friend. I've got to go to Scotland.'

'When?'

'Today.'

'Oh!' Elaine gave a small grumbling sigh. Marnie could hear her tapping her stubby fingers on a surface. 'Well, if you've got to go, you've got to go. I'll just have to try and find someone to cover. We can't have the museum closed while you're away, can we?'

'I was thinking, I know someone who might be able

6

to stand in. She's young, not quite twenty, but she's –'
Marnie broke off. 'Responsible. And she knows the
museum already – she's spent time there with me. She
loves it.'

'Who's this paragon?'

'Eva. She's my, um, niece, kind of.'

It was simpler than saying that Eva was her ex-
stepdaughter.

'I didn't know you had siblings.'

'No – well, it's complicated.'

'This Eva, when could she start?'

'Today, I'm sure. She's staying in my flat, so I could
show her the ropes before I go.'

'Hmm. Responsible, you say?'

'Yes.' Marnie said it more assertively this time, swallowing her misgivings.

'Does she know about this?'

'I thought I'd ask you first. But I'm sure she'll want to
do it – she's looking for work.'

That wasn't quite right, of course: for the past ten days,
Eva had been thinking about looking for work or, even,
planning to think about it.

'All right, then. If you vouch for her.'

'I do.'

'And, Marnie . . .'

'Yes?'

'Your friend, I hope she – he? – will be all right.'

'Thank you.' For a moment, the knowledge of what
she was going to flooded through Marnie and she stood
breathless, although she was half conscious that it wasn't
only fear she was feeling but a kind of mysterious, tingling

excitement. There were moments when certainty dropped away and you were left in a high and lonely place, dizzy with precariousness. She put out a hand to touch the table, pressed her bare toes into the tiles. She wanted to add something, but all she could think was 'His name is Ralph.' Saying his name out loud brought meaning closer. And when had she last spoken it?

Elaine's tone became brisk again. 'Right. Give this Eva my phone number in case of emergencies.'

'Of course. Thanks, Elaine.'

'Take care now.'

'I will. You too.'

Marnie made another pot of coffee, extra strong. She heated some milk and sloshed it into two mugs, adding a teaspoon of sugar to one. Then, holding both in one hand, she rapped sharply at Eva's door. Waited. Rapped again.

'Hnnuff?'

'Eva?' She pushed the door with a toe and it swung open a few inches before it was blocked by some unseen obstacle. 'Good morning.'

''Stime?'

'I've brought you both some coffee.'

Marnie squeezed through the door, wading over soft drifts of discarded clothes and occasional crunchy objects – a CD case, a mobile phone, a wallet – to the futon where Eva and her boyfriend Gregor lay. She could make out Gregor's soft brown locks, a single squinting eye, and one hand, outflung so that his fingers trailed on the littered carpet, but Eva was invisible. A sequined cushion, made by Marnie many years ago, lay squarely over her face, and the duvet was wrapped around her body. Only three toes, with dark purple nails, peeked out at the end of the bed. What was more, there was a third body in the room, sprawled on the floor dressed only in boxers and one sock, with a T-shirt of Eva's covering his face. An irregular snore whistled through it and his hairless chest rose and fell peacefully.

The curtained room was full of a sour morning smell, mixed with tobacco and perfume. Marnie wrinkled her nose. Until Eva had turned up, this had been her small workroom. Now all her tools and materials were stacked in shoeboxes and large bags under her bed and on top of her wardrobe. In their place, Eva and Gregor had scattered their things like farmers sowing seed. It felt like a mathematical impossibility: they had so few possessions yet they made so much mess with them.

'I wouldn't have woken you, only there's an emergency.'

A snuffling query came from under the cushion. Gregor's long fingers curled into a fist that was retracted under the covers. He gave a wounded sigh. The man on the floor shifted slightly.

'You've got a job. Eva, do you hear me?'

'Job?'

'Yes. You said you were looking for a job. Now you've got one.'

'I'm hibernating.'

'I'm putting two mugs of coffee down. I didn't know you had a visitor. Don't spill them. So this is where all my mugs have got to. Some are growing mould. Listen, I've got to go away for a few days.'

Eva pulled the cushion off her face, though her eyes remained screwed tightly shut. She aimed her blind glance in Marnie's direction. 'When?'

'Today. In a few hours. You're taking my place.'

The eyes opened a crack. 'I am?'

'Yes.'

'In your museum?'

'Right.'

'Oh.' The eyes shut again.

'Don't go back to sleep again. Eva! I'm turning on the light – are you ready? I'm going to take you there in, let's see, half an hour or so. I'll show you how everything works and leave you.'

'Half an hour!'

'Yes. Please, Eva. This is important.'

'Why?'

'Because I need to leave before –'

'No.' Eva struggled to a half-sitting position and pushed back a tangle of black hair. 'Why are you going?'

'I'll tell you when you're out of bed and dressed.'

'Marnie!'

'Ten minutes. I'll get you something to eat.'

''K.'

'Remember your coffee before it gets cold.'

'Yeah, yeah.'

Marnie retreated, pulling shut the door. In her own room, she put on a black corduroy skirt, thin T-shirt, pale grey V-necked jersey and a pair of old black boots, then pulled her holdall out of the cupboard. It still had its last air ticket attached to the handle and in a side pocket a small spray deodorant and a hairbrush. She added knickers, bras, several pairs of socks and toiletries. Hardly pausing to think, she selected a pair of jeans, three shirts, another jersey, the dressing-gown she'd just got out of. What else? Shampoo, toothbrush. Passport, with six years left before it expired. Four years ago she'd looked much younger – a kind of softness about her face that had since been chiselled away. She pulled her belted grey coat out of the wardrobe and threw it on top of her bag.

Knocking at Eva's door again as she passed, she returned to the kitchen and put two *panini* into the oven. A *panino* with Marmite and melted cheese was Eva's current favourite breakfast (previously, it had been a cinnamon bagel). She was a slender young woman, everything about her – wrists, ankles, thin face, shallow hips and narrow shoulders – delicate, almost breakable, but she ate with the gusto of a brickie at the end of a hard day. Marnie didn't know where it went: Eva rarely did any exercise and was as indolent as a cat lying in a puddle of sunlight.

Eva and her younger sister Luisa were probably the reasons why Marnie had stayed with their father, Fabio, for as long as she had. Perhaps they were the reason she'd fallen in love with him in the first place; that and the need that had filled her body, top to toe, to have a child herself. When she had first met the girls, they were nine and just seven: shock-headed, springy-limbed waifs with dark eyes who'd been motherless for a year and a half and who had about them, in their different ways, a neediness that had overwhelmed Marnie with a maternal desire to protect them that she had never quite shaken off, just learnt to hide. Luisa, mild and painfully shy, had trusted Marnie at once, climbing into bed between her and Fabio, slipping her small hand into hers on the way to school each morning, allowing Marnie to tie her unruly hair into plaits and choose her clothes with her; Eva had ignored her, then sneered at her in front of Fabio, trying to humiliate her out of her patience, then fought her, once even spat at her, like a wild cat, and finally accepted her in a gust of tears.

Marnie had steered both girls through hormonal rushes, friendship worries, periods, exams, first boyfriends, hangovers. She had taught them how to cook English food as well as Italian; how to use oil paints and watercolours; how to sew, knit, mend pots and change plugs. They had shown her Florence, Siena and Pisa, and corrected her Italian grammar. She had taken them sailing, as her own mother had taken her, and as the salty spume licked over her face and she saw them laughing while the little boat bucked through the waves, she told herself to remember this moment and call it by its proper name: happiness. She had held them when they wept. She had giggled with them. She had never had that baby with Fabio and bit by bit, like a fog gradually lifting, she had come to see that Fabio was off not-having-babies with other women as well, returning to her after each one with an exuberant, penitent tenderness that should have warned her long before it did. Leaving him was easy; leaving them was perhaps the hardest thing she had ever done – except that by the time she did, they were leaving too. And then, a few weeks ago, Eva had turned up on her doorstep with a small bag and a large, dishevelled Polish boyfriend. She'd come, she had said off-handedly, to stay for a bit and look for work before travelling – that was all right, wasn't it? And Marnie, hiding her grateful joy under an equally casual manner, said that of course it was fine; she should stay as long as she wanted.

She grated cheese over the *panini*, popped them back under the grill, then opened the kitchen door. 'Eva! Come on!'

'One minute.'

'It's been more than fifteen already.'

When Eva finally made it into the kitchen, her high shoes tick-tacking over the tiles, she was wearing a short, swinging green skirt over patterned tights, an orange long-sleeved shirt, half unbuttoned to show a pink top beneath it. She was festooned with necklaces, bright bangles jangled on her wrists and earrings rattled in her small lobes; a stud glittered in her nostril. Her fingernails were painted vermilion, her eyelids turquoise, her lashes dark blue, her lips a luscious red.

'Good Lord,' said Marnie, feeling suddenly cheerful in spite of the phone call. 'You make my eyes throb.'

'I thought I should make an effort.' Although her English was fluent, her intonation still pattered, a tuneful machine-gun.

'Who's the man on your floor?'

'I'm not sure,' said Eva, vaguely. 'He did tell me. We met him last night. He missed his last train home. Is this for me?' She took a large bite of *panino*, and threads of melted cheese attached to her pointed, determined chin.

Marnie saw that she had a small spiral painted – or tattooed? – on her collarbone. 'You look like an emergency flare. At least it's quite dark in the museum. That'll mute you a bit. Anyway, there might not be any customers to scare off. Some days are very quiet.'

Eva perched on a chair. 'So, tell me. Where are you off to, all dressed in black and grey like a nun?'

'To see a friend who's ill.'

'A friend? A man friend, by any chance?'

'Someone I knew a long time ago.'

'Before Babbo?'

'Long before.'

'A mystery. How ill is he?'

Marnie didn't reply: in the face of Eva's concern she found that she couldn't. There was a hook in her throat. She bit her lip hard and stared out of the window. Three young women rippled past in the increasing rain; a traffic warden, trudging head down; a father and his tiny child, who was swaddled in a colourful scarf and had a bobble hat pulled down over his brow.

'It's that bad?' said Eva. 'Oh dear. Dear-dear-dear.' She had a motherly side: she tutted soothingly and her small hand, heavy with cheap rings, was stroking Marnie's shoulder.

'I'm not sure when I'll be back. It won't be long. A few days. Maybe I'll be home tomorrow. I'll ring. You'll be all right?'

'Certainly I'll be all right.'

'And you'll –'

'And I'll look after the flat and not make too much noise at night and I'll make sure everything's all right at your work. Can I borrow your pink woolly jacket?'

'Sure,' said Marnie. 'I expect you to plunder my wardrobe. It makes me feel I'm still your stepmother.'

'You'll always be my stepmother. My other mother.'

'That's all right, then. We should make a move.'

But she tarried for a moment, then took a crooked striped mug from the sideboard and from the cupboard a small glass jar of whole nutmegs and a pot of local honey. Eva watched her with a glinting stare but didn't ask any questions.

The museum had a Dickensian pokiness about it that had probably been one of its contrary selling-points for Elaine. She had fallen for its quaint, uncomfortable Englishness, its warped shutters and narrow staircase, and was unfailingly delighted when other people – not her, because of her short stature – bumped their heads on its beams. It was squeezed between a sixties office building and a down-at-heel house that had been divided into several unsatisfactory flats. Its three narrow storeys looked out, at the back, onto a tiny yard. Marnie had been clearing it of its accumulated junk (a child's broken tricycle, a stack of assorted roof tiles, tins of hardened paint, a rotting door), and was planning to stock it with potted shrubs and perhaps an apple tree. She was going to buy a bird table, and she had even started a compost heap in the corner, which she fed with customers' coffee grounds, teabags and orange peel. Marnie had never managed to cure herself of her home-making compulsion. If she was staying in an anonymous hotel room for just one night, she would still unpack her bag into the drawers, line up her toothbrush, hairbrush, face cream and shampoo as if she was settling in for the long haul. Ralph used to tease her about it. He used to call her 'Mother Hen'. He would lay his thin, untidy body at her feet and tell her not to clear him up as well.

'The bulbs are always going,' said Marnie, unlocking the door. 'There are spare ones in the big cupboard.' She switched on the lights and at once the shapes hanging from beams and sagging on shelves came to life. She had never quite got used to the eerie effect of so many puppets watching her with their painted eyes, their sectioned jaws gaping and leering, their spindly hands dangling by their sides and their legs folded under them. She was quite well acquainted with them all by now: she knew their names, their ages (some of them were hundreds of years old), their origins. She could tell visitors which came from Sicily, which from Indonesia, which were home grown. She had repaired many of their costumes – this Japanese silk kimono, for example, she had stitched back together, and she had fashioned a new sword for one of the old wooden warriors in the back room and a fan for the courtesan, whose hickory cheeks were painted scarlet. The large, shabby dragon near the entrance, which children loved, had newly mended seams. She had polished Orlando's armour. Sometimes, when she was alone, she would gently lift one down from its perch and walk it over the floor, the lozenge-shaped feet drumming the boards, the arms lifting jerkily as if to ward off a sudden blow. Some were ornate – like the twenty-eight-inch princess from Burma – and upstairs many of the others were simple hand puppets. There were several topsy-turvy dolls among them and a few that reminded her of the papier-mâché puppets she'd made at school, dipping shreds of newspaper into water and glue, and laying them over the crudely fashioned Plasticine head. There were some inflexible figures, too, mounted on sticks, and others that barely earned the title 'puppet' at all. Her favourite was the small, blunt-faced dog from Papua New Guinea, whose crumbling, legless body was made of bark.

Marnie turned on the heating, stacked leaflets and post-cards on the front desk, showed Eva where the coffee and tea were, and how to operate the till. You could buy cheap puppets here – animals with foolish faces, villains with moustaches, kings with crowns and jesters with surprised eyebrows – and also the flatpack of a bright miniature theatre, complete with tiny cardboard characters you could colour yourself and move around on sticks. Marnie would have adored it as a girl: she tingled with nostalgia whenever she sold one.

'Do you think,' asked Eva, running a finger over the shelf where cardboard masks were stacked to inspect it for dust, 'that you and Babbo will ever –'

'No.'

'That's very – What's the word?'

'Unequivocal?'

'I don't think that was it. You shouldn't have left us.'

'I didn't leave you, I left him – and, anyway, I only left what was already long gone. You know that. In any case, this isn't the right time to talk about it.'

'I know. I always start talking just when the other person's about to leave. It's a bad habit. There must be some psychological explanation, but I don't know what it is.'

'Well, *I*'m going to leave now. You're sure you'll be all right?'

'Don't worry so. I'm grown-up now, remember?'

'And is Gregor –'

'Staying? Yes. You asked that before. But he'll behave, OK? We'll both behave. We won't drink all your wine and trash the place.'

'So I'll be going, then.'

'You will be, yes.' Eva slitted her eyes. 'Don't you have a plane to catch?'

'Yes.' She reached out and removed an imaginary hair from Eva's shoulders, just for the comfort of touching her and breathing in her familiar smell. Under the tobacco smoke, camomile, lemon and balsam, she was sharp and clean. They hugged. Eva's soft black hair rustled on her neck and her warm, grassy breath blew against her cheeks.

'Good luck,' said Eva, as she left.

As the plane took off, Marnie leant against the window; her forehead bumped gently against the smeary oval. The sky was a stewed brown. Through it, she briefly glimpsed a scattering of houses, patchwork hills and then the curve of the Thames. Somewhere down there her day was continuing but without her in it. Eva was sitting in the gloom of the museum, tapping her glossy nails or smiling at a customer with her full red mouth. Heavy-limbed, white-faced, silent Gregor was occupying her flat and filling it with his own smell of beer, tobacco, Polish food. Her mother was lying in her small plot of ground, beneath needles of winter rain. And the other two, of course – but they had died so long ago that their graves were shallow, grassy mounds, one so small that it was scarcely visible. Then there was David – he lay somewhere down there as well, although Marnie tried not to think about him too much, pushing his memory to the muddy floor of her consciousness, where occasionally it stirred, sending up dark clouds in which she could detect no shape, just a vague dread. Ahead of her were Ralph and Oliver: her past had flipped and lay waiting in her future. After months of peaceful inactivity, of repair and slow consideration, she was on a journey again. And although the journey was to say goodbye, she felt again a throb of excitement. Something was happening. Life was shifting under her feet.

Chapter Two

She had landed in a different world. She climbed from the plane into the grip of winter, which had not yet arrived in London and perhaps never would, not like this. She was hit by a bitter, stinging cold that made her nose ache and the tips of her fingers start to pulse, and she pulled her scarf over her chin and mouth. Though it was only mid-afternoon, the sun had sunk below the skyline and the moon had risen to float its tilted crescent above the frosted landscape. On either side of the runway, she could see fields; in one, horses were grazing, apparently undisturbed by the noise of planes, while another was ploughed and looked, in the twilight, like a lumpily frozen sea. Beyond, the massed shapes of pine and birch trees stood against the sky. Her worn boots slid on the tarmac, where ice glistened.

The airport resembled a shack, and already the baggage was being unloaded onto a carousel that looped jerkily round the arrivals room. Marnie went to the Ladies, through a rackety door into a room lit by a bare bulb. She examined her face in the mirror, not out of vanity or anxiety so much as to remind herself of what she actually looked like: she half expected to see a stranger staring back at her, or perhaps her younger self, the one Ralph had first known. But no, it was her all right, with crow's feet around her eyes, the first tiny threads stitched above her lip, the brackets faintly grooved between nose and mouth, the hair that had darkened over the years, the eyes that were – and had always been – calm. Indeed, she felt quite calm. Her heart beat slowly; her hands were steady; she felt clear-headed, though strangely distant from what was happening. She leant forward until she could see the flecks in her irises and the fine hatchings in her pale skin. Fabio had told her, long after she had moved in with him but before he had turned his eyes to other women, that when they first met he had barely noticed her, but that she had 'grown' on him so that one day he had realized he found her beautiful. And Ralph had once said that, more than anyone he had ever known, she could make herself invisible. When she had protested that she didn't do it deliberately, he shook his head, not believing her. 'You like to watch,' he had said. 'You stand in the shadows, seeing but not being seen. You're a *spy*, Marnie.'

Marnie left the toilet, picked up her bag from the carousel and, squaring her shoulders, walked through the swing doors and out into the hall, where strip lighting stuttered onto stained white tiles and a single car-hire desk. Everyone else seemed to know where they were going, swinging purposefully out into the chilly darkness to the vehicle that waited in the small car park over the road, or hugging a waiting partner. A small boy ran helter-skelter towards his returning mother; the paper bag he was clutching split, and small green apples rolled across the floor in all directions. He stopped and his mouth started to tremble. Marnie stooped and gathered them up, feeling a stab of envy for the woman who had a son waiting for her with apples in his hands.

Then she looked around her uncertainly. Would Oliver be here, and would she even recognize him? Would he recognize her? She swung her gaze from face to face, anticipating the flicker of acknowledgement. Nothing. She put her bag down, pulled her mobile from her pocket and turned it on: no messages. She walked to the door and peered out into the gathering night.

'Marnie Still!' It wasn't a question so much as a command.

Marnie turned and found herself looking at a bulky woman with coarse grey hair chopped into a crude pudding bowl around a face that was creased with numerous lines, like crumpled linen. Her eyes were a startling pale blue, and she looked like the pen-and-ink drawings of a squaw from one of Marnie's childhood books, but a squaw dressed in ill-assorted clothes – wellingtons over khaki canvas trousers, and a man's black suit-jacket (left pocket ripped open) on top of a thick grey fleece.

'Oliver couldn't come,' said the woman, in a thick accent. She seized Marnie's hand in her own broad, calloused one and squeezed it hard, so that Marnie's ring bit into her flesh. 'I'm Dorothy.'

'Hello. It's good of you to meet me.'

'Or Dot.'

'Sorry?'

'Now you're going to tell me I don't look like a dot. That's what Ralph always says.' At the name, Dot's stern face softened, so that she looked briefly girlish. It was an expression Marnie had often seen on the faces of ageing women when they mentioned Ralph – a kind of rueful helplessness in the face of his rawness and charm.

'Is Ralph –'

'Car's this way.'

It turned out to be a tinny little Rover with a caved-in passenger door that had been taped shut. Marnie, after putting her bag in the boot next to a rusty hacksaw and a tin of primer, had to climb over the driver's seat to get in. It stank of dogs and cigarettes.

'Heater doesn't work.'

'Never mind,' said Marnie, bravely, wrapping herself more securely in her overcoat. 'It won't take long, will it?'

'Good hour and a half, two hours.'

'Oh.'

'Bumpy road. And floods.'

Dot, it seemed, rarely spoke in complete sentences: verbs were lopped off and question marks removed, so that her words hurtled like a fast ball thrown over-arm when all you could do was shield yourself against its impact.

'Floods – has it been raining a lot, then?'

'Could say. Cigarette?'

'No, thanks.'

Dot inserted one into the corner of her mouth but didn't light it at once. She started the car, which snorted and rattled but pulled away, its headlights illuminating the narrow strip of road ahead.

'Are you a friend of Ralph's?'

'Friend?' A left turn onto a smaller road. 'Hope he would think so.'

'What's wrong with him?'

But Dot didn't answer. She depressed the car lighter, waited for it to pop out again, then pressed the red-hot filaments to the tip of her cigarette. An acrid smell filled the car and smoke trickled out of her small, closed mouth.

'Oliver said on the phone that he was dying.'

'Not a doctor.' This was practically a bark, accompanied by a baleful, smoke-stained glance.

Marnie realized the woman was close to tears. 'I haven't seen him for years,' she said softly, as much to herself as to Dot. The road was leading uphill now, onto a flat plateau where the wind buffeted the insubstantial vehicle. Though she could see little, she had the impression of land stretching widely away on either side. 'I didn't know he even thought of me any more.'

Of course he thought of me, she told herself. If he's in my mind, like a restless ghost, I should be in his as well. We can haunt each other.

Dot didn't reply. She leant forward over the wheel, cigarette held between the fingers of her right hand and smoke drifting in front of her weathered face. Marnie watched as the column of ash grew longer and finally crumbled into Dot's lap.

'Is it cancer?' she asked eventually.

'He's very thin. Never was much flesh on him, but just skin and bones now. Skin and bones and that laugh of his. I don't know how there's room in his poor body for laughter, but there is.' She turned her head sharply towards Marnie, as if she suspected her of being an impostor. 'You know how he laughs?'

'I do. Did.'

'Giggles like a little boy.'

'Yes.'

Dot dropped her stub onto the floor and jabbed at the

24

radio, which hissed and crackled, occasionally emitting a sharp burst of music. She turned the dial through equivalently nasty sounds, then turned it off again. Marnie took this as a sign that she did not want to talk – about Ralph or anything else. So she sat further back in her seat, her face sinking into the folds of her scarf, folded her arms for extra warmth, and looked out of the window.

The moon was the vaguest glow behind the clouds now, and she could only make out shapes, occasional houses in the distance. Sometimes an overtaking car (their flimsy Rover whined up hills, its gear stick biting at Dot's large hand) or one coming at them from the other direction would briefly light up the moorland. Sitting in this cold, smelly car beside the taciturn Dot, as they nudged their way through the vast darkness towards a dying man she no longer knew, Marnie was suddenly apprehensive. And something else, dark and heavy, made her chest ache. She felt homesick, she realized – not for her Soho flat, or for the Italian home she had made and then left, but more for her lost self, for her dead mother, her childhood spent in the ramshackle house near the sea where, when gales blew against the window at night, she would lie in bed and feel safe, bulwarked against the world.

It began to rain, at first in large, occasional drops, then in a downpour that defeated the wipers, whose blades whipped back and forth, their rubber fraying. The rain clattered on the roof and sprayed up around the car wheels in violent arcs. It almost felt as though they were underwater. Dot leant further forward, her nose nearly touching the streaming glass and her big body seeming to press against the steering-wheel. She had another cigarette stuck between her lips at a surprising angle. The smoke leaked into her right eye and ash collapsed on her collar, specking her neck.

'Do you want to pull over for a bit?' Marnie ventured, when the car skidded on the road's muddy verge for the third time, its wheels roaring frantically in the mud.

'Quite safe,' said Dot.

Marnie didn't feel safe at all, not in this tinny little car that seemed too light to hold the road, and not in herself. She pressed her forehead to the window and tried to find objects in the landscape that, in the darkness and the rain, looked more like an ocean than solid ground. Ralph had loved journeys such as this, when he didn't know where he was going, but Marnie didn't. She needed to plan things and always to be prepared. For a moment Ralph's face – the face of long ago – flashed before her, and she had a powerful sense that she was travelling back in time, towards the self she used to be.

The car bumped on through the night. Marnie shut her eyes. She let sleep creep up on her, felt herself sinking towards a dream in which Ralph appeared, wearing a jumper her mother had knitted for him. He was very young in this dream – just a child – and he was weeping copiously. She tried to hug him but suddenly he was no longer there and in his place was a stranger with a curled moustache and cold eyes, wearing a bow tie. He looked like Salvador Dalí, or a pantomime villain . . .

Then she was back in the car, and Dot was beside her, leaning implacably over the steering-wheel. She blinked several times to get rid of the dream, and rubbed her eyes with her fists; they stung with tiredness and with the smoke that filled the car. She felt befuddled and had no sense of how long she had slept: perhaps the cigarette that Dot had clamped between her teeth was the one that had been there when Marnie had closed her eyes, or perhaps it was several cigarettes later. Outside, the landscape was the same, black and wet and empty.

And then she must have fallen asleep again, for Dot was laying a hand on her shoulder and saying, in a loud but not unkind voice, 'Marnie. Marnie, wake up. We're here.'

Marnie sat up stupidly, pushing escaped strands of hair back behind her ears. The car had stopped in front of a small, whitewashed house at the end of a rutted track. The upstairs windows were dark, but downstairs lights shone behind the closed curtains and smoke was coming out of the chimney. It was still raining, steadily drumming on the car roof.

'Sorry,' she said. She was stiff with cold; her mouth was thick; she felt muzzy and quite unready for what lay ahead. 'What time is it?'

'Quarter to seven, give or take. Can you manage your bag?'

'You're not coming in?'

'Me? No.'

'But I –' Marnie stopped. What was there to say? 'Thanks very much for collecting me,' she said. 'I appreciate it.'

'Welcome,' said Dot.

'Before you go, tell me. Is he – no, I mean – I think I mean – will I recognize him?'

Dot looked at her with her pale, unblinking eyes. 'He's your friend.' She got out and held open the driver's door for Marnie, who clambered across, gasping as the cold rain slapped her face, making her cheeks sting and her eyes water. She collected her bag from the back, then watched as Dot reversed back up the track and disappeared. Icy water ran down her neck; her hair was already soaked. She turned to face the house, which was as simple as a child's drawing of home: very small and square, with two curtained windows upstairs and two down, a blue door, complete with knocker, in the middle. There was a birch tree with flaking silver bark to one side and on the other a woodshed, beyond which two small cars were parked nose to tail. She took a deep breath, picked up the bag and walked firmly up to the front door, avoiding the puddles that were collecting. She lifted her hand and hammered three times with the knocker, then stood back and waited.

What did she expect – Ralph to tumble skeletally over the threshold? Oliver, with his grave, assessing stare? Instead a small, brown-haired woman, as neat and sweet as a songbird, opened the door and smiled. 'You'll be the friend? I'm the nurse. I'm just leaving now. Mr Fenton's expecting you. He'll be out shortly. Rotten night, isn't it?' And with that she was gone, flicking up a small umbrella, like a benevolent Mary Poppins, as she stepped over the threshold, leaving Marnie to walk into a narrow hallway. The door clicked shut behind her.

Feeling quite unreal, almost dizzy with the oddness of it all, Marnie pulled off her gloves, unwrapped her scarf, took off her coat and hung it on a hook beside a jacket and waterproofs. She kicked off her boots, took a pair of old slippers out of her bag and put them on. The hall led directly on to the wooden staircase. On the left was a closed door, on the right a half-open one that gave on to what was clearly the main room of the house. Marnie walked cautiously into it, her slippered feet pattering softly on the quarry tiles.

'Hello?' she said softly. 'Oliver?'

The fire in the grate flickered, throwing a strange, guttering light. There was a deep armchair beside it, a book open face down on its seat, and on the other side a small, shabby sofa with a tartan rug folded over its back. Between them was a packing case that served as a table, and on it a bottle of whisky and an empty glass. There were piles of books on the floor, and also a laptop, whose green light was blinking. An improbably tiny kitchen was stuffed in under the beams at the end of the room: the stove, a metal, two-ring box above shelves of pots and pans, the sink piled with dishes, the small wooden table stacked with papers, magazines, letters, some of which hadn't yet been opened, and an odd assortment of tools at one end – secateurs, pliers, thick gloves, a trowel with mud still clumped on its wedged blade, a ball of twine. On one of the chairs there was a small saw. By the side door a laundry basket overflowed with sheets.

For a moment Marnie stood uncertainly, waiting. She thought she heard a voice from behind the other door, but it remained shut. Then she put another log onto the fire, went to the sink, rolled up her sleeves and started to tidy up. She stacked the dirty dishes on the table, scrubbed the draining-board, then ran a sinkful of water. When she was very small, her mother had stood her on a chair, tied an apron twice round her miniature frame, and instructed her on how she was always to wash glasses and cutlery, rinsing soap off everything, before moving on to mugs, plates, bowls, and finally pots and pans. She thought of her mother now, as she stood at the sink, arms up to the elbows in suds and steam rising into her face, which soon became warm and damp. When she felt lost in the world, as she did now, she would try to imagine what her mother would have done in her place, and sometimes experienced a ghostly sensation, like an echo ringing softly in her head, that she was occupying two lives at once, or that her own life was following the tracks her mother had laid down for her. Her feet in her mother's footprints; her voice repeating the words her mother had spoken; her thoughts snagging on her mother's presence, even though she was long gone and only came now in dreams and in memories.

She lifted her hands out of the foamy water and looked at them: strong, with a single ring on her right hand, short, unpainted nails and wide knuckles; they were her mother's capable hands, made for carrying and holding. If she could have seen herself at this moment in a mirror, her mother would be gazing steadily back at her. And 'Marnie,' she would say, in that low, clear voice of hers, which was also Marnie's, 'if you do something, do it with your whole heart or not at all.'

'Marnie.'

She swung round, scattering drops of water across the tiles. Her heart bumped painfully in her chest and her legs trembled, as if she was ravenous and needed to eat before she collapsed. 'Oh,' she said, hearing her voice rasp, feeling horribly shy and clumsy. 'Hello, Oliver.'

'Why on earth are you washing up?'

'Because it makes it easier if I can feel useful.'

'Useful?'

'What? Why are you looking at me like that?'

'You haven't changed.'

Marnie felt herself flush. 'I have, you know.'

'Of course. I didn't mean it like that.'

'No. It's all right.'

They stood at either end of the room, looking at each other warily, not sure whether to walk across and shake hands, hug each other, kiss the other's cheek – for were they strangers or reunited friends? Would she have known him if she had seen him across a room or glimpsed him on the street? It was like looking at an image superimposed on an earlier one so that she took in both, but neither quite clearly. She saw his slim shape, boyish and long-limbed – but he was no longer slim: he was solid. His face, which Marnie remembered as gaunt, had filled out and lost its eager smoothness. There was still that small dimple in one cheek when he smiled, but there were new lines and creases, new pouches under his eyes. His brown hair was still tousled, but shorter than it used to be and already threaded with silver. His chin was metallic with stubble. He wore faded jeans and a pale brown jersey, round-necked and with torn sleeves. His feet were bare. Time had creased, rumpled and frayed him. And he looked tired, Marnie thought, weary, as though a weight had been placed on his shoulders, preventing him from moving with the easy grace he had once possessed. She stared at him, biting her lip, then ran her wet hands down her skirt, pushed her hair away from her face and crossed the room to stand in front of him.

'So I came,' she said, then stopped. It felt important not to blurt out foolish, unconsidered phrases. But what could she say? Years of unspoken words blocked her throat; she could only utter tiny, foolish fragments.

'I was certain you would. Dot was there in time?'

'Yes. Who is she?'

'A neighbour. A lonely, cantankerous woman who loves her geese, her dogs – and Ralph, I guess.'

With the mention of Ralph, she felt on surer ground. It was why she was here, after all – to see him. That was the important thing and nothing must get in the way.

'She didn't tell me what was wrong with him.'

Oliver sighed and rubbed his hand over his face in a gesture so familiar to Marnie that she almost gave a small cry of recognition. 'Listen, let me show you where you're sleeping and then I can pour us a drink or something and we'll talk about it.'

'Is he in there?' She nodded towards the closed door, just a few feet from where they stood.

'He's sleeping right now. He's had a bad day and is all in.'

'OK, then, show me my room.'

He picked up her bag and she followed him up the steep, narrow stairs.

'This is usually Ralph's,' Oliver said, 'but we thought it best to put him downstairs, next to the main room, which is where he likes to spend most of his time.'

'It feels wrong to be taking his room.'

'Wrong?'

'Too strange,' she amended. 'Too intimate and sad.'

Oliver just looked at her. She could hear the words he

wasn't saying: this is strange, and this is intimate and sad.

'All right,' she said. 'Thanks.'

'The sheets are clean, and there are spare blankets in the cupboard if you're cold. The window looks out on to the loch. You'll be able to see it in the morning.'

'There's a loch?'

'Just a small one, hardly deserving of the name, at the end of the field. The bathroom's opposite – the tank's very small, I'm afraid. Not much hot water, but enough for a very quick shower. Shall I leave you to yourself for a few minutes? I'll be downstairs.'

'Fine.'

They were being so polite with each other, so formal and careful.

'Are you hungry? I've lost track of time.'

'Now I come to think of it, I haven't really eaten today. But I only need a piece of bread or something.'

'I'll make us a sandwich, shall I?'

'Thank you.'

Marnie listened to him going down the stairs, pausing outside Ralph's room before entering the living room. She pulled open the heavy curtains but could see nothing, only her face floating in the darkness. Watery night pressed against the glass like the sea, and she could hear the wind swelling round the small house; inside, the air felt thick and heavy. In the rippled light she took in the low bed, the knotted floorboards, the heavy wooden wardrobe, the charcoal sketch on the white wall that she remembered well, a teapot with a crooked spout on the window-sill, and on the mantel above the small fireplace a photo from long ago that she couldn't bring herself to look at – it was as if she was full to the brim with emotions, and the tiniest nudge would spill them over.

There was a bookshelf made from planks and bricks along the length of the room and she made out some titles: a Riverside Shakespeare, a biography of Chekhov, a thick *Guide to British Birds*, and another to trees, Pablo Neruda's love sonnets, a book about the Spanish civil war, an Italian dictionary. There were other books in piles around the floor: a Dickens novel, an anthology of poetry, a catalogue from the recent exhibition of Holbein's paintings (Marnie had been to it: maybe they had been there on the same day and had stood back to back staring at the large canvases), a pamphlet about melting glaciers, a book about imaginary numbers, an instruction manual for making mobiles, a book of chess games, another of magic tricks for a beginner. For a moment it was as if the Ralph of random enthusiasms and sudden obsessions was in the room, face ardent with the need to convert her as well.

A pair of shoes lay at the base of the bed. From where she sat, Marnie could see the darker smoothness rubbed into their inner soles by Ralph's heels and toes. A white shirt sleeve was caught in the wardrobe door. A bathrobe hung from a hook, and on an impulse she got up and buried her face in it, wincing as she inhaled the smell, half familiar and half strange. For a moment, she could barely breathe and to comfort herself she pulled her mobile out of her shoulder bag to phone Eva, but there was no signal.

Before going downstairs, perhaps as a way of delaying, Marnie unpacked the few things in her bag into the small chest. Most of the drawers were empty, only the top two containing a few T-shirts and some underwear. This she shut hurriedly, with a sense of intrusion. She took her toilet bag into the unheated bathroom, where she brushed her teeth and washed her face, first in hot water then cold. Then she made her way down the stairs, walking softly so as not to disturb Ralph.

Oliver was assembling sandwiches. He had cut several thick slices of white bread and was now spreading mayonnaise over each one, before adding chicken and slices of avocado.

'Why don't you pour us both a drink?' he said, without turning round.

'What do you want?'

'There's a choice of whisky or wine. I've been hitting the whisky in the last few days. There's a bottle of white wine in the fridge, if you'd prefer. Glasses in that corner cupboard.'

'Whisky's good. How long have you been here?'

'We came up a few days ago – and then it all went haywire.'

'Came up? Together, you mean?'

'Ralph doesn't live here, you know. He lives in Holland at the moment. It's just the place he comes when he can.' He gave that steady, penetrating glance again. 'It reminds him of a time he was happy.'

'I see,' was all Marnie could manage. Then she said, 'I didn't know. I don't know anything. All I know is what you said on the phone and that wasn't much.'

'Pour us that drink and we'll sit by the fire.'

'I haven't seen him for years and years, Oliver.'

'I know.'

'Of course you do. Is that too much whisky?'

'No. I think we both need it. There's ice in the freezer compartment of the fridge. Here you are, one very messy sandwich.'

'Thanks.'

They sat by the fire, Marnie in the deep armchair and Oliver on the sofa. She sniffed her whisky, the smell of muddy disinfectant, and took a good gulp. It burnt its way down her throat and she waited for her eyes to stop stinging before she bit into the thick sandwich: doughy white bread, rubbery strands of chicken, soft avocado. 'Lovely,' she said. For a moment, in the safety of the chair and the warmth of the fire, with Oliver's lived-in, well-remembered face looking at her with kindness, she wanted to weep. She wrenched herself back to Ralph and the present. 'Right, tell me.' Oliver took a breath. 'First off, why's he dying?'

'Pancreatic cancer. But it's everywhere now.'

'And there's no –'

'No.'

'He's so young. How long?'

'How long has he had it or how long has he got?'

'Has he got.'

'Not long. Weeks. Days. Maybe, even hours. The thing about cancer of the pancreas, I've learnt, is that it's difficult to detect – it can feel like indigestion at first – and it's hard to treat. He didn't know he had it until it had advanced to the liver and spleen. He's had radiotherapy, but it wasn't very effective.'

'Do you mean he's come here to die?' Marnie gripped

her whisky glass and leant forward. The heat from the fire warmed one side of her body, but the other was cold.

'I don't think he knew that when he insisted on this trip, but it looks that way, yes.' Oliver lifted his face and met her eyes. 'Are you sorry you're here?'

'No. I don't know. It feels so – so unreal. But, Oliver – I don't know how to ask this. Sorry if it comes out wrong. Am I supposed to be here until –' she stopped, took a sip of her drink '– until it's over?'

'You're not *supposed* to do anything.'

'All right, but is that what Ralph wants?'

'Ralph didn't even know you were coming.'

'What? He doesn't know?'

'No.'

'But that's – I mean, I thought he'd asked for me. Maybe he doesn't even want me here!'

'He wants you.'

'You don't know that. You just assume. Perhaps it'll upset him.'

'Marnie. In one way or another, Ralph has been upset all his life. He doesn't want to die without seeing you again. He misses you.'

Questions crowded her brain: is he scared? Is he angry? Sad? Is he ready? Has he had a happy life? Does he feel that darkness is descending and there's nothing he can do to keep it at bay? Will I know him, or is he transformed utterly into a yellowing, alien creature, skin hanging off him in tatters and those great eyes staring at me in love, in reproach, in torment?

'Is he in a lot of pain?' she simply asked.

'He's got a flask of liquid morphine that he swigs at

regularly, though if he has too much it gives him terrible dreams, not to mention agonizing constipation. And when we arrived and he took a turn for the worse, I got in touch with the hospice nearby and they send a Macmillan nurse round twice a day to make sure he's getting what he needs. She's very good.'

'I met her at the door.'

'Colette. We got him a hospital bed as well, so he can half sit or lie flat to sleep.'

'Are you going to stay all the time?'

'Yes. I've told them at work. I won't leave now.'

'You must be exhausted.'

Oliver pushed a charred log that had rolled away from the fire, releasing a splutter of bright flame. 'I'm OK,' he said. Then he added, 'He's my friend and this is his hour of need. He'd do it for me without hesitation. It's my – I don't want to sound pompous, but it's my privilege to do it for him.'

'Has he got no family?'

'No. Only the family he doesn't want, who don't want him. But you know what he's like – he's got good friends.' Oliver nodded at the unopened mail lying on the table. 'He's already had more letters in a few days than I receive in a year.'

'He isn't married, then?'

'No.'

'No children?'

'No children.'

'It makes it feel as if he's already dead, doesn't it? Talking about him like this. He's lying in there, just a few yards away, or at least you say he is, but I keep imagining that maybe no one's there at all, just a closed door. Or maybe it isn't him. And we're sitting here and talking about him as if he can no longer say anything for himself. As if he's got no words left, and he's empty, a vessel with no self inside.' She was seized by a sudden fear. 'That's not the case, is it?'

'It's still Ralph in there. But I agree, you should go and say hello.'

'I didn't mean that exactly. Anyway, isn't he sleeping?'

'He sleeps lightly, just on the surface. Night and day, he wakes and he sleeps, wakes and sleeps, and sometimes I can't tell the difference.' He swilled the remains of his whisky round the bottom of the glass, staring at the amber liquid. 'Sometimes I go in there and think he's dead. I have to put my ear to his mouth to hear the breathing. It reminds me of when my children were babies, just born. Such a fierce, light grip on life.'

Marnie stood up. She was seized by a sudden desire to lay a hand on his coarse hair, or to bend down and kiss the back of his neck. But, of course, she couldn't do that. She didn't know what note to strike with Oliver. They were virtual strangers although they had once known each other well, and now they had come together to wait at Ralph's deathbed. 'I'm glad I can go through it with you,' she said finally, and rather formally to cover her own awkwardness. 'We'll do it together. I'll just step in and see him.'

But she hesitated.

'You don't need to be scared,' said Oliver. 'It's just Ralph in there, your friend Ralph.'

It was almost exactly what Dot had said to her.

'I feel I don't know why I'm here.'

'I can't tell you that. To make him smile, to hold his hand, to clear up his shit, to wipe his brow, to tell him you love him. Maybe you're here to help him die.'

'I would have done better to have helped him live.'

She paused outside Ralph's door, listening. A liquid cough spluttered into the silence and for a moment she was back in her mother's house, listening outside her bedroom door as she lay dying. As quietly as possible she pushed the door open a few inches and stepped into the room. It wasn't entirely dark. An oil lamp stood on the wide window-sill in the puddle of its own yellowish light, and around it there were silent shapes: a tall cupboard, a squat table, a low iron bed.

She inched forward, her foot nudging against a large plastic bowl on the floor. At first she thought it was all a horrible joke or a dream and the bed was empty, for Ralph's body barely disturbed the duvet that lay over it. But then she heard him breathing: a rustling, unsteady whisper of air. And, anyway, there was a smell in the room, a human stench of decay overlaid with some piny air-freshener. For a few seconds the breathing stopped and Marnie stood arrested, a few feet from where he lay. Although she couldn't see it, she could hear the steady tick of a clock, and wondered how he could bear to have it by him, marking off the remaining time. She could make out his head on the plump pillow, a shock of dark hair in the half-light, a white patch of face. One hand was curled by his cheek. Then he breathed again, a sharp rasp before settling back into the light rattle of before.

She took the last few steps and sat very gently on his bed. He gave a tiny grunt. She remained there without moving or speaking, gazing down at him: even in the dim glow of lamplight she could see how thin his face was: his nose was beaky, his neck pitifully scrawny, his cheeks caved in; it seemed that his sharp bones should tear through his papery skin. He was stripped and sculpted, barely human any more.

Finally, she took the hand on the pillow and held it between both of hers, feeling how like a woman's ivory-and-paper fan it was, lying loosely hinged in her grasp. 'Ralph,' she said softly. 'It's me. Marnie.'

The eyes didn't open. The breath rustled and scraped. The figure in the bed made a sound that at first she took for choking, but then thought perhaps he'd said something. 'What?' she whispered, leaning forward so that she felt his breath, hot and sour, on her face. 'Ralph?'

But the figure on the bed was silent.

I said: I might have known you'd find me. Marnie Still. Coming into my room like a cat. Like a shadow slipping through the door to sit beside me. You always made so little noise. But I always knew when you were there. A room feels different when you are in it. The hot drumming in my head dies down. The air softens around you, the ground is firmer, things feel as if they're in their proper place again. You make me feel safe. Don't stop holding my hand: if you hold my hand, nothing can snatch me away. Your fingers are warm and strong and dear. I remember them. I remember your smell. Forests. Deep and clean. Runnelled bark, scent of sap and pine and earth; leaves that rot into the ground. Hundreds of years. Water spilling over rock, soaking into peat. Dappled light through green leaves. Moss like soft sponge underfoot; our feet sink down. If I could open my eyes, I would see your face. Grey eyes; clear, attentive. But even blind, I can feel you looking at me, and behind my closed eyes, I can see you. I know what you look like, underneath the years that have passed since we met. You'll always look the same, the serious, shining girl I loved. I love.

What do you see? Do you see a living corpse rattling his bones, eyes sinking deeper into their sockets, or do you see me? I'm still here, though I'm like a dry brown leaf hanging from a branch — one gust of wind and I could be lifted off to fly into the black space that doesn't end, goes on and on in every direction for ever and ever. Light years of nothing. Nights are the worst, and in the winter, nights are long. The small hours. No sound, except the tick of the clock, the whisper of the wind, the frail scrape of my own breath. Then I can feel the great darkness opening like a grave before me and the cold, cold stars. So lonely. But now you hold my hand and the darkness settles around me like a blanket. The clock sounds less foreboding, more like the pumping of a heart than the metronymic beat of time running out.

There, you're leaning towards me. I can feel the touch of your hair against my skin and your breath is warm on my cheek and now your lips are on my forehead. Just a touch and you withdraw. Your hand loosens its hold on mine. Don't go. Don't leave. I'm still here. Marnie.

Chapter Three

The wind woke Marnie. For a moment, she couldn't remember where she was; only that she wasn't at home in a city that was never dark like this, so dark that when you held your hand in front of your face you couldn't see it and when you shut your eyes the quality of darkness didn't alter. She fumbled for her mobile phone to find out the time and saw that it was only four in the morning. This far north, the sun wouldn't rise for hours yet. But she knew that she wouldn't go back to sleep now, and neither did she feel tired, although last night after seeing Ralph she had been stunned by weariness. She sat up in bed, groping with her hand for the bedside lamp, then blinking in the sudden light. The room came into focus. Her memory of yesterday sharpened and the shapes of her dream dissolved. From downstairs, she thought she heard a noise – but when she held her breath and listened there was nothing, only the rising moan of the wind.

It was very cold in the bedroom, so she dressed in her warmest clothes and slid her feet into slippers. Then she crept downstairs. The plates and dishes were still piled in the sink where she'd left them yesterday, and the fire had long ago gone out, leaving a dull pile of ash in the grate, stirring slightly with the draught that came from the hall.

She set about making the room comfortable; Oliver

had said this was where Ralph spent most of his time and she wanted him to be in a welcoming place. The water was tepid, so she boiled a kettle for the sink and methodically finished the washing-up. Then she wiped every surface. She found a broom in the tall cupboard in the hallway and swept the floor. There was something absurdly satisfying about collecting crumbs and debris into a small pile, then disposing of it. Later, she thought, she would wash the floor as well. She collected up the ash from the grate, though it was still warm, and laid another fire. 'Start with knotted balls of newspaper,' she heard her mother say. 'Then lay kindling wood over the top, like a kind of wigwam. After that, the larger logs. You never need fire-lighters, just patience.' There were matches on the floor and she put a flame against the edges of the wadded paper and watched as it licked the kindling.

When she was sure the fire wouldn't go out, she turned her attention to the piles of books and magazines, which she simply made into neater piles and pushed back against the walls. The gardening tools she put into a plastic bag in the hall. The laundry from the basket she stuffed into the tiny tub washing-machine, which rocked slightly as it ran. Her mother used to say that the sound of domestic appliances at work – washing-machines, dishwashers, vacuum-cleaners, coffee-grinders – was profoundly soothing, the sound of life functioning properly.

She ground some coffee beans, putting a hand towel over the grinder to muffle its noise, and made a pot of strong coffee. Then she looked in the small fridge. There wasn't much – the scant remains of the chicken, a few rashers of bacon, three eggs, a half-pack of butter, some milk and a tub of hummus. In a bin beside the fridge there were a few vegetables. Marnie took an onion and a couple of carrots and put them into a pan with the chicken carcass. She would make soup, she thought. Soup was good for invalids and, besides, there was something about the smell of a stock on the stove: it made one feel cared-for, made one feel that there was order in the world. And all the time – as she scrubbed, tidied and cooked in a parody of an anxious housewife – her heart bumped heavily in her chest and she kept glancing towards the closed door.

When she opened the curtains she saw a pale, smudged band on the horizon. Day was creeping towards her at last. She put a pan of porridge, half water and half milk, on the hob and stood there, stirring it unnecessarily just to have something to do with her hands.

That was how Oliver found her when he emerged from Ralph's room and stopped in the doorway. 'I didn't know you were up,' he said.

'I didn't know you were.'

'I wasn't. I slept on a camp bed in Ralph's room. I didn't want to leave him.'

'Is that where you always sleep?'

'Yes.'

'No wonder you look so tired.'

'Do I?'

'I'll make some fresh coffee, shall I? And there's porridge.'

Oliver took a few paces into the room. 'It looks nice. How do you do it?'

'I just cleared up a few things.'

45

'No, you were always like that. I'd forgotten.'

'A talent for tidiness,' she said, aiming for lightness but her voice had a crack in it. 'Is Ralph awake?'

'He's stirring.'

'Does he know I'm here?'

'Not yet.'

'Should I wait for you to tell him before I go in?'

'I don't know.'

'You need to tell me what we do here.'

'Do?'

'I mean, do we get him washed and dressed or can he do that himself? Can he get to the bathroom, or does he use a bedpan? That kind of thing.'

'We've only been here five days. But the nurse usually gives him a bed bath. And he hasn't been able to get to the bathroom for the last day or so. I think it's best if I deal with that side of things, though. He might feel it humiliating.'

'Fine. But you have to tell me what you need from me, all right?'

'All right.'

'If I'm here, I want to be fully here. If I stay, it's because it helps – helps Ralph and helps you. I'm not squeamish. I don't mind shit and vomit.'

'OK.'

'If Ralph doesn't want me here, I'm on the next plane home.'

'Sure.'

'Do you want porridge?'

'Please. I've been living off bread and cheese and Dot's chicken. And whisky. I haven't managed to get to the shops in the last few days – I went once, at the beginning, to the little stores a few miles away for milk and things. But let me get washed first.'

'Do you think Ralph would want some as well?'

'Marnie.' He looked at her, and his quizzical half-smile sent a sharp stab of memory through her. There was a small crease between his eyes. 'I think you should ask him yourself.'

'Oh. Yes, you're right. Now, you mean?'

'If you're ready.'

The lamp had been extinguished and the curtains opened. Ralph lay in the soft grey of dawn, propped up on his pillow. His arms were outside the duvet, palms upwards; on the fragile, breakable wrists Marnie could see blue veins. She imagined Colette, the nurse, putting her thumb there to feel the thready pulse. His eyes were closed and she thought, Is this what he will look like when he has died? But she could see that he was alive because he swallowed, his Adam's apple bobbing in his scrawny throat. She took a step forward, seeing outside the window the dull grey sky and heavy brown earth and, in the distance, the waters of the loch.

'Hello, Ralph.' The eyes opened, and locked with hers. She held her breath as she gazed at him, and the room seemed full of a dense, crowded silence. Then she crossed the room to squat beside his bed because she didn't want to be looking down at him. 'It's me, Marnie. I've come to see you.'

'You've grown your hair again.' His voice was unexpectedly strong. 'Good. I like it better that way.'

47

'Men always want women to have long hair.'

'Not true. It's children who always like their mothers to have long hair. Do you have children?'

'Not as such.'

'That's a very Marnie answer. Not as such.'

'I'm sorry, Ralph.'

'Sorry?'

'That you're –' She was going to say 'ill', but she saw the glint in his eye. 'Sorry that you're dying.'

'Me too. I think.' He started to cough and as his thin frame jerked on the pillow, Marnie watched him helplessly until he was still again. His face was waxy; there were hollows in his temples and blue shadows under his eyes.

'Can I get you anything, Ralph? Porridge? Something hot to drink?'

'Maybe. I don't know.'

'I'll be back in a minute.'

She almost ran into the main room, grateful that Oliver wasn't there. She put a small pan of milk on the hob to heat, then went upstairs to her room, where she collected the striped mug, honey and nutmeg from her case. Downstairs again, she stirred a spoonful of honey into the milk and grated in some nutmeg. She poured it into the mug, took a cautious sip to make sure it wasn't too hot, and carried it into Ralph's room.

'Here,' she said, sitting on the bed. His eyes opened again. She slid an arm under his shoulders, feeling every bone and sinew beneath the thin T-shirt he was wearing, and pulled him to a sitting position. He lay against her as light as a bird. 'Try to drink some of this.'

She held the mug to his lips and he took a sip, then lifted his head and smiled at her properly for the first time.

'Do you remember?'

'Of course I remember.'

After a few more sips, he lay back on his pillow and gave a small sigh. Marnie sat in silence for a few seconds. She didn't know what to do next, and was about to stand up and tiptoe from the room when his hand gripped her wrist. 'Marnie.'

'I'm here.'

'Don't go.'

'I won't.' She settled herself down on the bed.

'Talk to me. Tell me.'

Marnie, who had never been very good at talking about herself, looked out of the window for a few seconds, seeing how the bare trees bent in the wind. Then she took a determined breath. 'It's been such a time since we saw each other, Ralph. It's hard to know where to begin or what to say. What's that?'

'I said,' he wheezed, 'you're not at a fucking cocktail party.'

'You haven't changed.'

'Dying is the ultimate licence to be rude. Go on.'

'Right. I live in London now. On my own. Well, not on my own right at the moment because my stepdaughter, Eva, is with me. I suppose I should say ex-stepdaughter. Anyway, I have this flat in Soho and I work in a puppet museum. It's an odd little place, dark, full of nooks and crannies, and there are puppets everywhere, of all shapes and sizes. I walk in there in the morning and it's like being in a whole different world, a world peopled by these odd creatures who I feel I've come to know, though I'm not sure. They can surprise you. If I'm in the wrong mood they can seem quite baleful. Sinister, almost. Their eyes never close. Sometimes I dream about them. Disturbing dreams.'

She stopped. Ralph was looking straight up at the ceiling. She couldn't tell if he was listening to her. A small vein ticked on his temple. She tried again. 'Until quite recently I was living in Italy. Near Florence. But I had to leave, because — oh, well, because I did. I suddenly thought one morning, That's the wrong face on the pillow. I can't go on waking up to the wrong face for the rest of my life. Better no face at all. That's another story, though, and I don't know if you'd want to hear it, anyway. I'm just sitting here, feeling strange and talking about anything, nothing, words falling like stones into the silence, and I don't know what to say, Ralph. What do you want to know? How does one start? Perhaps I could read to you. I could read you a poem . . .'

'Tell me about us.' His voice was a croak.

'About us?'

'Our past. Memories.' She had to lean forward to hear his urgent whisper, frantic as an abandoned child's. 'Tell me about myself. Tell me about us. I can't bear the silence. Don't let there be this silence all around me. Don't.'

'Ralph.' She took his brittle hands in hers and leant over him, inhaling the smell of illness. 'Ssh, sweetheart.'

'Tell me.'

The sun was up now, though not visible in the dark

sky that promised more rain. Today would never get properly light, she thought. Dawn would continue until it became dusk, and night fell once more.

'Listen then,' she said.

Chapter Four

Marnie would never have met Ralph if she hadn't met David first. And she wouldn't have met David on any other evening but this one, when she was truculent and running late. She didn't want to go to the party; she didn't like the people who would be there and they didn't like her. She didn't belong. She was odd, they said. She didn't seem to care what they thought of her. She wore quaint clothes, bought from Oxfam or borrowed from her mother's unpredictable wardrobe, and carried her books in a shabby music case; she rode to school on an old sit-up-and-beg bike, lived in a house whose roof leaked, knew how to play the accordion, liked opera and sailing and old philosophers with shaggy white beards – knew how to knit, for God's sake. And, at a time when it was only just beginning to be diagnosed, she was dyslexic, though this wasn't what they said. They said *thick, stupid, dim, brainless, a twat, a retard, two sandwiches short of a picnic.*

And then, of course, as if that wasn't enough, there was her mother: older than most mothers, single, with a mane of dark, static hair and an uncompromising stare that could stop you dead in your tracks. She wore long skirts that trailed in the mud, jumpers she knitted herself, no makeup except, occasionally, smears of paint or clay on her cheeks that she had failed to rub off before leaving the house. They called her *witch, weirdo, madwoman* (though only behind her back, and even then furtively, as though she might suddenly appear out of nowhere). Of course, what had happened to her and Marnie was sad – but it was ages ago. They should have got over it by now. Life goes on, they said. And Marnie and Emma had learnt not to turn around and say, 'Yes, but *how* does a life go on?' Not in the same way, that was for sure, though from the outside it might look the same.

On this particular evening, Marnie had promised her friend Lucy that she would accompany her to a party, because Lucy – diligent, bookish, sarcastic Lucy, who wore rimless glasses and had read all of Dickens's novels at least twice – had decided that she needed to go out and needed Marnie to be there, as moral support and listening-post when she found herself stranded at the end of the room with no one to talk to, as she certainly would because that was what always happened to her at parties. Marnie struggled crossly into a pale grey dress that was too small for her and a slightly odd shape, now she came to examine it, but there was no time to change: Lucy would be waiting. She slid her feet into heavy ankle boots that didn't match the dress, and didn't bother with makeup. Neither did she brush her unruly hair.

'That's quite a short dress,' her mother said, in a neutral tone, as Marnie climbed into the car.

'I think I've grown out of it.'

'Mmm. Be careful.'

'What? Do you think someone's going to take advantage of me just because I'm showing my legs?'

'Your bottom.'

'I'm not showing my bottom!'

'OK.'

'I'll keep my coat on, then.'

'Marnie, I just said be careful.'

'I know what you meant, though.'

'I meant be careful.'

'I don't even want to go to this party anyway. I already feel trapped, stifled. I'll just stand in a corner with my arms folded and sulk.'

'That sounds like fun.'

So when David saw her, he saw a girl who didn't really exist – he saw the skimpy dress worn with clumpy leather boots as a quirky new fashion that showed her worldliness; he was struck by the pale face, half hidden by her heavy fall of hair and bare of makeup, which frowned rather than smiled or pouted; usually she was patient and polite, but tonight she was irritable.

Marnie knew David by sight; almost everyone in the room did. He was the boy from the grammar school across the road from the girls' high who used to go out with red-lipped, anorexic Lily. He was the boy who'd won the 1500-metre county championship and been in all the local newspapers and even on TV, talking about how he wouldn't mind being in the next Olympics, but he thought he probably preferred football to running. He had bright, thick blond hair and a square jaw, white teeth, a habit of hitching his thumbs into his belt and standing with his legs apart, like a cowboy. And that evening he came into the room, a casual late arrival, like a gun-toting outlaw with his posse of admirers, his glance roaming across the people in the room.

There was a shift in the atmosphere. Hardly realizing

that they were doing so, girls moved closer to him, raised their voices so that he could hear them, turned their heads slightly so that he could see their profiles, became more animated. He noticed Marnie because she seemed barely to notice him, and when he walked over to her, a slow smile growing on his handsome face, she stared at him impassively.

She had the beginnings of a headache; her glands were painful and her throat thickened ominously. She was coming down with a cold, and to make it worse, her period was due, giving her a low back ache, painful breasts and a skin that prickled with physical irritation. All she wanted to do was curl up in bed and listen to one of her talking-book tapes with a cup of camomile tea beside her and her cat lying on her feet. She had already telephoned her mother, asking her to collect her early.

'Can I get you a drink?'

'I've already got one.' She raised it in front of her and took a sip.

'OK, how about "Would you like to dance?"'

'No one else is dancing. And I'm not really in the mood.'

'What mood are you in, then?'

'The wrong one for a party.'

'What's your name?'

'Marnie.'

'I'm David.'

'I know.'

His smile strengthened. 'You know?'

'Yes. This is Lucy.'

He barely glanced at Lucy. Behind him, Marnie could

see her group of tormentors looking at them and, despite herself, gave a small grin at the confusion on their faces.

'Why are you smiling like that?'

'It's nothing.'

'Really, tell me.' He leant closer.

She smelt the beer on his breath, and his musky sweat. His features blurred. 'I've changed my mind,' she said. 'I'd like to dance. Once. Then I'm going home.'

'We'll see about that.'

'Don't,' she said sharply, set on edge by his knowing tone.

'Don't what?'

'Don't assume.'

'Sorry.' He sounded almost humble.

They stood in the centre of the room where there wasn't really any space to move and he put his arms around her. His hands were on her back; his solid body was too close to hers. His breath was warm against her cheek. She was hot and kicked off her heavy boots so that suddenly he was taller than her and had to bend his head to talk to her, his hair flopping forward. His words came fast and easy; he talked about nothing in particular with fluent self-confidence.

'I'm going now,' she said, when the music changed. 'Goodbye, David.'

'But you can't go yet!'

'I can.'

'Did I tell you you're beautiful?'

'Yes. Thank you.'

'Can I call you?'

'What?'

'I want to see you again. Give me your phone number.'

'Oh.' Marnie frowned, pushing her feet back into her boots. 'It's in the book.'

'Well, then, what's your last name?'

She hesitated, then shrugged. 'Still.'

'Marnie Still?'

'Yes.'

'What's your father's name?'

'I don't have a father.'

'Sorry,' he said, unabashed.

'But there aren't any other Stills.'

So it was that Marnie — untrendy, unsporty, outspoken Marnie, who made her own dresses and let her mother cut her hair — found herself going out with David Tinsley, heart-throb of the sixth form, hero of the football field and running track. Looking back over the years that separated her from that time in her past, she could see clearly that she had never really desired him — or, at least, only did so second-hand, because other girls, girls Marnie disliked, were so smitten with him and startled by her new status. And she could see, too, that she was the wrong girl for him, but that was precisely why he persevered: she wasn't impressed by him, she didn't come to watch him play football, she didn't spend hours in front of the mirror preparing for their dates, she didn't laugh at jokes that weren't funny, she didn't pretend to agree with him, she wouldn't cancel arrangements she had made with Lucy to accommodate him. She wasn't grateful that he had chosen her.

'When am I going to meet him?' her mother asked.

'You'll hate him.'

'Does that mean I can't meet him?'

'No. It's OK. I'll bring him back tomorrow. How about that?'

It was March and their stalwart little house near the coast was coming into its own, after weeks of winter when the brown sea leaked into the dun skies and water dripped through the ceiling onto the bath's rim. Now there were daffodils in the garden, the japonica by the front door was in flower, and there were sticky green buds just visible on the trees. The sea, which they could see from their windows and reach by a small track, was no longer sullen but a flickering blue-green, sending off diamonds of light when the sun came out. Every morning, Emma Still opened the windows to let the air in, and then Marnie could hear the swell of birdsong, liquid and full throttle. Sometimes she could see one of the birds in the bare branches of the trees, its tiny throat throbbing.

She had been born in this house, and she knew her mother would never leave it, although it was old and felt increasingly worn out: its beams sagged; its side wall was cracked; the heating was inefficient; slates slid off the roof whenever there was a storm. Then, rather than call in a builder, Emma would climb up and replace them, her hair blowing in the wind like a tattered banner. Emma was good at things like that: it was she who laid carpets, put up shelves, made curtains late at night, her foot pedalling the sewing-machine, her mouth pursed full of pins. She often enlisted her daughter's help; ever since she was small, Marnie had painted her own room, liking the sensation of laying wet, clean layers of paint over the stained surface.

The house was too large for the two of them, and it was quiet. Both Marnie and her mother were restrained, swallowing their emotions. Marnie felt the house's stillness as something almost tangible, its heaviness filling the rooms and pushing against the windows, and she sometimes imagined that the same kind of pressure existed inside herself and her mother, as if all the shouts and yells they hadn't uttered were pressed down inside them, making them less light-footed and carefree than other people, more deliberate. She didn't properly remember, but imagined, what it had been like when four of them were living here: not just Emma and Marnie, but Marnie's father, Paolo, and her older brother, Seth.

That was long ago. Marnie had been only three when Paolo and seven-year-old Seth had gone off on a fishing expedition, protective father and proud son, and drowned in the freak storm that locals still remembered. For years after she had dreams of them in the churning water, screaming for help, or under the waves with limbs flailing, lungs exploding and seaweed already stranded around their distorted, dying faces. Now she often found that she could no longer remember properly what they had looked like, or could only do so by thinking of the photographs that stood in the downstairs room: Paolo and Emma, with the sea going out behind them; herself and Seth squashed together on a swing in the garden, Marnie grave and Seth impish; the four of them together, Marnie with her eyes squinting against the dazzle of the sun and her hand holding Emma's blowing skirt. Paolo and Seth's real faces had faded, and the memories she had were fragmentary and unsatisfactory. For instance – and she didn't like to say this to her mother – when Seth came to her now, as he often did unbidden, he was invariably belligerent or derisory. There was the time when she'd trodden on his model aeroplane, made of balsawood and the glue still sticky, and he'd pushed her onto the floor and banged her head on it until fireworks fizzed inside her skull. Or the time he and his best friend Stephen had put cushions over her on the sofa and then sat on her to watch TV. She remembered – or thought she remembered – lying in stifling darkness, the boys' sharp bodies shifting on top of her, and trying not to cry. She longed for a happy image to surface, but the more she searched for one, the more it wormed its way down to the bottom of her consciousness.

Sometimes, in the silence, she would hear Seth's voice in her ear, but it was usually sardonic and not at all like the voice of a seven-year-old, more like the voice of Marnie's hidden *alter ego*. She was used to it now, so would no longer swing round wildly in an attempt to glimpse him before he was swallowed by her mind. With her father, it was worse in many ways, because she found that she remembered nothing at all: he was just a paternal myth, vague as fog. 'Did he read to me?' she would ask her mother. 'Did he lift me onto his shoulders? Did he tickle me, feed me, dry my tears?' and when Emma replied that of course he had, Marnie would picture Paolo sitting on the side of her bed, or hoisting her high in the air, and try to convert that into a memory. But all of her authentic memories, even before the storm, were of Emma, with her strong shoulders and her steady gaze, her calloused man's hands that would hold Marnie's, the creases and grooves in her face, like water marks on a cliff. Emma, like a rock after the tragedy, the momentous grief crashing against her determination not to collapse.

And she hadn't collapsed, thought Marnie. Not once – or not in front of Marnie. She had been a potter when her husband and son were swept out of her life, but had been unable to continue except in her spare time. To make ends meet, she had turned the house into a bed-and-breakfast. With spring approaching, the season for guests would soon be under way again. White cotton sheets would billow on the washing-lines or, in wet weather, be draped across the chairs; the fridge would be full of bacon rashers, packets of pork sausages, eggs bought from the farm down the road, beef tomatoes that Emma grilled, white button mushrooms and bags of coffee beans.

Marnie thought that of all the people she knew, her mother must be one of the least suited to running a B-and-B. Like Marnie, she wasn't naturally sociable. What was more, if she took against someone it was almost impossible for her to hide her feelings and, more often than not, she took against the unfortunate guests who pitched up at their house and were upset not to find an en-suite bathroom, a TV at the end of their bed and a coffee-maker beside it. Marnie had developed a kind of sixth sense for the kind of person Emma wouldn't welcome. She had only to see them getting out of their car and her heart would sink, for she could already picture her mother's firmly closed mouth and hear the stern clack of plates on the table in the morning, the leathery egg lying like a sticky insult alongside a split, charred sausage.

So it was when she brought David back to be inspected. Emma's mouth became a grim, closed line when he took her hand between both of his and said, 'I can see where Marnie's looks come from.'

Emma smiled, a curiously flat smile that showed her teeth sharkishly. He can't tell, thought Marnie. He thinks he's charming her. They climbed up the narrow stairs to her bedroom. Her mother's eyes were on them and Marnie was conscious of David's hand burning into the small of her back.

'That seemed to go OK,' he said, pulling her onto his lap. 'I think I'm good with mothers. Do you want to meet mine as well?'

Marnie didn't really: she knew this would end almost before it got going. 'All right,' she said.

That was how she had met Ralph. The first time she went to David's home – which was on the outskirts of town in a cul-de-sac of thirties houses all built of the same yellowish brick – it was a Sunday afternoon and an air of boredom glazed everything. Men were out washing their cars, and mothers pushed buggies along the streets with a slow purposelessness.

Marnie locked her bike to the fence and rang the doorbell; she heard a tune sound inside and, through the frosted glass, a shape appeared. 'Yes?'

The woman who stood there was thin and pale. Marnie thought she looked washed out – or rubbed out, perhaps, as if her edges were bleeding away and her colour diluted.

'I'm Marnie.'

'Yes?'

'I'm a friend of David's,' Marnie said politely. Surely David had told his mother she was coming for tea.

'Come in, then.'

David's mother stood back just enough to let Marnie squeeze past, like an unwanted salesman. But then David came down the stairs two at a time, his yellow hair bouncing. He draped his hand around his mother's sloping shoulders, and Marnie saw her face transform. It opened, sweetened, became girlish with pleasure. 'This is my mother,' he said unnecessarily.

'How do you do?' said Marnie. She held out her hand to take the woman's slim, unresponsive fingers. In the silence, she added, 'I'm pleased to meet you.'

'I've made a cake,' the woman said. Her eyes slid across Marnie's face. 'Why don't you come through to the kitchen?'

There, David said, in an offhand voice, 'This is my sister Grace.'

'Hello, Grace,' said Marnie. She bent down to take Grace's plump hand, reddened at the knuckles. 'I'm Marnie.' Then she glanced at David. Why hadn't he told her? Grace sat at the table in a wheelchair. Her legs were thin and floppy, like the tubular legs of a rag-doll, and her upper torso large and shapeless. She had a round, smiling face with a lopsided mouth and, under a block fringe of blonde hair, David's blue eyes blinked nervously round the room. Her hands twitched and fretted in front of her. She made a low-throated sound and lifted a hand into the air, like a conductor asking for silence. When her mother tied a baby's bib around her neck, she whimpered and tried to take it off.

'Where's Dad?' asked David.

'He's resting.'

'Nonsense. Here I am.' The man who stood in the door was an older version of David, but everything that was handsome in the son was coarsened in the father: his face was fleshy, so that his features seemed to have bunched up in its centre; his skin was weathered and broken, puffy under the blue eyes and in soft, grimy folds round his neck; his eyes were bloodshot, and Marnie thought there was a mean gleam to them; his waist strained over the belt, fastened too tightly on jeans that were too small.

'It's Marnie, isn't it?' He captured her hand in both of his and Marnie saw his nicotine fingernails and caught the sweet smell of alcohol on his breath. 'My son's got good taste. Takes after his father.' He gave a broad wink, his features twitching.

Marnie wondered if he might possibly be drunk. She smiled cautiously and tried to pull her hand free but he kept hold of it.

'Ah, to be young,' he continued. 'Young and free.' And he winked once more.

This time Marnie did pull her hand free and stepped back sharply, knocking into the table. David's mother hissed and tutted as pale brown liquid spurted from the spout of the teapot. Grace picked up a spoon and started banging it against her plate. David's face was impassive and Marnie felt a spasm of pity for him – he hated above all to be pitied, aiming always to appear impregnable, in control. He stood, she saw now, in front of a series of framed certificates that honoured his sporting prowess, as if trying to establish how he wanted to be looked at. The conquering hero, not the son of a drunk father and the brother of a damaged sister.

'Where's my mad brother?' he asked abruptly.

'In his room, of course. He knows you're here.'

'Shall we go and get him?' David said to Marnie. He pulled her out of the room and she followed him up the stairs.

'What's wrong with Grace?' she asked his back.

'She was born like that.'

'Yes, but –'

'This is Ralph's room. He's the real weirdo . . .'

He didn't bother to knock but pushed the door open with one vigorous bat of his hand. Marnie, peering into the room, was struck by its manic disorder. Where the rest of the house was clean and impersonal, this was like a thieves' lair. It was, she thought later, as if Ralph's feverish brain had been put on display. The floor was littered with disparate objects – a broken guitar, a legless chair, an ancient typewriter, a trouser press on which he had hung a tattered velvet coat, a cardboard box the length of a man's body on which was written in huge red letters 'RIP'. In the corner there was a life-sized model of a skeleton – or half of it: it had no skull, and most of the ribcage and one entire leg were missing so it had to lean back against the wall for support. Books stood in piles and the narrow bed was heaped with notebooks, bits of paper, folders. There were postcards everywhere – even on the ceiling. She saw all of this before she saw the room's occupant, for he was a skinny figure on his knees at the edge of the room, his back turned to them.

In front of him on the wall he had drawn a large, slightly misshapen rectangle.

'What do you want?' he asked, without looking round. He dipped a brush into a tin of paint on the floor beside him and lifted it, scattering drips across the carpet. He laid a thick daub of turquoise inside the rectangle.

'Dad'll kill you,' David said, with more than a touch of relish.

'Maybe.' The thin shoulders shrugged. Another lick of paint was laid down. He had black curly hair; one foot was bare, with a grubby sole; the other wore a white plimsoll.

'It's tea. And this is Marnie.'

Ralph laid the paintbrush on the upturned lid and turned round. Marnie saw a small, pale face, a shock of unkempt hair, flecked greenish eyes under heavy brows. She knew he was about the same age as her but he looked younger – and, even at this first glance, she had the impression of someone who was hungry, needy, restless and, like a flickering candle, never still.

'Hi, Ralph,' she said, stepping into the room.

He stood up in one movement and came towards her, half limping in his single shoe. 'Hello.' A smile flared briefly on his face and died.

'What are you painting?

'A window. It's really dark in here, and if I can't have an actual window, I thought I could paint a large one on the wall, with the blue sky showing, and clouds. Maybe a tiny plane in the distance. What do you think?'

'I like the colour,' she said shyly. He went on watching her, waiting for more. 'Like a spring sky,' she added. 'Or early morning, before it's got really warm.'

'That's what I wanted. Everything new.'

'Dad'll just make you paint over it. You know that.'

'You could have a bird on the sill too.'

'I'm terrible at art. I can't draw.'

'I could do it.'

'You could?'

'It's tea, Marnie,' David interrupted. 'Are you coming?'

'If you wanted me to –'

'Are you coming or not?'

'You could paint me a swallow! A bird that returns each spring.'

'OK.'

'Have you seen their nests of mud?'

'Marnie. He's just showing off, you know, trying to get attention. You shouldn't fall for it.'

Marnie watched Ralph's face flush. He stared at David, biting his lip, then turned away. She saw the muscles tighten at the nape of his neck.

'Tell Mum I'm not hungry.'

'Up to you.'

'So there you were,' said Marnie, bending closer to Ralph. 'A burning star in a dark house.'

And there you were. You stood in the doorway, with that funny little smile on your face, the one you wear when you're waiting to see whether to smile properly or not. I remember you on that day – or I think I remember, anyway. Perhaps I've made it more vivid in recollection: 'The First Time I Saw You'. I do that a lot. The past feels brighter than the present. But whether it's true or not, I can see now your soft, pale, slightly smudged face half hidden by your hair. Grey eyes, fringe that looked as if you'd chopped it yourself in an absent-minded moment, large mouth, determined chin, a few freckles on your nose – they would spread out when summer came. No makeup, except, I saw later, your thumbnails were painted dark purple. You were wearing – in my memory at least, that discredited thing – old jeans that were too large for you and were held up with a canvas belt, a smocked jersey, well-worn walking boots. You didn't look as if you'd dressed up at all, even though this was your first visit to meet the family. You weren't what I'd expected, not at all. I thought you'd be like David's last girlfriend: a stick-thin blonde, cool, vain and contemptuous. She would look at me and see someone wonky, nerdish, foolish, faintly amusing and pathetically small. But you – I had the sense that when you looked at me, you saw me, saw into me, and didn't turn away.

My mother never looked at me like that. She was always waiting to be dissatisfied, examining me with a discontented expression to see what was wrong with me – clothes all messy, hair too long and not brushed, face simply the wrong face because it wasn't David's, not his golden hair, his vicious baby-blue eyes, not his easy, charming smile; I was speaking the wrong words, feeling the wrong emotions, gripped by an anger she didn't begin to understand. My poor mother. I used to try so hard to win her. As a child, I would follow her around like a shadow, telling her I loved her, hanging on to her fingers, waiting outside the locked bathroom door, sulking when she paid attention to David, unable to sleep unless she had said good night, begging her for just one hug, driving her mad with my neediness.

'Where did you come from?' she would say sometimes, helplessly. 'How did I ever have a son like you?' I would dwindle when she looked at me, shrinking back into myself like a sea anemone poked with a stick: the puny middle child squashed between the heroic, worldly son and the pitiable innocent daughter.

68

I tried to say this to you once but I don't know if you understood what I meant: I felt that until you came along, nobody had looked at me properly and seen the person I wanted to be. I felt recognized. No wonder I fell in love with you, that very first meeting, when you gave me your smile and offered to paint me a bird. Head over heels in love, till death us do part. Death us do part now.

You can't hear me. You kiss my forehead and say, 'It's all right, my darling Ralph, it's OK.' Was that here, just now, or was it fished out from memory's pool, something that happened many years ago? Or perhaps it hasn't even happened yet, but is waiting for me in the diminishing road ahead. In this little room where I can smell the stink of my own decay, the past and future don't have the same meaning as they used to. Everything is contracting, like a pupil contracts in the light, until all that's left is an aperture the size of a pinprick. Just enough to see. But darkness is drawing in.

Chapter Five

Oliver raised the axe. For a second, it hung in the air above his head. He had one foot planted in front of the other and the muscles in his neck stood out. Marnie watched him. There was an expression of fierce concentration on his face, and she thought that, briefly, he had forgotten where he was and what was happening. Then he brought the axe down in a smooth arc and it cleaved the log, sending tiny splinters of wood flying. Marnie picked up the two halves, breathing in their clean sappy smell, and dropped them with a clatter into the wheelbarrow.

The nurse was still with Ralph, and for half an hour or so, she and Oliver had worked together in virtual silence, Oliver chopping the logs he had sawn up before she arrived and she carrying them to the wooden lean-to by the side of the house, where she stacked them in neat lines. The effort was strenuous and although it was very cold and blustery, threatening rain, both of them had taken off their jackets. Marnie did not ask why they were doing this, or for whom the wood was intended. It certainly wasn't Ralph: by the time it had lost its sap and was seasoned, he would be dead. But the physical exertion took away some of the awkwardness between them, and the consoling rhythms of daily life were continuing: wood was chopped and stacked; sheets were washed and floors swept; the soup was on the hob.

That morning, after sitting with Ralph, she had gone for a brief walk, her eyes watering in the cold. If she breathed in too deeply, the air hurt her lungs, sending little stabs of pain through her chest and up her throat. The lake lay at the bottom of the hill, beyond a small wood of pines and birches that creaked and groaned in the wind. Raindrops stung her cheeks; her feet crunched through the frosted brown leaves into the sodden mulch beneath. She remembered this landscape of lochs and pine forests from long ago, but then it had been summer, a watercolour idyll of blues and greens and the sun spinning a glittering kaleidoscope on the water's surface, sending up glowing fragments of silver.

Now everywhere was a dull impasto of brown, beige, grey and charcoal. Even the evergreen pines were drab and thin, and in the murky light the scene took on a ghostly aspect. Marnie had shivered and walked more briskly, wrapping her arms around her to hold in the warmth. The loch, when she reached it, looked brackish and sullen. She squatted at the edge where yellowish rushes sagged and put in her hand to feel the water, noticing how it was viscous near the shore, sludging to ice. In a few weeks, the whole lake would have frozen over; maybe snow would fall, to transform this colourless world into a place of brilliance and beauty.

She had picked up a flat, flinty stone and sent it spinning over the water. It bounced once, then disappeared.

'Why can't girls throw properly?' It was her brother's voice, bright and smug.

When she was younger, she had always tried to imagine what Seth would look like now, what he would be doing.

Her mother used to measure her and Seth, and then just her, each New Year's Day – she had stood Marnie against the door jamb and drawn a pencilled line where her head came to, jotting in her name and the year. Marnie would always step back and stare at the lines: hers continued to inch up the wood; Seth's had stopped at four foot seven and a half inches. At eight, she was about the same height as he had been at seven; at nine she was taller – but not really, for she would draw an invisible line where she thought he ought to have reached, and he was always ahead of her. Ahead of her in height, in reading and writing (as a dyslexic, she was years behind everyone), in maths, in French, in passing exams, in easy friendships, in knowing best. She could never catch up. She knew when his voice would have broken. When he would have had his first girlfriend. When he would have sneaked off to the beach to smoke a furtive cigarette. She imagined his face, smooth, then spotty and then stubbly with new manhood; his body, once so slight, had bulked out in her mind, the shoulders broadening. But at a certain age she had lost track of him. Now he would have been in his forties. What would he be doing? Once, a long time ago, she had asked Emma what she thought, but her mother had turned on her a look that had made her feel scared because it was as blank and eerie as the moon.

Hearing Seth's voice in her skull, teasing her, she grimaced and picked up another stone, bent low, scudded it across the lake and watched it skip rapidly several times. 'There,' she said out loud. 'But you'd be able to do it better, wouldn't you? Of course you would. It's not fair.'

But it wasn't Seth's voice she wanted to hear: it was Emma's. Her mother had always been good at knowing when to give advice and when to withhold it. She was never hasty. Marnie could see her face now, the considering frown corrugating her forehead. She would put her hands on her hips, legs slightly apart, and wait until she was sure of what she wanted to say.

'I don't know what to do.' Marnie had sat down on a small wooden boat that had been dragged up the shore a few feet and turned turtle, its oars tucked underneath its pot-bellied bow and a piece of canvas tied over its middle. 'I'm scared.'

But her mother didn't answer. Marnie had sat for what seemed an age but was probably no more than a few minutes, listening to the erratic slap of tiny waves on the shore and the ripple of her thoughts.

Now she threw a couple more split logs into the barrow, then straightened up to watch Oliver. As soon as she wasn't moving, the cold cut into her. 'Don't stop, but can I say a few things?'

'Sure.' Oliver let the cleaver thud onto a small log; it sliced into it like a knife through butter.

'I'm going into town with your car so we should make a shopping list. You need to tell me the things he can still eat.'

'Right. But I can do the shopping if you want. Or Dot will always go. She'd like to do something.'

'I'll go, if that's OK. And I've been thinking we should move Ralph's bed into the main room. That way, instead of shutting him into that little room – which feels a bit like death's waiting room, don't you think? – he can be at the centre of the life of the house. Everything will happen around him. We'll cook and wash and talk and read and play music. Even if he can't join in, he's there with us.'

Oliver paused to wipe a forearm over his brow. 'If that's what he wants,' he said. 'But he might feel a bit public. What about when he needs a bedpan or just wants to be hidden away?'

'I could easily rig up a kind of screen from the curtain in my room. We could pull it across when he wants privacy.'

'We can ask him anyway.'

'And we could both sleep in that room as well.'

'Really?' Oliver sounded doubtful.

'It just feels odd, leaving him.'

'If that's what you want.'

'I keep thinking he could go anytime.'

'Mmm.'

'We should talk to him, even when he looks as though he's asleep. Maybe he can still hear.'

'I do that now.'

'It all seems a long time ago, doesn't it?'

He didn't answer, just lifted the axe once more and swung it down, the blade glinting, his breath clouding from his mouth.

'It does to me, anyway,' continued Marnie, determinedly. 'A long time ago and yet impossibly close.'

Oliver rested the axe on the ground and wiped his forehead with the back of his hand. Marnie watched him, but at first he didn't look at her, just stared beyond her at the woods as if he could see something in them that needed his attention. Then he dropped his eyes to her. 'I don't know, Marnie,' he said. 'I don't know what I think about it.'

It was such a nondescript little sentence but for a moment it felt as if the distance between them had dissolved.

'Well,' she said, and smiled at him, but he didn't smile back. His face was tired and subdued.

'This is such an odd way to meet again.'

'Any way would have been odd.'

'Probably.'

'Imagine bumping into each other at a party, or the theatre or something.'

'Very awkward,' he agreed, but he still wasn't smiling and his expression remained troubled. Questions crowded into Marnie's mind. Are you married? How many children do you have? Have you thought about me? Who have you loved? Have you found contentment? She found she couldn't ask them.

'Have you always kept in touch with Ralph?' she said instead. 'I mean, after . . .' She let the sentence die.

'As much as he'd let me. Sometimes he'd disappear for a while.'

'Has he been happy?'

'Happy? No. That's not the word I would use. Joyful sometimes. Euphoric. Excited. Restless. Wretched. Despairing. In heaven and then in hell. You know.'

'Loved?'

'Sometimes.'

'And in love?'

Oliver laid his axe down carefully, resting the blade on

a stump. 'There are some things I don't know and some things I can't say.'

'Does he ever talk about me?'

'He used to. But for a long time now he hasn't mentioned your name.'

Marnie walked to the top of the hill on the other side of the lake. From here, it was just possible to get a signal. She listened to her messages, then pulled off her gloves and phoned Eva, with fingers that were rapidly turning numb in the cold.

'Hello!' a bright voice sang out.

'It's me.'

'Marnie! I can hardly hear you. You sound as though you're under water. Are you all right?'

'I'm good. Is everything OK there?'

'This place gives me the creeps. I keep thinking they're going to come to life.'

'But you're all right?'

'Fine. It's fun.'

'And is everything –'

'I can't hear you very well.'

'I said –'

'Marnie, I can't hear you.'

'I'll call later,' she yelled.

Marnie moved a few yards along the slope to get a clearer signal and phoned Lucy, who had left her an urgent message to call.

'Lucy?'

'Marnie? Hang on, don't go away. I'm just going to take this outside where it's private.' Marnie blew on her fingers, then pulled her gloves back on. 'There – can you hear me?'

'Yes.'

'I rang you last night and Eva said you'd gone to Scotland to see a friend who was dying.'

'Yes. It's Ralph.' There was a small intake of breath, and Marnie thought that this was the first time they had mentioned him for many years. He was their taboo. 'I'm sorry,' she said softly. 'I would have told you but I had to leave in a hurry.'

'I thought it was him. I don't know why. I just had this gut feeling.'

'I'm sorry,' Marnie said again.

'And it's true?'

'That he's dying? Yes.'

'So I'll never see him again.' It wasn't a question but a dull statement. 'I always thought . . . But you. You're with him.'

'Yes,' said Marnie, helplessly, hearing the bitterness in Lucy's voice.

'Are you alone?'

'Oliver's here.'

'Ah.' It was a sigh more than a word. 'Will you give Ralph a message?'

'Of course.'

'Tell him . . .' For a few seconds she did not speak. Marnie looked down the hill to the loch while she waited, watching the way the wind sent dark, tight wrinkles across its surface. 'Tell him I'm happily married, with two children, but not a day's gone by when I haven't thought of him.'

'I will.'

'Now I've got to get back to the meeting.'

'Of course.'

'I can't really believe it. He's always been so alive.'

What could she say? Marnie pressed the phone to her ear and was silent.

The nurse had gone. Oliver lifted Ralph in his arms like a baby and carried him to the sofa where Marnie sat. He laid him down, his head on her lap and the tartan blanket pulled over him. The fire flickered in the grate and there were flowers on the makeshift table in front of them, left by Dot. Marnie ran her fingers through his hair, which was soft and clean. The nurse had washed it that morning.

'OK?' she asked.

'Mmm.'

'Oliver will bring your bed through soon. Tell me if you need anything.'

'Will.' His eyes opened and he looked up at her. 'Nice smell.'

'I made us some chicken soup. Do you want some?'

'No. You. You smell nice.'

'It's just soap and woodsmoke. I thought maybe I could read to you, if you'd like.'

'Soon. Wait.'

'All right. Lucy sent a message.'

'Lucy,' he murmured.

'She said that she's happily married with two kids but not a day goes by without her thinking of you.'

'Good.' He giggled, and then his giggle turned into a

cough, making him twist on the couch. 'About happy marriage and children, I mean.'

'It is good, isn't it?'

'At least one of us got there in the end. One out of four.'

Marnie leant down and kissed his forehead and then on the cracked lips. She was aware of Oliver watching them from the doorway. 'We're here now, anyway.'

'Go on with the story.'

Chapter Six

Against her expectations and almost against her wishes, Marnie and David remained a couple. That spring, he passed his driving test and would proudly turn up to collect her in his father's blue Saab with black plastic seats and an air-freshener hanging from the roof. He rarely came in and Emma would stand in the doorway, hands on hips, and scowl as they drove off in a splatter of gravel. Emma and Marnie didn't speak much about David, but Emma was fiercer than usual about Marnie's need to study for her O levels, and ruder than usual with her B-and-B guests, charring bacon and breaking egg yolks, bashing her iron down on the sheets. At school, however, Marnie had acquired a kind of mysterious cool. The trendy girls no longer ignored her; they even invited her ('Oh, and bring David, of course') to parties. Marnie usually refused, very politely; she was ashamed of the secret glee that ran through her at being accepted when she despised the reason for it, and knew very well that she might be dropped at any moment. As a matter of honour, she wore the same odd cast-offs, didn't put on makeup, and made sure she spent more time than ever with Lucy, fierce, geeky, loyal Lucy, who would ring her up at night to talk about *Jane Eyre* and Edward Hopper's paintings, and who thought, and said, that David was – she hesitated, choosing her words to carry maximum impact – not who she would have expected Marnie to choose.

Not who Marnie had expected either. But she climbed into his father's car nevertheless, and let him drive her to the seaside, where he'd put his hand under her bra and murmur into her neck and she would think of the sound sea-shells made when cupped against her ear. Or to pubs, although he soon stopped doing that because Marnie would insist on walking home if he drank any alcohol, even though he railed at her for being prim, pious and stuck-up – she had given her word to Emma, she said, as if that was the end of the discussion. Or, every so often, to his house, where his mother still glowered at her for being the unworthy girlfriend of her flawless son, his father flirted in a beery, half-hearted fashion, and Grace smiled and smiled, dribble running down her chin.

She saw Ralph a few times only. She painted the swallow on his fake window-sill, silhouetted against his brilliantly turquoise sky. Once, in the car with her and David, he talked as if against the clock about his favourite authors, most of whom she had never heard of. And another time, waiting for David to arrive triumphant from some football match, she let him teach her the rudimentary rules of chess. That was when she told him about her dyslexia, how she still couldn't readily tell the time, recite the months of the year or spell – well, spell dyslexia, for example – and how she sometimes felt that she was wandering through a fog, feeling her way blindly. She dreaded the forthcoming exams, she said, woke up in a sweat of terror just thinking about them.

'Yet you're the cleverest person I've ever met,' he said.

His eyes glowed. His dark hair stood up in spikes. His cheeks were flushed.

'Me!' She laughed.

'You. Yes.'

'I'm not clever.'

'You are. You're clever in the only way that matters. The only thing wrong with you is –'

'What, then?'

'Nothing. Nothing's wrong with you.'

'That's incredibly sweet.' She smiled at him, but he turned away from her furiously, knocking the chess pieces to the floor and storming from the room in one of his unaccountable tempers. Yet she noticed how solicitous and respectful he always was towards Grace, even though he was uncontrollably rude with his father, and sulky or – much worse – pleading with his mother, like a small, disgruntled child.

The japonica flowers bloomed and died. The blossom opened and the leaves on the trees unfurled. The magnolia stood like a candelabrum at the end of their potholed drive. The sea looked blue from Marnie's window and the gutters no longer dripped rainwater onto the paving. Her mother had bought a cockerel and four hens, and each morning Marnie would be woken by the cockerel's braggadocio crowing. She would slide out of bed, pull on her dressing-gown and slippers and pad over the dewy grass to the chicken run at the end of the garden in search of eggs. Usually there were several, smooth and warm in her cupped hands, and she would bring them into the kitchen where her mother would be laying the table for breakfast.

It was on one glorious evening in May that she went to David's house for an early supper. Afterwards they were expected at the home of one of his football friends for a game of poker, though Marnie had no idea of how to play poker and if it was for money she only had about a pound in coins tucked into the back pocket of her jeans. If it turned out to be the loud hilarity of strip poker, as she was beginning to suspect, she would go straight home without even removing a hairband.

Everyone was there, and Marnie was seated next to David, with Mr Tinsley on her other side at the head of the table. Ralph sat next to Grace and talked to her about how many different kinds of French cheeses there were, while Grace chuckled and clucked softly at him, basking in his incomprehensible attentions. Mrs Tinsley put a plate in front of Marnie: three fat, undercooked sausages, a large heap of mashed potatoes, baked beans. She couldn't eat all that. Mrs Tinsley tied a bib round Grace's neck and put an over-heaped plate in front of her, too. Ralph stabbed a fork into one of the pink sausages, stood it upright and quivering, then announced loudly, 'I think I'm a vegetarian.'

'Nonsense,' said his father. He snapped the tab off the beer can in front of him.

'Since when, may I ask?' his mother said.

'Now.' He gave a nervous giggle. 'Too much pig on my plate.'

'If you don't like your mother's food, leave the table.'

'Dad.' Ralph turned towards him and pointed a trembling finger. 'You don't need to be personally offended by what is an ethical decision.'

'Ethical fucking claptrap. I'll show you ethical.'

'Just eat up and don't show off by making a fuss,' said Mrs Tinsley, in a long-suffering voice.

Grace picked up a sausage in her thick fingers and tried to push it whole into her mouth. Her left cheek bulged.

'After all,' said David, in the ironically patronizing tone he reserved for Ralph, 'you won't get big and strong without protein.'

'Like you, you mean?'

David smiled at Marnie, rolling his eyes, and sat back in his chair. He was wearing a new blue shirt with the sleeves rolled up and flexed one arm so that the muscles worked. 'Could do worse,' he said.

'I don't think I could.' Ralph's voice was very low, but they all heard him. The room filled with a thick, ominous silence. Grace gave a small moan and plunged her fingers into the mess of baked beans on her plate.

'Really?' David leant towards his brother and smiled his beautiful bright smile, a hundred watts of hostility. 'Well, at least I don't sit in my bedroom all day writing poems. Eh?'

'You've been going through my things!'

'All your sweet little secrets.'

'Shut up – just shut up.'

'Now, let me see if I can remember anything you wrote.'

'I said, *shut up. Fucking shutupshutupshutupshutup.*'

'Ralph, leave the room,' shouted his father. 'This moment.'

'How does it go? Ah, yes. "I woke but I was dreaming still . . ."'

At this point, Ralph erupted to his feet, plate in one hand, glass in the other and, before anyone had time to move, his meal was flying through the air over the narrow table and splashing into David's face, over his thick blond hair, across his ferocious smile, dribbling down his new blue shirt. A few beans found their way onto his freshly washed jeans. In the stunned silence that followed, Ralph almost listlessly tossed his glass of milk after the rest. For a few seconds, the scene was like a freeze-frame: his father halfway out of his chair, red-necked and purple-faced, his mouth open but not yet emitting the bellow that would follow; his mother's thin lips drawn back in a snarl of outrage; Grace, one hand flat in the squished remains of her food, her face slack; Ralph quite calm and waiting for the storm, a little smile playing on his lips. Marnie saw on David's spattered face the rage of a small child who had been made to look stupid.

Then somebody laughed. Clear as a bell, the sound pealed out in the room. Marnie jammed her hand to her mouth but the laughter spilt between her fingers. In the commotion that followed – people shouting and yelling, Mr Tinsley dragging Ralph from the room by his hair, Mrs Tinsley standing beside David and staring at her where she sat, Grace throwing her own dinner onto the floor with a companionable gurgle – Marnie's laughter grew weaker and at last stopped.

'Sorry,' she said feebly, with a final hilarious hiccup. 'I always laugh when I'm shocked.'

'We're done, you little bitch,' said David. His mother's lips tightened in sour approval and she wrapped an arm round his shoulders, transferring some baked beans to her pink jumper. 'I don't know how I put up with you as long as I did.'

Then he picked up a napkin, wiped most of the mess off his face and strode from the room. They heard the car door slam, the engine roar into life and David wrenching it out of the drive in an angry splutter of mud and gravel.

'Well,' said Marnie. She felt light-headed.

'I think you'd better go, don't you?'

'Probably.' A giggle rose in her throat but she swallowed it.

Mr Tinsley re-entered the room, a belt in his hand. On his face, which was redder than ever, there was a look of righteous satisfaction. Marnie stared at him until he looked away. She felt sick at the sight of him.

'She's just going,' said Mrs Tinsley.

'Goodbye, Grace,' said Marnie, walking round the table to plant a kiss on the top of her head. 'Tell Ralph he was perfectly justified. David shouldn't have snooped like that. And you shouldn't have beaten him,' she told his father. 'You're a nasty bully.'

'Just get out of here before I use this on you, too.'

'Oh. And tell David I'm really, really happy we're through.'

Cycling slowly home through the thickening light, Marnie felt peaceful. Her hair blew behind her and her limbs felt strong and unencumbered; she could feel the muscles in her calves working. She was glad it was over and that the conflicting desires and dislikes were in the past. She no longer had to push away his urgent hands, fend off unwanted invitations from girls at school, or visit his angry, unhappy house. She saw the sea in front of her, silver and grey in the soft twilight, and her heart lifted.

Her mother was in her work shed so Marnie made them both a cup of tea and went to visit her there. She was wrapped in a white apron and painting a large, shallow bowl she had made a week or so before; her sleeves were rolled up and there were smears of paint and clay on her arms. The tip of her tongue was on her lip, a sign of concentration.

'Here,' said Marnie. 'Cup of tea for you.'

'You're back already?'

'Yes. Can I help you?'

'Do you want to decorate a mug? It's a bit blemished so you can just do whatever you want with it.'

'Sure.'

It had been ages since Marnie had worked out there, among the unglazed pots, the smell of clay, paint and glue. She hesitated in front of the paints, then chose a terracotta red and dipped her brush into it. This was always the best bit, before you actually began.

'I don't think I'll be seeing David again,' she said, after several minutes, 'so I'll have plenty of time to help you in the house and revise for my exams.'

Her mother didn't reply at once. She bent forward over her bowl, her brow creased, considering. 'You're all right?' she said eventually.

'I'm really fine.'

'Good.'

'He wasn't very nice.'

'Hmm.' Emma laid an invisible stroke of paint along the rim and stood back. Marnie saw that there were flecks of grey in her hair. 'Shall we go on a picnic tomorrow, if the weather holds? Once I've got the B-and-B-ers out of my hair, we can row out to the little island. You can ask Lucy if she'd like to come.'

'I'll make the sandwiches.'

'That's settled, then. You need to make the paint a bit thinner, I think.'

'Sometimes I don't want to grow up. I want just to stay here with you, in our house by the sea, painting mugs and having picnics. It's an odd feeling – like being homesick for something I've still got.' She looked up at her mother, whose face was stern and sad and whose eyes seemed to go right through her. 'What did I say?'

'Nothing. Nothing at all.'

'You're thinking of them, aren't you?'

'Not really.'

'There's a certain look you have. It's like you've gone away.'

Emma sighed, laying down her brush and pushing her hair away from her face. 'Marnie, you don't have to feel threatened.'

'I don't!'

'Yes. You do. It's natural.'

'I wish –' Marnie stopped.

'Go on.'

'I wish you were happy. I want to make you happy.'

'You do make me happy.'

'No, I don't. I'm not enough.'

'You're everything.'

'Everything's not enough.'

Emma laid her dry, roughened hand flat against

Marnie's cheek. There was a fine dust in her hair. 'Everything is everything. Don't ask for more.'

It wasn't until the next morning, after Marnie and Emma had made breakfast for the Lake family from Leicester, and cleared away the congealed remains, after they'd stripped the beds and put the first of the sheets into their ageing, noisy washing-machine and Marnie was making ham and mustard sandwiches, humming to herself, that she heard.

Emma came into the kitchen and took the knife from her hand. She made her sit down at the table, and then she told her that David had crashed his car the night before, skidding out of control round a corner and smashing into a wall. He had died immediately.

For some time Marnie didn't say anything. She sat quite still, aware of her mother's eyes fixed on her, and looked at her hands, which were gathered uselessly on her lap. She heard herself swallow and then the old clock, ten minutes fast, tick loudly. She saw David's glaring face, spattered with orange baked beans and yellow-white potato, and she heard her gleeful laughter ring out. Before her mother could move, she had picked up the bread knife and sliced it down her own arm, watching the red line well with drops of blood.

In the night, there was screaming. I had never heard anyone scream so loud. I thought it was in my room, inside my own skull. It sounded like an animal being slaughtered, but it went on and on without let-up, and then it suddenly stopped. For a while there was silence, which was almost worse than the screaming — thick and menacing, like an animal about to pounce. A panther with a mouthful of blood. Blue lights on my ceiling. Cars in the drive. Voices shouting. Someone running. I lay quite still. I didn't want to move because I thought my body would break apart if I did. I was falling down an endless hole inside myself. Do you know how it feels to be so scared that all the clichés come true — your heart's in your mouth, your stomach turns to liquid, you're on a slippery slope, the ground opens up under your feet, the world stands still?

At last I went into the corridor. My back still stung from the belt. There was nobody in my parents' room or David's, but Grace was in her bed, awake and with the covers pulled up to her chin. I sat by her and held her hand. I can still feel her fingers, warm and squashy and passive, in mine. I already knew. I talked to Grace about all sorts of things, fragments of whispered nonsense in the darkness. She wasn't listening, she didn't hear; I thought as long as I talked, nothing could really happen. But, of course, it already had.

I mustn't think of that now, the cold, cold night before dawn.

When I first kissed a girl who wasn't you — that's another story — I closed my eyes and pretended I was kissing you once more. I was coming home at last. I was loved by the only person I wanted to be loved by. Her taste was your taste. The way she had her fingers in my hair: that was you. It was you pressing up against me like that. Then the music stopped; the kissing stopped. I opened my eyes and it wasn't you, it was this stranger — wrong shape and wrong size and wrong smile and wrong way of saying my name.

That wasn't the only time either. With Lucy, I was often with you. You were always the third in our affair, if affair is the right word for the strange, intense and doomed romance that had more to do with things that could never be said than with simple desire or pleasure. I think she knew that. Did you know? Of course you did. You always knew. And the last time I slept with a woman – and by 'slept' I mean just that, side by side through the night – I dreamt of you, and when I woke up, I lay in the darkness, hearing the steady breathing of the person next to me and feeling her warmth just a few centimetres away, and willing myself to continue the dream I didn't want to leave. I already knew of my cancer by then; I'd known for several weeks but told no one, not even Oliver. (And we'll come to Oliver later, won't we? I can feel him just over the horizon of your story. His shadow's already there.) I went through each day with this secret growing silently inside me, taking me over bit by bit. It felt odd that the whole world looked different to me and yet apparently nobody could tell. We're all alone, aren't we, Marnie? Even in the middle of sex we're alone but trying feverishly to lose ourselves in the other in order to pretend that we're not.

Anyway, on that strange night with a woman I had known for many years, I tried to dream that you were with me at last, and that when I turned on my side I would be able to see your face looking at me, grey eyes to lose myself in, and you would hold out your arms and I would slide into them and be safe at last. And I did turn over and, for just one self-deluding moment, it was your face, oh, God, your darling face, that I was looking at, your arms that were around me, holding me so tight under the sheets. Do you know what it feels like to be homesick for the whole of your life?

But who was I seeing when I was seeing you? It was so many years since we'd met; you were a memory, a ghost. Was it the you of our childhood, or the person you'd become, whom I no longer knew though often imagined? I don't know and it didn't matter.

Dreams have their own logic. It was simply you. And then not you. The sickening knowledge that you still weren't there.

You're here now. I've missed you so badly. God, Marnie, I've missed you so very much.

Chapter Seven

Marnie borrowed Oliver's car to drive to the shops. She took with her both his and Ralph's mobile phones so she could check for messages once she was out of the dead zone. They lay on the seat beside her, mysterious packages that she had permission to open. The blustery wind blew the rain sideways; it streaked across the windscreen so she viewed the scene in front of her through a watery curtain, the moors blurred and sodden, the branches of the trees whipped back, the heavy sky bearing down on the barely visible hills.

The town that Oliver had directed her to was small and unprepossessing; the houses had a surly air, with grey slate roofs and mean windows. It lay huddled against the side of a hill, and at first glance looked closed down for winter. The windows were unlit, the doors firmly shut, the streets deserted. But Marnie saw that smoke rose from a few chimneys, quickly swallowed in the wet grey air, and when she drove up the main road, the bakery, the butcher's and the general grocery store were open for business. She parked and turned off the engine. Almost at once the streams of rain made it impossible to see anything out of the window, and she sat for a moment in her private fug, listening to it clatter on the roof and splash onto the tarmac. Then she turned on both phones and waited for a signal to appear.

She started with Oliver's, jotting down the messages in her notebook. Jenny (it sounded like a girl's voice, perhaps his daughter): 'Where are you and when are you coming back?' Sylvia: 'How's Ralph?' Roger: something to do with a case he was waiting to hear about, get in touch ASAP. Tony: please ring. Jenny again. Mal: 'How about that meal?' Lorrie: Christmas arrangements need to be finalized – was Lorrie his wife, his ex-wife? No name but a soft and intimate voice, and Marnie felt displeasure jolt through her: 'Call me, sweetheart.' Professor Goodman: something about a meeting he had cancelled. No name again, saying caressingly: 'Oliver, Oliver honey, I need to speak to you. Please!' For a moment, Marnie considered not passing on the message from Oliver's other, real, world where women called him 'sweetheart' and made arrangements to meet up.

Then Ralph's. She listened to a world of strangers leaving messages, Dutch accents, English ones, a southern American drawl. Telling Ralph they were thinking of him. Asking Ralph if they could come and visit. 'I love you, hon,' said a woman on the brink of tears. Someone was praying for him. Someone else said not to forget how important diet was; it was never too late. A few clearly didn't know that he'd left and were trying to make arrangements to come round that afternoon, the next day, whenever he felt strong enough to see them. Margriet had baked his favourite cake. Mark had made him a CD of birdsong. At last Marnie turned the phone off and stared at the paper covered with names, messages, numbers, realizing more strongly than ever how far she and Ralph had moved from each other and how unlikely it was that she should be with him as he lay dying.

She sighed, buttoned her coat and got out of the car. Stinging needles of rain hit her. Before she made it across the road to the bakery, she was wet through, and her hands were so cold she could scarcely open her purse to find change.

Back at the house, Oliver had put more wood on the fire and already drawn the curtains against the encroaching darkness; the wind rattled the window-panes and hissed through the keyhole, but inside it was warm and full of soft light from the fire and the oil lamp. Ralph was half sitting, half lying on the sofa covered with the rug, and he and Oliver were playing chess. Though his hand, when he reached out to move a pawn, was like a bird's claw, he looked quite different from that morning, as if in the couple of hours she had been gone he'd filled out: there was colour in his cheeks and his eyes glittered with a morphine-gaiety that Marnie was learning to recognize. His hair lay in clean, soft curls around his thin face. When he saw Marnie, he smiled at her, the sweet smile of his boyhood. And Oliver lifted his head and gave a small, rueful smile too. Both of them were looking at her with tenderness; for a moment, she felt as if she had never been away.

She sat at the table chopping vegetables as they played. Nobody talked. Occasionally Ralph chuckled when he thought he had gained an advantage. The chess pieces tapped softly on the wood, muted by their felt bottoms;

Marnie's knife clipped against the chopping-board. The fire crackled, and garlic sizzled briefly in oil. The kettle gave a breathy whistle as the water boiled.

Marnie added the vegetables to the pan, pulled out a mixing-bowl. There were no scales in the small kitchen, but she estimated the weight of the sugar and flour, then beat them together with a wooden spoon. Behind her, Ralph coughed, a terrible hack that made her wince, and she heard Oliver's quiet, soothing voice. She took the eggs from their container, holding their porcelain coldness in her cupped hands and remembering how as a girl she would collect them each morning from the chicken run. Sometimes they would still be warm from laying. She cracked the first sharply against the edge of the table and let it plop into the jug she had put ready for them. She doubted Ralph would be able to eat any cake, but it felt good to be preparing it for him while outside the night closed in and the weather pressed up against the windows. The clean tang of lemon zest, the fine cloud of flour as she sifted it into the mixing-bowl, the smell of baking that would fill the room, bringing back their childhood, holding the future at bay. Unexpected happiness flowed through her, so strong it made her throat ache and her eyes water.

'He's asleep,' said Oliver at last, rising from his chair.

'Who won?'

'Nobody yet. We can finish it later. But he always wins so I imagine he will this time. That smells good.'

She took off the apron she'd wrapped round her waist and untied her hair, shaking it loose, then moved across the room to where Oliver stood. Together they looked down at Ralph, who was lying in a crumpled heap on the sofa, one arm hanging down, the fist uncurling; there was a small smile on his lips.

'He seems so much better,' said Marnie, putting his arm carefully on the sofa, pulling the blanket over him, shifting his feet back a bit. He stirred and murmured.

'Sometimes he is.'

Marnie turned towards him – or perhaps it was Oliver who turned first and put his arms round her, holding her fiercely against his solid warmth, resting his chin on the top of her head and breathing into her hair. She laid her cheek against his chest and felt the strong beat of his heart. She imagined Ralph's heart, fluttering and scrabbling like a dying bird, and leant closer in to their embrace. Oliver's shirt smelt of smoke.

'I always thought I'd see you again.' he said, into her hair. His voice was almost a groan.

Then they drew apart.

The doctor, when he came that evening, had the broad shoulders of a rugby player and sandy receding hair. His face was pouchy and pink, and covered with smudgy freckles that made him look as if he were dissolving. But his eyes behind his glasses were sharp. When Marnie walked with him to his car, asking him as soon as the front door was shut if Ralph's sudden improvement didn't allow room for hope, he paused.

'Ms Still –'

'Marnie.'

'Marnie. Cancer's not predictable, and stranger things have happened.'

'But?'

'But – here, sit in my car awhile. We can't stand about chatting in this storm.' They climbed into it and he turned on the engine to give some warmth, then an internal light. He looked at her with a tired, kindly expression. 'What do you know about your friend's condition?'

'I know it's pancreatic cancer – and I know that's not good.'

'It's a nasty bugger, shaped like a slipper. Difficult to detect because the pancreas is behind the stomach and deep in the abdomen. Difficult to treat. According to his doctor in Holland, it had spread to several adjacent structures before it was discovered.'

'Adjacent structures?'

'That is to say,' he coughed, 'colon, liver, lung. To name some.'

'I see.'

'Ralph has had radiotherapy. Surgery was not appropriate in his case, and chemotherapy would not have been effective. Now all that can be done is to relieve the symptoms.'

'His morphine.'

'Yes. That has side-effects. Drowsiness, of course. Serious constipation and stomach cramps. On occasion there can be bad dreams, even waking hallucinations.'

'Poor Ralph.'

'But he doesn't have to suffer much pain. And if he needs to go into hospital –'

'He doesn't,' said Marnie, quickly. 'He's doing well. We're doing well.'

They sat in silence for a few seconds.

'In that case . . .' he said eventually.

'Of course. And thank you.'

'If you need anything . . .'

'Yes.' She opened the car door. 'Dr Gray?'

'Mmm.'

'How long?'

'I can't answer that. But I would say not long at all.'

That evening, Ralph tried to escape. He staggered from his bed, clutching the blanket round his waist, his spindly legs sliding under him. Marnie and Oliver tried to hold him back but panic made him strong and he thrashed out against them. Marnie felt his hot breath on her face and his bones slipping under her fingers. His open palm landed with a slap on Oliver's cheek. One of his fingers viciously poked him in the eye. He was gabbling obscenities at them, telling them that, oh, God, oh, dear fucking Jesus, they had to let him go; it was his last chance. Momentarily free of their restraining hands, he pressed up against the window, fumbling at its catch and half sobbing.

Then, suddenly, he stopped. His body sagged and his face, which had been drawn back in a snarl of fear, collapsed. He looked like a baby and like an old man, bewildered and alone. They wound their arms carefully round his breakable body and led him back to his bed, which they'd made up beside the sofa, laid him down, covering him with his duvet and leaning over him to tell him that it was all right, everything was all right, there, dear heart, they loved him and they weren't going to leave, he was safe. They called him 'darling' and 'sweetheart' and nonsense names, holding his hands, stroking his clammy brow. His panting subsided, though his caved-in chest still rose and fell rapidly.

After a few minutes, Marnie boiled milk and added nutmeg with honey; she held the striped mug to his lips and let him take tiny sips. His eyes were closed, the lids faintly blue, and he smelt fetid and damp. Oliver put on a CD of Chopin's *Études*, then poured two tumblers of whisky and handed one, without a word, to Marnie. After a while, Ralph relaxed into sleep and Oliver went upstairs, treading slowly and heavily. Marnie sat on the floor beside Ralph, holding his hand and letting the music wash over her while she drank her whisky, which tonight seemed to have no effect. She thought of Ralph's expression as he had rattled at the window: he had looked like a cornered animal.

He whimpered in his sleep and his limbs tightened in a spasm. Marnie put her hand on his clammy forehead and murmured something meaningless. 'You're all right,' she whispered, though of course he wasn't. She felt a very long way from anywhere safe; an ill wind blew through her. She didn't know how she was going to endure this, and for a moment she imagined walking out into the icy darkness and simply leaving Ralph and Oliver in this little house to face what was coming without her.

'Marnie.'

She must have fallen asleep. The fire had burnt low in the grate and she felt chilly and stiff. Her back was sore from sitting in the same position. 'Yes,' she whispered.

'I just wanted to know you were still there.'

'I'm still here.' She clambered to her feet, put a couple

more logs on the fire, then knelt to blow strength back into the dwindling flames. She pulled the tartan rug off the sofa and wrapped herself in it, shivering. There was still some whisky left in her tumbler so she took a swig. 'I'm not going anywhere.' She leant her head against the edge of Ralph's bed, feeling sleep thin and recede. 'Listen . . .'

Chapter Eight

At first Marnie had said she would not go to David's funeral. The memory of their last meeting, the sound of her laughter sending him storming out of the door and into his car, stayed with her. It didn't matter how often her mother told her that David had been on his way back from his friend's house when he died and that he had been drinking: her own guilt was lodged in her. She had spent hours trying to compose a letter of sympathy to his parents, and in the end had simply put, in her careful, crooked handwriting: 'I am so very sorry for your loss, with best wishes Marnie Still.'

She had recurring nightmares about it, waking up with a terrible lurch. She found that she could hardly bear to eat, although she tried to make herself because she did not want to play the part of victim and walk around the school with hollow cheeks. She would take half an hour to swallow her toast and marmalade in the morning, every mouthful like wet leather and nausea rising in her stomach; her mother studiously avoided fretting over her, but nevertheless Marnie was sometimes aware of her eyes following her.

At school she was regarded as a tragic heroine – her handsome boyfriend had died, leaving her bereft – and her refusal to accept such a role only seemed to enhance her reputation. She was surrounded by girls who wanted her to confide in them, but the only person she talked to was Lucy, who would listen to Marnie, her flat, clever face tipped slightly to one side. She never offered words of false comfort. Lucy had disliked David; she had found his particular brand of good looks faintly repellent and his sporty, cocksure friendliness had made her pinched and grimly pedantic in his presence. It was Lucy whom Marnie rang when she decided, at the last minute, that she should go to the service after all, although she wasn't certain why. She didn't want to go alone, though: she needed dry-eyed, unsentimental Lucy to be there with her.

Marnie borrowed a black skirt from her mother, which was too wide at the waist and came down almost to her calves, and black boots that were a bit too small for her now and pinched her toes. She pulled on a long black jersey, tied her unruly hair back as neatly as possible, and put a thin silver chain round her neck. She barely recognized herself in the mirror, pallid and ungainly in overlapping layers, and on an impulse she took her mother's green-handled sewing scissors with their long blades and cut through her fringe, which she'd nearly succeeded in growing out. Now her face looked naked, and somehow younger under the asymmetrical slant.

Outside, the sky was a marbled white and turquoise, the leaves on the trees were still clean and pale, the sea in the distance glittered and spun. This didn't feel like the day of a funeral – in films, they usually happened on grim winter days, in black-and-white. Seth and Paolo had been buried in March, just on the cusp of spring; Emma, when asked, said merely that it had been raining, but not heavily.

Marnie remembered only small and seemingly random patches of the day, as if she was catching glimpses of her own life through a thick, enveloping fog. She remembered needing urgently to pee, shifting from foot to foot but not daring to ask her mother, who was holding her hand so tightly she thought the bones would snap. She remembered – she thought she remembered – how weirdly small her brother's coffin was and how a large lady in a purple dress bent down, displaying a deep and mysterious cleavage, to give her an extra-strong mint that had made her eyes water. Did someone – the vicar? – say something about how, when an adult dies, we remember and mourn their past, but when a young child dies we mourn their lost future, all that might have been, or had she read it later somewhere and added it to her paltry collection of memories? She remembered a tall man, whom she had discovered later to be her grandfather, dressed in a thick black suit and weeping so noisily and violently that everyone else's grief seemed muted by comparison.

Seth and Paolo were buried together in the local churchyard, Seth's portion of ground pitifully small, his inscription brief to match his brief life ('Beloved son and brother, for ever missed'). Emma and Marnie used to go together to visit the twin graves every weekend and put flowers there, but gradually Marnie had ceased to accompany her mother and Emma continued her vigils privately, almost furtively, as if she did not want to force her grief on her daughter. Marnie still went sometimes, always alone and at odd times, drawn by emotions she did not fully understand. She would stand looking down at the graves with their simple headstones, which were already becoming worn with time and settling into the landscape. There were always flowers there; she wondered how often Emma came and how long she spent with her lost husband and son. Sometimes, to her shame, she felt a pang of jealousy, imagining the three of them huddled together out there, week after week and year after year, while she got on with her ordinary life.

David's funeral took place at the same church. The lozenge-shaped hole had been cut into the ground, ready for his coffin, for his parents did not want him to be cremated. Marnie saw, as she and Lucy walked up the lane towards the church, that a large number of people had already gathered and was relieved; she preferred to be hidden in the crowd. Many of the people there were young; some she knew, at least by sight; a few were from her school and those especially she wanted to avoid. Several of the girls were holding on to each other, buckle-kneed and starting to cry, or at least pressing tissues to their eyes.

Marnie lurked behind a large bush and put a restraining hand on Lucy – who was dressed in an ugly tweed jacket with oversized leather buttons that looked ancient and equestrian, though as far as Marnie knew she had never so much as offered a sugar cube on an open palm to a horse. 'Let's wait until the last minute,' she whispered. She wiped her forehead with the back of her hand, feeling hot and oppressed in her thick black garments. The skirt itched against her waist and her feet felt cramped and sweaty. 'I want to be right at the back.'

Lucy nodded. 'Sure.'

'What are you wearing, anyway?'

'This? I found it in Mum's cupboard, though I've never

seen it on her. I didn't know what I was supposed to wear to a funeral. Horrible, isn't it?'

Marnie felt a dreadful mirth working its way up her throat. She frowned sternly and concentrated on those filing past them into the church: a steady stream of people, old and young, dressed in sober clothes and on their faces a look of solemn anticipation. 'Why are we here?'

'I'm here because you asked me,' said Lucy. 'And you're here because you knew David. Quite well.'

'Not very well, really. In some ways, we were strangers.' She remembered his mouth clamping down on hers and his hands warm and solid on her back, then his splattered face as she had last seen it, harsh with dislike; in the days since he had died, it had taken on a hard-edged, over-lit quality. It loomed out of nightmares like a curse.

Lucy took Marnie's hand in hers, which was small and dry, with bitten nails and a callous on the middle finger from the press of her fountain pen. 'You're right to be here,' she said. 'Don't torment yourself. He crashed the car because he was in a giant strop. You didn't loosen the brake pads or whatever, did you? Everyone today will describe him as some kind of saint. He wasn't. He was a bit of a jerk, to be honest.'

'Ssh.'

Lucy's voice had risen on the last words, and a few heads had turned towards them.

'Sorry. But it's just moral luck. Bad luck.'

'What do you mean?'

'He was being a bully and you giggled at him. What's so terrible about that? If he hadn't died, you wouldn't feel your behaviour had been wrong, would you?'

'Maybe not, but –'

'*Ergo*, it's not.'

It was what Marnie wanted to hear – and why she'd brought Lucy with her, if she was honest. But it jarred: it was the wrong day for a beginner's lesson in moral philosophy.

'It's very kind of you to try to make me feel better, but it's not that simple, Lucy. Anyway, I don't want to be thinking about myself right now. It's not right somehow. It gets in the way of the main thing, which is nothing to do with me and my stupid guilt, or if not guilt then – shame, I suppose. I want to think about David and his poor family and feel sorry that he's dead – not *bad*, sad. That's what I'm here for. I want to feel sad.'

'Right. Sad. But they're about to close the doors.'

Standing right at the back of the thronged church, Marnie could not immediately see the chief mourners, only the bobbing heads of those in front of her. She stood on tiptoe and caught a glimpse of the coffin, with a large bouquet of flowers placed on top, and of the vicar's white surplice. It was hard to make out what he was saying. His words distorted in the high spaces of the church, and the woman in front of them rustled in her bag for lollipops that, at regular intervals, she popped like a dummy into the mouth of her small, fidgety daughter. There were hymns but Marnie, whose mother, as far as she could recall, had never taken her to a single religious service after the one when they had buried Seth and Paolo, didn't know the tunes. The densely printed words in the hymn books ran together when she squinted at them, turning into meaningless and shifting squiggles under her dyslexic stare. She tried to follow the lines with a finger, but was always several phrases behind, so she gave up. People seemed to her to be singing two different tunes, and there was a self-satisfied baritone somewhere near the front at least four notes ahead of everyone else. She frowned and bowed her head, trying to concentrate on the organ music.

She was waiting for sadness to well in her at last. No one else seemed to be having trouble. Muffled sobs and gasps filled the church. People sniffed and blew their noses. Someone near the front, whom Marnie couldn't see, was weeping quietly and steadily. David's headmaster gave an address and the sounds of grief swelled, like a river about to burst its banks. Chas Fulbright, David's best friend, made a clumsy little speech that was addressed not to the congregation but to the dead boy – he recalled football triumphs and kept calling him 'mate'. Choked with tears, he couldn't get to the end.

Finally, after a shuffling hiatus and an outburst of dry coughs, a violin started up. Marnie, pressed against the wall with a cold radiator digging into the small of her back, could not see who was playing, but the music, full of scraping errors and mis-hit notes, affected her in a way that none of the words had been able to do. She was thinking of the raw hole cut in the ground outside, narrower at its base. Soon David would be lying near her brother and her father, alone through all the cold dark nights ahead. No one would ever see his broad white smile again or hear him give that boisterous laugh. She let herself picture him standing in his characteristic posture: his strong runner's legs slightly apart, his head back and his blue eyes gleaming with assurance, looking as if he owned the earth; it had irritated her then, but now it seemed tragic. Her eyes pricked; she ran a finger cautiously round the rims, anxious that no one should see her weeping and offer her sympathy she did not deserve.

Then it was over, and the crowds bunched together to let the Tinsley family through. At last Marnie could see them at the top of the church near the pulpit, standing in a black-clad group: Mr Tinsley in a thick suit that was too tight, straining at his shoulders and held together by a single button at the front. His face looked redder than ever, eyes bloodshot, lips pulpy. It was only now, seeing his inflamed face, that Marnie understood what David's death meant and a trickle of horror worked its way down her spine. At his side stood Mrs Tinsley, desiccated and almost yellow in her unbecoming mourning clothes. Her face was bonier than it had been, and her body under the coat was all angles and sharp joints; she looked suddenly old. Grace was slumped in her wheelchair, head sunk between her shoulders and one arm trailing over the side, the hand clenching and unclenching. And there was Ralph. His ill-made suit was enormous on him; inside it he seemed shrunken. Someone had taken the scissors to his hair, giving him an ugly convict's cut that made him look like a mutinous, wretched ten-year-old.

'Oh, God,' Marnie whispered. She felt Lucy's hand take hers for comfort. 'Poor things.'

The coffin was carried out of the church by six of David's school friends, lumpy and awkward in their borrowed clothes. The Tinsley family followed it, walking slowly through the hushed congregation, Grace's wheelchair bumping on the uneven floor. Mrs Tinsley's burning eyes briefly met Marnie's before they both glanced away, but Ralph stared at her as they passed, then turned his head to keep her in sight for longer. At last they were gone, out of the cool, still church and into the soft breathing warmth of the day.

It must have been about a week afterwards, and already late. The long shadows that lay across the garden were being gradually engulfed by night. After a cloudless day, the air had a sharpness to it. Marnie and Emma had eaten boiled eggs with buttered toast, then poached pears and yoghurt for their supper, and had laid the table for breakfast the next morning. It was a quiet week: they only had an elderly couple with them who had come in at seven thirty that evening and gone to bed well before nine.

Emma retired to the little room at the back of the house, more like a cupboard, where she struggled to keep up with her paperwork and bills, and Marnie went upstairs to finish her homework. Her O level play was *The Tempest*, and she was trying to write an essay on how Prospero changed from the first Act to the last. She knew what she wanted to say, it was putting it into correctly spelt words and separating them out with punctuation that remained hard for her. She put on her pyjamas and dressing-gown, then sat at the little table Emma had rescued from a skip and Marnie had painted green; she gazed helplessly at what she had already done. She saw how her writing tipped, slid off the lines, and felt certain it was riddled with errors that remained invisible to her. Emma always told her to read things out loud and listen to where she drew a breath, so she tried that now: '"When we first see Prospero in Act One . . ."' Should there be a comma after 'Prospero'? She put it in anyway and continued, '". . . he is an angry man full of thoughts of –"'

She broke off, hearing a soft, insistent rapping at the front door. She looked at her watch, frowning. It was nearly ten o'clock. The rap came again, slightly louder, and Marnie sighed, tightened the belt on her dressing-gown and went down the stairs. She pulled open the door.

Later, she tried to describe to Lucy how she felt when she saw Ralph. 'He was like a stray puppy or something,' she said. 'Kicked around and beaten and scared, but putting his trust in you all the same. It was all I could do to stop myself picking him up.' He was wearing old trousers with paint on them and a thin T-shirt, plimsolls with no laces, no socks. His brutally cut hair stood up in spikes. A yellow, blue and black bruise flowered under his right eye, which was bloodshot.

'Ralph!' she said. 'What on earth –' Something in his expression stopped her dead. 'Won't you come in?' she said politely, and stepped back.

For a moment, Ralph simply continued standing there. His face was quite blank. He stared at her without moving.

'Ralph,' said Marnie. She put a hand on his arm, but it was like touching a steel girder.

'I don't know,' said Ralph at last, then stopped.

'Don't just stay out there. You'll freeze. Ralph?'

'It's just –' he said.

'Let me,' said a voice behind her. Emma was still wearing her reading glasses and had a pencil tucked behind her ear. 'You come with me,' she said to Ralph.

Her voice was matter-of-fact, solid enough to lean against with no fear of falling, but in her eyes Marnie saw a melting tenderness that made her look away quickly, as if her mother was suddenly naked in front of her. She didn't like it and, for an instant, she wanted to push Ralph out into the cold and slam the door on him.

'This is Ralph,' she said to Emma. 'He's David's brother. I told you about him . . .'

But Emma wasn't listening. She put her arm round Ralph's stiff, thin shoulders and drew him into the house, leaving Marnie to close the door behind them.

'Get a jersey,' she said to Marnie, sitting him down at the table. He lifted a hand and cupped the battered right side of his face, ashamed.

When Marnie returned, Emma had put the picnic rug over his lap and pulled off his shoes. She pulled the jersey over his head and he sat there unresisting. 'When did you last eat?' she asked. Ralph looked at her blankly. 'Right, I'm going to make you a hot drink for a start.'

She turned away to the stove and Marnie hovered awkwardly. 'I'm very sorry about David,' she said at last. It sounded so formal.

He hunched further into himself and said nothing.

'Here,' said Emma. 'Hot milk with honey and nutmeg. Drink it.'

Ralph lifted the mug and took a small sip, then put it down on the table with a clip. Marnie thought that if she reached out and touched him, he might shatter into hundreds of sharp fragments.

'He'd better stay the night,' Emma said to Marnie. 'Do you want to go and make the bed up?'

'All right,' said Marnie, obediently, fighting down the urge to weep so that she, too, not only Ralph, would feel Emma's gaze turned on her with such concentration. 'On the sofa?'

'No.'

'But the B-and-B guests are –'

'He can sleep in the attic room.'

'But –'

'It's fine, Marnie. Take the sheets I washed this morning from the boiler room. You could put a hot-water bottle in as well.'

'OK.'

Marnie climbed the stairs with the warm sheets, her legs heavy under her. When she pushed open the attic room's door, the air smelt woody and unused. She didn't immediately turn on the light, but felt her way into the small room and stood there, her eyes straining in the darkness. A small patch of night glimmered through the skylight; she could just make out the shape of the bed and the chest on the other wall. Hugging the linen, she buried her face in the crisp cleanliness. She was finding it hard to breathe normally. It was as if she had a heavy weight on her lungs. It had been a long time since she had come into this room; sometimes she almost forgot it existed. She couldn't remember when she had last pushed the door open and put her head round to peer in at the empty spaces. Perhaps Emma came up here sometimes, just to sit. She didn't know. There were things they didn't talk about; too many closed doors.

At last she turned on the light and busied herself, shaking the first sheet flat, and letting it settle over the low bed, pulling it tight and tucking it under the mattress with the hospital corners Emma always insisted on for the B-and-B guests. Then the second sheet, the blue blanket doubled up for warmth, the pillow inserted into its case. She plumped it and turned down the covers to make it look welcoming. She did everything quickly, efficiently, holding the strangeness at bay. The room had been cleared out long ago, nothing personal left there, but there were still barely visible lighter squares on the walls where posters had once been stuck. Footballers? Dinosaurs? Marnie didn't know. She couldn't remember. She had never tried to remember and didn't want to begin now.

She collected the hot-water bottle from the bathroom and started down the stairs to the kitchen to fill it. But then she halted. She could hear her mother's voice, low and steady, the way she often talked to Marnie, and she had the sudden sensation of being an intruder in her own house.

Emma was sitting beside Ralph at the kitchen table, holding a cold compress against his cheek.

'I've done it,' said Marnie.

'Thanks.' Emma met her eyes. She gave her a small, approving nod and a smile. 'Are you tired?'

'I'm not sure.'

'It's late and you've got school tomorrow. Perhaps you should go to bed.'

'Maybe I will,' said Marnie. All of a sudden her head felt thick with weariness. 'I'll just fill the bottle.'

'I'll wake you at the usual time.'

'Good night. Good night, Ralph.'

He looked at her then, his eyes burning in his puffy,

discoloured face. On an impulse she went to him and bent down to kiss his forehead, but he lifted his face and she found herself kissing his lips, very quickly and lightly. They were hot and dry, like a feverish child's. 'It wasn't our fault,' she said. 'We are not to blame.'

She lay in bed and listened to the sounds downstairs, trying to make out words. There was the chink of china. Footsteps. She thought she heard the front door open and shut, but perhaps she was imagining it. And, anyway, it merged with her dream in which someone was standing at the foot of her bed, calling her name. It was Seth, of course, who often visited her in her sleep although sometimes in strange disguises; this time he was telling her he'd come home and why didn't she get up and make him welcome, but for all her efforts she couldn't move her limbs or open her gluey eyes. Wasn't she pleased he had come back after all these years, he asked, and did she want him to go away again?

But no, not Seth after all, for how could it be? It was her mother, telling her it was morning, time to get out of bed, another beautiful day outside, look – the gush of light flooding her room as Emma drew back the curtains – and the cockerel outside crowed and crowed again, the mighty show-off in his harem.

The smell of bacon, coffee, toast. Marnie pushed herself upright and rubbed her eyes. Her dream was still a vapour trail in her head.

'Is Ralph –'

'He's cooking breakfast,' said Emma, 'and entertaining our guests.'

'Is he OK?'

'He seems entirely fine,' replied Emma, drily. 'You can judge for yourself. Come on, or you'll be late.'

Ralph, enveloped in Emma's white apron, was wielding a slatted steel spatula, which he lifted high in the smoky air as Marnie entered. 'Don't talk yet!' he said. 'One moment.'

He slid the spatula under the blistering egg and deposited it on the plate beside him, its yolk oozing out over the charred rashers of bacon that had shrivelled to a quarter of their normal size. Marnie couldn't work out how he had managed to use so many pans or make quite such a mess. When she walked on the tiles, they were sticky underfoot.

'There we are, Mr Lomas,' Ralph said, putting the greasy plate in front of the old man with a flourish. 'Egg sunny-side up, kind of – it's a bit broken I'm afraid – bacon, sausage, grilled tomato, mushrooms and fried bread. The egg, like your wife's, is fresh from the hens that run free in the garden. You can hear the cockerel if you listen.'

'Thank you,' Mr Lomas said faintly, tapping the hard strips of bacon with his fork.

'While you're eating that, I'll do your toast.' He picked up the bread knife and ran his thumb down its serrated edge. 'Brown or white? And there's home-made marmalade, home-made raspberry jam or local Suffolk honey.'

'I'm not sure we'll be able to manage the toast, dear,' said Mrs Lomas, beaming fondly at him. 'Thank you all the same.' She turned towards Marnie. 'Your young brother has been looking after us extremely well,' she said.

'Well, actually . . .' began Marnie, then stopped. What was the point? 'I'm glad,' she said. 'I'll wash up. Just tell me if there's anything else you need.'

'We'll be on our way soon.'

'This place is great,' hissed Ralph, joining her at the sink where she was stacking pans. 'I woke this morning and I couldn't believe it. It feels like I've stepped into a whole new world. You can see the sea. I can't imagine what it would be like to see it at the beginning of every day. Or do you get used to it? Tell me you don't. It must change each time you look at it, different colours and moods. Look at the haze on it now. It'll burn away later.

'Once I took Grace to the seaside, just her and me. I pushed her all the way – about eight miles it was and on that busy road most of the way so cars whizzed by. I could feel the heat of their exhaust on my skin. I was so tired I thought I'd have to give up. My muscles were burning and I felt dirty and sick. I took her to the shingle beach, you know the one, and of course I couldn't push the wheelchair over the shingle to get to the sea and it goes up a kind of hill there, so we couldn't even see it from where we were and it wasn't nice weather any more. I was nearly crying, I was so tired and hot and cold at the same time. Maybe I was crying. I used to cry pretty easily when I was younger. I couldn't control it at all. David used to jeer at me. Well, he wasn't the only one, of course, people at school jeered as well, but David was worse because he was my brother and he was meant to stick up for me and he didn't. I think he was embarrassed by me

– he didn't want a cry-baby brother. Probably when I was born he thought he could have a clone of himself to play football and cut worms in half and do press-ups with. Instead he got this runt who wrote poetry and cried at sad films. Funny that, when I haven't shed a tear over David. I want to. I really badly want to cry. I sit in my room and concentrate on crying, but the more I try the more impossible it gets. They think I don't care. They look at me and I can see the violent disgust in their faces. But, really, it's because I'm frozen up inside and maybe I'll always be like that. For ever and ever.'

'Ralph,' said Marnie gently. She put one hand on his shoulder and felt him shudder at her touch. Behind her the Lomases stood up from the table, scraping their chairs across the floor.

'Sorry. Sorry. Where was I? Yes, the beach. I thought about carrying her, but Grace is really heavy, you know – and she's this dead weight too, which makes it even worse. Then this really nice woman – she looked a bit like your mum actually. What if it was your mum? – helped me. We lifted the chair and carried it right to the edge of the water and Grace sat there and chortled. It was really nice to see her. You think she's always happy, I bet, a big, happy, mindless lump – that's how most people see her anyway – but usually when she smiles and stuff, that's not anything like happiness. I think it's more like anxiety, actually. I think she's like this clumsy, eager bundle of fear and she's always waiting for something terrible to happen to her but hoping for something nice. Like a dog. I love dogs. When I leave home I'll have a dog. A mongrel. I'll get it from the rescue centre and make it feel safe again. Dogs are unconditional – you know that whatever else happens they'll be there for you. OK, but this day Grace was really happy. I took off her shoes and socks and splashed water on her feet, which are always purple – bad circulation, Mum says – and kind of turn inwards, pigeon toes. You've probably never noticed – well, of course, why would you? I heard an ice-cream van on the road and I left her sitting on the beach and ran and got her a double cone with a Flake stuck in and when I got back the tide had come up and the water was round her ankles. I gave her the ice cream and she took out the Flake and pressed the cone against her mouth so the blob of ice cream just spread out across her whole face and she made a lovely sound – a kind of gurgle of contentment, which made me feel contented too. As if I was doing something good. The water came up even more. The nice woman was gone by then and I had this thought that we'd just have to go on sitting there while the tide rose and rose. I imagined Grace's head stuck up through the waves and she'd still be smiling and her face covered with ice cream and chocolate and salt – though, of course, it wouldn't have been like that. I'll dry the dishes if you want. Then it was – What do you call it, when the tide kind of stops still?'

'Slack water.' Marnie wanted him to stop talking in that terrible eager fashion, his thin body practically pulsing with energy. She wanted to hug him to stillness.

'Slack water. Yes. It was slack water, and after that the sea went down really quickly. I could feel it sucking under the shingle. Then it was gone. Just wet pebbles and the sky was grey and it was over.' He stopped and the life seemed to go out of him. 'Oh, well,' he said, under his breath.

'Shall we have some breakfast now?' Marnie asked, when she was sure he'd run out of words. 'I have to go in ten minutes but I could make some toast.' She grinned. 'With home-made marmalade, home-made raspberry jam or even local Suffolk honey.'

He smiled back. His face, she thought, was as mobile as a kaleidoscope. Its expression continually broke and re-formed. Now he looked young and soft, and she was seized by an emotion that later became very familiar when she was with Ralph: the desire to rescue him.

'Toast and jam, please.'

'Do your parents know you're here?'

He shrugged.

'Ralph?'

'Your mother phoned them last night. I didn't want her to but she insisted,' he said shortly. 'She said she'd drop me back there this morning.'

'Were they all right about you being here?'

He shrugged once more.

'Your eye, Ralph, how did that happen?'

'I don't want to talk about it.'

'But –'

'*I don't want to talk about it,*' he repeated fiercely. He thrummed his fingers on the work surface while she sliced bread and put it under the grill. 'She showed me how to throw a pot before I went to sleep.'

'Mum?' So the sound of the front door opening and shutting had been the pair of them sneaking out to Emma's work shed and kiln at dead of night.

'She said I could come back and paint it.'

'That's good.'

'Is it? You don't mind?'

'Why would I mind?'

'I can think of dozens of reasons. Hundreds.'

'I don't mind,' Marnie said, though she wasn't sure that she was speaking the entire truth. Ralph continued to look at her questioningly, so she went further: 'I'd like it.'

'You'd like it,' he repeated, his face lighting up. 'Really?'

'Your toast's ready. Yes.'

'So, you see,' said Marnie, wrapping the blanket more closely round her and shivering, 'I thought of you as – Ralph? Ralph?'

There was no reply, but she could hear his whispery breaths. The fire was no longer burning; she poked at the ash and the embers flickered briefly. She swilled back the last of the whisky and looked at her watch. It was four in the morning: it was hard to imagine that anyone else in the world would be awake like her, keeping vigil.

She went to the door, pulled on her boots, picked up the torch and opened it, recoiling as she felt the lash of cold wind on her skin. It whined and snarled in the trees and skimmed over the ground, sending up stinging bits of grit. Drops of rain dashed themselves into her face. She reached the woodshed, turned on the torch and shone it inside. She found some pieces of kindling, then lifted as many seasoned logs into the cradle of her arms as she could before scurrying back into the house. The single dim lamp in the main room lit her way.

She crouched by the fire, fingers already numb, and

blew life back into the embers before feeding the new bluish flames with the thinnest pieces of kindling.

Beside her, Ralph's breath rose and fell.

So began the happiest time in my life.

I didn't come back at once. I made myself wait at least a week, holding the image of your house by the sea in my mind, like a painting: you in your school uniform and your hair in ridiculous plaits; your mother with her lined face and watching eyes. I would crouch in my room, under the swallow you had painted for me, and listen to the sounds of the house. My father bellowing. My mother querulous, then weeping, wailing. The flat slap of a hand against a cheek; I could almost make out the 'plack' of each separate finger as it landed and my own face would sting with shame that I didn't go to help. Then as often as not, someone would be retching, vomiting, groaning into the early hours of the morning. A cough. Grace doing her head-banging on the pillow in the next-door room, bang, bang, bang, until I thought she must hurt herself, but I knew that was how she shut out the anger and despair. And behind all the ugly noises, of course, lay the relentless silence. David's room, which my mother dusted every day, making sure not to disturb the trophies and the medals on his shelves, nothing altered from the day he had died, was the black hole at the heart of the disordered house. No music came from there, no laughter. No door slamming and no young, bold voice calling out orders.

It's only now, all these years later when it's too late, I can see that my father was a disappointed and unhappy man. I can remember him when I was much younger, not even at school, and he was different. He was in the army then, and wasn't drinking — or not so you'd notice it in the lurch of his steps and the red glare of his eyes. I think he was very like David, and when he was

David's age — the age David was when he died, I mean — he was probably the golden boy of his school, too: good at sport and good with girls, a broad-shouldered, blue-eyed charmer. Then he got a job, he got a wife, he got the taste for booze, he got debts, he got kids — and only David turned out the way he wanted. I was a runt with my nose in a book and Grace was 'a dribbling retard'. His words. I don't know which of us disgusted him most, but it was easier to focus on me. Even he could see that turning on Grace would make him an unforgivable bully. He wasn't anyone's hero any more, except mine for a while before I saw him beat my mother and clip Grace round the ear.

I used to want very badly to please him. I remember he would go fishing on a Sunday sometimes — the kind of fishing I don't understand, when you throw the fish back in once you've caught them instead of frying them in butter over a campfire . . . the way we did that time, do you remember? But I used to accompany him anyway, and occasionally he would let me hold the segmented black rod, his pride and joy, which stood in the scullery with the box of lures beside it, and try to throw the line out over the water with that flick of the wrist he had taught me, in those days before I'd seen him hit Mum and raise his fist to Grace and weep with maudlin, drunken self-pity at the kitchen table. Now, I make myself think back to him by the scummy stretch of river, when his face was thinner and his eyes were clearer and his laugh didn't sound snarled and vicious. I remind myself that he wasn't a bad man, really. He knew we despised him. The rot of failed dreams got into his soul.

After David died, when Dad beat me, I would close my eyes and will myself to imagine I was walking down your garden, past the clucking hens, in through the back door to the warmth of your kitchen. Sometimes you can separate yourself from what's happening to your body. Herbs, coffee, oranges, toast, soap suds, paint and glue. Two women sitting at the table, not talking but together somehow. Maybe you were decorating a pot. Maybe you were playing your accordion or doing your homework with that frown of concentration on your face that you always have when you're writing. I would try to hear the scratch of your pen nib on thick paper as the belt came down. You would look up as I came in and you would smile at me. The buckle ripped bits of skin; the pain spurted upwards, into my teeth and skull, down my fingers, every bit of me bright with it, but I wasn't going to cry out. He was never going to make me cry again. I would sit at your old table and put my hands on the knots of wood and feel the sun spill warmth through the open window onto my bare arms and everything was going to be all right. There was another world out there.

A week or so later, on a Sunday, I finally returned to see you. I didn't call in advance: I was scared you would say no or put me off until later. I walked all the way, about seven miles, but it was good because, although it had rained in the night, it was a fine, clean morning, blue and green and gold. I set off early, before my parents were awake and while it was still cool, and took my time. Even now, as I lie here on what will be my deathbed, I remember how I took my shoes off when I got out of town, and walked in time to certain songs. Held my breath between pairs of trees. Walked backwards for a bit. Jumped puddles. Made out shapes in the small clouds on the horizon. You know how often the best time is just before something happens, when anything is possible? I felt I was doing something momentous, although I knew that for you and Emma it would simply be a visit from a boy they barely knew and had very probably not thought about since they last saw him.

It was only when I got to your house that I let myself feel at all nervous. What was I going to say when you opened the door? I made myself think of opening sentences. 'Hi, Marnie, I was just passing . . .' *Silly, how could I be just passing when the lane dribbled out at the end of your drive? It never occurred to me that you wouldn't be there, but so it proved. I walked up the track, past the beech tree and the silver birches, the hens in their run, the rose bushes and the peonies that were beginning to wilt. I noticed how well cared for everything looked. There was a vegetable plot — later, I helped dig it over and plant things — which was laid out in sprouting rows, with a coiled yellow hose beside it. A wooden bench looking out over the sea, which on that day was turquoise.*

I knocked and there was no reply, and no sound inside the house. I pushed open the letterbox and peered inside at the wooden floorboards; knocked again. I went to the work shed where Emma had shown me how to throw a pot and knocked on its door as well, though I already knew that no one was there. So I sat on the bench to wait. I hadn't even brought a book with me, or a pad of paper. I rolled myself a cigarette and smoked it, then buried the butt in the soil. I did a headstand and made myself stay in it for two minutes, while the blood pounded in my head and I started to feel weird. Then I thought I might as well do something constructive, so I went to the vegetable plot and started to weed it. There weren't many weeds to pull out actually; just a few dull green shoots at one end, and a few darker ones dotted around. I wished there were more — I wanted you to come back and see that I'd transformed the plot. When I was done, I turned on the hose at a tap on the outside wall of the house and watered it carefully and then, because I was so hot by now, and wretched with disappointment that you weren't there, I held the hose over me and let the water stream off my head and down my body until I was wet through.

That was when you and Emma returned, walking along the drive with a man between you, laughing. You shaded your eyes against the sun when you saw me to make out who I was. For a moment I thought you wouldn't even recognize me. You were wearing frayed denim shorts, a red T-shirt and sandals, and your hair was tied loosely back; as you came closer I could see you had new freckles across the bridge of your nose and your bare arms were tanned. Emma wore a green skirt and a battered straw hat. She was carrying a lidded basket. I didn't take much notice of the man, except to see that he wasn't young, and he held a rug under one arm.

'Ralph?'

I put the hose down and the water gurgled into the grass beside me. I shook my head and sprayed little drops around my face. 'I was just passing. No, of course I wasn't. Hello. You said you didn't mind. So I came. I, um –'

'Why have you pulled up all of Mum's –'

'Hello, Ralph,' interrupted Emma, moving forward and giving me a swift kiss on the cheek. She didn't seem to mind that I was soaking wet. 'How nice to see you.'

'Weren't those weeds?'

'Never mind that now.' She moved away to turn off the tap. 'Come and have some coffee with us. Or would ginger beer be more to your liking?'

'If it's not too much trouble.'

'Of course not. Do you want me to find you some dry clothes?'

'No. I'll dry off soon enough.'

'Why don't you and Marnie sit out here and I'll go and fetch the drinks? By the way, this is Eric. He's from Scotland but he's staying with us for a few days while he visits his mother.' She smiled at Eric and added, clearly for his benefit not mine: 'He used to be a B-and-B guest, but he's our friend now. Eric, this is Ralph.'

'Hello, Ralph.' Eric grasped my hand. He must have been about fifty then. He had beautiful silver hair and weathered skin with lines radiating out from his eyes as if he had spent a lifetime smiling, though on that morning he seemed grave and treated me with a respect that was new to me and made me immediately like him. His handshake was firm enough to make me gasp. 'I'm pleased to meet you.'

You gave me a sideways glance and then, taking the rug from Eric, shook it out and sat down on it with long, slender legs folded under you.

'We had a picnic breakfast by the sea,' said Emma. 'If we'd known you were coming . . .'

I sat down next to you. My clothes stuck to me and I could feel your eyes on me.

'Shall I go?' I whispered, as Eric and Emma disappeared into the house. 'Was I wrong to come?'

You know the thing about you, Marnie? You're kind. You've always been kind. You gave me a proper smile at last and wriggled your feet out of their sandals.

'There's loads of breakfast left. Do you want something to eat?'

'Eat?'

'You know. When you put food in your mouth and chew it for a bit and then swallow it.'

'What is there?'

'Scones. Strawberries.'

'That'd be nice.'

'Here. Help yourself.' She pulled the basket across and opened the lid for me. 'You're wet through.'

'What did I pull up?'

'Lettuce. Broad beans, I think.'

'I wanted to help.'

'Oh, well.'

'Sorry.'

127

'Are things all right at home?'

I muttered something, not wanting to let the darkness of home seep into this summer brightness.

We sat in silence for a while. I pulled the hulls out of the lush strawberries and ate them one by one, slowly. Emma brought out two glasses of ginger beer and a towel. She told me I had to stay for lunch.

'You're lucky to have a mother like yours,' I said, when she'd gone.

'I know.' You crossed your legs and tucked both your feet under your thighs. Your thick dark hair shone in the sunlight; there were tiny beads of sweat on your upper lip. I stared at you, a throb of happiness in my fingertips and in my skull. You seemed so self-possessed and perfect, sitting in a lotus position, your palms turned upwards on your knees, the soles of your bare feet grubby.

'Do you think that if you started from that tree stump there you could get all the way to the sea without touching the ground?'

'You mean climb along trees and walls and things?'

'Yes.'

'I don't know,' you said dubiously, wrinkling your nose. 'Probably not.' Then you pulled your hair more tightly into its ponytail and put your sandals back on your feet. 'Let's try.'

It didn't feel as though we were sixteen years old, more like seven. We climbed into small knotty trees, leapt from boulder to log, teetered along the crumbling remains of dry-stone walls, scraped our knees and hands, got grit in our eyes, felt the salty wind and the sun burn our cheeks and shoulders, reached the beach by cheating and taking our shoes off to use as stepping-stones across a patch of bare ground. Then we swam in our clothes, shrieking at the cold and giggling and pushing each other under the water, before lying back and gazing up at the slab of clear blue sky above us. You were better at swimming than me, like a dolphin. I watched you and for a moment I forgot about David, about Dad in his cups or Mum with a face that shrivelled when she looked at me.

I stayed to lunch. I dipped a neat brush into a pot of aquamarine paint and laid the colour over my wonky bowl. I sat in the garden and played chess with Eric, and lost, and played again; neither of us spoke, and I could hear you and Emma indoors, though I couldn't make out the words. You brought out cup cakes, each topped with cream and a strawberry, and tea in a pot with a crooked spout that Emma had made long ago and you had decorated with tiny patterns. I still smell the fragrant steam as you poured. Such a perfect summer evening, soft and warm, with lengthening shadows on the lawn and mysterious pools of shade collecting under trees and shrubs. Salt was gritty on my skin; my hair felt thick and sticky. There were swallows in the eaves of your house, butterflies in the buddleia, dragonflies over the small pond near the steps, broody clucks of hens. I felt swilled through with joy. Rinsed clean.

I didn't want to go home. I thought of asking if I could stay in the small bare room you'd put me in last time – I hadn't yet discovered that it was your brother's old room; it took you months to tell me – but I didn't, because I knew Emma would insist that I rang my parents first. Eric drove me home after you'd made me cheese on toast. He insisted I borrow his book of chess moves to study and that made me happy, because it meant I had an excuse to come back soon.

I returned three days later, after school, and stayed until after dark. I came again very early on the following Saturday; Eric had left by then, and his place had been taken by a grumpy couple. I helped Emma cook breakfast for them: they could barely restrain themselves from bickering with each other over the eggs, sunny-side up. Emma didn't help either. She was clipped and glacially polite, *her face stony with dislike; the toast was burnt and the coffee tepid and she banged plates down in front of them. It was a side of her I'd not seen before, quite scary. Later, you and I pegged sheets and pillowcases onto the washing-line. The laundry billowed in the fresh breeze, revealing and then concealing you. So I hold you in my memory: in your denim shorts again, green paint on your knee, with a raggedy, round-necked grey jersey and a funny little cap pulled down over your forehead. Thick brows, pale clear skin, strong arms lifted above your head, candid eyes; now I see you and now I don't.*

And I kept going back, sometimes on consecutive days, and bit by bit it seemed perfectly normal that I should turn up and just join in with whatever you were doing and perhaps that was what I loved most – you were my alternative family, the one I could have had in a parallel universe. Shelling peas. Learning French verbs or chemistry formulae. Collecting eggs from the hens. Washing dishes. Cooking lemon cakes or flapjacks. Reading books – you never lost the habit of reading the difficult passages out loud to yourself in a whisper; even when you were silent your lips would move. Painting – you were doing Art O level and your final exam was coming up: you tried to teach me perspective and line. I still have the portrait you did of me in charcoal. It's in a frame above my bed in my room in Amsterdam. The me I want to be because you caught a look in my eyes – and I was looking at you.

It was a long summer, because we did our O levels in June and then were finished with school for ten long weeks. Do you remember the day you took me out in the sailing boat Emma had stashed under a tarpaulin near the shingle beach? It occurs to me now – and I wonder that it never did then – that it was the boat Paolo and Seth had died in. I don't know why she never got rid of it and I don't know how she let you go out in it. She was always determined not to infect you with her fear – though she insisted we wear enormous padded yellow life-jackets and if there was much wind she refused to let us go out.

The boat was a wooden tub with a gashed snub nose, a stubby mast and an ancient, ill-fitting main that we had to tie into place with bits of garden twine. Water gushed in through the bottom as soon as we heaved it into the sea. There wasn't really room for both of us, and my job seemed to be to sit on whichever side was tipping into the sea while loose ropes lashed at me, the sail flapped like a wounded gull and grey waves surged over the boat's rim — wrong nautical term, I'm sure; I never got the hang of the vocabulary. You sat at the tiller in your yellow life-jacket, entirely calm, but I yelled and giggled and cursed, and toppled into the bottom of the boat where I would bang my shin on the centreboard or slither like a beached fish while the boat bucked and thwacked its way through the choppy waters. And so again I hold you close in my memory: your thick dark hair whipped back in the wind, your grey eyes scanning the waves, a tiny secret smile on your face.

Marnie Still: all the memories of you that I've kept and guarded for this day. Painting your room — I was hasty and slapdash; you were meticulous. Picking mushrooms in the wood near your house, then cooking them with Emma, who taught me the Latin names that sounded to me like incantations. Teaching you, or trying to teach you, how to use full stops and commas in your writing — the only time I've known you almost hysterical, like a bat that's lost its sonar. It was the first time I'd seen you close to tears — it was just before we received our exam results, I suppose, though I didn't make the connection at the time. Then, just after we'd received them, when I did well and you didn't, getting drunk together in your room with the bottle of vodka I'd swiped from my dad: you were very subdued so the alcohol just made you floppy and sad. I so badly wanted to comfort you but didn't know how. Smoking cigarettes on the beach together, though you never really took to it. Riding our bikes along the country lanes with a picnic in the panniers: Emma lent me an ancient one that must have once belonged to Paolo, though she never said and I never asked; once I had that, it was easier to get to yours after school and cycle back late at night, the light screwed onto the handlebars throwing a dim, unsteady beam in front of me. Playing chess with Eric when he returned in the autumn to see his mother again and – having spent hours in my bedroom learning moves on my plastic travel set with several pawns missing – winning this time. Digging your garden over until my hands were blistered. Chopping wood, like you and Oliver have just been doing but I'll never do again. Learning how to light fires in the hearth, how to cook – you and Emma said very sternly that every man should be able to cook at least as well as women, it was his moral duty, so I mastered risotto and white sauce and omelettes and sponge cakes, and graduated to curries and casseroles and, my greatest triumph, lemon meringue pie. You taught me how to knit, for Christ's sake! But I never learnt how to make a room feel like a home, the way you and Emma could – just a few deft touches and a space was transformed. You're doing that here now. I'm dying in a home.

It was as if I had split myself into two people: there was the raw, surly Ralph, who truanted from school to avoid the bullies, who lived in the dark and disordered house in town, who locked his bedroom door at night for fear his father would crash in with his meaty fists and his ruined face and stand over him, breath reeking and curses spewing from his mouth. And there was the Ralph who slipped out of that nightmarish world and turned up at your house, terrified of his new happiness, terrified he might lose it and be back where he had started, except the darkness would be even darker now that he had known the light. Because of my fear, I tried to make myself indispensable and endlessly entertaining. I'd store up facts I'd learnt and stories I'd heard, remember jokes. When I skipped school I'd go and sit in the library and read all the newspapers. I imagine I must have been exhausting to have around sometimes, pouring out anecdotes and opinions.

I never talked of my family when I was with you. I thought of my other life as a virulent infection I didn't want to spread. I was ashamed, I suppose. I remember one evening, after you'd gone to bed – you always loved to sleep, you said you needed at least nine hours, preferably twelve – it was cold outside and I had made a fire for Emma. I was telling her about a philosophy book that I was reading, something about the nature of certainty, when she laid a hand on my arm and said, 'Can you take your shirt off, please, Ralph?'

'My shirt?'

'Yes, please.'

My cheeks were burning. 'No, Emma. Don't.'

'It's all right,' she said gently. 'I won't tell Marnie. But I need to see.'

'How did you know?' I said wretchedly.

She just smiled at me. I wouldn't have done it for anyone else, but I unbuttoned my school shirt, took it off and turned round, feeling ashamed and exposed. She put up her hand and touched the bruises with her cool fingers. I shuddered. 'It's only when he's drunk. He doesn't know what he's doing.'

'Mmm.'

'He's unhappy.'

'I'm sure he is. Does he hit your mother as well?'

'Sometimes.' My voice was a whisper. 'I don't stop him.'

'And Grace?'

'No.' I put my shirt back on and crouched beside the fire. 'What are you going to do? You're not going to do anything, are you, Emma?'

'I'm going to think about it. I can't just let this be . . . I'm sure you understand that. Do you always go to school?'

I mumbled something.

'Ralph?'

'No,' I said, not meeting her eyes. 'Sometimes I skip it. I go to the library, though. I read books. I teach myself things I'd never learn at school.'

I didn't want to tell her that, even though I was now in the sixth form and nearly seventeen, I was still miserable at school, where I was pushed around and jeered at. It was bad enough that she knew my father bullied me; I couldn't stand for her to know that my peers did too.

'Listen to me. You're going to have to promise me something now. You're going to go to school every single day, do you hear? You have less than two years left. Education is what will open doors for you and take you into better worlds. You go to school, you do your work, you pass all your exams and you're off into the wide world.'

'But, Emma . . .'

'What do you dream of being?'

'Me? Well, I don't know. My A levels keep all my options open, I guess. Sometimes I want to be a mathematician because I love maths – it's like a secret language I can speak – and sometimes I want to be a writer, or a film maker. Or a doctor, perhaps. The other day I was thinking that maybe I could be a geneticist; I was reading this book and – what? You're laughing at me.'

'Only in a nice way,' she said. 'Now I'm going to make you a cup of tea and then you're going to cycle home – unless you want to stay the night here.'

'You're very nice to me, Emma.' I wanted to lay my head in her lap and let her take care of everything for me. Tears pricked at my eyes but I blinked them away. I still hadn't cried about David, you know, or about anything since the day he had died. It was to be months before I finally cried. I guess you're coming to that, aren't you? In your own good time.

Of course it wasn't just some idyll. I had the blindness of an adolescent (I grew up slowly and reluctantly; I was still a child, really — you were so much more mature than I was) but I was aware of money difficulties. Your beloved house was old and coming apart at the seams. Things were always going wrong with it — the boiler broke down and had to be replaced; the damp course couldn't prevent wet seeping into the bricks; a crack crept ominously up the wall next to the front door and Emma used to measure it to see how fast it was lengthening and thickening. Wherever it was possible, you didn't call in workmen but did the job yourselves and, of course, I joined in, sanding down woodwork on Saturday mornings, helping you repoint the exterior and then paint it, spending back-breaking hours laying the gravel on your drive so that cars didn't damage their undercarriage on the deepening potholes.

Sometimes B-and-B guests showed their disapproval of the house's shabbiness. They wanted deep-pile carpets, colour TVs, en-suite bathrooms, fitted wardrobes with lights that came on when you swung open the door; instead they got a lavatory across the way, an ancient radiator that rumbled and belched and gave out very little heat, a rickety cupboard, old pockmarked beams, and a glorious view across the field to the sea. They wrote cool remarks in the visitors' book and we knew they'd never return. Emma would mutter, 'Good riddance,' as their car pulled away, but later she would put on her glasses and go into the tiny room that served as her office to rifle through receipts and bills. She could be very morose;

when she was like that, it was as if the sun had gone behind a cloud and the whole landscape chilled and darkened.

You, too, sometimes withdrew. Even though you were still polite and friendly, I had the feeling that you weren't really there. There were times when your down-at-heel lovely house, usually so warm and welcoming, was empty and sad, haunted by absences I didn't understand at first, and by deep, uncanny silences. You told me about your father and brother long after we were friends. It was nearly Christmas and there had been a light sprinkling of snow so we had walked down to the beach. Everything looked unfamiliar: there were patches of snow dappling the shingle, the sky was low and white, the sea a dull pewter and the tiny waves made no sound as they licked at the shore. Your voice was muffled when you spoke. I didn't say that Emma had told me already, after she saw me looking at the family photograph. I wanted to hear it in your words.

I'm making it sound as though it was just you and me and Emma, occasionally Eric (which was how I preferred it). There were others: the guests, of course, especially in the late spring and summer — even when they had retreated to their rooms we were aware of them there and couldn't entirely relax. Then Lucy was often with us, and I knew she and you spent a lot of time together when I wasn't around. I first met her the third or fourth time I visited, arriving unannounced to discover the two of you in the kitchen making a chocolate cake heavy enough to sink your boat. You two were licking out the bowl and turned simultaneously as I came in; on your faces there were chocolate smears and gleeful smiles. You looked like two naughty little kids. I felt a sharp stab of jealousy: you never looked like that with me.

I was jealous as well of Lucy's relationship with Emma: Emma treated her like a grown-up, asking her opinions and listening to her replies respectfully. But I couldn't feel angry with Lucy for long.

She was fiercely clever, sardonic, waspish, loyal and — yes — good. A good woman. I see her now with her smudged glasses on her small round face; her thin wrists, knotted shoulders, knobbly knees. She would lob dry comments into the conversation and wait to see what would happen. She would look at me with her disconcerting gaze and grin quickly, as if I'd passed some kind of test. Soon I liked her enormously — liked her passion for politics, her radicalism, her shyness. I liked her because she loved you but generously made room for me. And I liked her, of course, because she liked me. All right — she loved me.

Then there was Grace. One Saturday, unable to bear the thought of her sitting all day in front of the television while my parents bickered and slammed doors and the air boiled with unhappiness, I pushed her all the way to your house. I forgot to take her to the lavatory before we left, and to pack a drink, so she arrived hot, distressed and smelling of urine. Emma helped me wash her down and then you lent her some old clothes and we lifted her onto the lawn and she sat there, slumped among the daisies, smiling and cooing like a pigeon. You made her a daisy chain and hung it round her neck. I brought her back several times that year. You and Emma always kissed her forehead in greeting, and you talked to her as if she could understand what you were saying. You told her things; you teased me through her. 'Tell your brother his hair needs cutting,' you'd say. 'Tell your brother he needs to learn to clear up his own mess after cooking.' And perhaps you even confided in her because she couldn't react or reply. All your secrets were safe with her.

It's curious, but in that first year or so of knowing you, I never thought about you sexually. I adored you, but in a fervently romantic and chaste fashion. If we touched, it was in a rough-and-tumble way: arm-wrestling, pushing each other under the waves; sometimes you tucked a casual arm through mine. We behaved a bit like children with each other — to begin with anyway. Of course, you had been David's girlfriend, but I couldn't bring myself to think about that or to imagine him holding and kissing you. It horrified me to think of you gripped by desire. Anyway, he was dead and buried — my brother lying a stone's throw from yours.

I don't know when the innocent time came to an end, but I suppose it began when Oliver arrived.

Chapter Nine

Marnie stood by the window, trying to see signs of the storm that was raging outside in an orchestra of discordant sounds. The wind howled and she could hear the violent creaking of trees; rain pinged like bullets against the glass. As far as she could tell, there was still not even the faintest band of light on the horizon. She didn't hear Oliver come into the room on bare feet and jumped when he put a hand on her shoulder.

'Oh!' she said, turning in relief. 'You startled me.'

'Bad night?' His voice was quiet and held a note of tenderness that Marnie felt spread through her body.

She didn't answer immediately but looked at him. Very gently, he reached out a hand and brushed a tear from her cheek.

'I don't know,' she said at last. 'I was scared.'

'Of him dying?'

'Just scared.'

'You should have woken me.'

'No, you needed rest.'

'So do you. You look all in. I'll take over here. Go and lie down for a bit, try to sleep.'

'I don't think I can at the moment. Shall I make us some tea?'

'That would be nice.'

'Anything to eat?'

'Maybe later.'

He went and sat beside Ralph and held one thin hand between both of his warm, solid ones. 'Hello, my friend,' he said very quietly. It was impossible to tell if Ralph was asleep or not. 'Here I am. I'll stoke up the fire in a minute. Dot's bringing some portable heaters so the house won't be cold any more. You just tell me if you need anything, OK? Marnie's making us tea now. Marnie and her cups of tea, eh?'

Marnie put tea leaves into the pot and placed the kettle on the hob. While she was waiting for it to boil, she went to wash her face and hands. The face in the mirror was strained but composed. She pulled a comb through her hair, wincing as it tore into the knots.

'I had such dreams,' said Oliver, as she came back into the kitchen.

'Did you?'

After the horrors of yesterday evening, there was a new ease between them: the awkwardness and self-consciousness had dropped away, leaving in their place a solemn intimacy. They both felt they had moved to the next stage; that death had come much nearer, was crouching in the room with them.

'Disordered. I was dreaming but I knew I was dreaming.'

'I know that feeling. Here. Your tea.'

'Thanks.'

Marnie sat down on the other side of Ralph. With her free hand she stroked his hair. 'Did you hear the storm in the night?'

'Yes. And it's not really died down, has it? When it's

blown itself out we'll go and see what damage it's done. There'll probably be some trees down.'

'This morning I think I'll wash the windows.'

'Really?' Oliver sounded dubious.

'It seems silly to you, doesn't it? Washing windows he can't see from his bed, scrubbing floors he won't be walking on, making soup he can't drink and cakes he can't eat.'

'No, it's lovely. It wasn't like this before you arrived. Whenever he wakes, you're there, as if you've never been away. You're making life go on right until the last moment. All the small, ordinary things that seem like irritating chores until we're losing them.'

'Look, it's getting light.' Marnie bent nearer to Ralph. 'It's daytime now. The night's over.'

The storm abated. Outside, large and small branches littered the ground. A little tree had been ripped up by its roots, creating a surprisingly deep crater. Several tiles had come off the roof and the entire landscape looked as if it had been subtly rearranged. But now the clouds that had swirled with such force in the sky, like an inverted ocean, were breaking up and behind them lay pale blue. Marnie, freshly woken from her nap, walked cautiously across the sodden ground towards the loch, whose waters had been churned to a muddy brown. She turned back to look at Ralph's small house, standing stubborn and plain, surrounded by trees. Smoke was coming out of the chimney. She knew that Oliver was sitting in there, holding his friend's hand and talking to him. Soon she would go and join them. They would read poems and drink tea and do the small domestic tasks that were, in their intimate dullness, oddly pleasurable: pairing socks, washing Ralph's sweat-drenched T-shirts, rubbing wax into the wooden table, then buffing it with a soft brush until it had a honeyed glow, putting out crusts of bread for the birds that were struggling through the winter. All of a sudden, she was pierced with a shaft of joy that made her gasp and put her hand to her heart. Why should she be happy when she was watching over Ralph's deathbed? Yet she was exquisitely aware of feeling more finely tuned to life than ever.

She turned on her mobile and listened to messages. Lucy had called but only to say hello; a couple of friends were asking where she was and why she hadn't been at home for the last two days; Elaine reported that Eva had opened the puppet museum rather late on the two days she had been there, not until eleven o'clock, and Luisa – Eva's less flamboyant sister – was saying she wanted to join Eva and Marnie for Christmas, if that was all right. She knew from Eva that Marnie was away but she would arrive at the airport in four days' time and make her way to the flat.

'I miss you,' she said at the end. 'Marnie?' There was a pause, as if she thought that Marnie was actually listening to her speak. 'Marnie?'

Marnie called Eva at the museum.

'Hi!'

'That's a rather casual way to answer the phone. I might have been anyone – I might have been Elaine, for instance. What's that noise?'

'Marnie! Hang on, let me just turn that off. Greg? Turn the music off, will you?'

'Is Gregor with you?'

'He's helping out,' said Eva. 'That's OK, isn't it?'

'Does Elaine know?'

'Should she?'

'I'm not sure.' There was a crash and a loud laugh in the distance. 'Eva – is anyone else there as well?'

'Um – the others have come to keep us company.'

'Others? What others?'

'Oh – you know.'

'I don't.'

'It's OK, Marnie. Everything's good.'

'You can't just turn the museum into a party place.'

'They're dusting.'

'Dusting?'

'It's all cool.'

'Why don't I feel reassured? These others – are they staying in my flat?'

'Kind of.'

'Kind of. Right. How many?'

'Oh – not a lot.'

'Eva!'

'It's all right. We haven't trashed the place. They didn't have anywhere to stay. What could I do?'

'But –' Marnie closed her eyes, imagining her tidy flat, where everything had its proper place and pictures hung peacefully on white walls, full of strangers and in violent disarray. 'And Luisa's coming too?'

'Yes – are you pleased?'

'What about Fabio? Doesn't he feel deserted?'

'Uh-uh, he's going to be staying with – Actually, you probably don't want to know this right now.'

'Probably not.'

'Anyway, we can have a family Christmas, you and me and Luisa.'

'I don't know when I'll be back, though. I'm staying until the end.'

She stood for a moment after the conversation was over. A family Christmas: a light at the end of this dark passage. Lucy had wanted to change the world and had wanted Ralph; Ralph had wanted reckless adventures and Marnie. But all I ever wanted was a family, she thought: tall sons and beautiful daughters and somewhere to call home.

She didn't go back in immediately, but walked into the wood over the soft floor of fallen needles, until she found a well-shaped pine branch that had been ripped down during the storm. It was dark among the trees, almost like night, and shining drops of water fell noiselessly from the canopy above. Marnie held up her pine branch for inspection: it would have to do.

The wind was still blowing strongly, and now clouds raced across the sky, the blue patches widening all the time, a glister of cold brightness rolling across the land-scape. The nurse had been and gone, and there was a barely discernible smell of shit and disinfectant in the house. Oliver sat by the side of Ralph's bed reading poems in a low voice. Ralph's eyes were open, but Marnie could see immediately that he was drifting in a drug-induced drowsiness.

'Hello.' Marnie took off her coat, blew on her hands to warm them, then kissed Ralph's head carefully. Everything about him seemed infinitely frail and breakable. If she touched his skin, she half expected bruises to appear; when she lifted his head – so unnaturally large and heavy in contrast to his disappearing body – so that he could sip a mug of tea, she feared his neck might snap in her hands.

'What have you got there?' asked Oliver.

'Our Christmas tree.' She held it up.

'Gone by Christmas,' said Ralph, hoarsely.

'You're here now and so are we. This is our Christmas. I thought I'd decorate it for us.'

Marnie lifted the branch into a plastic flower-pot she had found in the woodshed, then packed it in tightly with stones collected on her way back from the woods. She put the pot on the packing case and stood it at the end of Ralph's bed, so he wouldn't have to turn his head to see it.

'Now you're here,' said Oliver, standing up, 'I'm going to dash over to Dot's. I'll collect the heaters and she's bought ice cream, as you asked, and also I'm going to borrow a DVD player and some old films I asked her to find for me. *The Lady Vanishes*, *His Girl Friday*, that kind of thing.'

Marnie nodded. She wanted to tell him not to be long, but held back the words. She had the sense that Ralph was slipping away from them, minute by minute. She could almost see him go, like a figure receding into the fog and then there would come a moment when he would be invisible. He rarely spoke now, and when he did the words seemed wrenched out of him by an enormous effort.

Oliver piled more logs onto the fire, then left, and Marnie put the kettle on to boil – she seemed to be making pots of tea on the hour. She rifled through the drawers and the piles of books and notepads stacked on the floor, and found some stiff card, as well as scraps of coloured tissue. She ran up the stairs to Ralph's old bedroom and took her sewing case and pastels out of her travel bag, then returned to the kettle's whistle.

'Shall we have music?' she asked Ralph. He didn't answer, though he looked at her all the time, following her movements with his enormous eyes. 'How about Haydn?' She pulled the CD out of its case and inserted it into the player. Violins filled the room in a minor key. She poured two mugs of tea for them, then sat beside Ralph and put a hand on his forehead briefly. She took out the sewing scissors and picked up the card. 'Bells?' she asked. 'Reindeer? Maybe just shapes.'

She cut a tiny spiral and laid it on the cover, over Ralph's chest. Soon dozens of paper shapes littered the bed; they rose and fell almost imperceptibly with his shallow breathing. She lifted Ralph's head gently and let him take a few sips of tepid tea, wiping his mouth with the hem of her shirt. Then she took her pastels and started to colour the card: blue, pink, green. She used a thick needle to pierce a hole in the top of each one, then threaded cotton through it and hung it from the pine branch. It was like being back at primary school. She twisted shreds of coloured tissue paper into fraying ribbons and tied them on as well, then added shreds of tin foil she took from the kitchen drawers.

'How does that look?'

'Nice,' he managed, or that was how Marnie interpreted the wisp of sound that came out of the side of his mouth.

Now the music was slower, more muted. It seemed to Marnie to possess a sombre, meditative quality and to be full of a sense of yearning. A kind of sorrow lodged in her throat; it was very like the homesickness she used to feel as a child. She rose from the chair and went to the low drawer beside the oven where she had noticed a bag of tea-lights. She took it out, tore open the thick plastic with her teeth and started to put them on every available surface.

'We'll light them later,' she said, 'when it starts to get dark. Now it's quite light for the first time since I arrived and rather beautiful outside – cold but almost clear. Look, I'll pull this curtain right back and you can see it better. I was in the wood, Ralph, just now, and there were shafts of light falling through the trees onto the floor of pine needles and moss. It was lovely. Mysterious, like a sacred place. I thought . . .' She stopped, hearing how her voice was thickening. 'I thought how precious you've been to me, even when we haven't seen each other for so long.' She stopped and looked at him. His eyelids were flickering. 'Can you hear me?'

He made no answer. She sat back in her chair, watching all the hanging shapes turn slowly on the pine branch, and listened to the music, which had speeded up without her noticing, sounding urgent now, as if it was reaching some kind of climax. From here, she could see how the sun broke in and out of clouds, so that the landscape was in continuous motion – now sombre and fantastical, now luminous. There was no clock in this room, and she didn't know what time it was; the implacable movement of minutes and hours had been replaced by light and dark, by half-dreams, poems read aloud and the quiver of flames in the grate, casting shadows over the room.

The music slowed once more and Marnie realized that she was listening to Haydn's 'Farewell Symphony' in which, at the end, the musicians take their leave one by one. She had seen it performed once, long ago, in a church. There had been candles on the stands, which were snuffed out as the music died away and the musicians left. She sat motionless in her chair by the bed, scarcely daring to breathe. Now the oboes had departed, now the horns; then the double bass stopped and the cello. Finally only two violins were left playing, muted notes of farewell. Then silence. Marnie, her hand on Ralph's, fixed her eyes on the brightness outside. She didn't know if he was awake or sleeping, but she continued their story nevertheless.

Chapter Ten

Marnie was seventeen years old when she met Oliver; apart from David, she had never had a boyfriend. And even with David, she had never been in love – not head-over-heels, heart-dislodged-and-burning-in-her-throat, sleep-deprived, enchanted, sick-and-stomach-churning, yearning-and-dreaming-and-foolish in love. Sometimes she thought there was something wrong with her, something missing, which meant that she would always hold back, retreating to her haunted house, her haunted mother, clinging fast to her childhood.

It was a drab Sunday in January – the kind of meagre day that never gets entirely light and passes slowly and restlessly in unsatisfactory tasks. Marnie had spent the morning helping Emma pack mugs and bowls in bubble-wrap, in preparation for a pottery stall the following week. Her fingers had whitened in the cold of the shed. After lunch she had tried to do schoolwork. Ralph and Lucy were doing their best to help her master grammar but, still, words turned to shapes as she stared at them. She hated punctuation, that was the fact of it. She was incapable of spelling. So instead, sitting in her room, she doodled on her English textbook, then picked up her art folder. She was taking Art and Textiles, and with those she felt at home. Sometimes, sitting in front of the fire while Emma sat nearby reading a book and Marnie pulled her needle through material watching a pattern grow, she felt a sense of contentment that was tangible and in the present: everything concentrated on the tiny, even stitches.

Now she picked up her charcoal. She was working on a series of sea views in black and white. The one she had in front of her now showed the hulk of an old boat – only its ribs left – half hidden among the long grass at the sea's edge. She and Ralph and Lucy had come across it on one of their walks a few days ago, and she had pulled out her sketchbook at once, drawn by its skeletal body in stark lines against the grey waves. Ralph and Lucy kept telling her to hurry up: they were freezing in the wind that lashed across from the east, flattening the reeds and blowing spray off the small waves. Marnie had told them they should go on without her, but they had dithered, throwing stones into the water and peering over her shoulder to see her drawing. Long-legged waders picked their way over the sand and shells, occasionally giving out muted, melancholy whistles. Lucy's face was blotchy in the cold; her eyes in their new contact lenses watered and she pulled her coat closer about her. Ralph was ridiculously underdressed, as he almost always was – in the ill-fitting, striped velvet trousers he'd insisted on buying in the charity shop, a collarless white shirt that showed his sharp collarbone and a long, beaded scarf that flapped behind him; he didn't even have a jacket. He hopped from foot to foot like a sea-bird, gabbling non-sense, his skin startlingly pale and his dark hair blowing about his face.

Perhaps, Marnie thought, she might draw in their

figures, just a suggestion at the very edge of the drawing to soften the bleakness of the scene. She was seized by a sudden tenderness for the two of them, their loyalty and unworldly enthusiasms. They made a strange, lopsided trio, she thought, not cool at all, thank goodness. Even though Lucy had recently started to make an effort with her appearance and was gradually acquiring a sleek, androgynous style, with her men's jackets and the baggy trousers held up with braces, she remained geeky, sarcastic and peremptory. At school they called her a 'nerd' and made jokes about her behind her back, but they largely left her alone because they were cowed by her quick tongue and fierceness. Ralph – Marnie's mouth twisted into a painful smile – was mercurial and gauche, tripping over himself in his eagerness, endlessly knocked back and endlessly resilient. In many ways, he seemed much younger than his years; still like a child full of impatience and greed. It was only in the past few weeks that she'd glimpsed another Ralph, a brooding young man with a thin face and beautiful eyes, but that was because she had seen him through Lucy's smitten gaze. She let her charcoal trail a line down the margin of the page, where her two friends had hovered by the boat – bending down to pick up a dried cuttlefish, seizing a minute cowrie shell for Emma's collection that she kept in a large glass jar in the bathroom, throwing a lank piece of seaweed at each other – then made a faint mark to suggest their presence, though only she would know what it meant.

When there was a knock at the door, she immediately knew it was Ralph, though she hadn't been expecting him today. No one else announced themselves like he did: a rapid, impatient hammering, as if he had something urgent to impart and couldn't wait a second longer. She put her sketchbook on the table, careful not to smudge the charcoal before she had time to fix it, and went down the stairs. But when she opened the door, it wasn't just Ralph who was standing there. At once, she felt uncharacteristically self-conscious: her jeans were torn at one knee and balding on the backside; the old flecked jersey had once belonged to Paolo and came down almost to her knees, her ancient slippers were squashed flat at the heel. She was dusty, and covered with charcoal, and had twisted a scarf around her hair so that it didn't get in the way of her work.

'Hi, Ralph,' she said, noticing that he was holding an open can of spaghetti hoops in one hand and a spoon in the other.

'Marnie,' he said, and scooped a large spoonful of spaghetti into his mouth. She could tell that he was in one of his hyperactive moods: his whole body was practically steaming with restless energy. She felt that if she stepped any closer, she would be able to feel the heat he was giving out. 'This is Oliver.'

Marnie allowed herself to look at Oliver then, though she had been aware of him from the first, standing beside Ralph and waiting to be introduced. He was a calm presence – that was what she was first struck by. She didn't notice that he was tall and, though quite slim, seemed substantial next to his wispy friend, or that he had grey eyes like hers and soft brown hair that fell to his shoulders, or that when he smiled bashfully at her and held out his hand he had a single dimple in his cheek.

Later, she would think he was beautiful – and later still, she would realize that he was quite ordinary-looking, really, except never ordinary to her. But what she was struck by that first time, as he stood shyly beside Ralph, was that he seemed so blessedly real, so reticent and un-neurotic. Though her heart rose in her chest like a bird, she was at the same time oddly at rest in his presence. She felt recognized. That was it. She looked at him and she was in love and she would never be able to work out if there had been a gap between the moment of seeing him and the moment of loving him. To her, it felt as though she had been carrying the love inside her, like a precious, unopened package, waiting for the knock on the door and on her heart.

Marnie heard the door open and shut, then Oliver came quietly into the room. She didn't look up but her voice faltered and she came to a halt. She couldn't tell if he had heard anything. He didn't look at her, but plugged in the portable radiator, put the ice cream into the freezer compartment and the groceries into the fridge and the cupboard, then went out to fetch the TV and DVD player from the car. When he came back, he put them on the floor and went up the stairs, moving slowly and heavily. Ralph's eyes were open. He half raised his head and looked at her with a self-mocking smile.

'I don't think you can stop at this point,' he said. His voice was strong, his smile mischievous.

'Later,' said Marnie.

'But you know I can't afford laters.'

Marnie took a deep breath, acutely conscious of Oliver

in the room above. But what does it matter, after all these years? she thought. It's all so long ago and we were barely more than children. Life has flowed on, like a broad, deep river, carrying us, dragging us down, separating us, and that time stands far behind us, shining with the clarity of something lost. And yet, here with her two old friends at last, she felt she was back in her past – no longer a forty-year-old woman with a botched history of love, a tendency to dote on damaged men she thought she could save, but on the threshold of life and trembling with unblemished hope.

Chapter Eleven

Say you believe in love at first sight. It has to be mutual, surely: he falls in love with her and she falls in love with him – isn't that the rule? If it happens to one, it's because it's happening to the other as well: a two-way exchange, a duet and a symmetry, eyes meeting, a connection struck and held, an invisible thread that ties each to the other. His mouth dries and so does hers. Her heart leaps and his does too. When he feels her come into the room, the air stills around him; when she knows his eyes are on her there's a blissful tingle up her spine, a shudder that runs through her and turns her stomach to liquid. They are both wretched, sleepless, moonstruck, unsteady, euphoric, foolish, weepy, turned inside-out and upside-down. It can't be just her, feeling this. It wouldn't make any sense.

Why not? says Seth to her, as she lies in bed that night, after Oliver and Ralph have left. Her dead brother's voice is loud and clear in her head and she turns her face to the wall, squeezing her eyes shut and wrapping her arms around her knees because it is cold in her room; there are already small flowers of frost gathering on the windows. But Seth continues: What makes you think you're so different from all the other millions of people in the world who love without return? Look at Ralph, for goodness' sake. Look at Lucy.

'Be quiet,' she mutters out loud.

She doesn't want to look at Ralph or at Lucy: she dreads disrupting the fragile equilibrium of their triangle. The soaring of her heart makes her feel like a traitor. She doesn't want to think about how Ralph was this evening, his face shining with excitement, words pouring out of him, showing her off to his new friend, showing his new friend off to her, watching each with the same kind of proprietorial pride and anxiety. He had met Oliver, he said, because they both played chess in the school club – Marnie hadn't even known Ralph belonged to a chess club or played competitively. 'Ralph beats everybody, even the people who are supposed to be teaching us,' Oliver told her, and Ralph glowed, his eyes bright and his cheeks flushed.

Although Ralph has never confided in Marnie about school, just as he rarely speaks about home, she thinks she has a fair idea of what he endures there, day after day: hulking boys, good on the football field and not in class, who jeer at him for loving poetry, for wearing dandyish clothes, for being a sissy and a wimp and a dreamer. It's as if David's place has been taken by dozens of replica Davids who pursue him everywhere he goes. Once she asked him about friends and he flushed to his forehead and muttered something under his breath because he didn't want Marnie to pity him; when he is with her, he needs to be someone other than the distraught, urgent and vulnerable young man wearing weird clothes and his father's punishing marks. He always strives to rise above the panic and the darkness that threaten to engulf him: he's the entertainer, the helper, the boyish and loyal friend, and he seems to have no idea that Emma and Marnie can read his moods. As soon as they see him at the door, they know from the expression on his face, the stoop of his shoulders, how he is. Now, in a demonstration of his normality, he had brought Oliver to them: handsome, quiet Oliver, who came from a close-knit family, played tennis, spoke French, visited New York once a year. He was here to prove that Ralph wasn't a freak and a loner, after all. Did he never imagine what might happen?

Of course he imagined it, you idiot, hisses Seth. Don't you see? Don't you begin to understand your friend after all this time? A part of him, perhaps a hidden part, knows what he's doing, even as he's appalled by it. Why else do you think he was so frantic this evening, so simultaneously overjoyed and wretched?

Say you know that if something happens between you and Oliver, your friend will suffer. He will think it's natural and right that you should prefer Oliver to him, for under his vivid surface he's bony, gawky, lonely and sad. His mind is full of dark corners where nightmares lurk.

Say that, day after day, your head is filled with two faces – one of the modest, moderate young man whose mouth you want to kiss so badly it's like a fever inside you, the other of the frail friend whose exuberance has brought light into your life but whose needs and sorrows press down on you. He's suffered too much in his short life and he has become your responsibility. You know exactly what the look on that face will be if you hurt him. He trusts you.

Which is worth more, asks Seth in the dark hours, a

fling or a friendship? And she pulls the covers over her head in joyful despair because she is seventeen and in love and she knows it is only a matter of time now. The way he flushes when he sees her, the way that the silence between them is heavy and full of meaning, the way their gazes linger. When his hand touches hers by chance a shiver passes through her. He must feel the same. He must he must he must.

'Is something going on between you and Oliver?' Emma asked, one evening, studiously avoiding Marnie's eyes. She was hemming a summer dress she was making for Marnie; her glasses were perched on the end of her nose and she had her silver thimble on her forefinger.

Marnie was trying to revise for some exams, which were coming up, but at the question, a little jolt ran through her. 'What do you mean?'

Emma looked at her, amused. 'What do I mean?'

'No. I mean, nothing is. Nothing at all. Why do you ask?'

'I just wondered.'

'Why did you wonder?'

'It doesn't matter, Marnie.'

'Please tell me.'

'The way you look at each other, that's all. But I know it's none of my business. I don't want to pry.'

'How do we look at each other?'

'As if you like each other, my darling.'

'Of course we like each other. We're friends,' said Marnie, crossly. But hope flared inside her and her skin felt suddenly warm – Emma had noticed. She wasn't just imagining it.

'He's very nice.'

'He is, isn't he?'

'So if you did happen to like him –'

'There's nothing going on.'

'So, if you did happen to like him, Marnie, I'm telling you it's all right. You're allowed to.'

Marnie felt something inside her collapse. 'But –'

'I know how it must feel. And I know you're scared as well, after David. But I'm telling you, it's all right. If you need it, which you shouldn't, I'm giving you permission.'

But it didn't work out like that, after all, because what Marnie didn't know at the time was that Emma had already discovered a lump in her breast. She didn't tell Marnie about it; she didn't tell anyone at all. She went to her GP who referred her, and she had a biopsy and only when she knew that it was cancer did she sit her daughter down, at the end of the day, and tell her calmly that she had discovered it very early, there was no sign of spread and that after her radiation and her advised course of chemotherapy, she was sure she would be all right. Nothing would change, except perhaps she'd feel sick and put on weight because of the medication (an unfair combination, she had always thought); maybe she'd lose her hair. But none of that was going to be a problem – she'd just have to loosen her belt and buy herself a few hats. Maybe a trilby, what did she think? Marnie's exams would not be disrupted; the B-and-B guests would come in spring; it would be an inconvenience, that was all. Marnie wasn't to worry.

'Do you understand?' She leant forward across the

kitchen table that separated them. They had just finished eating scrambled eggs on toast, a comforting winter meal; a few drops of rain pattered on the window.

Marnie looked at her mother. Her thick dark hair was peppered with grey. She looked at the new wrinkles, the crêpy skin under the eyes, those faint brackets around the mouth. Her mother's face was so familiar to her and so dear that she had stopped noticing it; now it came to her with a jolt of dismay that Emma was no longer a young woman. She wanted to go to her and bury her head in her warm lap and feel Emma's hands on her head and sob and tell her not to be ill, not to get old, never to leave her, she couldn't bear it. In her mind she was clinging to Emma and howling for help. But instead she looked into her mother's eyes and gave her a small nod. 'I know you're going to be all right. You'll come through this.' She took care to keep any note of panic out of her voice, matching her tone to Emma's. 'Tell me exactly what to do and I'll do it. You know that, don't you?'

'Yes. And thank you, Marnie.'

Their gazes remained locked. Marnie understood that they were each keeping steady for the other's sake. She knew that fear must be coursing through Emma – fear of her own death and fear for Marnie, as well, who had already lost her father. And, of course, Emma must be imagining what Marnie was feeling now: the terror that was pressing down on her so that it was almost impossible to remain sitting upright in her chair with her hands folded tranquilly on the table and that small, fixed smile on her lips. It was as if her innards were coming apart – her stomach had turned to liquid, her heart was spiky and sharp and didn't seem in the right place any more, her throat was thick and breath rasped through it unevenly. One leg trembled and she had to push her foot onto the floor to keep it still. She felt dizzy, as if suddenly conscious of the earth spinning under her. Leaning over, she took one of Emma's hands in hers and raised it, pressing her lips to the knuckles; there were hot tears in her eyes but she blinked them away.

'Why you?' Marnie wanted to say, but she could already hear her mother's matter-of-fact response: 'Well, now, why not?'

They were such a little family, the two of them.

She was wrong: it wasn't just the two of them, after all. Looking back at those months now, Marnie remembered how full the house became, how crowded with activity and hope. She discovered she wasn't alone. Even now she could feel a swell of gratitude towards her friends who, effectively, became her second and chosen family, gathering round to take her and Emma through the hard spring and out free into the summer.

She was flooded with memories. Lucy – no cook at the best of times – making ginger snaps as hard as rock because ginger was supposed to be good for nausea; arriving at the crack of dawn each Saturday to help Marnie clean the house, scrubbing baths and lavatories. Ralph weeding the garden with a gusto that left the vegetable plot bare and all the climbing plants pruned to death, or lighting oversized bonfires that sent billows of acrid smoke over the fields and down to the beach. Ralph and Lucy taking it in turns to sit beside Emma as she lay in grim nausea and read poetry to her. Oliver, who had passed his driving test, taking Emma to hospital for her treatment and waiting there with her; and later, when the B-and-B season had begun, turning up with his mother who – seeing sheets draped steaming over all the chairs – insisted she would be responsible for the laundry for the next few months. Ralph and Lucy arriving in the morning before school to help Marnie cook fried breakfasts for guests while Emma lay upstairs with her window wide open, gagging on the smell of bacon. Oliver and Ralph climbing onto the roof to replace slates that had blown off one windy night: Marnie remembered standing in the garden and watching them balance precariously, their shapes outlined against the sky. All four of them repainting Emma's room the day she had to spend the night in hospital – they were at it for more than ten hours, and when they'd finished they lay side by side on the floor with cans of beer, looking at the pristine ceiling and not saying anything, exhausted and satisfied.

She had come to know Oliver better over those months. He was the youngest in a large family and his three older sisters, who had cosseted him through his childhood, had all left home. He was reserved and self-deprecating – Marnie had never heard him brag of his achievements and it was only through Ralph that she learnt he was good at languages and popular at his school. He was very protective of Ralph, who in some ways had become the younger brother he'd always wanted (he told her he hated being the youngest in the family, the one who was always looked after, and she told him she didn't really like being the only child – she didn't mention Seth).

He liked sour apples and dark chocolate, beer with a head of froth and glasses of cold milk; she would see the tiny white moustache on his upper lip and her heart would swell. He liked *Dr Who*; his favourite novel was *The Woman in White*; he could play the guitar and if he sang along his voice was husky. He could beat them all at arm wrestling. He had a scar on his knee from a hockey game. He knew lots of jokes but told them badly, so they missed the punch line and then he would blush as they laughed at him. Marnie would see him blush and understand that he was vulnerable like her, anxious like her. Hope would grip and leave her as shaky as a convalescent.

Once, while they were sitting in a bus station late at night after a concert, he said he had visited Ralph's house and been appalled by it. He and his parents, who were already dreading their son leaving home, had invited Ralph to move in with them. But Ralph wouldn't leave Grace alone. Everyone, it seemed, needed to care for someone. Even Ralph, whom they all feared for, had Grace who needed him.

'And you, Ralph.' More than two decades later, Marnie turned to him on his deathbed. 'Do you remember how you even went and shaved your head, you bloody fool, to keep Emma company? God, you looked a sight.' Actually, he had looked both grotesque and beautiful, like a sexless alien with his gleaming skull and enormous eyes. How Marnie had loved him then; tenderness overwhelmed her. She remembered throwing her arms around him, pulling him close to her and kissing his bald head where she could see blue veins running just under the surface. She remembered how still he had gone in her arms, tense with hope, so she had very carefully let him go and stepped away. She shook her head to clear the picture and grinned down at him. 'And then she didn't lose any hair after all. It just got a bit thin.'

His eyes had closed again but she saw a smile quiver on his bloodless lips.

In a way, they had been the happiest of times, in spite of the cancer. Every day felt precious. Every emotion was heightened, yet also simplified. All that Marnie had felt about Oliver was put on hold. He was simply on her team, and they were working together in the stout old house.

Spring had come and was going. Oliver, who was taking his A levels very soon, didn't come so often, although twice a week his mother still collected the sheets. He would be going to university the following term, and as the months passed Marnie allowed herself the sense of lost possibilities. Summer came, spreading golden light over the sea and the fields. The roses bloomed in the garden and the evenings were long and soft. Emma's treatment was nearly over. She sat in a deck-chair near the beech tree and read novels, or simply stared out at the sea shimmering in the distance. It was the first time that Marnie could remember her mother not being occupied.

One day, when Emma was at the hospital and Marnie, who had come back early from school, was alone in the house, she had gone into Emma's room and sat cross-legged on the floor in the fuzzy rectangle of light that lay across the wooden boards. She rarely came in here; she and Emma were careful of each other's privacy and this was Emma's world. She looked at herself in the long mirror and saw how like her she was becoming. Standing up, she opened the wardrobe, pushing her hand into the fall of clothes that hung there, pulling out dresses she had never seen on her mother. This pale green one – had Emma worn it with Paolo, before she had children? Marnie tried to picture her, younger and carefree, no grey in her hair or lines on her face, twirling round and letting the skirt balloon out. Or this one: a little black dress that belonged to the kind of glamorous cocktail party Emma never attended now, from an era before Marnie's time. Had she put on pearls and drunk champagne in it? Marnie buried her face in the soft material, inhaling a smell that was unfamiliar to her, then held it against her body, scrutinizing herself in the mirror. She stood on tiptoe and stared into her face, trying to see beyond it to her mother's younger face, the face she would have worn before she had children, before she'd lost her son and her husband. She hung the dress back carefully and picked up a pair of pink shoes with high heels and a delicate ankle strap. Had Emma once been the kind of woman who wore these? She kicked off her sandals and inserted her feet into the shoes. They were slightly too big for her. She wobbled, unaccustomedly tall and splay-footed, before the mirror, in her mucky jeans and grass-stained T-shirt, her slightly grubby feet sliding about in the shoes.

Like a toddler, she pulled open the top drawer of the chest near the window and peered at the cosmetics. Emma rarely wore makeup, maybe a bit of mascara now and then, a dab of lipgloss; most of the items in the drawer looked old and abandoned. Marnie pulled out an ancient red lipstick – again, when had her mother worn such a thing? – and unscrewed the top, winding up the sticky stub and colouring her own lips scarlet. She dabbed silver on her eyelids and put blusher on her pale cheeks. In the mirror an unfamiliar woman gleamed at her, over-defined and defiant. She looked horrible, someone Marnie would go out of her way to avoid.

There was a black-and-white photograph in the drawer, which Marnie examined. It was slightly faded, with a brown ring to the side, as if someone had put a coffee cup on it. A couple stood in front of a low brick wall. They were smiling self-consciously at the camera. The man was in a suit, dark-haired and dashing; he had a beaky nose and his arm was round the young woman. She wore a skirt that stopped just above her knees and a crisp blouse and looked absurdly young. Her hair was brushed behind her ears. Marnie held the picture up to the window so that she could see more clearly the way her father's fingers pressed into her mother's waist; how her mother's smile crinkled her eyes; how she wore the chain round her throat that she still wore today. Marnie sighed and put the photo back, then went into the bath-room and scrubbed her face until it smarted. She took the nail scissors and cut a triangle out of her fringe.

One evening in June she went with Ralph to the church-yard. The sun was low in the sky and all the colours – the grey of the church, the green of the grass, the flowers and the deep blue sky – were rich. There were butterflies among the gravestones and birds sang from the trees. A soft, blurred chortle of wood-pigeons filled the air. Marnie led Ralph to where Paolo and Seth were buried, and they sat on the grass together and looked at their mossy names carved into the stone. Somewhere behind them, with a shadow slanting over it, was David's plot. They both took off their shoes. Marnie wriggled her toes in the cool grass and tipped her head back.

'I keep thinking,' she said, 'that soon there might be three of them lying here.'

'Emma's going to be all right, Marnie. You've heard what the doctor says. There was no spread.'

'I know. But all the same –'

'Yeah.'

'And then what would happen to me?'

'You mean –'

'Where would I go? What would I do? They'd all be here together and I'd be on my own. And I can't even read properly. What will happen to me?'

'No! You'll never be alone. I'd look after you.'

'You!' She'd almost laughed, then met his burning stare and realized he was in earnest. 'How could you look after me, Ralph?'

'I'd look after you,' he repeated. 'You'll never be on your own.'

'Oh, darling Ralph,' she said, and started to weep, still cross-legged and rocking backwards and forwards on the grass, hugging herself and tears pouring unchecked down her cheeks.

'Don't, Marnie, I can't bear it. You never cry. Please don't.'

'Sorry. Sorry. I don't know why, it's stupid, I haven't

really let myself think, and now it's nearly over and it looks like it might be all right after all, well – sorry. I can't seem to stop.' She felt her face pucker and tears slide down her neck and onto the collar of her shirt. She felt salt on her lips. She was dissolving. She screwed her eyes shut but could still see the orange sun behind her closed lids.

He knelt behind her and put his arms round her, holding her tightly. She half turned and pressed her face into his shoulder, feeling how bristly his head still was. Now he was stroking her tangled hair and wiping tears from her stained cheeks and murmuring words. Nonsense words she didn't want to hear, about how he loved her, adored her, always had – no, she mustn't listen, mustn't cross that line, but still his arm was round her and holding her tight, his hand stroked her hair and her tears wet his T-shirt; his breath was against her cheek.

He was going to kiss her and she was going to let him – because she was tired and upset and for once in her life all her defences were down and sadness had flooded in, because in his eyes she was unique and lovely, because Oliver hadn't kissed her, because it was summer and a blackbird was singing its heart out above her, because she was surrounded by dead people and she was scared to death herself, because life seemed to be slipping by too quickly and she wanted to halt it, because the words he was whispering into her ear were comforting her: she had saved him and he would save her. Falling back into the grass, she heard him: he would always be there for her, always, no matter what happened, and no matter where she was or who she became. Seeing his face above hers, one hand pushing her hair back: always, Marnie, don't forget, don't ever forget.

She stopped and let silence fill the room. She gave a small sigh and took Ralph's hand. She felt his pulse tick feebly under her thumb. A clock running down.

Don't worry, my dear heart, my sweetest love. I knew you didn't mean it to happen. I knew it was just a kiss. A single kiss in the graveyard because you were sad and scared and I was there. I can close my eyes and be back there. Bats in the sky as the sun went down. A smell of cut grass and cool evening, fresh and earthy. Your face screwed up with misery, and fat tears streaming down your cheeks: I had never seen you like that before. You who were so calm and self-possessed, so kind and collected, always the one who was giving and never receiving, out of my reach. When I saw you cry, snotty and hiccupy and trying to catch your breath, your face creased and plain like a woebegone child's, I wanted to tear my own heart out of my chest and lay it at your feet. Anything. I would have done anything for you.

I put my arms around you and I held you, and when you turned your darling wet face towards me, I kissed you. Kissed you in the churchyard as the sun went down. But I knew you didn't mean anything by it. It wasn't really me you were kissing. It didn't give me hope. It was your gift to me. Don't feel bad. Never feel bad.

Chapter Twelve

Marnie went upstairs slowly, hauling herself up each step; her bones ached and her eyes stung. Her face was puffy. She allowed herself to imagine her bed at home – the pillow plumped up, the duvet cover turned back, the room orderly. Although, of course, it wouldn't be orderly any more: Eva and her friends would have taken it over; makeup would be ground into the carpet, apple cores would be shrivelling on the bedside table and overflowing ashtrays lying on the desk. In the bathroom, she stripped off her clothes and stepped under the shower, shivering in the chilly air. The water came out in an unsatisfactory dribble, too hot at first but quickly cool. She hastily washed with the nub of soap that wouldn't lather properly in the hard water, and rubbed shampoo vigorously into her hair, rinsing it off as best she could in the little splutters of now cold water. It was a relief to wrap herself in a towel and, scooping up her dirty clothes, go into Ralph's old bedroom. She could hear that Oliver was setting up the TV and DVD. He was channel-hopping and bursts of studio laughter, gunfire, music drifted up the stairs.

She rubbed her hair dry and lay down on the bed, under the covers. The wind had died away and the sky outside was now a hard, flat blue; the trees and ground glinted with frost. She felt used up and all she wanted to do was close her eyes and shut out the world. But she found she couldn't sleep. Her mind was still racing. She could hear Oliver's voice as he said something to Ralph, though she couldn't make out any words. Then, from outside, there was a sudden frantic cawing, as if a bird was in distress somewhere in the woods. The rest of the day stretched in front of her, with nothing in it but Ralph dying. She needed to fill it with small and comforting tasks: the sheets that had to be washed, the cake she planned to bake because, although no one would eat it, and the last one was still hardly touched in the tin, the smell would fill the downstairs room, the tomato soup she would try to coax down his throat, the ice cream he wrinkled his nose at – or perhaps she should make him some custard, he had loved Emma's, the phone calls she would make on the hill behind the house, theoretically to ensure her flat was all right in her absence, but really to hear Eva's familiar, jaunty voice, the sudden cackle of laughter.

She would get through to the evening, and then – like an old married couple – she and Oliver would drink whisky as a black-and-white movie flickered in front of them and Ralph lay beside them, like their ill child, his head propped on a pillow, his eyes opening and closing. They would bend over him to make sure he was still breathing, adjust his covers to make themselves feel useful. Did the day stretch in front of Ralph too, so that he longed for it all to be over, the pain and the fear, or was he clinging to each second as it went?

The drawing on the wall was a seascape in charcoal. As she looked at it, it blurred, so it almost seemed that the waves were moving and that she could taste the salt on her lips. When she told Ralph the story of their past, she realized how partial her recollection was, and how bright clusters of memories glowed in the darkness. Marnie's childhood had been strangely cut off from the outside world, she a quaint, unworldly figure in drab second-hand clothes. All the events that were shaking up the country had seemed to be taking place beyond the world in which she lived, however much she tried to involve herself. She wanted to be part of the history that was happening. Lucy took her on marches; together they made banners and badges; she read books about politics; she signed petitions about women's right to choose. Once, she and Lucy had gone to Greenham Common and linked hands round the fencing, shouting slogans, though Marnie remained self-conscious, awkward among the fervent crowd. Ralph gave her numerous compilation tapes that he had made of new music, insisting that she listen – and she did. She went to concerts with friends, sat in the mud at a festival or two, smoked a joint occasionally, though it never had much effect except to make her feel dizzy.

People talk of the soundtrack of their lives. Hers was the sound of the sea, the waves sucking up the shingle, the wind riffling the grey water, the wild call of birds. Her most vivid recollections through her early years and her teens were not of wild parties or sexual encounters, but of the house: the compact kitchen where Emma would stand at the hob, with plaster in her hair and paint on her muscled arms; the fire burning in the grate and Emma beside it, sewing or reading; Ralph and Lucy up in her room, rain falling outside and the sea a roiling brown mass in the distance; collecting eggs still warm from the hens; sitting on the lawn with a sketchbook and the sun on the nape of her neck. Friends came into her world; she didn't willingly go into theirs. She had hung back, watching, waiting. Watching for what and waiting for what?

'You were a funny little thing,' Emma said, her long-dead voice as clear as if she was in the same room. 'Quiet, apparently self-possessed. Very protective of me; even when I wanted to protect you. Protective of everything, really. Remember the graveyard of animals you had – every bumble bee and fallen bird and mouse? And then there was Ralph. You felt responsible for him, however much I tried to tell you not to be. You thought you could rescue him, didn't you? Or was it Seth you were rescuing, over and over again?

'Too many ghosts,' continued Emma's voice, the voice of her own thoughts. 'Even I'm your ghost now. You can't let me go; you can't let any of us go. You carry us with you. But Ralph isn't a ghost yet, Marnie. So what do you think you're doing, lying upstairs mourning him already? There will come a time for that, but it isn't now.'

Marnie sat up. She almost believed she would see her mother at the end of the bed, arms folded, looking at her with those shrewd grey eyes. Standing, she saw herself in the small mirror, and for a moment she thought it was Emma. Same dark hair, sprinkled with grey; same eyes with tiny wrinkles raying out; same inscrutable expression, a mouth that looked as if it would smile at any moment. She put on clean underwear, then her long skirt and the baggy grey jersey she had worn so many times it was nearly bald at the elbows. She towelled her damp hair, and twisted it on top of her head, thrust her feet into her slippers and went purposefully down the stairs.

Although it was not even three o'clock, the light was thickening and the sky fading to a steely grey. Marnie passed Oliver, sitting with his hand on Ralph's and a book open but unread on his lap, and went to the door. She recoiled from the biting cold, which hit her as she opened it and stepped across the threshold. It scoured her cheeks and made her eyes water, though in the chill the tears were viscous. Her breath smoked in front of her and she could feel the hairs in her nostrils begin to freeze and her hair to become crisp. The temperature must have dropped several degrees in the last few hours. The moon was already up, low on the horizon. It was a yellow crescent, but the entire sphere was also unusually clear, with its craters and seas. The serene, inhuman beauty of the sight made Marnie's spine tingle, whether with terror or joy she could not tell. She stood watching it until her toes were throbbing in her slippers and she couldn't stand the cold any longer, then stepped back into the house.

'It's ridiculously cold outside,' she said to Oliver, noticing how tired and wretched he looked. 'It must be – oh, I don't know, minus ten or something.'

'It gets very cold here. I've been up in the winter before. We spent a couple of New Years here. It went down to minus fifteen, I think. I remember being struck by how hostile the environment felt, so icy and dark.'

'It's a bit like that now.'

'What is?'

Ralph's voice surprised her. 'I didn't know you were awake.'

'Sometimes I don't know if I'm awake or not either. I can't tell if I'm dreaming.' He sounded quite chirpy, though his words slurred and his skin was an ominous chalky colour. There was an odour about him that caught in Marnie's nostrils; soap wouldn't remove it. He was rotting before he had died. 'You, for instance. I think you're in my dreams. I slide away from you into sleep and then you're there as well. Who can say where one state ends and the other begins. Not me. It must be the morphine. Morphine's a wonderful thing, you know. I wish I'd discovered it before. You should try some.' And he actually started fumbling around in his covers for the silver flask of liquid morphine he regularly swigged from.

'It's OK. I'll stick to the whisky.'

'Things feel quite far away, but in a good way. Pain ebbs, like a tide going out. Things don't matter so much.'

'That's good.'

'Dying, for instance. It's not so scary.'

'That's good too.' Marnie had to fight the urge to tell him that of course he wasn't dying; that he was going to be all right.

'Except there are these pictures sometimes.'

'How do you mean?'

'Horrible.'

'What pictures?'

'I don't know. Things sliding together. Falling. Melting. Slime. Nothing stays the same. Makes me feel sick. Oozing inside.'

'Do you feel sick now?'

'No.'

'There's a beautiful moon outside – that's what I was saying to Oliver.'

'Can I see it?'

'From your bed, you mean?'

'No.'

'But, Ralph –'

'I want to see the moon.'

Oliver lifted his head. 'We can't move him,' he said quietly.

'I want to see the moon.'

'Why not? What can we do to him?'

'Look at him.'

'I'm here, you know,' said Ralph. His voice was sinking to a whisper now. 'And I've nothing to lose. Like you said, look at me.'

'Stop it.'

'Ollie – look.' He tried to raise himself but couldn't. His temples had caved in and his eyes were too big for his face. For a moment, Marnie barely recognized him.

'Why not wait and ask Colette?'

Oliver turned to Marnie. She put a hand on his arm reassuringly. 'What for, Oliver? If Ralph wants to see the moon, then of course he must see it. Wait.' She practically ran into the small room where Ralph had been when she first arrived – was it only two days ago? It felt like weeks, months. She took two blankets out of the chest of drawers and hurried back.

'Right. We're going to wrap him up warmly and carry him outside. Put a jacket on and then let's get going.'

Oliver rose to his feet. 'If you're sure.'

'Stay awake for a bit, Ralph,' said Marnie. It seemed to her a matter of urgency that Ralph's wish should be granted.

Oliver, bundled up in a thick jacket, knelt down beside him and gently drew the covers off him. Marnie tried to keep her expression neutral as she saw how bones jutted through flesh, which hung in bruised, yellowing folds. He was a heart, lungs, liver and kidneys in a cage of brittle ribs, held together by rags and tatters of skin.

'Take his other side and lift when I say.'

Marnie crouched beside Ralph, breathing in his body odours and the reek of his breath, and slid an arm under his shoulders. 'Say if I'm hurting.' She felt the sharp knobs of his spine. His head bobbled on the strings and wires of his neck.

They stood carefully with Ralph heaped between them, as light as a child. Marnie thought he might come to pieces in their hands, an arm slithering from its socket, the ribs detaching themselves. With one hand, she groped behind her for the blankets; then she and Oliver arranged them over him.

'Right, the moon,' she said.

Ralph didn't reply but his eyes were wide. She and Oliver edged forward, the blankets dragging on the floor. When she pushed the door open, the wind sprang at them like a wild animal, snarling viciously. She heard Ralph give a single whimper. She and Oliver shuffled around awkwardly to fit through the door without bumping their cargo. It seemed impossible that they wouldn't drop him.

'It's probably easier if I carry him,' said Oliver.

Marnie nodded, biting her lip. She didn't want to relinquish him. Oliver scooped him gently into his arms and Ralph lay there, his body hardly disturbing the drape of the blanket, his oversized shaggy head resting against Oliver's chest. Oliver pressed his lips to his forehead and kissed him. 'It's your fault, mate,' he said. He was grinning widely, though a tear was running down each cheek, trailing into his thick stubble. 'You wanted the moon and now you're going to get it if it kills you.'

'You can see it best from here.' Marnie led them up the shallow slope. Low clouds were gathering, but from there the moon was quite clear. Low in the sky, and casting its yellow reflection on the loch, it looked enormous and very close — as if you could reach out and touch it.

'A cold rock,' said Oliver.

'Can you see it, Ralph? Isn't it extraordinary? Eerie.' A small sound escaped him but she couldn't make out the words. 'Let's get you back inside, shall we? It's getting cold. Or do you want to wait a bit? Ralph?'

'Bit.'

'A bit longer?'

'It's a bitter night,' said Oliver, 'but as long as you want. You're not exactly heavy nowadays. You always were a bit of a shrimp, though, weren't you?'

Ralph didn't answer. He lay like a baby in his friend's arms. The three of them waited in the silence, the wind wailing in the massed trees, and stared at the moon without speaking. Then Oliver turned and made his way slowly back into the house. It was only the afternoon still, but the darkness was closing in and the cold gripped like a vice.

'Right,' said Marnie, as soon as the door was closed and Ralph laid back on the bed. 'It feels beautifully warm in here, but heap all those blankets over him anyway, Oliver – he looks turned to ice – and put more wood on the fire. I'm going to see if he can get some soup down him.'

Ralph couldn't swallow any, though he managed a few painful sips of herbal tea before he let his eyes close. Marnie stood for a while, looking at him in the glow of the firelight. His breathing became soft and even; she could almost feel him sinking, layer after layer, into a deep, far-off land. She hoped his dreams would be good there.

Only when she was sure he was unreachable did she turn to light all the tea-lights she had put out earlier. Soon tiny yellow flames were flickering and winking on every surface, casting strange pools on the mantel and sills. Marnie's makeshift Christmas tree was illuminated by their glow, the tin foil glinting.

'It looks like a magic grotto,' said Oliver.

'A bit over the top?'

'A lot over the top. In a good way.'

They sat down at the table with mugs of tea.

'Do you like Christmas?'

'Kind of. I used to love it as a kid, and then I used to love it when I had small children. Made a big thing of it – tree and stockings and turkey and board games. But when we divorced, we shared out the day in that bureau-cratically fair and correct way – you know: you have the kids until two p.m. precisely, and then off they go to their second celebration. We all hated it. When Mona suggested we alternate, it was a relief.'

'Whose turn is it this year?'

'Hers. Probably just as well, in the circumstances.'

'What are they called, your children?'

'Lottie, Will and Leo.'

'Good names,' she said, to cover her sudden self-consciousness. What she really wanted to know was what his marriage had been like, why it had ended, had he been sad, was he with someone else now, had he thought of her, over the years . . .

'She told me to go,' he said, without her having to ask. 'You know what I was thinking about, earlier? I don't know why, but I was remembering the times when the children were still quite little and they would make us breakfast in bed. It would always be on a Sunday morning, sometimes at an ungodly hour when no one wants to be awake. We'd hear them creeping downstairs together, giggling and bickering, trying not to wake us although they always did. Then we'd lie there and listen to them in the kitchen, clattering things around, arguing with each other about who would make the toast or who would carry the tray. Quite often they'd smash things. We couldn't go and help them – we weren't supposed to know what they were doing. Then at last they'd come up the stairs, glasses and plates rattling on the tray, hissed commands from Lottie, and they'd push at the door and find us lying with our eyes squeezed shut, and we'd wake with such surprise! Look, how wonderful! Thick, half-done toast with leathery crusts, smeared with Marmite and margarine, undissolved granules of coffee floating on the surface of the tepid water, a flower pulled up by its roots in a glass. They'd sit on the floor and make sure we ate it. Mona always hated those breakfasts, but she'd heroically swallow it all under their beady stare. Then they'd disappear to watch cartoons on the TV or something – there'd be mess everywhere and it would still be only six o'clock.

'What I'm saying is that I didn't realize how happy I was, on a cold winter morning, bleary with tiredness, crumbs in my bed, swallowing cold coffee. Three little kids in four years, and both of us had full-time jobs, careers to follow, ladders to climb. I thought I was doing fine by them but, looking back, perhaps I wasn't. I used to make sure I came home before they were asleep, but that's easy – they would already be tucked up in bed and all that was left for me to do was the pleasurable bit, the bit that makes you think you're being a good father when really you're not. You go and read a story to them, give them a goodnight kiss, pull the covers up a bit, turn out the lights. I could say I didn't have a choice but that would be a cop-out. You usually have more of a choice than you let yourself know. I could tell you about the number of meetings I cut short, meetings I didn't go to, important dinners I didn't attend in order to be a good enough father. I should have done better somehow. Been more vigilant. It's a sad fact that you don't know what you've got until you lose it. When the marriage ended and I was alone and free – well, freedom was what I didn't want. But I didn't know that until it happened.'

'I think –' began Marnie.

'You know what I realized, during those first months, when suddenly I was living in silence, cleanliness and order? What is precious are the tiny things, the things

181

that irritate you so much when you have them – being woken in the night when one of them has a bad dream, changing a nappy, wiping snot off a nose, reading them the same bloody book for the fiftieth time, running along bent double beside them while they learn to ride a bike, cutting their nails, picking them up when they fall over, knowing all the mundane facts of their days. I even found myself missing hearing them squabble and scream. How could I not have known it before? How could I have been so stupid, so ignorant and so blind?'

He stopped and drew a hand over his face. Marnie watched him, but didn't speak. He looked weary; his kind face was furrowed. Whenever she had thought of Oliver, she had imagined him peaceful, successful, contented: beautiful wife, clever and affectionate children, a life well lived.

'I don't often talk about these things,' he said eventually. 'But here, with Ralph dying and you beside me again after so many years, so changed and yet so the same, I feel a different person somehow. No, that's wrong – I feel myself in a way I haven't for many years, though it's so sad that it's taken something like this to bring me back to myself. There are things that I suddenly want to say.'

'Like what?'

'I don't know. Feelings.'

'Feelings,' said Marnie. How did anyone penetrate the mystery of feelings? They made up a tangled world that lay beneath the surface. She had loved her mother, that was certain; she loved Lucy; she was unconditional about Eva and Luisa; she felt towards Ralph such complicated tenderness that it made her heart burn. But had she once loved Oliver, or had that heady feeling been just a youthful infatuation, romantic and unreal? Had she loved, say, Gilbert, who had taken her out of her old life and shown her a new one? Or Fabio, with whom she had lived for so many years and had once thought she would live for ever? And if she had – and, yes, she thought she had – she remembered the uprush of passion and delight; she remembered the blissful feeling of newness and then the solemnity of intimacy with those different men – why had it ended? Where did love go? Did it burn away like morning fog, or was it still there lodged inside her? All those hopes and all those broken promises.

'Yes,' said Oliver now. 'Like – well, like you. I didn't forget you. I always believed we would see each other again. You were very dear to me.' He grimaced on the quaint word but Marnie found it touching. To be dear to someone is not nothing.

Some things she still could not say to Ralph, even now so many years later, when it shouldn't matter any more. After she had kissed him in the churchyard, she had left him and cycled away, hot with desire, guilt and confusion. She had not gone straight home but instead made her way to Oliver's house. She had only been there once before, but she remembered how to get there – or, rather, her feet pedalled her there even while she was trying to work out the directions. She still remembered it: the soft breeze on her cheeks, the bars of shadow falling over the lanes, the dappled green light in the trees. Sweat on her bare arms and her heart expanding with delight and dread.

Oliver lived on the edge of town, in a square pink house that gave the impression of a certain kind of middle-class comfort – slightly shabby, thrifty, faded and ramshackle, and cluttered with possessions picked up over the years. Clumsy children's pictures in cracked frames, a decorated wooden chest in the hall that surely must hold memorabilia, mottled mirrors, fringed shawls sliding off scarred coffee-tables, a grandfather clock that no longer told the time, a cracked, slightly stained leather sofa, family photos everywhere. It was the kind of house she yearned for, wrapped in the weight of its own history rather than haunted by it.

She swung off her bike and, before she had time to think about what she was doing, rang the bell. Oliver's mother opened the door. She had a glass of red wine in one hand and was wearing a striped blue apron. Her feet were bare.

'Marnie? How nice to see you.' Her expression suddenly changed. 'But is everything all right? Your mother?'

'She's fine. Really. And you've been very kind. More than kind. Especially since we were practically strangers.'

'Nonsense. I only washed a few sheets. We wanted to help. And don't call yourself a stranger – you're Oliver's friend, and mine now, I hope.'

She laid a hand on Marnie's shoulder. Marnie felt tears filling her eyes; one rolled down her cheek. She blinked furiously. She didn't want to weep, to let the strange feeling that filled her dissipate.

'Thank you,' she managed gruffly. 'Is Oliver around?'

'He's in his room. It's Maths tomorrow.'

'I won't disturb him for long.'

On her way up the stairs she passed one of Oliver's sisters, already home from university. She was wearing a sleeveless green dress that swung round her knees and her blonde hair was piled artfully on top of her head. She looked cool and glamorous; a subtle perfume wafted off her. Marnie imagined how she must appear to her: young and anxious, dressed in shabby clothes, hair crudely cut, no makeup, smelling of sweat and grass, not flowers.

'Hi!' The young woman flashed a bright smile at her. 'You here for Ollie?'

'Yes. I'm Marnie.'

'Go and persuade him to take his head out of his book for a bit.'

Marnie knocked at his bedroom door.

'Come in.'

What was she doing here? The urgency she had felt had died away, leaving in its place a sense of her own awkward foolishness. Oliver was sitting at his desk, his head resting on one hand, hair flopping softly over his face. How could she ever think that someone like him would want her?

'Marnie!' He jumped up, startled, scattering papers to the floor. His face flushed.

'Sorry. I shouldn't have interrupted you.' She knelt down to gather the papers, scrawled with incomprehensible formulae that looked to her like hieroglyphics.

'Leave them,' he said. 'They're only doodles, really. But is everything all right?'

She stood up. 'Yes.'

'Your mum?'

'It's fine. I just –' She took a deep breath, feeling the blood rush to her cheeks. 'I just wanted to see you.'

'Shall I get us a drink or something?'

'It's all right. I shouldn't have come, really. I know you've got your maths exam tomorrow.'

'No – I'm glad you did.'

'I'll leave in a minute.'

'You don't have to.'

'Nice room,' she said, because there was nothing else she could think of. From the window, she could see their overgrown garden, lush and verdant, a tangle of yellow roses at the end.

'I guess.'

'Have you always lived here?' She knew he hadn't, of course – he had come from Cumbria when he was six.

'This is weird. Are you making small-talk with me?'

'Yes. I suppose so.'

'Why?'

'Because – because I'm nervous.'

'Nervous?'

'Yes. I –' She was going to say that she had come here to kiss him but the absurd words of intention stuck in her mouth; she swallowed them back. The gap between them seemed enormous, though two paces would bridge it. And Ollie looked so stupidly friendly and courteous. How could she think of kissing him? He was untouchable.

'Why are you nervous, Marnie?'

'I can't say.' Now he had stepped forward so that he was just a few inches from her and looking into her face. She could no longer breathe properly. He was so much taller than Ralph; his shoulders were broader, his face calmer and his hair softer – when she made herself reach up to touch it.

'Tell me.'

'I don't know the words.'

She heard him give a small sigh, as if he was very tired – or as if he had understood something difficult. She didn't know. Then his mouth was on hers and his hands were on the small of her back, her arms were holding him close at last, and closer still, but it could never be enough. She closed her eyes for a moment, so she could be nobody, then opened them again, so that it was her, Marnie Still, in the arms of Oliver Fenton at long last. She could see his eyes, his dark lashes, or were they hers?, the pale blur of his skin; feel the press of his fingers. She slid her arms under his shirt. So this was what it was meant to be like. Until now, she hadn't known.

'Ollie.' A bright voice floated up the stairs; there were the sounds of rapid footsteps coming up. 'It's me, Lou. Can I come in?'

'Shit,' he muttered, and abruptly let Marnie go, stepping back and wiping the back of his hand across his mouth as the door was flung open. Marnie, dazed and blinking, saw a young woman with blonde hair standing in the doorway. She was long-legged and skinny and was wearing tight grey jeans and a black vest-top. There were bangles on her wrist and a small tattoo on her bare shoulder.

'I'm a bit early,' she said, dumping a leather shoulder bag on the floor. 'Is that OK?' Then she put her hand on his shoulder and kissed him full on the lips. It was as if Marnie was invisible. She shrank back against the wall and wrapped a lock of her hair round her fingers.

'Sure,' said Ollie. Then: 'Sorry – this is Marnie. Marnie, Lou.'

'Hi,' said Lou, in a casually friendly voice, plonking herself down on Oliver's bed and kicking off her shoes.

'We're going to do a spot of last-minute revision,' mumbled Oliver, not meeting Marnie's eyes.

'I was just leaving anyway,' she said, her voice a strange low growl. 'Good luck tomorrow.'

'Thanks. I'll see you out.'

'Don't bother.'

'It's not a bother.'

He walked with her down the stairs. 'Marnie,' he said at the front door, 'I never planned –'

'I did – but it doesn't matter now, does it?' She allowed herself to look him full in the face. She knew her own was flaming with shame and anger.

'It does. Listen, I really like you. I always have.' He picked up her hand and held it against his mouth. 'The thing is, Ralph –'

But she snatched her hand away furiously. Oh, she didn't want to think about Ralph in the churchyard; she didn't want to think about kissing Ralph, falling back on the grass in his arms and seeing how love lit up his thin face. 'What's Ralph got to do with anything? That's just your pathetic excuse. Don't be such a hypocrite.'

'That's not fair.'

'Who's Lou, then?'

'She's a friend.'

'I don't believe you.'

'OK. OK. She likes me and I like her and I thought because of the way things were with you and –'

'Shut up. I don't want to hear. You don't understand anything, do you? I'm just a stupid, stupid fool.'

'Marnie, please.'

'You shouldn't have kissed me.'

'I've been wanting to kiss you from the moment I met you.'

'Well, you've had your chance. It's not going to happen again.'

'Dear to you?' she said now to Oliver, shaking away the memory that was two decades old but still made her feel ashamed.

'Yes.'

'Well, it was a long time ago,' she said. 'We were very young.'

'It doesn't feel so long ago.'

'Time's strange like that, isn't it? I used to think we changed and left the past behind us, but I don't really believe that any longer. It's more as if we carry all the parts of our lives inside us. I'm the ten-year-old me and the seventeen-year-old me, the twenty- and thirty-year-old me all at once. You know, when I was in the wood earlier, I could remember so vividly what it was like to be a small child in wellies crunching over the frosty ground at home that for a moment it was as if I *was* that girl. There was no distance between the memory and the event, if you see what I mean. I just *was* ten.'

'Yes.' The word was almost a sigh.

And now, for a moment, she was seventeen and wanting so badly to take his face between her hands and kiss his eighteen-year-old mouth and pull his youthful, slim body against hers that she was breathless with the old desire.

'There's been so large a gap,' she managed, her voice slightly uneven. She had the dangerous sense of being suddenly unstoppered: she could say anything now and forbidden words would pour out of her. 'But I'm glad you've thought about me, because I've thought of you, too. Of course I have. You and Ralph, and Lucy too, and those days we spent together. Sometimes the memory has been so vivid it's been almost impossible to believe that that time is safely in the past, that I can't reach back and be there again – be that person again. Young, with everything ahead and everything possible. But also there have been times – weeks, months – when I haven't thought of you at all. You disappeared from me or, at least, became a speck on the horizon. It's an odd feeling – to know you and not to know you, to feel close to you and yet far away as well. In fact, it feels a bit like a dream, unreal at any rate, to be here with you, watching Ralph die.' She gave a small, choking laugh. 'Sorry, I feel a bit drunk. Drunk on air, drunk on emotion. Shall we have the whisky a bit earlier tonight?'

'Why not? We're not in any real time zone here – it's like at an airport.'

Waiting, thought Marnie, and gave an involuntary shudder. Waiting for a flight and he'll be on it and we won't. We'll head back to normal life without him.

'Do you know what I most remember about you, back then?' Oliver was asking.

'What?'

'You were always kind.'

'Was I?'

'Through and through. Kind and reliable.'

'Does that make me sound a bit boring?'

'No! We all felt looked after by you – like I feel looked after by you now, here. You were the one we turned to, the one we wanted to do well for. You know, every so often over these past years, out of the blue, I've found myself thinking, Marnie would be proud of me now. Does that sound odd?'

'It sounds nice. It makes me want to cry a bit.'

'Lucy used to say you were an enzyme.'

'What?'

'An enzyme – apparently it has a settling, stabilizing property. I don't know, I didn't do chemistry. She meant that when you were with us, we felt we were better people, or behaved better at any rate.'

'Well, I don't know about that. Fabio – the man I lived with for many years – he used to say I was often invisible. It sounds to me that you're saying almost the same thing.'

'No. You were never invisible to me.'

Ralph shifted and whimpered and they turned; his face was twisted in a rictus of pain and his body stiffened under the covers. Marnie squatted beside him and put a hand on his forehead. 'Ralph? Sorry. We're here. Don't worry. Everything's fine. Ralph?'

But his eyes were closed; he snored, tiny wheezes escaping his half-open mouth.

'I don't know if he hears or not,' Marnie said. 'I talk to him, I tell him things, and I don't know if he can hear me. What's going on inside his head?'

'I don't know,' Oliver replied. 'But he can't hea

at the moment. He's dreaming. I wonder what he dreams of.'

'He doesn't look unhappy.'

'No,' said Oliver. 'And that's one thing about Ralph – you can always tell when he's unhappy. Everything shows on his face.'

'There were times I could hardly bear that,' said Marnie.

'I know. Remember?'

'Yes.'

'It sounds terrible, but every so often, I find myself writing his obituary in my mind. Trying to sum him up, or something. But he always escapes me. There are these great gaps that I can't fill. There was a time when he was everyone's golden boy, with his book, his TV appearances. You should see the fan mail he got sent. He showed me once: boxes of letters from women who thought they understood him. And then he dropped out big-time. You know all that, though. He more or less disappeared from view. If you Google him, he just seems to stop in the nineties. There was a time when I didn't know where he was and I still haven't found out what he did during that period. He would never tell me. Maybe it was too terrible to speak about – or maybe he just liked keeping parts of himself secret. I don't know. I feel so sad when I think about it. I wish I could go back to that time and find him

ne of Oliver's hands between both of
her. She felt the moment open between
e times when anything can be said and
freighted with meaning and has to be

used softly, with great care. 'I know that feeling,' she said.

'I should have helped more,' he said. 'He was my closest friend and there were times that I just let him go. Just thought, sometimes, I wonder where dear, hopeless Ralph is now?'

'And you have no idea?'

'Well, I know that for a bit he lived in a squat. During the late nineties, he worked with homeless people – probably because he always felt at heart that he was a homeless person himself. I've never known anyone as desperate to find a home and as panicky about being tied down. Maybe that's why a certain type of woman always fell for him – you must have noticed. They wanted to rescue him and mother him. My wife is quite a judgemental woman in many ways, but she used to go completely soft over him – he could get away with anything.'

'Like Emma.'

'Yeah, I guess. Or Dot. Anyway, for a bit he taught chess in secondary moderns in the north, Sunderland – that was at the time Sunderland was officially the poorest place in England. I visited him there once and he was living in this condemned tower block, on the twelfth floor or something, but he had an allotment and he appeared quite happy, if one can ever use a word like that to describe Ralph. I don't know what happened or why he moved, but he did. Everything always felt precarious with him. I never felt he was safe.

'There was a time, several years ago, that he seemed almost settled. He was working for an arts organization and living with a woman called Carrie, who is a GP in Leeds and has three children. They must be teenagers now, or older. She adored him, in a Lucy kind of way – shone when he was with her and seemed always amazed at her good fortune. And he was wonderful with those kids – it was a revelation to me. I suppose a bit of him is still a kid. He didn't patronize them or talk down to them, but was very respectful and yet at the same time insanely playful. He was always going on jaunts with them, or playing football, or making weird inventions. I remember once when I was there he painted the climbing frame and swings in the garden with them. They wore shorts and had bare feet and took all the old half-used tins of paint, of every colour, and went mad. They ended up daubed in strange colours, giggling and clowning around, and he was the most hysterically excited of them all. I looked at him and thought, You're going to explode one of these days. Nobody can be like this ... I thought it might last with Carrie, if only because of her children. But it didn't work out. He always wanted to be settled but at the same time he was restless, hungry for something else. He was endlessly destroying the things he cared about. It's my belief that he never felt he deserved to be happy. There was a trip switch in him: when he reached a certain level of contentment or peace, he flipped.

'In the last few years, he lived in Amsterdam. He went there with a woman called Elsa who was a journalist on a glossy monthly. I met her a few times and they came and stayed with me a year or so ago. She was much younger than him but seemed rather calm and nurturing – like Carrie, really. She wanted children. There was one evening, when Ralph was out, that she confided in me. She thought that if she got pregnant, Ralph would understand how much he wanted to be with her and to have his own family. Maybe she was right, maybe it could have worked. I don't know why he left her either. He worked as a carpenter in Holland – I had an idea that that was a kind of way of recapturing what Emma had done with her pots. He loved Emma, you know. He talked about her even after he stopped talking about you. She was the mother he never had.'

'I know,' said Marnie. 'I always knew that.'

'Her death was a great blow. Hers and Grace's.'

'I was going to ask about Grace.'

'She was the one person he ever felt responsible for. Even when he lost contact with the rest of us he kept in touch with Grace. After she died, I think it was the last tie to – well, to normal life, obligations. He suddenly had a terrible freedom.'

'Terrible? He always wanted freedom – remember how he used to lecture us on it? He even read *The Outsider* to me once. Every time I was about to fall asleep he'd prod me and say, "This is important, Marnie! Pay attention."'

'Terrible because it was as if the last rope tying him down had broken, and he could simply be – be blown away. I suppose I used to think he would kill himself, just because there was nothing stopping him.'

'Did he try?'

'I don't think so. I don't know, though. He never said. There were lots of things he didn't say. I knew him intimately, he was – is, for God's sake – my best and oldest friend, and yet I sometimes feel I don't know him at all. I tell you this, though: when my marriage broke up, he was really very good to me. I think he liked being needed. Usually he was the one who needed.'

'That's true – he was always happy when he could help me with my work, or Mum with things in the house or the garden. He used to try so hard to be useful to us.'

'People would say – do say, every so often, like in those "Where Are They Now?" pieces in a Sunday supplement – that Ralph did not live up to his potential. Perhaps that he even ran away from it, because for some reason he couldn't bear to be a worldly success. For Ralph, the important things in his life were probably all the ones that he never told anyone. Things inside his head. Feelings, perceptions, torments, joys. Who can say? He would call himself a failure, but I wouldn't. He was always adorable. Is. Is adorable.'

'Yes. He is.'

Oliver got up and went to the window, drawing open the curtain to peer outside. 'I think it might snow tonight,' he said. 'It has that heavy feeling.'

'What if we get snowed in?'

'We'll think about that if it happens. But Dot has a tractor that can get through anything. We'll be fine.'

'Are we doing the right thing here?'

'It's what he wanted.'

'I feel so – so unqualified.'

'What qualifications do you need?'

'You know what I mean.'

'Of course. It's scary.'

'Right.' Marnie stood up. 'I'm going to make some custard. Ralph used to love Mum's custard – he'd eat bowlfuls. I know he won't manage any, but I'm going to anyway. And then we can drink whisky and watch one of those films. What's the choice?'

'*His Girl Friday, The Lady Vanishes, The Thirty-Nine Steps, Bringing Up Baby*. Optimistic, smart, fast films.'

'You choose. I'll make us some sandwiches, shall I?'

There was a brisk knock at the door, which opened, and Colette stepped into the room, her cheeks bright pink, steam curling from her rosebud mouth.

'Good evening. My, it's cold out there and –' She stopped mid-sentence. 'Why, gracious me,' she said quaintly. 'You've done everything up. It looks like Fairyland in here.'

Marnie laughed self-consciously, feeling foolish. 'I wanted Ralph to have a taste of Christmas. Maybe I went a bit too far.'

'It's lovely – don't you think so, Ralph? But I think I'll need the overhead lights on, don't you? Now, how are you? Let's be having a look at you.' She pulled off her coat. Drops of water sprinkled the floor.

'We'll be leaving you for a bit, then,' said Marnie.

'Grand.' Colette was bending over Ralph.

Oliver and Marnie climbed the stairs together to Ralph's room, and sat side by side on his bed. Oliver put an arm round Marnie's shoulders and she leant against him. He smelt of woodsmoke and was warm and solid. He pressed his lips to the crown of her head, and she put one hand flat against his chest to feel the steady beat of his heart. He pulled her closer and she felt his breath against her cheek.

'It doesn't seem fair, does it?' she asked. 'Being happy.'

*

Ralph woke, half woke, into the soft golden fuzz of the room. He blinked at all the tea-lights that were guttering and throwing strange shapes, and his dry lips twisted into a smile. 'Oh, Lord, have I died and ended up in a kitsch heaven?' he whispered. 'God's going to be very pissed off with me; I haven't been very nice about him.'

'Hi, Ralph.'

'You've been decorating.'

'Kind of.'

'Might have known.'

'How are you?'

'Can't see you properly. A blur.'

'Can I get you anything?'

''S OK. Where's Ollie?'

'He's just taking a shower. We thought we'd watch a film all together. Would you like that?'

He made an indeterminate sound. Marnie leant forward and picked up his hand. 'It's going to snow,' she said. 'But it's warm inside. Warm and cosy.' She was prattling foolishly. She pressed her lips to his hand and continued, 'We'll sit by you and watch an old film and play music and we won't leave you.'

'It'll be me leaving you.' Ralph made a dry, choking sound that Marnie realized was the remnants of his old laughter. 'That's never happened before, has it?'

Chapter Thirteen

When her treatment was over, Emma announced that they would go on holiday that summer. 'Eric's invited us to stay in his summer cottage in the Highlands.'

'What about the B-and-B?'

'We'll have to tear ourselves away from it.'

'Can we afford it?'

'That's not your concern – but, yes, we'll be fine. I think we've earned it.'

'Doesn't Eric need the cottage?'

'He'll be there too.'

'What about his wife?'

'She won't be. As a matter of fact, he doesn't live with her any more. They've decided to separate.'

'Oh!' said Marnie. 'I see.' And she thought, with a wild lurch of apprehension, that perhaps she suddenly did see, though she wasn't sure she liked it. She stared at her mother accusingly, but Emma returned her gaze, refusing to drop her eyes.

'It's by a loch, very remote and beautiful. There's a boat.'

'Just you and Eric and me?'

'Yes. Is that a problem?'

'No. No problem. And I'm – well, I'm glad you can have a proper rest after everything. It's just – can I invite Lucy? I know she's not doing anything in the summer.'

'Of course. As a matter of fact, I was going to suggest that myself. What about Ralph?'

'What about Ralph?'

'Do you want to ask him as well?'

'No!' said Marnie, crossly. 'I do not. It would just make everything too complicated. I don't want to be worrying all the time. I want to be selfish.'

'OK, no Ralph.'

Eric's house was wooden and snug. From its two large front windows you could see the small loch, which, on the evening they arrived, glowed in the sunset, still as a mirror in which was reflected the fringe of trees and the few streaks of cloud; the back looked out onto the forest, which stretched away, cool, dark and mysterious.

Emma stayed in the wooden guesthouse that Eric had built on the side of the main house, with its own separate entrance, just big enough for the double bed and a basin in the corner. She never mentioned her relationship with Eric, and Marnie, watching her, couldn't tell what was going on between them. Her mother went to bed every night in the guesthouse, alone; each morning she would emerge from there, washed and dressed and looking refreshed. They still behaved courteously to each other, and certainly never touched or held hands. But there was a new shine to Emma, a softness and restfulness that hadn't been there before. And sometimes Marnie would intercept a glance between them, a smiling look of intimacy. It was like being the mother, not the daughter, she thought: first nursing Emma through her illness, and now spying on her love life, if that was what it was.

Lucy and Marnie shared the bedroom next to Eric's, with a ceiling that sloped almost to the floor so that they had to crawl into their beds to avoid banging their heads. For the first two days Ralph – for of course Ralph had come too: Marnie was unable to leave him behind – slept in the small room next to the kitchen on a fold-out divan, but then he moved out into the one-man tent Eric hauled out of the attic. It was missing one of its poles so that the back sagged, and it leaked copiously if the rain was heavy. Mosquitoes whined in its darkness and there was a faint smell of mildew, but Ralph was absurdly cheerful about all discomfort. He had never been on holiday before, apart from a miserable week spent in Frinton a few years before, and he had never slept in a tent. He crawled into it each night with an air of ownership; in the mornings he emerged like a badger coming out of its sett, his face sprouting the unsatisfactory beginnings of a wispy beard.

He had packed a motley collection of entirely inappropriate clothing: a thick, moth-eaten greatcoat, a balding velvet jacket, a pair of white drainpipe trousers he'd picked up in a thrift shop for a couple of quid, which quickly became so filthy he folded them into a wad and used them as his pillow, and cowboy boots from the same shop, which pinched his feet. Eric lent him an ancient pair of canvas shorts to keep him going, and these he wore day in, day out, though they were voluminous on his spare frame and he had to keep them up with a piece of rope he found in the bottom of Eric's sailing boat. He looked more like an abandoned waif than ever, with his skinny legs and bony knees poking out of the flapping shorts and his matted hair.

When Marnie looked back on those weeks, they had the quality of a dream, without context, disconnected from the past or the future. There in the north, in the middle of summer, it never seemed to get dark. Dawn broke softly almost as the dusk faded away; the horizon always seemed rimmed with a faint luminescence. In the evenings, shadows stretched long fingers across the grass, light thickened, coolness gathered in corners. Marnie, Lucy and Ralph would often swim at midnight, lying on their backs in the water and gazing up at the sky. Or they would take the rowing boat out into the middle of the loch and sit there for hours, talking and falling silent, maybe throwing a line out in a hopeless attempt to lure the bony perch that had long since retreated to the reeds. During the day, they would laze around on the shore or take the sailing boat out, though the wind was rarely strong enough to fill its sails. They sometimes walked in the forest, feet sinking into the soft moss. The light splashed through the pine trees and birches and birds sang invisibly above; often a woodpecker tapped somewhere in the distance, and the hollow sound reverberated through the woods.

Emma and Eric were there, of course, but often they got up early and spent their days searching for wild mushrooms in the woods or going for long walks with binoculars and returning with tales of red kites and reed warblers. For much of the time, Marnie, Lucy and Ralph were alone, in days that seemed to have no boundaries. As if by unspoken consent, they left behind the prickly discomforts of their adolescence and behaved like children. It didn't seem strange to Marnie to lie on her stomach and let Ralph unhook her bikini and rub sun lotion into her warm skin; when they wrestled in the water – her bare limbs tangling with his and his laughing, bristly face close to hers – she did not draw back from him, or worry that he might want to kiss her again. Lucy, her small face tanned and her hair growing out of its spikes into a soft muss, forgot to be sardonic; she almost forgot to be in love with Ralph, as if they had all regressed into a state of innocence. There was safety in the threesome.

Several times, Eric took Ralph fishing. Marnie would always carry in her memory the picture of the pair silhouetted side by side on the boat with their rods. Sometimes she could hear Ralph's laugh ripple over the water, a sound of pure happiness. She did a sketch of them in charcoal and years later, looking at it, she could still hear the accompanying laughter and it would bring back Ralph as he was then, suspended between boyhood and manhood, uncertain and oddly beautiful, energy coursing through his gangly frame and his face lit with joy.

Everything changed when Oliver turned up. He had told Ralph that he might 'drop in', because he would be visiting his sister who lived in Edinburgh, but no one had taken him seriously. It felt as though he had dropped out of their world. None of them had seen him for more than a month: straight after his exams he and two friends had gone backpacking round Europe. Marnie had received one postcard from Barcelona saying simply, 'Eating tapas and thinking of you, O xxx'. She had it in her bag now and every so often, when she was alone, she would take it out and look at the line drawing of a naked woman on the front, and at the neat italic handwriting on the other side, relive the moment when she had put her arms around him and felt his mouth press down on hers, before his girlfriend had pranced in. That was the last time she had seen him, although he had phoned her twice, asking if he could come round. Both times, aching for a sight of him, she had said, no, she was busy, then cursed her own obstinacy and pride. And – proud himself, perhaps – he had not persisted.

He arrived in the evening, when the sun was low and the light thick and golden. Apart from Eric, who was in the house cleaning the parasol mushrooms that he and Emma had gathered, they were outside, sitting on the grass. Ralph was making a big fuss about gutting the two perch he had caught, shouting in mock horror as he drew soft purple strings out of their bellies, Lucy and Emma were reading, and Marnie was trying to draw the birches that half hid the view of the loch. It was warm and windless. Marnie still remembered what she was wearing then – her old denim shorts and a halter-neck bikini top, bare feet, a chain around her ankle. Her hair was in a single French plait that Lucy had braided that afternoon after they'd swum and was coming undone. She even remembered that Emma had put on a wide-brimmed hat and, in her long skirt, looked like an out-of-place Edwardian lady.

It was Marnie who saw him first, though she didn't recognize him at once; he was just a figure in the distance, carrying a large rucksack. But then he drew closer. He raised a hand and she gave a small gasp, leaning forward and shading her eyes to make sure.

'What?' asked Lucy, looking up from her book.

'I think –'

'But that's Ollie! Look, Ralph, it's Oliver.'

Ralph dropped his fish into the bucket with a wet plop and stood up; he was bare-chested and his shorts were stained with grass. Marnie saw how he flinched in shock, then wrenched his mouth into a broad smile and ran forward, shouting a loud hello, overdoing the delight. Marnie rose, too, but remained where she was, watching Ralph, who looked suddenly small and scrawny, approach his friend and hug him. She was oddly breathless. Her heart thumped and her hands were sweaty; she wiped them down her shorts and pushed her hair off her face. What did she look like?

'Hello, Marnie.'

So there he was in front of her, a shy, tentative smile on his face. He was taller than she remembered. His hair was lighter, bleached by sun and salt, and longer. He was wearing a stained T-shirt and she saw how his arms were tanned and strong. He looked older, as well – as if he'd left them all behind.

'Ollie,' she managed. Her voice was husky.

'I hope it's OK that I've turned up out of the blue like this. I was quite close and I thought I couldn't not. Lucy, hi. I like your hair, by the way. Emma, did you know I might come? Ralph said I should. Is it all right?'

'Of course.' Emma got out of her deck-chair and went over to kiss him on both cheeks. Marnie saw she looked concerned beneath the smile. 'I didn't know, but that doesn't matter. You're always welcome, as long as you don't mind not having a bed.'

'Ollie doesn't need a bed. He's been roughing it all the

way round Europe without one,' Ralph gabbled. 'He can have my bed, or my tent, and I'll take the bed, or he can share my tent with me. Whatever. How did you get here anyway?'

'I hitched and then walked the last few miles.' Oliver slid the rucksack off his back onto the ground and rubbed his shoulders. 'It's very hot.'

'You must be knackered. Have you had an amazing time? You're going to have to tell us all about it.' Ralph turned to Emma. 'He's been everywhere, you know, all the places I dream of going to one day. Paris, Rome, Budapest – did you know that Buda and Pest used to be two cities? – Prague.'

Ralph was still boasting on his friend's behalf, thought Marnie, and she was painfully touched by his generosity, which was exaggerated, self-destructive. She touched his shoulder and smiled, and he gazed at her for a few seconds, his eyes wild. She could almost feel the panic steaming off him.

'Do you want something to drink?' she asked Oliver. 'Aren't you thirsty?'

'I'd love some water. Thanks.'

At that moment, Eric came out of the house with a tray and glasses. 'White wine?' he asked. 'Or I could make a jug of Pimm's as a treat?' He didn't seem surprised to see Oliver, whom he had never actually met.

'Oliver's come to stay for a day or two, if that's all right with you,' said Emma. And she went up to him and put a hand on his shoulder, smiling into his face. Such a small gesture yet it had the clarity of an announcement, and Marnie saw Ralph's mouth half open and Lucy give a small acknowledging smile. It was as if a line was being drawn under the past ten days. They were all grown-ups again, and back in the real world where secrets pulse under the skin. She was suddenly conscious of her bare legs, the skimpiness of her bikini top.

'I'll get you some water,' she said, and practically ran into the house. She didn't immediately go to the kitchen but went upstairs to the bathroom, where she washed her face in icy water, then pressed her forehead against the mirror over the basin, closing her eyes. She thrilled to the knowledge that Oliver had come. She wished he hadn't. She ached to be near him, and she wanted him to disappear at once, leaving the lovely simplicity of the summer intact.

The weather, which for two weeks had been warm and clear with occasional brisk showers, was now oppressive. The heat was thick, ominous; at night Marnie would lie on her duvet with the window open, feeling the faint lick of a breeze on her skin. A storm was on its way. Every so often a couple of fat raindrops would fall from the saturated air. The sky was no longer blue, but a brownish yellow. Sometimes in the distance they would hear the distant rumble of thunder. They had three days left. Summer was running out and already a few of the birch leaves were tinged with gold. This far north, said Eric, the summer came late and left early – a brief interlude between seasons of cold and darkness.

Nothing was the same. They swam, rowed on the loch, went fishing with Eric, sat over barbecues as the light faded and bats flitted between the trees, stayed up late over games of cards with bottles of beer, as they had before. But Marnie was only pretending to be her old self, moderate and sensible – the one who rigged the boat, made the tea, cleared up the enthusiastic mess Ralph made in the kitchen when he was cooking; the one who didn't talk much but stood quietly back, letting everyone else take centre stage. Under the familiar surface she was electric with desire and dread. She could feel her blood coursing through her veins and hear the pumping of her heart, which felt swollen and tender in her chest. Her skin tingled. She lay awake at night, Lucy breathing deeply beside her, and thought of Oliver.

She got up in the morning, and when she saw him her legs were loose and trembly and there was a strange heat in her belly. She couldn't eat properly. One gulp of wine and her head spun. She noticed the dimple in his cheek, the way his hair curled slightly at the nape of his neck, the golden hairs on his arms, the tiny scar under his left ear, the way his eyes crinkled when he smiled, the way he bit his lower lip when he was thinking. Sometimes their hands touched; sometimes their eyes met and she would feel as though she was falling. Sitting in the boat together, his foot lay against hers. Once, he pushed a lock of her hair out of her eyes, in front of everyone and looking straight into her eyes. She heard the tiny involuntary sound she made in the back of her throat and for a moment she thought she must put her arms round him and draw him to her. She was sick with desire, weak and boneless. If he touched her, her flesh would burn, would melt. She felt that Emma was watching them and Ralph, too – and this made her awkward and self-conscious. She couldn't remember how to behave normally. Everything she did was an act she was putting on, a parody of her old self that surely could fool nobody.

Chapter Fourteen

Ralph and Lucy were playing chess, lying under the shade of a tree on their stomachs with the small board between them. They had just eaten a late breakfast, sitting outside at the rickety table covered with a blue tablecloth. No one had spoken much: they were bleary from sleep and soporific in the heat; surely it must rain soon. Marnie poured herself a last half-cup of coffee, then piled the plates and breadcrusts onto the tray. Oliver was sitting opposite her. He was wearing a white T-shirt and his only pair of jeans. His hair was tousled; his cheeks were thick with stubble.

He slid a hand – strong, long-fingered, leather thong round the wrist – over the table and covered hers. A jolt went through her. She didn't move and didn't speak. Behind her, she could hear the faint click of chess pieces on the board, a murmured comment from Ralph. She lifted her gaze and met Oliver's; couldn't look away. She tipped her hand so that now they were palm to palm. Their fingers curled together. She closed her eyes, opened them again and saw Oliver still watching her.

'If you do that,' Ralph said, 'it'll be checkmate in two moves. Do you want to take it back?'

Marnie sighed, pulled her hand away and stood up with the tray. In the kitchen, she filled the sink with hot water, then very slowly washed the crockery. There were footsteps behind her but she didn't turn round. She went on washing up, the cutlery now, the coffee cups. Her entire body was molten; it seemed impossible that she should still be upright. There was a hand on her waist but still she didn't turn; she leant back slightly, with a sense of languorous delight. His lips were on her bare shoulder and she shuddered; now his hands were on her breasts. She twisted to face him, put her soapy wet hands in the tangle of his hair and held him back for a few seconds so that she could relish this moment before they kissed, before she pressed herself to him and felt the burn of his stubble on her face, before he was holding her so tightly that she thought all breath would be squeezed out of her, but that it could never be tightly enough.

'My gorgeous Marnie,' said Oliver, and kissed her again; she tasted blood on her lip.

'Someone will come in,' she managed at last. 'Stop.'

And, sure enough, they heard voices coming towards them, Lucy laughing.

'What are our plans for today?' asked Ralph, as he bounded into the kitchen. 'We've got to make the most of the short time we've got left.'

'I agree,' said Marnie, smiling dazedly. Her lips were sore; her entire body throbbed. Surely it was obvious.

Of course it was obvious. I knew as soon as he arrived. He was my very best friend and when he came over the hill I was shaken with wretchedness — gutted, that's the word. I saw the way he smiled at you and I saw the way you looked at him and . . .

In the forest, in the soft green light, dim and aqueous, he pulled her out of sight behind a tree and kissed her again, hard. She felt the bark dig into her back and her skin flowered under the press of his fingers.

'Come on, the two of you!' shouted Ralph. 'Don't lag.'

. . . the two of you, the two of you. And me . . .

In the boat, staring up at the lowering sky, feeling the weight of the air pressing down on her summer body, and one of his feet was pressed against her dusty calf. Her body was soft, boneless, hot. She heard Ralph talking, Lucy replying; their words buzzed over her head. In the distance, she saw a falcon falling out of the sky. Let this moment never end.

. . . let this moment end. How long was it possible to sit at the bow of the boat, feet dangling in the water, creak of oars in the rowlocks? I was a marble statue weighing down the frail vessel, words bubbling out of my stiff, grinning mouth. Misery is heavy, cold and dull . . .

By the side of the loch, eating ginger cake and drinking ginger beer. 'Where will we all be in ten years' time?' said Lucy.

'Here,' said Ralph. 'We'll all be here, of course, sitting by the loch together.'

And he lay down and put his head in Lucy's lap. Marnie watched as Lucy closed her eyes as if in pain, and ran her fingers through the mess of his dark hair.

'But really, where?'

'You don't want to know,' said Marnie. Her hand moved across the grass and the tips of her fingers touched Oliver's.

'How true.' Ralph's voice was almost a whisper. 'What a curse, to know your own future.'

What a curse to know your own future, I said. What a curse . . .

And he said, 'Marnie . . .' She stopped him, putting her hand across his mouth.

'Tonight,' she said. 'I'll come to you tonight.'

'Where?'

'In the woods, by the fallen tree. As near after midnight as possible – when everyone is safely asleep.'

'You promise?'

'I promise.'

. . . he put his bare foot on your bare foot. Your eyes flicked upwards to his face and then away. You leant across the table and poured a glass of water and I watched as you drank it. He watched as you drank it. I saw the way your throat worked, and tiny drops of water spilled on your chin. You wiped your hand across your mouth. You had your hands on the table, on either side of your plate heaped with food that you weren't eating. I looked at your thin wrists, with a white strap mark round the left one where your watch had been. Slender tanned arms, covered with tiny grazes from two weeks spent scrambling through the forest. Prominent collarbone. Swell of breasts. Dark, unkempt hair in a tumble round your face. Thick brows; tiny white scar glancing through the right one. I have learnt you. Can anyone love you the way I have loved you? No no no no no.

Ralph insisted that they sat outside at dinner, under the threatening sky. He said that soon enough they would be back in their indoor lives, like pale grubs. His voice was angry and full of tears, and Marnie saw Emma look at him anxiously, putting a hand on his shoulder as she passed.

Emma and Marnie cooked that evening – a roast chicken with different salads and garlic bread, followed by a cake topped with wild strawberries that Emma and Eric had gathered that afternoon. They stood in the small kitchen together and every so often a raindrop would splatter against the window.

'I feel I've hardly seen you,' said Emma, crushing garlic into butter and mashing it.

'I know. But it'll all return to normal soon.' Marnie didn't want her mother to ask her intimate questions or look at her with her penetrating stare. She sliced open a slightly stale baguette and spread the garlic butter on it, then wrapped it in silver foil.

'You've had a good time?'

'A lovely time.'

'Is Ralph OK?'

'Fine.'

'He seems a bit –'

'He's all right. He gets odd sometimes, you know that.'

'Yes,' said Emma, doubtfully. She started to shred lettuce into a large bowl.

'Shall I open some wine?'

'You and Oliver –'

'I don't ask about you and Eric.'

'You can ask me anything.'

'But I don't want to.'

'Be careful, that's all.'

'I'll be careful,' Marnie replied lightly.

She didn't want to be careful: she was sick and tired of being careful, tactful, practical, sensible, diligent, thoughtful, considerate, *good*. She didn't want to think about other people's feelings, Ralph's feelings. Not now. Not tonight. This was her night. No more holding back and no more waiting. She was hollow with longing; desire sluiced through her; excitement and fear trickled down her spine; her mouth was dry; her skin pulsed. Tomorrow, she would be a different person. She would be Marnie whom Oliver had loved.

They carried the meal outside on trays. Eric poured wine but Marnie only took a few sips. She already felt drunk. Her legs trembled. She felt slightly sick and couldn't possibly eat the food on her plate. She pushed it around with her fork. Chicken was impossible. She chewed a lettuce leaf, drank some water. Emma cut the cake, still warm and steaming from the oven, with a long knife. Tiny strawberries scattered over the plate and Marnie put one in her mouth. They had a mineral sweetness and she would never again taste one without remembering this particular evening.

'. . . are you even listening?'

'What? Sorry?' She smiled dazedly at Ralph.

'Lucy suggested a midnight swim. Our last. Yes?'

'Oh. Maybe. I feel a bit tired. I thought an early night for once.'

'Come on, Marnie. Don't be a party pooper.' This from Lucy. 'We're all going. Aren't we, Ollie?'

'Are we?'

'Yes.'

'There's going to be a storm tonight.' Eric was looking

up into the hot brown sky, frowning. 'Don't leave anything out.'

'Don't swim if there's lightning,' said Emma.

'Don't worry.'

'Don't tell me not to worry!' Her tone was sharp. 'I'm serious here. You're not to go into the water if there's a storm.' There were years of anxiety in her voice.

'OK. Sorry.'

'I'm trusting you with this.'

'What about Ralph in his tent?' asked Lucy. 'He'll be swept away. Should he come inside? He can put his mattress in Ollie's little box-room, can't he? There'd be room.'

Marnie tried not to show her dismay.

'I'll be fine,' said Ralph. 'I'd quite like to be out in the tent in a storm. Why don't you join me, Ollie?'

'I'll think about it,' said Oliver, casually. 'I'm not quite as bonkers as you.'

'No – go on. Join me.'

'It's a one-man tent.'

'That doesn't matter for one night. We'll squash up.'

'It leaks when you touch its walls.'

'So?'

'Well – we'll get wet.'

'Like drowned rats,' said Lucy, cheerfully, trying to dispel the tension.

'I'll see.' Oliver stood up. 'Let's go swimming at once, shall we, if we're really going to do it? Before the storm.'

The four made their way down to the shore. Before they even arrived, the rain was falling. The sky was now so dark it was maroon. The loch looked chilly and sullen, its colour barely distinguishable from the sky. Marnie shivered. 'Are we really going to do this?'

'Last one in,' said Ralph, 'is a – what? You lot decide.' And he pulled off the T-shirt he was wearing with his swimming trunks, and walked onto the jetty. His bony body glimmered palely. He gave a loud hoot and jumped high in the air, arms up and legs apart. For a moment he seemed to hang there, like a bird. Then he hit the water with a splash. They all watched as he struck out for the centre in his wild, energetic crawl.

'OK,' said Oliver. He turned so he was facing Marnie, and took off his shirt. He took a step forward, nearly touching her, and put up a hand. He touched her cheek very gently, then grazed her lip with a thumb. Marnie stood quite still, rain dripping onto her head, running off her bare shoulders. She knew Lucy was watching them.

'Whatever the weather,' he said very quietly, so only she could hear.

'Yes. Whatever the weather.'

There was such a storm across the land. Thunder cracked and broke in the heaving purple sky and lightning streaked garishly across it, illuminating the lake, the trees, the stony and grassy ground, making everything unearthly. Rain fell in a thousand bullets onto the water, sending up small explosions. It torrented through the trees, turned the path to liquid mud, and clattered noisily on the roof of Eric's house, which was stalwart under the onslaught. Usually I love storms, great winds, deluges, hail. All my life I've loved them. But not that night, because its buffeting violence seemed to be my own internal turmoil. As if I had been turned inside-out and all that I hid, all that I kept secret, was blowing around in the open and there was nothing I could do to stop it . . .

Marnie lay in bed. Outside, the thunder was now only a distant rumble and the rain had almost stopped, although she could hear the steady drip of water from the trees. On other nights, there had been a moon, stars, a band of light on the horizon so that as evening faded morning was already on its way. But tonight it was quite dark. She strained her eyes and could make out no shapes. How would she see her way to the fallen tree? Beside her, Lucy shifted and muttered something thickly.

'Lucy?' whispered Marnie. 'Are you still awake?'

Lucy didn't answer, except to let out a tiny snore. She would give it another few minutes and then go. Now the time had come, all desire seemed to have drained away, leaving only a dull sense of dread. She shivered under her thin covers. It seemed that the languorous blue heat of summer had gone in a single day. It was wet and muddy outside, with a sighing wind, but Oliver would be waiting. She had promised.

Very cautiously, she sat up in bed and pressed her face to the small window. In the garden, she thought she could see a faint, blurred spot of light – Ralph's torch, dim behind the canvas of the tent. He was still awake, then. She imagined him huddled in his sleeping-bag. What would he be doing? Reading? Writing in the diary he scribbled in each day? Lying gazing up at the sagging roof above him, the drops of water oozing through? His face flashed before her as it had this evening: she knew that he knew, and she knew – while trying not to – that he was wretched and lonely and angry and scared.

She inched her legs out of the bed and stood up. The floorboards creaked. She pulled her old grey cardigan over her cotton pyjama shorts and bra. Holding out her hand, she groped her way towards the door. The room seemed to have rearranged itself – everything was in the wrong place. The door had moved. At last she was on the landing, one foot cautiously in front of the other, down the stairs, hand pushing on the banister to lighten her weight on the steps. Around her there was silence. She fumbled under the stairs for where she had left her wellingtons, at first finding the wrong ones and pushing her feet into a pair that were far too large, like paddle boats. Perhaps she should turn the light on – but she didn't dare. She was beginning to make out vague shapes, and felt along the chairs standing at the kitchen table for her waterproof. When she put it on, it felt cold and clammy against her skin.

The door to the tiny room where Oliver slept was shut – what if he had drifted off to sleep? Marnie tiptoed towards it, as far as it was possible to tiptoe in damp wellington boots, catching her hip on the edge of the table and almost yelping in pain. She pushed at the door.

'Oliver?' she hissed. There was no reply. Holding her breath, she could hear no sound of his. 'Are you there?' She reached out and found the divan-bed, patted it for Oliver's body. Nothing. He was gone then, and she felt a stab of panic because it meant she had to go too.

The door swung open onto a gust of cold, spitting air. The ground was spongy and sodden beneath her feet, and when she took a few paces she could actually hear the gurgle of water beneath the surface. When the breeze strengthened, a sudden shower was shaken from overhead branches. Marnie tipped her head and stared up into the moonless, starless sky. She felt that she was standing in a different world from the sunlit summer one of yesterday. It felt larger, less friendly, full of blankness and emptiness, swilled around by slanting rain and cold winds. Her boots slipped in the thick mud.

At the end of the mown grass stood the small tent, but Marnie could no longer see it. Ralph had turned out the torch. She moved very slowly forward towards the pitch black of the forest. Where dark met darkest, there Oliver was waiting. Marnie put her hands under the waterproof and did up the buttons one by one, in an act of demureness that struck even her as comic. Never mind, he wouldn't be able to see it – he would see nothing and neither would she: they would be blind except for touch. She pushed her hair back. It was so quiet she could almost hear the beat of her heart. She touched her face, as he had earlier, to remind herself.

An owl gave a single muffled hoot.

No, not an owl.

A sea-bird far from home called, its melancholy cry melting into the sob of the wind.

Not a sea-bird, no. Oh, no.

Marnie stopped in her tracks and listened. There it was again. She put her fist to her mouth.

A boy gave a sob in the night. It was a piteous sound, half animal in its grief, and it curled into her heart.

And again. Had she ever heard anything so abandoned?

Slowly she turned and went in its direction. At the mouth of the tent she knelt and pulled off her boots, then unzipped the flap and crawled inside. 'Ralph,' she whispered. 'It's me. Don't cry. Please don't cry. It's all right.'

Ralph made an indistinct noise. She couldn't tell if it was a word or not.

She put out a hand and touched a bare leg. He was lying on top of the sleeping-bag.

'What is it? Please tell me.'

Another sob tore out of him, then another.

She crawled further up the tent, found his shoulder and touched it. Her fingers felt for his face, his wet cheeks. 'Is it because of me? I can't bear it if it's because of me.'

'Please go,' he managed.

'I can't go and leave you like this.' She leant forward and kissed his damp forehead.

'Stop,' he whispered. 'I don't want your pity. Anything but that.'

'I don't pity you,' she said. 'You're my dear friend. I love you.'

'Oh Christ oh Christ oh Christ.' Or that was what she thought he was saying. He had turned away from her and put an arm over his face; his words were choked.

Marnie took off her waterproof and lay down next to him in the musty darkness. The floor was lumpy and water seeped through the canvas where it touched her back. She very carefully put her arms around his body, naked except for boxers, and felt him go absolutely still. Through her cardigan, she could feel the serration of his spine. He smelt like grass, soil, woodsmoke. His skin was damp.

'It's all right,' she said. 'Just go to sleep. I'll stay with you until then. Everything's all right. Really.'

'Marnie,' he gulped, and then he was crying in earnest. Crying as a tiny child cries, holding nothing back. His body shook in her arms. She could feel the grief ripping through him in great waves, which broke over him. Sometimes there were words. He said, 'David,' and he said, 'Grace.' He mentioned his father – except he called him 'Daddy', as if he was a small and trusting child again, not a young man whose father beat him and whose mother ('Mummy,' he said, shuddering in Marnie's arms) blamed him for his brother's death.

'Oh, goodness,' he gasped. It was such an old-fashioned, unlikely expression, which Marnie had never heard him use before, and for some reason it made her feel almost unbearably tender. The buttons of her cardigan were pressing against his back and she wriggled out of it and tossed it to one side, then pressed her warm, half-naked body against Ralph's cold flesh, her legs against his, held him close in the thick darkness. She needed to go, she needed to calm Ralph and find Oliver, put everything right that was wrong – but everything Ralph had stored up was gushing out of him, a torrent of misery, rage, guilt and despair. Marnie thought his body must break under the pressure of the black flood that was roaring through him. She imagined him as a landscape that was disintegrating, whirled around with fallen buildings and hurled boulders. She whispered into his shoulder that she was there.

She pictured Oliver standing by the fallen tree, waiting. How long would he wait? She thought, Please don't go, please stay for me, to be there at the end and hold me in the sheltering calm of your presence. She squeezed her eyes tight shut and prayed that Ralph would stop weeping and release her from this torment, but still the sobs continued until she barely heard them; they rose and fell with the wind outside and with the beating of her own heart. She didn't know what time it was, had no idea of how long she had lain there with Ralph, holding his thinness against her, listening to him sob, to the drip of water outside the tent, the strange creakings and sighings of the trees, the occasional rustle as if there were animals outside in the undergrowth.

They lay there for a long time. The wind died down and Ralph stopped crying. At last there was silence, inside and outside the tent. Marnie stirred and loosened her clasp.

'I haven't cried until now.' Ralph sounded exhausted. 'Not since he died. I thought I'd never be able to cry again. That there was something wrong with me.'

'Well, you certainly made up for it.' Marnie tried to keep her voice light. She eased away from Ralph and sat up, feeling the sodden roof of the tent against her. She was chilly now, and tired, depressed. She groped for her cardigan, damp from the rain that had seeped in through the canvas walls, and started to pull it over her head, getting her hair caught round one of its buttons. She took if off carefully, untangled herself, and started again. There was no need to hurry now. She knew she was too late.

There was a sound outside, and before either of them knew what was happening the tent flap was pulled aside and a torch shone in on them. Marnie sat caught in its beam, in her bra and pyjama shorts, her cardigan around her neck. Beside her Ralph crouched in his underwear, his face puffy and creased from weeping, his hair matted round his face.

'What?' she started. 'Who's there? I can't see.' But she knew anyway; she didn't need light.

The torch swung round and now the beam pointed back into Oliver's face.

'Me,' he said. 'Who else?' Then he dropped the beam and they were all invisible again, in an ominous silence.

'Ollie!' said Ralph. 'Shit.'

'Oliver.' Marnie tugged the cardigan down over her stomach and scrambled towards him. 'Listen ... wait, don't go. Please don't go. This isn't – I was on my way –'

'Crap,' he said coldly.

Then he was gone. She sat at the mouth of the tent, watching the wavering light cross the grass towards the house.

'Fuck. Fuck fuck fuck.'

'Sorry. I'm sorry, Marnie.'

'Shut up.'

'I didn't mean to – you didn't need this. I'm so, so sorry.'

'Don't keep saying sorry.'

'No, sorry. Oh, bugger.'

'I ought to go.'

'I've ruined everything.'

'No,' she said dully. 'There wasn't really anything to ruin.'

'I'll tell him. You were comforting me, just being kind. He'll understand. It's me. I ruin everything. I'm like a plague-carrier or something.'

'Stop. Shut up, will you?'

'People should keep away from me. I ought to have a bell to ring, warning of my approach.'

'I said, shut up.'

'Yes. Sorry.'

It was no longer absolute darkness: a new dawn was breaking. The wind of the night before had blown the clouds back and, through them, Marnie could see the stencilled shape of a crescent moon and, just beneath its horn, a single pale star. A narrow band on the horizon glowed orange and pink – after the storm, it was going to be a beautiful day. Her boots were outside, toppled into the grass, and she pushed her feet into them, feeling how wet and gritty they were inside. She picked up her waterproof.

Taking a deep breath to calm herself, she said, 'It wasn't your fault, Ralph. Don't think that. It's no one's fault and it doesn't matter anyway.'

'You're just being kind.'

'No. I chose to be with you and I'm glad I did.'

'Really?'

'Really. Now try to get some sleep.'

'I won't sleep. But don't worry, I'll stay here and you go and talk to Ollie.'

'Yes.'

In the gathering light, she trudged towards the house through the slushy grass. A light had been turned on downstairs: Oliver in his little room. At the front door, she kicked off her boots and stepped inside, turning on the overhead light and blinking in its dazzle. She felt grimy and dejected. Her cardigan was inside out and streaked with mud; her feet, she saw, were filthy. She didn't want to think what her face looked like. But she went through the kitchen and knocked on the door of Oliver's room, quietly so that no one upstairs would wake.

It opened and Oliver stood, blocking her way in. His face, usually so warm, was empty of expression. Behind him, she saw that his rucksack stood beside the divan and clothes were strewn around it.

'What are you doing?'

'Don't speak so loud – everyone will wake up.'

'I don't care,' she said, but in a furious whisper. 'Tell me what you're doing.'

'What does it look like? Packing.'

'Why?'

'I'm leaving.'

'But we've got one day left,' she said stupidly.

'You have – not me.'

'Aren't you going to travel back with us?'

'Why would I want to do that?'

'Ollie.' She stepped forward, but he still didn't budge. She put a hand up to touch his arm, then let it drop. 'It wasn't what you think.'

'What do I think, Marnie?'

'Please. Don't speak like that. You think that I was – was with Ralph.'

'You were with Ralph.'

'Not like that.'

'Naked. I saw you, remember?'

'You don't understand.'

'While I waited in the forest. Waited for hours in the rain and the wind.'

'I know.'

'You promised.'

'I wanted to come.'

'Yeah?' His voice was hard. 'It didn't look like that.'

'Oh, stop trying to punish me and listen. I heard him crying. I couldn't bear it.'

He looked at her for a few moments. 'I really cared about you, you know. It doesn't happen to me very often. I fell hard.'

Marnie winced. 'Don't say it like that, as if it was all over.'

'Over? It didn't even begin. Maybe that's how you like things – the bit just before anything happens.'

'Ollie. What do you think I should have done? He was sobbing his heart out. Ralph, your friend, mine – I couldn't just walk past and put it out of my mind. I couldn't.'

'He's in love with you.'

'What's that got to do with it? He's still my friend.'

'He's in love with you and so was I.'

'Don't say *was*.'

'Grow up, Marnie.'

'It's you I chose. *Choose*, for God's sake.'

'You didn't, though, did you?'

'So.' Marnie folded her arms across her chest. Anger was rising in her. 'That's that, is it? You're going to pack your bags and leave because one night went wrong? That's how much you cared about me?'

'Not just one night. You're not being honest. You didn't want anyone to know about us. You wanted it to be some furtive secret, not out in the open. You're scared.'

'Scared? Of what?'

'You tell me. Sex. Needing someone. Being vulnerable.'

'Hurting Ralph.'

'Hurting Ralph, yeah. Disappointing your mum in some way. I don't know. Not being the good little girl any more. Growing up, being an adult, making your own decisions.'

'OK. Maybe you're right. Maybe I am scared. But I was still going to come to you. It wasn't going to stop me.' The fight went out of her. She was too tired and dispirited, too cold. There was no room in her for desire or even affection. She sat down heavily on the divan beside a pile of dirty clothes and rubbed her eyes. 'Fuck off, then, Ollie.'

'Right.' He picked up the clothes and pushed them into his rucksack, then slung in a couple of books.

'Have a good life.'

'Don't worry. I will.'

And that was it. He put his rucksack on his back and went out of the room. She stood up and followed him as far as the front door, where she watched him walk up the track and over the hill. It seemed a long time ago that she had seen him arrive and she remembered how her heart had flown into her mouth with fear and delight. For a moment she thought she would run after him and pull him back, but she didn't. Instead she sat down at the kitchen table and rested her heavy head in her grubby hands. Summer was over.

'Marnie? Marnie?'

She must have dropped off to sleep. She raised her

head blearily to see her mother and Eric standing in the room, both in dressing-gowns. They looked like a married couple, she thought, and rage surged through her. 'What?' she retorted crossly.

'What's going on?'

'Why should anything be going on?'

'It's half past five and you're asleep in the kitchen covered with mud.'

'So?'

'Why are you up?'

'No reason. I just couldn't sleep.'

'Are you all right?'

'Of course. Why shouldn't I be?'

Emma tightened her dressing-gown and looked at her shrewdly. 'I'm going to make you a mug of hot chocolate and then you're going to get into a nice hot bath.'

Marnie shrugged, dangerously close to tears. 'You don't need to bother.' She paused, then said coldly, 'Both go back to bed, why don't you? I don't want to get in your way.'

'Don't be absurd. What were you doing outside? Are the others up as well? What's wrong?'

'I thought you were going to make me hot chocolate and run me a bath, not ask me endless pointless questions.'

'Here comes Ralph,' said Eric, who was standing by the window, 'looking like something the tide washed up.'

It was true that Ralph, when he came in, looked truly awful. He had pulled on the oversized, grubby shorts and a T-shirt that clung to his body, making him appear malnourished, with thin, sloping shoulders and a scrawny neck. His hair was in a clotted tangle, his face was puffy from lack of sleep and still tearstained from his crying jag. His eyes were bloodshot and there were dark shadows beneath them. More than all of that, he looked drained of life – his restless energy and turbulent enthusiasm had leaked away and he was empty. He moved a bit like a sleepwalker, and came into the house dragging his sodden sleeping-bag behind him. His bare feet shuffled.

'Hello, Ralph,' said Emma, gently, her eyes darting between the two of them. 'I'm making Marnie some hot chocolate. I'll get you some too.'

Ralph sat down at the kitchen table opposite Marnie and gazed at her but she didn't look up. She wanted to feel sorry for herself, not him.

'I've got a better idea,' said Eric, suddenly. 'Ralph and I are going to go fishing. Early morning is the perfect time, and it's our last opportunity. We'll take hot chocolate in a flask and I'll make us honey sandwiches for breakfast. We'll bring back pike for lunch – OK, mate?'

Marnie saw the look her mother gave him. She watched how their eyes locked before they turned away. They love each other, she thought. My mother loves Eric and he loves her back. They are a real couple. She didn't recognize the feeling that flooded through her, didn't know if she was angry, resentful or glad that, after all these years of silent grieving, Emma was able to feel this kind of happiness again. She suddenly understood that this was what the holiday had really been about: not her with her blind, feverish longings and adolescent terrors, but Emma and Eric carefully finding each other in the forests and the meadows. She lifted her head and gave her mother a watery smile. 'I'm fine,' she said. 'We're both fine, aren't we, Ralph?'

'Are we?' He gazed at her pleadingly.

'Yes.' She took a deep breath and laid a hand on his arm reassuringly.

'Marnie?'

'Yes?'

'I wish you'd marry me one day.' Ralph's eyes widened in shock even as he spoke the words; he hadn't known what he was going to say and he actually put a hand over his mouth after he'd spoken.

The words hung in the silent room. Marnie closed her eyes and pressed her hands together, willing the moment to pass. 'I'm seventeen,' she said, trying to turn it into a joke. 'And you're mad.' She turned to Emma and Eric and tried to sound casual; her face was rubbery with tiredness. 'Ollie's gone.'

'Gone?' Emma's eyebrows shot up. 'Gone for good?'

'Yes.' She waited for her mother to ask why, but she didn't. She had always been wise like that, knowing when to hold her tongue. She just gave a little nod, as if in recognition.

Eric took Ralph out onto the loch, whose waters were still opaque from the previous night's storm. From the first floor, Marnie could see them, cut-out figures against the washed turquoise sky. It was as if Oliver had never been there – except for the ache in her eyes and throat, the exhaustion that made her bones heavy. She lay in the hot bath that Emma had run for her and listened to the sounds from the kitchen: the china clinking and doors being shut; a tap running. She imagined her mother there

– her dressing-gown sleeves rolled up and her hair pulled severely back, a look of concentration on her strong, handsome face as she stood at the sink or wiped the table clear of crumbs – and she felt safe again, and young. She didn't want to grow up, anyway. She could do without the heavy, coiling lethargy of lust, the gulping and hyper-ventilating elation of what, for want of a better word, she called love. The water lapped around her and her skin felt soft and clean. Emma was making things orderly; Eric was taking care of Ralph for her; Lucy was peacefully asleep in their room, her sharp features softened by hope-ful dreams. Marnie's father had been dead for nearly fourteen years; her brother too; they lay under the turf hundreds of miles away, but they were here too. Everyone was here. Marnie closed her eyes and tears bubbled under the lids.

Once I had a dog. I keep expecting her to be here now, laying her muzzle on my arm, looking up at me with penitent brown eyes. She was a stray, a ragbag of breeds, and I got her from a rescue centre when she was a year old with sharp ribs, a matted coat and a trembling fear of loud noises, motorbikes, other dogs, crowds, men with beards. I called her Gretel. She spent her first few months cowering in corners and under chairs, panting and whimpering. Bit by bit she gave me her trust. After six months, she was devoted to me. When I came into the room, she would be hysterically happy, dashing around and throwing herself onto the floor in front of me, where she would lie with her belly exposed and her tail thumping, her eyes rolling back to show the whites. When I went out of the room, she would weep – there's no other word for it. She followed me everywhere. She looked at me with wounded adoration.

I had her for five years. It was – this sounds ridiculous, and you know how I always hated that sentimental attitude to dumb animals – one of the most important relationships of my life. I guess you could say that during those years, some of the darkest years of my life, Gretel was my best friend. Maybe she saved me from – what? What am I saying? Would I have killed myself without her? All I know is that I couldn't collapse when I had her to look after. She needed me, not just to feed her, take her for walks, but to be there for her. I couldn't leave her, not when she was so unconditionally in love with me. Sometimes I would wake in the mornings and think, Why should I get out of bed? Then I would hear her whining and scratching at the door downstairs, asking to be let out, and I would make myself go down to her. In the evenings, she would rest her head on my lap as I sat in my chair and read, or just stared out of the window, and that physical contact took the edge off my loneliness.

One day she simply disappeared. We were on one of our walks, a regular cross-country circuit that took an hour or so and she knew well, and a rabbit ran across our path. Gretel ran after it, her tail streaming out behind her and her ears back. She disappeared like an arrow and I never saw her again. I spent weeks, months searching for her. I imagined her lost and waiting for me to find her. I imagined her stolen and whining for me to rescue her, or injured and knowing I would come to help her and take her home. Every so often I would think I saw her, although I knew I hadn't, and my heart would jolt with the hope that I knew would be crushed. Years later, I would get sudden false glimpses of her. I still dream of her.

Why am I thinking of her now? I suppose because I'm dying and I often wake and think she's here with me, lying on the floor. Perhaps she is, in a way. When there's no future, the past crowds in on you. I can hear the thump of her tail on the floor and feel the grizzled softness of her muzzle. She loved me and I loved her, and that was the only balanced equation of my life.

Chapter Fifteen

While Oliver read poems to Ralph, Marnie cooked. It was just for the two of them; she knew that Ralph would never eat another meal, and the most she could try to do was spoon a few drops of soup down his throat; even that seemed painful for him to swallow. She held his head up and he fixed his cavernous eyes on her.

She boiled water and dropped tomatoes into it, then scooped them out after a few seconds and removed their skin. She roasted peppers in the oven and peeled off their blackened skin as well, then chopped the soft flesh into strips. She crushed garlic and fried it in a small amount of olive oil, then shook in some dried herbs. She added the tomatoes and peppers and the smell, pungent and rich, filled the air.

'Look,' said Oliver, suddenly. Marnie, raising her head from her task, saw that the quality of light in the room had changed. 'It's started to snow.'

She rinsed her hands and joined him at the window. The flakes fell slowly, dissolving on the ground.

'It's not settling yet.'

'No – but I think it's getting heavier.'

'Do you remember the time when we all went tobogganing down the hill by our house? We didn't have a sledge, just bin-bags and an old metal tray.'

It had been cold and bright, the sun sparkling off the

crust of unbroken snow, giving out no heat. Marnie could still recall how it had felt swooping down the hill, faster and faster, and ending up with her face buried in a snow-drift, cheeks stinging, ice trickling down her neck, stiff scarf rubbing against her chin, the balls of her feet numb, fingertips throbbing, in bliss.

'I remember it vividly,' said Oliver. 'Ralph ended up in a thorn bush.' He turned. 'Do you remember, Ralph?'

Ralph didn't answer. His eyes were half open but it was impossible to tell if he was awake or asleep.

Marnie went over to him, held one translucent hand. Was he lying there listening to their words, or had he gone beyond them now? She wondered what thoughts and memories were in his mind. She could picture him on that snowy day, careering down the hill, head thrown back, snow glistening on his dark hair, mouth open in a shout of delight, utterly reckless and abandoned to the moment, and now he lay in front of her, a pile of bones under the sheet. Was he still inside that crumbling body, the same wild and lonely boy whose face used to light up when he saw her, whose words would tumble out of him, whose mind would fizz with sudden new enthusiasms, whose raw need and clumsy generosity had once touched and tormented her?

She was filled with images of the past, which she had forgotten but for years must have lain dormant, waiting for this moment. Ralph making a mobile for Grace, using a metal coat-hanger and the stones he used to search for on the beach, sometimes for hours on end, with holes at their centre. He said that each stone represented a wish and it would slowly spin over Grace's bed, keeping her safe from harm. Ralph trying to do cartwheels on her lawn – he'd kept at it until his gangly body straightened out and his legs described a smooth circle through the air. Ralph barbecuing mackerel over the fire in Scotland, very serious, wrapped in the striped apron that Eric used to wear. Ralph on his knees in front of Emma, his face in her lap, and Emma's hand softly stroking the tangle of his hair – when had that been and why had he been crying? She couldn't remember now, didn't want to. She concentrated on images of happiness, as if by remembering them she could communicate them to Ralph. Riding on the rusting old bike that Emma had given him, his greatcoat streaming out behind him. Learning how to toss pancakes, half-cooked shreds of batter flying through the air. Reading to her when she had tonsillitis and had two weeks off school – Rosamund Lehmann's *Dusty Answer*, she could still hear his voice, and *Catcher in the Rye*. Singing, badly. Playing the guitar, badly. Trying to learn to play her harmonica. Striding through the surf towards her with Lucy on his shoulders, his face split into a grin. He had a capacity for silliness that had allowed Marnie to be silly as well. He'd given her a childhood.

'How have I managed without you all these years?' Marnie said now, bending forward and kissing his clammy forehead, his damp head. Then she said, 'I know it's only just been done, but shall I wash your hair again, ready for our Christmas celebrations?'

He didn't reply but he gave her a small, affirmative smile.

She filled a bowl with hot water, and lifted his head up

to slip a plastic bag and then a towel under it. She used her own shampoo, which smelt of lemons, and lock by lock washed and rinsed his hair, rubbing it dry as she went along. She noticed grey strands among the black. When she was done she shaved him as well, taking great care not to nick him. His skin was loose on his wasted face. She put a dry towel under his head and patted Oliver's after-shave onto his smooth cheeks, breathed in appreciatively. 'Very fragrant,' she said.

Ralph's eyes opened and he gave her a little grin. She kissed his forehead and said, 'Now for your nails. They're turning into talons.'

She did his fingernails first, collecting the thin crescents in the palm of her hand and dropping them into the bin. Then his toenails. His feet were bruised, as if he'd put them in a mangle, and she rubbed cream into them, holding them between her hands and massaging them gently. She had done this for her mother, during her last illness. She remembered painting Emma's cracked toenails red on the day before she died.

She returned to her cooking, and Oliver to reading poems. His voice was quiet and she only caught a few words. She boiled water for the pasta, chopped cucumber and tore lettuce leaves, grated Parmesan, made a salad dressing. If she kept busy, she would be all right. Oliver came over and opened a bottle of wine, poured her a glass and raised his own to her silently. Inside, the Christmas lights glowed and flickered. Outside, the snow was falling more thickly. It streamed past the window and gathered in small heaps on the sill.

When Marnie stepped outside for a few seconds, she

looked up, suddenly disoriented in the vortex of white. Flakes landed on her upturned face and melted there, sliding down her cheeks. She put out the tip of her tongue to catch one, the way she used to as a child – and for a fraction of a moment, she thought she saw her brother running towards her with a snowball in his hand. How the imagination tricked one. There were ghosts in the woods and by the water. The world was white and muffled in silence; the pines above her creaked slightly under the new weight of snow.

Back at the hob, she added the pasta to the boiling salted water, dressed the salad, drank her wine, feeling it course through her. Every time she looked up she saw Oliver sitting by the bed in the pool of light, and Ralph lying inert beside him.

'It's ready,' she said at last. 'Shall we eat it with a film?'

'Sure.'

So they sat on either side of Ralph, the television at the end of his bed, and watched a black-and-white movie in which the wisecracking guy got his wisecracking girl. Marnie didn't even try to follow the plot. The figures on the screen made animated gestures, Ralph's eyes flickered open and closed again, the snow fell steadily and the fire burnt down in the grate until only the embers glowed. She ate her pasta slowly and drank more wine. Oliver handed her a whisky and she took a single burning sip. If she closed her eyes, she knew that she would be overcome with tiredness, but she didn't want to close her eyes, because it seemed to her that it would not be long now and she had to be awake: she had to be there and accompanying him until the very last moment when he would cross the threshold and they would no longer be able to follow.

Chapter Sixteen

No one mentioned Oliver any more: it was as if he had never existed. Emma simply said that if Marnie ever wanted to talk about – 'No, thanks!' snapped Marnie, banging round the kitchen, attacking the surfaces with Vim, exaggeratedly busy. 'There's nothing to say, so why should I say it?' Lucy, after an initial attempt to draw her out, had become tactfully silent on the subject. And Ralph – once he had begged Marnie to meet up with Oliver, he wanted them to be together, and Marnie had told him coldly that it was none of his business and he should stop interfering – proceeded to behave as if he did not have a friend called Oliver Fenton, although Marnie knew for a fact that the two of them had met up the day after they had returned from Scotland to sort out their quarrel. It didn't help. The more that she made him into a taboo, the more she thought about him. She even had disturbing and erotic dreams about him, and would wake in confusion.

The day before she went back to school for her final year, the phone rang and when she answered it was him.

'Marnie?'

'What?' she snapped. Oh, but she had longed to hear his voice. She pressed the receiver to her ear, closed her eyes.

'Can we meet?'

'No.' Why did she say that?

'I'll be on the beach – by that old rotting boat – in about twenty minutes.'

'I won't.'

'I'll wait for an hour.'

She hung up and prowled irritably round the house. Emma was in her shed and neither Lucy nor Ralph was there, although Ralph had asked himself round for supper that night. He wanted to cook for them – already Marnie felt tired just thinking of the mess and drama he would create when she wanted a peaceful evening and an early night.

She found herself standing in front of the mirror, looking critically at her image, wrinkling her nose at her dishevelled hair and shabby clothes. She found herself taking a shower, even though the water was tepid, and she told herself that she had been going to wash her hair anyway, before going back to school. Nothing to do with him. She wasn't thinking about him. She wasn't going to look at her watch. She looked and saw that he would probably be there by now, waiting for her. She towelled her hair dry and pulled on her oldest jeans and a green shirt that Oliver had once said he liked. Her cheeks burnt. What did she care whether Oliver liked it or not? She brushed mascara onto her lashes and bit her lips to bring colour to them, then went into the kitchen. She had been about to make a cake before Oliver phoned; the bowl of sifted flour stood ready, three eggs, two lemons waiting to be zested. She took the margarine out of the fridge and weighed four ounces into the scales and grinned savagely at herself, making a lemon cake in the kitchen like an obedient suburban housewife while the young man she loved – yes, oh, yes, she did, she did, why not admit it to herself? – waited for her outside.

There was a clock on the wall and she didn't look at it, wouldn't, but out of the corner of her eye she could see the minute hand advancing.

Why not? Why not?

Four ounces of sugar added to the margarine; she beat them ferociously with a wooden spoon until the mixture was pale and light. The sky outside the window was a pale, cool blue. She cracked the eggs into a bowl and whisked them, hard, until they frothed. Zested the lemons into the flour, grazing her knuckles.

He wouldn't wait. If she didn't come, she knew he wouldn't stay.

She pushed her feet into her walking boots and her arms into the black woollen jacket that had seen better days. Ran from the kitchen and out, down the garden, towards the sea, which rippled and shone. The shingle crunched under her feet. Autumn was nearly here; there was a lash to the wind that made her eyes water. Shallow waves foamed over the pebbles and sucked back. She slowed as she saw the ruined hulk of the boat in the distance, trying to get her breath.

He was looking out at the sea, his arms wrapped round himself for warmth. She stopped and then, when he turned and saw her, moved forward again until she was a few feet from where he stood.

'I thought you wouldn't come,' he said, not moving.

He seemed tired, thinner than she'd remembered him.

Soft brown hair, steady gaze, lanky frame. Just an ordinary young man, nothing remarkable, but hers. Was it possible that he could feel the same as her, that his heart was also bursting with fierce joy? In a few moments would he be holding her tight? She put it off, standing her ground. 'I wasn't going to.'

'So why did you change your mind?'

'Because I had to see you.'

'Marnie —'

'I was just hugging him. He was so upset.'

'I know that. He told me.'

'You're going away soon.'

'Yes.' He looked at her, waiting.

'I can't bear it,' she said, in a small voice.

In two steps he was beside her, or perhaps it was her who crossed the distance between them, she couldn't tell. All she knew was that his arms were tight round her and hers round him and they clung together, pressed to each other blindly. Now his hand was in her hair and he pulled back her face until they were staring into each other's eyes, not smiling, not saying anything. Behind them, she could hear the slap of the water, the lonely call of a bird. His arms went under her coat, her hands were beneath his shirt and feeling the warmth of his back, the sharpness of his spine. Too many layers, but at last they were peeled off and he laid her down on top of them, so she was protected from the sharpness of the shingle. The wind was chilly on her bare skin but then he was covering her and it was too late to tell him that she'd never done this before, he was the first, she didn't know, he had to be careful, it hurt . . . She closed her eyes and put her arms on his shoulders, on his back; she opened them and saw the pale sky and Oliver's face, frowning as if he was concentrating. This was something to get through, she understood, like a gate into another place in her life. And when it was over he pulled the strands of her dark hair from her face and kissed her mouth, her cheeks, her forehead, her neck, smiling at her at last. Then he pulled his jacket over the top of both of them and they lay curled up together, his arm pillowing her head.

'Oliver,' she said at last, and he raised himself on one arm and looked at her.

'It's all right.' He spoke before she could say the words. 'We won't tell Ralph. We won't tell anyone. This is just us, you and me.' He traced a line round her jaw, ran a thumb over her lip.

'When are you going?'

'Thirteen days' time.'

'Thirteen days.'

So began Marnie's secret life. She was surprised by how easily she could be two people. At home and at school she was the same Marnie Still, quiet, stubborn, attentive, self-contained. She got up early each morning and fed the hens, collected their warm eggs, bits of feather sticking to the shell. She sat at breakfast with Emma, eating porridge with Demerara sugar, or toast with marmalade, and drinking tea – or on days when there were guests, she helped her mother fry bacon, grill fat pink sausages until their skins burst, and wash dishes smeared with yolk. She went off to school on her bike, her bag slung over her shoulders, her eyes watering in the wind that whipped up from the sea. She bent over her desk, chewing her lower lip, mouthing the words on the page silently to herself because, however hard she tried, reading remained difficult, letters squirming on the page and rearranging themselves; she was painfully aware that she was seventeen and read aloud like a ten-year-old. She met up with Lucy between lessons, sat over cups of instant soup in the sixth-form common room where they would gossip, exchange confidences, make plans, arrange when to go out together and when Lucy would next come round.

With Ralph she was reassuring, warm, friendly. She watched hope flower in him and hated herself. On the evening that she had first met Oliver again, Ralph came round for supper and they cooked it together, with the giggling ease they had not had for months. She had teased him, and seen how he flushed with delight, taught him how to make a cheese soufflé, listened as he told her about imaginary numbers, played cards with him before he went up to Seth's old room under the rafters. With her mother, she was always pleasant and unconfrontational, but shied away from proper discussion and Emma's discerning gaze, and spent more time than usual in her room.

And then: she would sneak out of school during her lunch hour and meet Oliver; skip lessons and meet Oliver; hurry to his house as soon as the last bell had gone, breathless with desire, and he wouldn't say anything when he opened the door, just take her hand and lead her up to his room, lay her down. A couple of times she waited until Emma was asleep at night, then went to the beach where they'd met on that first day to find him there, waiting for her again in the cool salty darkness, under the hazy moon. The world receded, became a pale blur in the background. Only Oliver was vivid. Alone in bed she would replay how he had looked, what he had said, how he had touched her, pushed back her hair, how he had lain in her arms. She would never forget those secret days. Even at the time she understood that a new self had at last been born, unfolded in delight, and that when she was very old she would look back and remember how softly beautiful she had felt, how flush-full of love, tenderness, melting desire.

She had always thought she was an honest person, but deception came easily. She told Ralph that she was busy because she had to do catch-up study, Lucy that she was helping Emma more than usual but soon things would be back to normal, Emma that she needed to use the school's darkroom to develop her photographs, or that a few girls she hadn't been friendly with before had invited her round. Once, in town with Lucy, they had bumped into Ralph and Oliver together, and the four had stood in a self-conscious huddle on the pavement. Neither Oliver nor Ralph had said anything to her about their patched-up friendship, but Marnie didn't mind: indeed, she felt an illicit thrill that they were all hiding from each other. Nobody was in plain sight – except perhaps Lucy, who looked between the three of them with her beady, deceived gaze.

Now she understood that the reason she kept Oliver a secret was not just an over-protective impulse towards Ralph. It had begun that way, certainly, but she had gradually discovered that she liked her life to be hidden from view. She didn't want to be an official couple, whom other people had opinions about ('What do you make of Marnie and Oliver?' 'Oh, it can never last'). She loved sitting in her room until she was sure the house was silent and all its other inmates asleep, then creeping down the stairs, avoiding the one that creaked, three from the bottom, opening the door to the night tang, feeling for him in the spooky darkness. If Ralph knew, he would be wretchedly happy for them – she could already see the look on his thin face; if Lucy knew, she would be sceptical, curious and sour; if Emma knew, she would understand too much about her daughter's life. Marnie did not want anyone to understand her life – except Oliver, to whom she offered fragments of her history like gifts.

A few days before he left, she said to him, 'I've been thinking of Seth recently.' Then she waited, feeling the familiar bulky anxiety lodge in her throat and stomach.

They were in his room, sitting on the floor with their backs against the bed, eating toast and Marmite. She was wearing Oliver's thick striped dressing-gown, which smelt of him, and their legs were tangled. It was early afternoon, hours before either of his parents would come home, and outside it was raining steadily: it pattered on the roof and streamed down the window, so that she felt they were cocooned inside a bright, warm space while the world outside was wet, grey and cold.

Oliver didn't answer immediately. He shifted his position so that he was sitting up straighter, and then he picked up one of her hands and held it between both of his own, fiddling with her fingers. 'You've never talked about him before,' he said finally.

'But you knew, of course?'

'Yes.'

'From Ralph?'

'No. He's never said anything to me.' Marnie was surprised, but at the same time felt a surge of affection towards her friend, who let her tell her own stories. How many other people could she say that about? 'My mother told me, after I first met you.'

'Your mother?'

'It's just one of those things that people round here know.'

'You mean, "Do you know what happened to those poor Stills? No wonder they're a bit odd."'

Oliver grinned wryly. 'Something like that.'

'But you never said anything. Why not?'

'*You* never said anything, Marnie. I was waiting.'

'Well, now I have.' She sighed and put her head on his shoulder and he stroked her hair. 'If I was writing an essay about it, I'd probably say that being with you has stirred up lots of things in me that I've never really thought about – or, at least, tried not to think about. Like a muddy pool.'

'What have you been thinking?'

His voice was measured, quiet; if he'd pushed her or expressed his own opinion, Marnie knew that she would not have continued. 'Stupid things, mainly – like, if he was alive, what would he be doing, what would he look like, would he have a girlfriend and what would she be like, would we get on, would we actually like each other.

One of the things I sometimes feel is that he'd look down on me, wouldn't be bothered – I'd still be his silly baby sister, still tagging after him, petitioning him for favours. Would he like *you*? And things like, what would my relationship with Mum be if she had a son as well? Would he be her favourite? Would I be less special to her? Or does she resent me because I'm alive and Seth's dead? Does she ever look at me and think it should have been the other way round?'

'The one thing I can be absolutely sure of, Marnie, is that your mother never thinks that.'

'Are you? When someone dies, they become perfect, especially when they die young. That's what happened with David – look at how Ralph's parents reacted. Ralph never stood a chance when David was alive, but dead – well, he's like a god. Seth was little, sweet, clever, innocent and unblemished, the first-born. And then there's me – no, don't say anything – and I can't compete. Oh, I know it shouldn't be about competing, but sometimes I feel like that. And then I feel so guilty for feeling like that. Not just guilty for being alive when he's dead – it's like I'm jealous of my brother, jealous of someone who died in a terrible accident when he was seven! What kind of person would feel that?'

'A normal one?' Oliver suggested.

'You know why Mum adores Ralph so much, don't you? He's her replacement son. The moment she set eyes on him, it was like love at first sight. I saw it happen.'

'For both of them.' It was barely a question.

'Oh, yes. She needed a son and he needed a mother. He's the only person who makes her melt. I don't.'

'And that makes you feel . . .' He paused, waiting for her to fill in the gap.

'I don't know.' Marnie stood up and went to the window. Outside, the large garden was soggy; the trees at the end were turning golden. She leant her forehead against the cool pane and looked out at the falling rain, the grey and blurred horizon. 'Ralph's like my – I was going to say burden. That sounds terrible and I don't mean it like that. More like my penance. I suppose he's my family now. He has this hold over me.'

'I know,' Oliver said wryly.

'You're going to say we have to tell him.'

'But we do. Every time I see him, I feel rotten.'

'Not yet.'

'It's not some dirty secret, Marnie. We're going out, that's all.'

'Can we wait till Christmas, when you come back for the holidays?'

'Three months.'

'But you won't be here, anyway, so you won't have to be feeling rotten.'

'That's not how it works.'

'By Christmas, he'll have taken his Cambridge exams and done his interview. I don't want anything to get in the way of that.'

Oliver stood up and joined her at the window. 'Do you think that if he gets into Cambridge, he'll be all right and you won't have to worry about him any more and, miraculously, you'll both be free of each other?'

'Kind of,' she admitted.

'You know how ridiculous this is?'

'Yes.'

'And if Ralph knew, he'd be furious and humiliated that we were hiding from him.'

'Yes.'

'OK, then.'

'Really?'

'You know, this is the first time you've talked about the future.'

'What do you mean?'

'About us having a future, beyond the next few days.'

'You mean, you going away?'

'Yes.'

'Do we?'

'How can you ask?' He put his hands on her shoulders and turned her to face him. 'I've never felt this way before.'

'Never? What about all the other girls before me?'

'Which other girls?'

'I don't know. Like . . .' She pretended to search for her name, though it was branded on her heart and even now she would remember her bright smile, her air of confident propriety. 'Lou.'

'Oh, Lou.' He spoke dismissively. Marnie's heart lifted in delight.

'Who, then?'

'Marnie, I don't know what you think but I haven't had loads of girlfriends.'

'Haven't you?'

'No. I'm quite shy, you know. A good Catholic boy.'

Marnie pushed her hand through his hair, kissed him half on his mouth, felt his lips smile under hers. She felt

Ralph recede, their betrayal soften and fade. This was what mattered: here, now, in this room.

'How many, then?' she said.

'You want numbers?'

'Well, it's only fair. You know about me: there was David and that's all. One before you, and I didn't even like him very much and we certainly didn't sleep together.'

'At school,' said Oliver, 'everyone talks about sex as if it's easy. You listen to boys, even the nasty ones and the fat ones and the spotty ones, and you'd think they were having sex all the time. They'd boast about it and compare notes and name girls who were up for it. I didn't understand how they could be so confident. Now I think most of them were probably just making it up, but then I'd ask myself, "Why is it so simple and so casual and meaningless for them when for me it's so . . ."' He trailed off.

'So what?'

'Different. I dunno. Complicated. Scary, even. I didn't know how to talk to girls, even though I've got all these bloody older sisters.'

'You always talked to me all right.'

'I saw you standing there in your shabby clothes, your hair all messy, paint on your face. How could I resist?'

'You did resist, though – for ages.'

'I told you, I'm shy. Anyway, one, since you asked.'

'One?'

'And that wasn't even Lou. It was a pissed, unhappy girl at a party who I'd never met before and never saw after. I behaved just like the oafs at school who used to brag about doing it in the cupboard under the stairs.'

'So, one pissed girl and then me.'

'Are you disappointed?'

'Do you know what I am? I'm happy.' She wrapped her arms round his neck. 'I'm so happy I feel blurred. I've lost my boundaries.'

At that moment the doorbell rang.

'Ignore it,' said Oliver, his lips in her hair, his hands undoing the belt of the towelling robe she was wearing. 'We've got at least two hours before Mum gets back.'

So it was that they were lying on his unmade bed, naked and entwined, when they heard Ralph's voice, calling Oliver's name, saying he knew he was there and he should just take a look at what he'd brought him. Before they even had time to cover themselves with a sheet, he burst into the room, sopping wet and carrying a tall, cumbersome parcel wrapped in brown paper. He was shouting something about a going-away present, which he hadn't been able to resist – it was a bit like the one he had only much better. Even after he had seen them, and his face was full of wild distress, a few words still managed to escape.

'I hope it'll fit in the car,' he said feebly, looking away as Marnie sat up and brought the sheet under her chin. Carefully, he stood the parcel upright just inside the door.

'Ralph,' said Oliver, 'we were going to tell you.'

'It doesn't matter.'

'It does matter.'

'No. You don't need to say anything. I'll let myself out. I left the spare key on the table by the way.'

He backed from the room, pulling the door shut behind him.

'Shit,' Oliver said. He stood up and started to pull on his clothes.

'What are you going to do?'

'Run after him, of course.'

But he didn't need to, because the door was flung open again and Ralph stood in the entrance and now his face was blazing with fury. 'What did you think? That I wouldn't be able to cope? Better to protect me? Is that it? Sweet Ralph, helpless, hopeless Ralph. Treat him like a child.'

'No!' said Marnie, although, of course, that was what she had thought.

'What? What? You thought I was in love with you and would be too upset to deal with the truth, so you could just go along and pretend that nothing was happening. You're my *friends*. God, you must have laughed. And you,' he said, jabbing a finger into Oliver's chest. 'I told you you should go and make it up with Marnie – I pleaded with you – and you said maybe one day. And all the time you were fucking her?'

'It was wrong,' said Oliver. He cast a single stony glance at Marnie, then turned back to Ralph. 'I know it was wrong. I'm sorry.'

'That time we all met and you two pretended you hadn't seen each other since Scotland? And, Marnie, when you said you didn't care about Oliver any more? And you even flirted with me – yes, you did. You know it's true. You played with me, like a cat with a fucking mouse. Why? That's – it's not right. It's *wrong*.'

'Ralph,' said Marnie. She got out of the bed, keeping the sheet draped around her, and went to him, tripping over the folds in her haste. 'Please. It was my fault.'

'You didn't trust me, either of you.'

'That's not it,' said Oliver.

'Yes. You thought I'd collapse or something. Maybe I would even have been pleased for you – at least you could have given me the chance, allowed me some kind of control over my own life. You had power over me and you abused it.'

'Ralph –'

'*Both* of you. You've ruined everything.' He turned to Oliver. 'Have a good time at university,' he said. 'I'm sure you will.' Then he kicked at the vast parcel and it fell to the floor with a dry, rattling sound. 'You fucking shit.'

Marnie wasn't sure how it happened. Later, she couldn't piece together the events in the right order or say who hit whom first. But suddenly the two of them were throwing wild, ineffective punches at each other, their faces puckered as if they were about to burst into tears. They looked farcical, ugly.

'Stop it!' she cried, trying to pull them apart while still holding her sheet in place. 'What do you think you're doing? This is stupid. Look at you both. Stop!'

They didn't reply. She heard their laboured breaths. Their feet pattered on the floor. Then Ralph's fist landed on Oliver's right cheek, just under his eye, and Oliver staggered backwards, banging into his desk and slipping to the floor with a comical look of surprise on his face.

'Jesus,' said Marnie, in disgust. 'I don't believe you two.'

'You don't have to,' said Ralph. 'I'm off. You can forget I ever existed. 'Bye.'

This time he did not return. They heard the front door open and close. There was absolute silence in the room. Oliver crawled over and knelt down by the parcel, tearing away some of the paper. 'He's given me a skeleton,' he said. 'A life-sized skeleton.' He sounded as if he was about to cry. 'He must have spent every last penny he had on it.'

'What did you both think you were doing?'

'I'm not even doing medicine. One of the arms has come off.'

He didn't look up as Marnie pulled on her clothes and left, walking out into the gathering darkness, knowing it was over.

It doesn't matter any more, sweetheart. It really doesn't matter. All that frenzy and all that sadness, all that bitterness and rage and despair. That's all finished with and you're beside me again. Peaceful. The three of us together. Who'd have thought it would come to this at last?

It's still snowing outside, isn't it? I imagine the moon glowing on a white world. Sound muffled. Eerie quiet. If I was out there now, I would lie down in the snow and look up into the sky's vertiginous fall; it always makes me feel that it is me who is floating upwards into space. I would pick up a handful and crunch it into a solid ball. Perhaps I would pull on my skates and push out onto the ice of the loch, the blades sinking through the few inches of snow and cutting into the ice with a slight hiss. I would hold out my hand and feel the single flake melt on my palm.

Go outside for me now.

Do it for me. Do all the things I will never do again.

Chapter Seventeen

Marnie looked up. Oliver was fast asleep in his chair, his head tipped forward and his mouth slightly open. He looked older when he slept, and heavier. Ralph's eyes were also closed; Marnie couldn't hear him breathing. She stood up and leant over him. His eyelids were blue, his lips almost white. She picked up one hand and with her thumb found his reedy, erratic pulse.

The television screen was blank, a single white line flickering down it. She turned it off. The fire had nearly gone out but, with Dot's portable heaters, the air was still warm, and the embers glowed, brightening and fading. The Christmas lights shone above the bed, giving a ghostly appearance to the tableau of the two sleeping men. Marnie picked up the rug she had wrapped round herself earlier and laid it across Oliver, taking care not to wake him; she smoothed the covers on Ralph's bed, making sure his arms were safely under them – when they lay on top, he looked more than ever like a corpse arranged by an undertaker.

She was far from sleep. She wasn't even tired any more; she'd passed through all the stages of weariness and come out the other side, preternaturally alert, ready for whatever might happen, her senses tingling and every sound – the muffled thumps of snow falling from the eaves outside, the barely audible crackle as the embers lit an unburnt twig, the far-off hoot of an owl and the even-more-distant reply of its mate – amplified inside her.

She picked up the plates and glasses and padded across to the sink to rinse them quietly while she waited for the kettle to boil. Then she made herself a cup of camomile tea, which she took to the window to drink. When she pulled open the curtain, flakes drifted past the window. Although she couldn't see it from where she stood, she knew that there must be a moon because everything – the soft floor of snow, the dark mass of trees, the rise of the hill beyond – was bathed in a spectral light. She heard the owl call again, closer this time.

Marnie pulled on her coat and slid her feet into her boots. She slipped her phone into her pocket, wrapped a scarf round her neck and pulled on her gloves. When she opened the door, a dim rectangle of light fell across the hall floor. Outside, it was not as cold as she had been expecting, though her breath curled in the air. The sky had cleared and, yes, the moon was low on the horizon, half swathed in cloud. She pulled the door shut carefully behind her and stood in the windless quiet. Nothing moved. The trees were motionless, etched against the sky. Above her, small icicles hung from the guttering. When she moved forward, out of the shelter of the house, her shadow lay across the blue-white ground; her boots creaked on the snow. The world was mysterious and beautiful.

Marnie walked a few yards further on and turned back to look at the little house, its downstairs windows illuminated and a thread of smoke curling out of the chimney. Then she set off up the hill, her footprints the only marks in the snow and the owl's shriek closer. Now she could see the loch, which lay in an oval of perfect whiteness beneath her. She had come up here to make a phone call, but she could hardly bring herself to do so. The real world – at least, the world from which she had come – seemed so very far away, a dream. The past was nearer to her than the present. She stood in this monochrome clarity, imagining Eva, a colourful bird making her untidy nest in Marnie's flat, her raucous, urban, smoke-filled days and her cluttered, dancing nights, and felt giddy with distance: not just the distance in space, but the distance in experience. There was her stepdaughter – or ex-stepdaughter – with her Facebook network of virtual friends, her magazines and text messages and iPod of ten thousand songs, her refusal to make plans beyond the next half an hour, her painted nails and painted lips and teetering heels, her instant experiences, her incomprehensible vocabulary, her days streaming past in a clatter of noise and excitement. And there was Marnie, waiting at the bed of her friend with no phone, even, with time slowed down to take in the whole of her past, with the world receding.

Finally, she pulled her phone out of her coat pocket, took off her gloves and turned it on. It could have been any time – midnight, three, an hour before dawn – but she saw that it was only ten o'clock. There were a couple of text messages from Eva, saying 'R U OK?' and 'Rng l8er', and some voicemails, but she didn't want to listen to them just now.

First, she rang Eva's mobile, but it asked her to leave a message. Next she rang the flat and, just as she was about to give up, a voice answered. A young woman, but not Eva: she had a gravelly smoker's voice and a London accent. Marnie asked to speak to Eva, but was told Eva wasn't there right now, could she take a message? In the background. Marnie could hear several other voices, music playing.

'Who are you?' she asked.

'Sorry?'

'I'm Marnie – I own the flat. Who are you?'

'I'm Corrie,' the voice said warmly. 'It's really nice of you to let us all stay here.'

'But I –'

There was a scream of laughter, and Corrie, whoever she might be, said, 'Sorry, emergency. Got to go. Whoops!'

Marnie gazed for a few seconds at the mobile, grimacing. Then she scrolled down the address book until she came to Lucy.

'Hello?' Lucy's husband, voice curt as if she had interrupted him in the middle of something.

'Fred? It's me, Marnie.'

'Marnie!' His voice took on a note of solemn warmth, so that Marnie could tell he knew where she was and what she was doing. 'How are you?'

'OK. At least, I think so.'

'You want Lucy. Hang on, I'll call her. You take care.'

'Thanks.' Marnie waited. She heard him calling Lucy's name, and then Lucy was on the phone.

'Marnie – is he . . .'

'No. He's still alive. Though I can't believe it will be much longer.'

'Is he in pain?'

'I don't think so. He sleeps, mostly.'

'Are you all right?'

'Yes. I don't know. I've been thinking about everything. The past. All the things I've done wrong.'

'You don't need to –'

'I know it's a long time ago, but it doesn't feel it. I just wanted to say sorry.'

'You said sorry at the time. More than once.'

'Well, I'm saying it again.'

'Marnie, listen. I'm happy. Much happier than I would have been if things had worked out differently.'

'You've been a good friend to me.' Marnie listened to the emotion swelling in her voice. She felt that there was an ocean of tears behind her eyes, and if she started crying now, she would never be able to stop. 'The very best.'

'We've come through,' said Lucy.

'It's snowing here. And there's an owl. Lucy, I'm scared.'

Without knowing that she was going to, she lay down in the snow and gazed up at the flakes that spun towards her. It made her feel giddy, as if it was she who was floating upwards, leaving the earth behind. She stood up again and collected a handful of snow, squeezed it into an icy ball and dropped it. Then, holding out her palm, she let a single flake fall onto it and melt.

Chapter Eighteen

Ralph simply disappeared. One moment he had been there, oppressively so, knocking on the door, running up the stairs to find her and share his enthusiasms, his face eager and besotted. The next he was gone. At first Marnie assumed he was in a miserable rage and keeping his distance. But that evening, when she plucked up courage to phone his house, his father said, with belligerent drunkenness, that he wasn't in; the next morning she waited outside his school to catch him as he went in but he never arrived.

For the first time since David had died, she made her way to the Tinsleys' house and knocked on the door. It had taken her three attempts: for several minutes she had lurked on the road, trying to summon the courage that seemed to have drained away from her, leaving her knees shaking and her heart hammering with dread. She waited for the door to be opened, and was partly relieved when it looked as though no one was in. Then she heard shuffling footsteps and stood up straighter, arranging her mouth into a cautious smile.

The door opened a few inches and a small, pinched face was pushed into the gap. Hair dyed to almost the same colour as the skin; faded blue eyes; pouchy cheeks; heavy vertical lines along the upper lip; deep brackets around the mouth. She smelt of cigarettes and Marnie saw that her teeth were stained. She looked decades older than her age. Beyond, the hall was piled with rubbish bags and junk. For a moment, she considered running away – simply belting down the path and leaving this house that stank of misery and neglect and that Ralph had returned to night after night, never really telling her what it was like.

'Yes?'

'Mrs Tinsley. It's Marnie Still.'

'I know exactly who you are.' She did not open the door any wider.

'I've come because I'm worried about Ralph.'

'You are, are you?' The words were like a sneer.

'Have you seen him recently?'

'You're the one who sees him, not me.'

'Was he here yesterday night?'

'It wasn't enough for you, pushing my eldest boy to his death, but you have to take my only remaining son away from me.'

'I haven't,' said Marnie, helplessly.

Suddenly Mrs Tinsley pushed the door wide open. She stood there, hands on her hips, and looked at Marnie appraisingly, then curled her lip. 'I can't see it myself,' she said. 'Can't see what's so good about you. Never could.'

Marnie flushed but held her ground. 'I just want to make sure he's all right. He was upset yesterday. I was worried about him.'

'Upset?' She gave a brittle laugh that cracked in the middle into a rasping cough, painful even to hear. '*Upset* is the way Ralph's made. It's his middle name, didn't you know? What have you done to him?'

'Nothing.'

'I'll know who to thank if he's come to any harm.'

Angry retorts crowded into Marnie's mind. He's already come to harm, she wanted to say, and you haven't lifted a finger to protect him. You've stood by while his father beat him. You've withheld your affection, your approval, your most basic duty of care. You've made him feel low, worthless, loveless, cursed. You've blamed him for his brother's death. You made him believe that he was the one who should have died.

But she remained silent. Mrs Tinsley reeked of unhappiness: a stale, flat, rancid hopelessness. Her bitterness against Marnie seemed the only spirited thing left to her.

'Have you seen him?' she asked meekly.

'Since yesterday? No.'

'That's all I wanted to ask. Thank you.'

She turned to go but Mrs Tinsley called after her, 'If you see him, tell him to come home.'

Emma listened and did not interrupt. Marnie talked without meeting her gaze: she stood at the window, looking out at the grey sea. It was a blustery day and the waves bucked, kicking up spray.

'So you're worried he might do something stupid?' Emma asked, when she finished. It was typical of her, thought Marnie, gratefully, that she didn't make any comment on the rest of the story, but immediately focused on Ralph's plight. Everything else would come later.

'He's probably fine, I know that, and I don't want to make everything worse by turning it into a drama,' said

Marnie. 'But you know what he's like. He was –' She searched for the word, remembering his face as she had last seen it, working with furious distress. 'I don't know,' she finished lamely. 'It was awful.'

'Hmm. And is Oliver looking for him as well?'

'I don't know.' She didn't want to think about Oliver: she felt as though a door had closed on them. 'Where could Ralph be? If he wasn't at school, wasn't at home, isn't at Ollie's, hasn't come here, where else would he go?'

'Have you tried Lucy?'

'Lucy? No, but I don't think he'd go there.'

'Probably not – but he might turn to her, if he felt let down by you two. She's very fond of him, isn't she?'

'Yes,' said Marnie, miserably. One corner of her mind was noting how much her mother knew about things she had thought secret. 'She is.'

'Call her, and then I'll phone the police.'

'The police!'

'Marnie, I'm quite sure they'll say that he's seventeen and is overwhelmingly likely to be fine but that they'll keep an eye open for him.'

'Do you think he's overwhelmingly likely to be fine?'

'Yes,' said Emma, firmly. 'I do.'

'You don't think he'd –' She couldn't finish the sentence.

'No.'

Later, after Emma had spoken to the police, the two of them went out in her car. Marnie sat hunched forward, gazing anxiously out of the front window as they drove through country lanes and round back-streets. Every so often they would see a figure who might perhaps have been Ralph – although they always knew it wasn't. They didn't talk, except to make suggestions about where to try next.

'This is hopeless,' said Marnie, at last. 'He could be anywhere.'

'You're right. Shall we head home?'

'It's getting dark, and it's so windy and wet.'

'Don't torment yourself – it doesn't help anyone.'

'We can't just give up. Can we go and look on the beach?'

Emma hesitated, then said, 'If you want. Let's go home first. We can collect a torch and walk down from the house. As long as you understand that he very probably won't be there.'

'What if we can't find him? What will we do then?'

'We'll wait for him to find us, all right?'

'Yes. You're being very nice to me.'

'How did you expect me to behave?'

'All of this is my fault. Ollie's right. It's because of me.'

'Marnie,' said Emma, glancing at her, 'once we know that Ralph is safe, we can talk about what happened. I'll say this, though. The fact he's disappeared doesn't mean that what you did was any better or worse than it would have been if he had behaved more calmly. You mustn't judge yourself by the way he reacted.'

'Thank you,' said Marnie, numbly.

The torch's battery was running low so it cast only a dim light, wavering on the path in front of them. The rain was heavy now, slanting in the gusts of winds, stinging their cheeks. The long grass whipped against their legs and the ground squelched beneath their feet. Marnie felt her shoes fill with water. The sky was covered with cloud, so there was no moon.

'Shall we go this way?' she said, when they reached the sea. 'That's where Ralph and I usually go when we come down here.'

'Towards the wrecked boat?'

'Yes.'

Their shoes crunched over wet shingle; a stone's throw away, waves crested and broke onto the shore, foam shining in the half-light. Emma swung the beam of the torch in faint arcs around them. 'There's the boat,' she said, as they approached it, 'but I don't think he's here.'

'No.' Marnie stood beside the hulk and stared across the lumpy waters. 'Ralph!' she called. Her voice disappeared into the wind and breaking waves. 'Ralph!' she tried again, shrill and high with panic. 'It's me, Ralph! Where are you? Ralph?'

'Ssh.' Emma took her hand. 'He's not here, which you knew he wouldn't be anyway, but that doesn't mean he's not all right. He's probably somewhere safe and warm, with no idea that you're out here in the darkness searching for him.'

'Yeah.' Her voice trembled. 'I guess.'

'Stop tormenting yourself.' She squeezed Marnie's fingers. 'It will be all right. Everything seems worse at night.'

'Will he be back by morning?'

'I can't say that.'

'You promise he's all right, though?'

'I'm not going to promise anything – but he will be all right.'

'Everything's such a mess. Why can't things be simple for once?'

'Oh,' said Emma, wryly. 'Well, that's life, you know.'

'Is it like this for everyone?'

'I don't know. Everyone's different.'

'What about you?'

'Me?' Emma looked out over the sea. 'I don't know, Marnie. It's complicated.' She paused. 'I used to come here a lot with your father, you know.'

'Did you?'

'Mmm. The boat wasn't so rotted away then, of course. We'd often walk here before supper. He used to skim stones. In the summer, we'd sometimes strip off and swim from this point – does it still shelve more deeply here than further along?'

'Yes,' said Marnie.

'He was a good swimmer. Much better than me. I never thought he could drown. It was right here –' she patted the slimy, decaying wood '– that I told him I was pregnant with Seth.' She gave a soft sigh. 'He was a very emotional man, your father.'

'I don't remember him.'

'When you were born, he cried.'

'Did he? Because he was happy?'

'He always wanted a daughter. He used to call you "*Carissima*". Dearest. He would get up at night and sit by your cot, making sure you were all right.'

'You've never said any of this before. You never speak about him.'

'There are some things I find hard to talk about. I should have done. Instead, I've shut them away and the longer I didn't speak, the more impossible words became. He was very proud of you.'

'Really?'

'And he would have been very proud of who you've become.'

Marnie stood for a while, listening to the slap of the curling waves on the shingle. Her chest ached. 'Sometimes,' she said at last, 'I feel you love them more than me.'

'I know you do.'

'And that nothing I can do will ever match up to them.'

'I've tried to behave towards you as I would have done if they hadn't died. I didn't want our relationship to be always intense and tragic. I was wary of oppressing you, or being too soft on you. I wanted you to have a normal childhood.'

'I have.' Marnie gave a little shiver. 'Is it over, then?'

'What? Your childhood?'

'It is, isn't it?'

'Wait until you leave home, then say that.'

'What will you do?'

'When you leave, you mean? Oh – there's lots of things. Make more pots, for a start.'

'What's happening with Eric?'

Emma didn't reply at once. She pulled her coat more tightly round herself and stared out at the dark sea. Then she said, avoiding the subject, 'Speaking of Eric, I should call him about Ralph. Come on, let's go home before I freeze to death.'

'Mum.'

'Yes?'

But Marnie didn't know what she wanted to say. Her eyes filled with tears and she blinked them away in the darkness. Emma linked arms with her and they walked slowly home.

Marnie thought she would never go to sleep, not with Ralph still missing and perhaps out in the cold, wet darkness. Emma made her a boiled egg with toast and butter, then a mug of hot chocolate, which she drank in front of the fire. She could hear her mother talking on the phone, a low murmur whose words she could not make out. In bed, she lay with her eyes open, listening to the rain against the window, the wind in the trees, the sea's incessant murmur in the distance. She thought of their small house, illuminated in a world of black sky and dark water, and wrapped her arms round herself for comfort. Ordinarily she loved the sense of their snug isolation, but tonight it scared her.

She woke when Emma put a hand on her shoulder and shook her gently.

'What? Is it morning?' But her windows were still dark.

'No. It's just before four. But I thought you'd want to know.'

'Ralph?'

'Eric's found him.'

'Eric! Where?'

'At his summer house.'

'What on earth was he doing there?'

'I don't know. Eric's bringing him back tomorrow.'

'So he's all right?'

'Cold, wet, shame-faced. But fine.'

'I'll kill him,' said Marnie, as relief swept over her. 'I'll wring his stupid neck for making us so worried.'

'Go back to sleep now.'

'Plus,' Marnie said, and she snuggled back down in her bed.

'Yes?'

'Plus he's gone and ruined things.'

'Think about it in the morning, not now.'

'We ought to ring Ralph's mother.'

'I already have.'

'What did she say?'

'Not much. She cried.'

Ralph came back the day that Oliver went away. Marnie didn't see either of them. Instead she went for a long walk with Lucy along the coastal path, while Oliver's parents drove him with his belongings – including a battered life-sized skeleton – to start his new life at university, and Emma spent the day with Ralph and Eric. Marnie never discovered what had gone on between them, but she imagined her mother had been stern, calm, practical.

When she eventually did meet Ralph, several days later, he was subdued and at first could barely meet her eye. He apologized, rather formally, for causing her concern and for reacting so melodramatically; he said he had been selfish and childish, and of course he understood that she wanted to keep certain parts of her life private. He had no wish to harm her relationship with Oliver. He spoke as if he'd learnt the words by heart. With equal formality, she had accepted his apology and said that she, too, was very sorry: she had never meant to deceive or hurt him. They had hugged, but lightly and carefully, and kissed each other's cheek.

Marnie wanted to rail at Ralph and weep, hurl objects and insults at him, tell him that of course he had bloody harmed her relationship with Oliver – what did he think? Instead, they were kind and well behaved. She felt that something was coming to an end. Suddenly her world, bounded by the sea on one side and the town on the other, was crumbling, its borders dissolving.

Or, as Lucy said rather drily on their walk along the coast, 'The fellowship is being broken up, isn't it?'

'No!' said Marnie.

'If it ever was a fellowship.'

'What do you mean?'

'They're both in love with you. It's always been like that. Do you think I'm blind? And then there's me, on the edge, being the plain best friend.'

'That's not right.'

'Isn't it?' Lucy stopped for a moment and gave her an odd, glinting look.

'You're not plain, for a start.'

'Now you're just patronizing me.'

'I'm not!'

'Marnie,' said Lucy, patiently, as if she was talking to a small child. 'In this context I'm plain – or, at least, invisible.'

'That isn't how I see things at all.'

'No? I wouldn't mind, except –' She stopped. The

273

wind ruffled her short hair and blew the sea into corrugated shapes.

'Go on.'

'Well, you know anyway. It's really odd, isn't it, how some things are never said out loud, even though everyone knows, and everyone knows the others know too? Ralph is besotted with you, Oliver's always had a thing about you –'

'I don't think that's quite right,' Marnie broke in. 'And, anyway, he's gone away now. That's all over.'

Lucy ignored her and continued, 'And you like Oliver and I've always had a thing about Ralph. Which isn't a good idea. It's like *A Midsummer Night's Dream*, isn't it? Except there's no dark wood and no magic potion, and Ralph's not going to wake up suddenly and realize he's mad with love for me instead of you. Well, is he?'

'I don't know,' Marnie muttered.

'The thing is, if you weren't there, then maybe he'd like me – sometimes I think so, anyway. We get on really well – we've probably got more in common than you two. I keep thinking that if he'd just *look* . . . But with you around, he can't see anyone else. We're all in the shadows. So, of course, I should be glad about you and Ollie, because theoretically it gives me more of a chance. Except it doesn't seem to work like that. I sometimes think it's like a weird formula – the more one of them loves you, the more the other does. You don't even have to do anything, whereas I – I work so hard and it's all for nothing.'

'I'm sorry,' Marnie said hopelessly.

'I've been really jealous of you, you know. I mean, *really* jealous. It's not a nice feeling – it's like being poisoned.'

'You should have said.'

'I'm saying now, aren't I?'

'We're going to be all right, though, aren't we?' Marnie asked, in a small voice.

Lucy stopped again, glared at her distressed face, then tucked an arm through Marnie's. 'Yeah, we'll be all right,' she said gruffly. 'Now, let's go home.'

The word brought tears stinging to Marnie's eyes, and she wiped them away with the back of her hands and sniffed loudly. 'OK. Home.'

Home. What do you think of now when you say the word? Do you think of the place you live now, alone? Or do you think of your old house by the sea, and Emma still there? Perhaps you go even further back and think of the time when it was the four of you together, the time you can't even remember but you know is there, under everything, an image of happiness and loss? Do you still get homesick, the way you used to?

Homesick. Sick for home. It's one of the most desolating feelings that I know, the hungry ache in the pit of your stomach, that acute missing. It's not like missing a lover whom you know you will see again soon so that absence becomes painfully sweet, anticipating the reunion. It's just grim, heavy, cold. It hurts. Thoughts hurt. Knives in the chest, in the head. You can move around in the world, and talk and smile and make all the right gestures, and it's a bright charade. Sometimes I couldn't do it any more. I remember once walking away from your house and just stopping. It was too much effort to keep going, putting one foot in front of the other, forcing my eyes open, swallowing, breathing. I couldn't. I simply couldn't endure it. I lay down in a field and curled up like a foetus, arms round my knees, head tucked in, eyes squeezed shut. I don't know how long I stayed like that. There were blades of grass against my face, and soil and bits of leaf and twig. I could hear myself breathing, and I could hear birdsong, wind and, in the distance, the hum of traffic. I thought that I could feel the earth moving.

How odd it is, this business of being alive. Things matter so much. Emma used to tell me to stop caring so deeply about the smallest upset – but how can you persuade yourself not to care? Sometimes I think what a relief it will be to die, to be done with it.

When I think of home, I think of your house, with you and Emma in the kitchen and the smell of bread baking; Lucy is sometimes there too. Or Eric's house in Scotland, that summer before it all went wrong. Or here, which became my refuge.

Is it still snowing outside? There was a poem I used to read to you – what was it? Something about flowers blooming behind the window-pane. I can't remember any longer. I imagine the snow falling, covering the world with its white, blank beauty, erasing everything. My thoughts are spreading, fading, disappearing. Images move through my mind and one by one I watch them pass. Faces that will not come again.

You touch my hand, my head. Maybe this is home. This moment, now.

Chapter Nineteen

Marnie stood up and went over to the window. She opened the curtains and moonlight streamed in, flowing like a silver river across the floorboards. For a moment the two sleeping men were illuminated by it, while the rest of the room lay in shadow. They looked like figures in an old painting and Marnie stood quite still, watching them both. They didn't stir. Embers glowed and faded in the hearth.

Outside, the snow had stopped, and stars pricked the clear sky. Tiny icicles hung from the guttering and the branches of the trees. So still, so flawless, serene and inhuman. The owl shrieked, close to the house, and then again. Marnie imagined the sound it made echoing through the forests and over the icy loch. Perhaps Dot, in her house on the other side of the hill, could hear it too. She pressed her face to the cold pane and tried to make out its shape in the trees. Perhaps it was calling desperately for a mate; she hoped it would find one soon to put it out of its demented loneliness.

After Oliver, there had been Leo. She was never in love with him, never felt that rush of agonizing yearning, but she wanted to erase the memory of Oliver's tender face, of Ralph's wretched, needy expression when he looked at her. Cold turkey, she told herself. Pretend you're OK, pretend you don't miss Ollie and want him, pretend it didn't really matter. After a bit, it won't be pretending any more. Leo, she realized later – and maybe even knew at the time – was everything the two of them weren't. Tall, bendy, almost like a rubber band, with long dirty-blond hair tied back in a ponytail and a cigarette in the corner of his mouth. He wore a moth-eaten army coat that swamped him, and a long scarf trailed round his thin neck. He was lethargic, indolent, pessimistic, sardonic, moved slowly and dragged his feet along the ground. He smoked without using his hands, puffing billows away from his face, and drew patterns on the backs of his hands and up his arms with indelible marker. The world and everyone in it, including himself, seemed a source of gloomy amusement to him. If Marnie was using him to get over her confusion and grief, she was sure he wouldn't get too worked up about it. Anyway, he didn't last long. They drifted apart just after Christmas, without regret or rancour, and Marnie never saw him again, although even now when she saw youths who drifted along pavements with their heads bowed and tatty clothes, she was reminded of him and of her strange last year at home.

Next came Bill, who wore round glasses and cropped his hair short above his pale, creased brow. He was insistently intellectual, hungry with the need to impress. Marnie fell first for the way he talked, in eloquent para-graphs that sounded profound – until she discovered he was quoting Beckett or Baudelaire to her. Then she fell for his insecurity, the anxiety that lurked under his surface. But it wasn't enough.

For the first year at art school, when she wore black jeans, jerseys, and was thin for the first time in her life, there was Magnus. He was an Icelander who worked in a bar near her halls and was studying film. He was dark-haired, solid, bearded, unfailingly courteous, slightly mysterious, unreachable. He bought her flowers every Friday, and took her to jazz concerts in dark cellars, where his friends kissed her hand in greeting. In the spring, she went with him to Reykjavik to meet his family and to see the sulphurous plains, the bubbling springs, the black sand and thick light breaking over the vast, whale-inhabited sea. It was as though she had stepped off the edge of the world and she felt such a rush of homesickness for Emma and her little house, where there would be a candle in the window if she was expected, that she could barely move for the pain of it. Later, she tried to put down what she had seen and felt on canvas, the dark surge of yearning amid the spooky lunar landscape, but could never quite capture it. She was working in oils now. Her hands smelt of turpentine; her clothes were daubed with paint. There were flecks in her hair.

She sat in her grotty little room, with Magnus's yellow roses on the broken-legged chest of drawers, and wrote to Ralph, knowing that the pages were probably thick with misspellings, grammatical failings and random punctuation.

Don't you think that very often our words aren't heard? They bounce off the surface, don't take root. I remember sometimes, with you or Ollie or Lucy, I would summon up the courage to utter something, and when at last I said it, it seemed tame, unremarkable, as if its meaning had been lost somehow. I'm sure everyone feels like that, not just me. It's as if you have to write

something down or turn it into a picture or something, in order to
describe it properly. We've never really talked about what
happened and that was partly because I simply didn't know the
right words for what I was feeling and I probably still don't. And
partly because I was scared – I don't know why really. I don't
want to lose things. I don't know if I'm angry or guilty or sad, or
all three. I don't know what I felt about Ollie. Or you. There are
all these rolling emotions inside me and there aren't words for
them – or at least, I don't know the words. Perhaps you do.
You're better at these things than I am. You're better at almost
everything except drawing pictures, tidying rooms, having
confidence in yourself. I guess what I want to say is that
I love you and I miss you. I miss you and I miss how everything
was and in spite of everything, if you ever need me or are ever in
trouble or distress, you have to tell me. Because I'll always,
always be your friend and even if years go by and we don't meet,
I'll still be here.

She didn't send the letter, of course. She sent a postcard instead, with a Rembrandt self-portrait on one side, and on the other her scrawl saying simply: 'Am really having a good time and learning a lot. Hope that you are too and that we meet in the summer. Thinking of you and sending my love, M xxxxx'.

She wrote to Oliver as well. She had been to a party: her feet were sore and her head throbbed with tiredness, but she knew she wouldn't sleep. There was a buzz of sadness and unsatisfied excitement inside her. She sat in her flannel pyjama trousers and a thick hoodie, her back against her bed, her pad of paper on her knees, her feet on a hot-water bottle.

Dearest Ollie, It's that strange time of night, when it's nearly dawn but it's still quite dark. The curtains of my room (it's horrible, a box with just enough space to cram in a bed and a chest and a desk and me) are open and I can see a few pale stars above the rooftops. I've been thinking about you – I've always been thinking about you ever since we met and you stood in the doorway with Ralph and I thought you were the loveliest person I'd ever set eyes on – and wondering if you've been thinking about me and if we can meet again, try again. Can we try again, or is it too late? I don't know why it all went so wrong.

I shouldn't be writing this, I know that, but I can't stop myself, maybe because it's so late and so quiet and my head and my heart and my body and my bones and my blood are full of longing to be with you again and have you hold me the way you did and I was so happy, for a few days I was so happy. It's been such a long time since we met. You've probably got a girlfriend. I've got a boyfriend. His name is Magnus and he's much nicer than I deserve and he treats me well and I like him a lot (and so does my mother!). But it's not the same. Everything was unfinished between us and I feel I can't bear it. Though of course I can bear it. I just want to know if you feel the same, ever. It's horrible, not knowing anything and having to make everything up in my head, in the silence. Maybe you never even think about me. Maybe I was just a little blip, a few days between two stages of your life. Maybe you barely remember what I look like any more and I'm fading away with every week that passes – I had a boyfriend after you left, and when I try and remember his face, I can't properly. Perhaps that's what it is like for you. I used to think that love – real love – had to be reciprocated, but I don't believe that any more. The world is much more complicated than that. And I used to think that you reap what you sow, but now

I don't believe that either. Sometimes it's just stony ground; sometimes it's not fair.

The words were untidily large and covered several sides of paper. Marnie took a sip of water from the glass on the floor in front of her and wrote on:

The thing is, my dearest darling beautiful Ollie, I know I will never send this letter to you, so I can say anything I want. The truth, for instance. The truth is that I am still in love with you and I don't know what to do about it. I thought that without you around, the feeling would gradually disappear and in a way it has. It doesn't hurt so badly, not usually, not the way it used to when I would feel sick and ill with missing you. Only sometimes, like tonight when I've drunk red wine and danced and now it's too late to do anything except sit in my room and feel self-indulgent and weepy, remembering how it used to be, just for a few days. Such a tiny scrap of time. Why am I feeling like this tonight, when I've been dancing and laughing?

I don't know why we never saw each other again. Pride? Can pride be stronger even than love and hope? I guess so. I kept thinking I would go round to yours. Or that I would get on a train and track you down at university (except I kept thinking you'd be there with some woman and I'd stumble in on you and you'd be embarrassed and I'd be horribly humiliated and ashamed, a bigger version of the way I felt when I came to your room that time – do you remember? – or a version of Ralph finding us). In the end I didn't even write. Actually, there was one time when I went to your house, but there was no one there. All the windows were dark. Anyway, I kept telling myself that you should come to me, because it was you who left me. And you

*never did. Do you know that feeling when you wait for the phone
to ring, or the letter to drop through the letterbox, or someone to
knock at the door? A dry feeling in your mouth all the time, a
racing pulse. You go round pretending to be you, smiling and
laughing and saying the right things at the appropriate time,
and always you're waiting. I'm waiting.*

*And if we did meet, maybe we wouldn't even like each other
any more. Maybe there'd be nothing and we would be polite
strangers who'd known each other in a different life. But that
would be all right. Actually, it would be a great relief because at
least I would know. I could put it all behind me and get on with
life, wholehearted again.*

*I'm trying to say I'm sorry about everything. And can we
meet? I think of you all the time.*

Marnie stared at the letter. It looked as though a giant
spider had been dipped in ink, then scuttled across the
pages. She read what she'd written and grimaced. She
didn't even know if the words were true or not – or, at
least, if they were true beyond this moment, the small
hours, when even London seemed asleep, all the roar of
life stilled and only her awake, with the pool of light from
the bedside lamp making the darkness seem darker. She
tore the pages in half, then half again, and screwed each
piece of paper into a tight ball before chucking them into
her wastebin.

She took one of the postcards from her collection in
the desk drawers (Fra Angelico's *Annunciation*, which she
had seen when she and Emma had been to Florence just
before she'd left; they had spent hours in the monks' cells
where he'd made his restfully beautiful frescos and this

one was her favourite; even looking at it touched and calmed her) and wrote, as neatly as she could, 'Dear Ollie, I thought I would get in touch again, just to say I hope you are well and happy. I'm at art school in London now. Maybe one day we can meet? Love Marnie (Still).' She examined what she had written with distaste and tossed the card into the bin, where it lay, picture upwards.

She wrote to Lucy on the back of a Picasso line drawing.

Dearest Lucy, I'm having a wonderful time and there's nowhere else I'd rather be, and yet I'm always wishing you were here too. I keep thinking of things I want to tell you or show you. It takes ages to make new friends, doesn't it – especially when the old ones are so close and so dear and know what you mean before you know it yourself? I hope you're happy. Come and see me if you have time, Marniexxxx

That one she might send. It said little enough.

She climbed into bed and lay with her eyes open, staring into the darkness. Doesn't everyone want someone to whom they can tell all the intimate secrets of their heart? That's when you're finally home.

'I'm very sorry,' she said to Magnus.

'I thought we were good together.'

'We were.'

'What changed? What went wrong?'

'Nothing!'

284

'Then I don't understand.' His handsome, open face creased in bewilderment.

'It's me,' she said hopelessly. 'I just – I can't do it.'

She went home for the weekend, taking a bin-bag of laundry. It was as if she had never been away. Her bed was neatly made up, one corner turned down ready for her to climb into it. The book she had been reading when she went away was still there, waiting for her on the bedside table. Her old sketchbook still lay on her desk, with the soft pencil beside it; when she opened it, she saw that she had been halfway through a drawing of her mother. They ate cauliflower cheese and, after supper, sat in front of the fire while Emma read and Marnie mended the ripped knee of her jeans and sewed up the hem of her favourite skirt. Then they played patience together, while outside Marnie heard the waves breaking on the shingle.

'I finished it with Magnus,' she said, gathering up the deck of cards and shuffling them. Emma looked up, not speaking, attentive. So Marnie continued, 'Because he liked me more than I liked him.'

'Was he all right?'

'I think so.'

'Nostalgia's a dangerous thing, you know.'

Marnie sighed. 'You shouldn't do that. It feels like I've got nowhere to hide.'

'Why do you want to hide?'

'Everyone needs to hide sometimes – especially from their mother.'

'I finished things with Eric as well,' Emma said softly.

'No! But why? You were so happy.'

'Because – because I liked him more than he liked me.'

'Oh.'

'He's gone back to his wife.'

'Oh, Mum.'

'It's all right.'

'So here we are.'

'Indeed. Here we are, the two of us.'

Now Marnie looked across at Oliver, still sleeping in the moonlit room, his head tilted back, his mouth slightly open, his eyes flickering under their lids. He had no idea, she thought, of the havoc he had visited on her life all those years ago.

Suddenly his eyes half opened. Marnie couldn't tell if he was looking at her or not.

'Marnie?'

'Yes. It's me. Are you awake?'

'I don't know.' He blinked at her in bewilderment. 'I had this dream.'

'What about?'

'I don't know. I can't remember.'

'Was it a good dream?'

'Maybe. Maybe it was good. I feel . . .' he rubbed the side of his face '. . . strange.'

'Do you want anything? Tea or hot chocolate or whisky?'

'Let me get it. You're always looking after other people.'

'Hardly!'

'You are, though. It's what you've always done.'

'I don't know that I like the sound of that – someone who rushes around being helpful.'

'Being attentive. Caring. You would have made a wonderful mother, you know.'

Marnie went to sit on the floor beside Ralph and put her hand on his clammy forehead. She picked up one hand and held it very carefully between both of hers, rubbing her thumbs over his knuckles. 'It was all I ever really wanted,' was what she didn't say, because it hurt too much. 'To have children. Sons and daughters, grand-children for Emma, running around on the lawn outside our old house. I used to imagine it in such detail it almost seemed true to me. Leaning over their cots at night, holding their little bodies on my lap, that sweet, sawdusty baby smell, milk blisters on their lip. Picking them up when they fell over. Knitting them odd little outfits. Cooking meals for all of us to eat together. Teaching them the things Emma taught me. Passing things on. Loving them and being loved by them, the way you'll never love anybody else and no one else will ever love you. Even now I can't believe it won't happen, although of course I know it won't.'

What she said instead was: 'Life doesn't turn out the way you expect. But I was lucky. I had Eva and Luisa. And I've been like an honorary aunt to Lucy's kids.'

Oliver got up and went to the cooker. He poured milk into a pan and put it on the hob to heat.

She said to his turned back, 'Why did you never try to get in touch with me?'

'Oh.' His breath came out in a sigh, but he didn't turn. 'I don't know, Marnie.'

'You don't know? Is that all?'

'I could say it was because I was too proud, and that would be true. Or hurt: true. Or furious. Or let down. Or ashamed. Or because of Ralph. Or because I thought you didn't care enough. Or because I made myself forget about you. Fell in love with other girls and left you behind, just like I assumed you'd left me behind. All true. I don't know which is truest. I used to think about seeing you again.'

'Did you?'

'I used to imagine it, and sometimes you'd run towards me and we'd fall into each other's arms. Other times you'd barely recognize me and it would simply be humiliating. Ridiculous. This boy you never thought about any more, harbouring fantasies about you.'

'I wrote you letters.'

He turned to face her. 'I never got any from you.'

'No – I wrote them to you and then I threw them away.'

'You should have sent them.'

'I don't think so. They were more like letters to myself. Maudlin meanderings.'

'I wish you'd sent them all the same.'

'Well, it was a long time ago.'

'You mean, when we were young and foolish?'

'No. We were young, but we weren't foolish enough. If we'd been foolish we wouldn't have stood on our dignity and pride. I would have sent the letters, telling you I wanted you back. You would have tracked me down and thrown stones at my window to call me out.'

'I guess it takes courage to be foolish.'

And they both looked towards Ralph, whose face glimmered bone-white in the moonlight.

How long had it been since he'd spoken? They were running out of time, and as sand seems to pour through the hour-glass more and more quickly as it reaches the end, so it felt to Marnie that Ralph's life was slipping past at gathering speed and only the last glistening traces of it remained.

Chapter Twenty

Running out of time, and time running out. Just a few grains left in the neck of the glass and the past lying in a domed heap beneath, all accounted for and done. So skip the next three years, and go to when Marnie was working in a theatre in the suburbs, painting sets and finding props for under-rehearsed productions of *Oh! What a Lovely War* and *Anything Goes*.

She had recently returned from Normandy, where she had gone to be with a man, briefly her teacher and many years older than her, who was renovating a collapsing farmhouse there and trying to escape his sense of self-disappointment – 'Your father substitute,' Lucy had commented waspishly when she had first met Gilbert. Marnie had stayed long after she knew the relationship was over, because she had gone out in the first place in the teeth of her mother's silent anxiety and Lucy's articulate disapproval, and it hurt her pride to come crawling back.

In fact, it was Ralph who had finally rescued her. Perhaps he had read between the lines of her jaunty postcard, or perhaps he had talked to Emma. Whatever the case, he turned up one wet and windy morning in April, with no luggage, just a passport in his back pocket and a tatty copy of *Paradise Lost* in a plastic bag. Marnie was on her hands and knees in the kitchen, laying tiles. She was tired and filthy: her clothes were caked with dirt, her ripped fingernails were black, her head itched with grit. The only operating shower was a nozzle on the wall of the downstairs bathroom that gave out a thin dribble of tepid water, and there was a faint smell of sewage that made her feel doubly unclean.

Rubble lay everywhere, and dust rose in clouds: Gilbert had started work on the principle that if you demolished everything to begin with, you would be forced to reconstruct it. He had wielded a pickaxe like a madman when they first arrived, knocking down walls and levering up stone floors, and then he and Marnie had had to live in the building site he had created. Wires poked through skirting-boards, wallpaper hung in shreds, and there were holes in the ceiling through which you could see the roof beams. To make matters worse, it had been raining for what seemed like weeks. Marnie had dreamt of blue skies and apple blossom, picnics of bread and Camembert on the lawn, the sun shining down on their labours, the lovely old house emerging from its years of neglect. Instead, the garden was a bog and water dripped or streamed into almost every room. French plumbers and electricians swarmed everywhere, but progress was slow.

Gilbert started drinking earlier every day, until he was opening the first bottle at midday. He worked erratically, and the more Marnie laboured, the more resentful and critical of her he became. Marnie began to see his sadness as self-pity, his dreams as self-deluding bluster. She realized she couldn't save him and that, after the first flush of love had died down, she didn't really like him very much. Yet she didn't leave: she felt she had made a promise to herself and to him and she didn't feel able to break it.

And then Ralph turned up, sodden, filthy, starving and full of a bright, glad energy that immediately changed the atmosphere of the house.

'You!' she said, scrambling to her feet, shading her eyes with her hand, as if he might turn out to be a trick of the light.

'Me! You look a wreck.'

'Thanks. You don't look so great yourself.' He did, though – he looked fabulous.

They'd laughed into each other's faces. Happiness bubbled through her and she opened her arms to him.

'Even your scalp's got dirt in it,' he said, as he pressed his lips to the crown of her head.

'Why are you here?'

'To see you.'

'Yes, but –'

'I was sitting in the library, waiting for a book I'd ordered to arrive from the stacks, and I suddenly thought, I have to go and see Marnie *now*.'

'Just like that?'

'More or less. So I got on a ferry to Calais.'

'Why do you look as though you've been sleeping in hedges?'

'I have. I walked from Calais.'

'You walked?'

'It was part of the deal.'

'What do you mean, "part of the deal"? What deal?'

'I said that if I walked all the way, everything would be all right.'

'Said to who?'

'To myself,' he replied patiently.

Marnie gave a little giggle. Tears were brimming in her eyes. 'You're mad.'

'D'you think?'

'Either you're mad or everyone else is.'

'That'd be it. Don't cry, Marnie, or I'll cry too.'

'Sorry.' She wiped her hand across her grubby face. 'God, I've missed you, Ralph. We haven't been like this for ages, have we?'

'No. But that's OK.'

'And you really did that for me?'

'Of course. So, is everything all right?'

'It is now you're here. It hasn't been.'

'I can see,' he said. 'You look a bit down to me.'

'Do I?'

'Does she?' said a voice behind them, and Gilbert came into the kitchen, carrying several baguettes and a plastic bag bulging with bottles. He was wearing baggy trousers and a crumpled shirt; his face was unshaven. He looks like a bulldog, thought Marnie. 'And why would that be?'

'Ralph, this is Gilbert. Gilbert, Ralph.'

'Ah – Ralph.' Her heart sank: he was already slightly pissed. 'The famous Ralph. Were we expecting you?'

In the first weeks of their affair, Marnie had talked to Gilbert about Ralph, confided in him. Now she wished she hadn't. She recognized the cruel gleam in his eye.

'Hello,' said Ralph. 'No, you weren't – I just came on a whim. And, yes, she does look a bit down. I don't know why, although I could make a guess.'

'I am in the room, you know.'

'Sorry,' said Ralph. He didn't look sorry. A smile was

293

pushing at his lips; he looked as though he was about to start giggling.

'Do you both want coffee? Then I'll show you round, Ralph.' Marnie pushed stray strands of hair back from her face. She wished she could jump into a cold, fast-running stream and wash herself fresh again.

'Or wine. When in France and all that,' said Gilbert, and without waiting for a reply, he pulled a bottle out of the carrier-bag and a corkscrew out of his back pocket.

'Not for me, thank you.'

'Only after six, is that it? Like Marnie here. You don't mind if I do? You're much younger than I thought you'd be, Ralph. Are you still a student?'

'No.'

'How long are you gracing us with your company?'

Marnie winced: Gilbert always used florid language when he was spoiling for a fight – a kind of heavy-handed, blundering sarcasm that soured his face. But Ralph didn't seem to mind. Today he was impregnable.

'That depends on Marnie,' he said, and turned towards her. 'I want to ask you something.'

'Yes?'

'Ask away,' said Gilbert. He poured himself a large glass of red wine and held it up to the light. 'We're all ears, aren't we, Marnie?' And he put an arm round her, pulling her roughly to him.

'Privately.'

'Charming.'

'Let's go next door,' said Marnie, extricating herself.

'No, no. I'll leave. I know when I'm not wanted.'

'Sorry,' said Marnie, as the door shut behind him. 'He's

not always like that. He can be –' She stopped, frowning. What could he be? Tearful, sentimental, impassioned, scared, frail, failed. That was the trouble: she could always see the unhappiness behind the bluster. It was the unhappiness that kept her here. 'What did you want to ask?'

'Do you want to come back with me?'

'Come back with you?'

'Yes.'

'You mean now?'

'Why not?'

'Because –' She stopped and looked around her. 'I don't know,' she said weakly.

'I've come to rescue you,' he said, quite seriously. His face was illuminated.

'What if I don't want to be rescued?'

'Tell me to go and I'll go.'

'He's not a bad man.'

'Just bad for you.'

'Bad for himself. Disappointed.'

'Come on, Marnie. You can only save yourself – that's what you've always said to me.'

'I did, didn't I?' She stared at him, hope running through her, like cold water over a dusty plain. 'God, Ralph – am I really going to do this?'

'I don't know. Are you?'

'Yes. Yes, I am. I should get changed.'

'Why? You're going to get dirty all over again, walking. Just put on some proper shoes, if you've got any.'

'We're going to walk?'

'I thought so, and hitch. St Malo's the nearest ferry. And it's a lovely town. We can have a meal there.'

'Oh! All right. I mean, good. Yes! I'd like that. God, this is weird, though.'

'Get your passport and warm clothes and we'll be off. George is waiting outside.'

'George! Who's George, Ralph?'

'A friend. He came with me.'

'You never mentioned him!'

'You'll like him. He's quite eccentric. Very optimistic about life.'

Marnie felt light-headed. She stared around the wreckage of the kitchen. 'I have to go and tell Gilbert.'

'Leave him a note. Paint it on the wall.'

'No, that would be very wrong.'

'Go and tell him, then. Shout if you need us. We'll be in the garden.'

'It's pouring with rain.'

'It'll be pouring with rain on the road.'

Marnie used to think – used to say, in conversation with friends – that happiness and unhappiness were not each other's opposites. Unhappiness was a condition: you almost always knew when you'd got it. But happiness was more elusive, a sensation that was fleeting and mysterious, not to be confused with pleasure or contentment. You couldn't pursue it, and you rarely knew that you were happy, only, once it was over, that you had been. You looked back and said, 'Yes, there, then, with that person, in a world now gone.'

But it wasn't like that with Ralph. Just as his unhappiness was a tangible burden, dulling his eyes and slumping his shoulders, practically crushing him, so, too, his happiness had an animal quality. You could see it in his gaze, hear it in the way he spoke, almost smell it on his skin. Sometimes Marnie thought that if she closed her eyes she would still be able to tell his mood at a distance by feeling it vibrating in the air, in the atmosphere he cast. On those two days in France, Ralph's happiness streamed off him. His feet were light, his voice strong; he sang, laughed, leapt over puddles in the road, vaulted over gates, teased George (who idolized him, stared at him when he thought no one was looking with a hopeless expression of worship), told jokes and nonsensical stories, got them thoroughly lost.

After their first embrace, he didn't touch Marnie, except to jump her down from stiles or to see her into cars that sometimes stopped for them – although only if the two men hid behind a tree and Marnie stood alone to lure them to a halt. With his companion like an absurd fellow knight beside him, he was saving her, redeeming them both from the ways of the past. The road, winding through lush fields and tiny villages, led them to a different future. When they finally arrived in Portsmouth, filthy and light-headed with the triumph of their journey, Emma, who had been alerted, was waiting. She waved to them from her rusty little car with the split plastic passenger seat. At which point Ralph and George simply left them.

'Don't look at me like that!' Marnie snapped at her mother as they drove away.

The room was very crowded; it hummed with voices, peals of laughter, a hubbub of civilized camaraderie.

Everyone looked prosperous and at home – those young men with high cheekbones and eloquent hands; those older men with intelligent dark eyes and rumpled suits; all the beautiful young women, thin as storks, with silky blonde hair or chic crops, aristocratic noses, clever dresses, modulated voices. They held glasses of pale golden wine and reached out for canapés of spiced prawns and tiny goujons of sole as they passed. She wished Lucy had come with her. Then they could have stood in a corner together, stuffing themselves with crispy delicacies and uttering spiteful, comforting remarks about everyone else in the room.

This was a new world, thought Marnie, one to which she did not belong. She was an outsider, awkward and unworldly. If she spoke her voice would betray her, for she lacked irony and sophistication and – especially after her wretched months in Normandy – confidence. If she were to put anything down on paper, for God's sake, her skewed, misspelt writing would shame her. She looked down at what she was wearing: the long velvet skirt with a ragged hem; the scuffed boots; the cotton jacket with big buttons and a cinched waist that she'd picked up in a charity shop. She had come straight from the theatre, hardly stopping to brush her hair. She wore no makeup and probably had paint on her face. Her hands were worn and calloused, with nails cut short.

She stood in the doorway, clutching her bag and think-ing that maybe she would turn and make a run for it before anyone saw her. Ralph wouldn't mind; he wouldn't even notice. She scanned the room for a sight of him. Yes, there he was. He was wearing a beautiful black jacket and jeans and talking to a young woman with apricot hair. As Marnie watched, he threw back his head in amusement and, even from this distance, she thought she could hear his laughter. So he was at home here, too, she thought. And as she looked at the familiar figure and saw him for the first time as others must see him, it came to her that he was beautiful. He wasn't the scraggy, undernourished boy she had always seen him as. For a moment, she gazed transfixed: his black hair in a nimbus round his head, his slim figure, his thin, pale face, which could look so haggard but which this evening was mobile and expressive. He made everyone else seem dull, weighed down. The feeling that had flickered, illicit, inside her since their Normandy adventure returned more strongly and she practically gasped as she recognized it – for this was *Ralph*, after all, Ralph who was like her younger brother, Ralph who was like a puppy with eager eyes, Ralph who loved her with one-way adoration. No. It wasn't possible.

She hitched her bag onto her shoulder and turned to go.

'Marnie!' From across the room he had seen her and came rushing over, nimbly side-stepping outstretched hands. 'Marnie, I didn't know if you'd come.'

'I was about to go,' she admitted. 'All these scary people.'

'Scary? Rubbish. Come and meet some of them.'

'No – listen, this is your evening. These are your guests.'

'I don't know half of them. To tell you the truth . . .' he lowered his voice and leant towards her '. . . part of me wants to run away.'

'You can't.'

'I've got to wait for my editor to make his little speech and then give a little speech in return – after that, why not?'

'Because you're why everyone's here.'

'Me and the drink and the gossip and the feeling of belonging to some circle or other . . . Ollie was going to come, you know.'

'Ollie!' She couldn't keep the alarm and the hope from her voice.

'But his father's ill, so he pulled out. He asked after you.'

'Oh.'

'I said you were just the same, but better. Look, there's George. Come and talk to him while I do my duty, but don't you dare go.'

'All right.'

'Promise?'

'Promise.'

'Have you read his book?' George asked. He was wearing a suit that was a little too tight for him and his face shone with sweat and earnestness.

'I've just started,' said Marnie. *Dreaming of Home* had been sent to her by the publisher the previous day; she had read the first few pages immediately, but had found herself so overcome with distress that she had been unable to continue, although she carried it in her bag and was conscious of it in the way that one is conscious of a love letter or a bomb.

'It's extraordinary,' said George. 'Completely extraordinary. It's going to be a sensation.'

'Is it autobiographical?' asked Marnie.

'It's more like a deeply personal meditation – and a weird philosophical ragbag, too, of course, with all the things he's ever been interested in thrown in – on the meaning of home. It reads like an intimate confessional memoir, you know, with that voice that feels as if it's talking directly to you – except Ralph doesn't talk about himself in the book. Doesn't talk about himself, but you feel he's in every line. I'm in awe of it. And deeply jealous, of course.'

'Do you want to write?'

'Me? No. But I want to *have* written and be at a party like this, with a book like that on the table and critics talking about me as the new bright hope of British literature.' He laughed. 'It's hard to be jealous of Ralph, though. He's so . . .' He paused, looking searchingly at Marnie. 'What's the word?'

'Sweet?'

'Good God, no! He's too scarily strange to be sweet. But he's adorable, isn't he? Everyone adores him.'

'Do they?'

'I do,' George said frankly. 'But I think the word I was looking for was vulnerable. He's very vulnerable.'

'Yes,' said Marnie, glancing across the room at Ralph, who was now talking to a man with a tape-recorder. 'He is. He always has been.'

'Don't hurt him,' said George.

Marnie was taken aback and didn't immediately reply. She took a glass of wine from a passing waiter and drank a deep, cool mouthful. 'I don't intend to hurt him,' she said finally. 'He's my dear friend.'

'Since getting back from Normandy,' said George, 'he's been extricating himself from a relationship.'

'I didn't know. He didn't say,' said Marnie. 'I haven't seen very much of him in the last year or so, and not at all since France. You two just disappeared.'

'Sophie. There she is.' George nodded in the direction of a tiny woman, whose dark eyes and blue-black hair gave her an Oriental appearance. She was wearing ballet pumps and a very short orange shift. She made Marnie feel large and clumsy. 'A linguist. She speaks about a hundred languages. Postgraduate at Cambridge, like Ralph.'

'Oh.' She didn't know what else to say.

'She was very upset,' said George, and Marnie felt he was accusing her of something.

At that moment someone knocked a knife against a glass, and someone else called for attention. The room fell silent and the crowd tightened in a circle around Ralph and a man with thick white hair, who introduced himself as Ralph's publisher and friend. He talked, without notes, for about ten minutes. Marnie, standing at the back, could only catch half of what he said, although she did hear the word 'brilliant'. He told an anecdote about his first meeting with Ralph, in which Ralph had apparently arrived at his office wearing odd shoes. A ripple of affection ran round the room. Marnie looked at the faces around her: it was true, they did all adore him, she thought, and a stab went through her – of what? Desire, tenderness, pride, fear.

Ralph's talk lasted a much shorter time, just a minute or so. He thanked his publisher and his agent – who was clearly the woman on his right, beaming at him as if he was her beloved son. Then he said that friends from all parts of his life were in the room and that, perhaps, was what home meant to him: where people he loved were gathered together. He raised a glass to everyone, and everyone raised a glass to him. Cheers and applause burst out and conversation built up again, until the room was once more buzzing. George introduced Marnie to a man with a thin, quiet face, who turned out to be one of Ralph's old tutors, then to a woman with flaming red hair and a chipped front tooth, who told a long, breathless story about how she had arrived late because a man with only one leg had fallen down the Underground escalator, which she was travelling up, and she'd taken him to have a drink but it turned out that he . . . At this point, Marnie lost track of the story.

An older woman with hair the colour of cigarette ash and an attractively low voice arrived and introduced herself as a friend of Ralph's who had always wanted to meet Marnie. She had seen one of her pictures in Ralph's room, and made Ralph tell her the story behind it. Marnie knew the canvas she meant: the charcoal drawing of the shingle beach in winter, the old hulk in the centre and just the suggestion of Lucy and Ralph's figures to one side. She remembered working on the sketch of it; she could feel the sting of wind on her cheek and her hair lashing her face. She could see Ralph and Lucy as they were then, shabby, young and overexcited, tipsy on new relationships and hope.

'Shall we go, then?' As if on cue, Ralph appeared at her side.

'Go where? And are you sure you should leave?'

'Always leave a party before it leaves you,' he said. 'Anyway, it's beginning to break up. Shall we have dinner?'

'I'd like that.'

'There's a place near here I've been to that does fish. It's very simple. Is that OK?'

'Perfect.'

'Right, let's make a break for it before anyone stops us. If someone calls my name, pretend we can't hear.'

They dashed from the room, down the broad stairs, through the double doors and out onto the street. It was early summer and the day was only just starting to fade, taking on the fugitive air that Marnie so loved; a time of vague shadows and promise. She slid an arm through Ralph's, feeling shy, solemn, nostalgic, washed over by a lovely melancholy. She stole a glance at Ralph, and found he was looking at her, so she looked away again. Was this really happening? Once, long ago, they had kissed in the churchyard; she had let him kiss her. She remembered falling back on the grass and the way he had gazed at her then. She heard his words: *Always, Marnie, don't forget, don't ever forget*. But she had gone from there to Oliver. No, she didn't want to think of Oliver. Not on this night, when a door she hadn't even known was there was opening onto a new landscape.

She ordered salmon, though she didn't think she would be able to eat it; he asked for cod and a bottle of house white. They smiled at each other across the table, picking at hunks of bread. She couldn't remember a time when just the two of them had been to a restaurant together, in all the years they had known each other. Pizzas with Lucy and Oliver; chips and sandwiches in service stations on the way to Scotland; bowls of tomato soup in the café near home; that dinner when he'd got his scholarship to Cambridge, and Emma had taken them out to celebrate and had, for the first time that Marnie could remember, let herself weep. But this kind of meal – alone, at a table in a corner, with the evening pressing up against the window: it had never happened before.

The wine, when it arrived, was dry and light: it flowed through her veins, dissolved her self-consciousness. 'I saw you differently tonight,' she said.

'How so?'

'I saw you in your own element.'

'Hardly.'

'No – you know. For them, you're the scholar, the writer, the young man of promise.'

'Whereas you see me as – what?'

'Ralph,' she said simply. But, of course, it wasn't that simple, not at all. 'What I mean is that when you know someone's past, it's hard to disentangle them from it. That's why we have to leave home, isn't it? We have to get away from our family and friends' versions of us. You especially.'

'Why me especially?' She couldn't read his expression.

'Because your past was quite . . .' she hesitated '. . . extreme. With David dying. With Grace. With your father as he was.' She waited for his expression to close, as it always had done when she mentioned his father, but his face remained open, attentive. 'So there was an extreme version of yourself that you must have had to escape.'

'You mean neurotic, needy, dependent, volatile, fragile, unstable, unsafe?'

'That kind of thing,' she acknowledged. She took another sip of wine.

'Is that how you see me?'

'No. Or, rather, yes, in a way – I see it behind the you I see now.'

'Like ectoplasm or something.'

'I guess. Like a ghost. Ralph the boy who turned up on our doorstep and Ralph the man.'

'And you see them both.'

'Inevitably.'

'But you do see Ralph the man?' he persisted.

She knew what he meant and held his gaze. 'Yes. And perhaps that's new to me.'

The fish arrived. Marnie took a few mouthfuls, between sips of wine. She saw that Ralph was hardly eating either. He gave her news of Grace and she told him about Lucy. She looked at his hands, close to hers on the table; his bony wrists. She described the theatre where she was working, the motley collection of actors, some ageing, cynical and on their way down; some young, full of dreams and high-flown ambitions. His generous, mobile mouth and flecked greenish eyes. He described the strange life of a Cambridge scholar, the way that some of the dons had never left the town since they arrived and now cycled around it in their flapping gowns, like benign creatures from an earlier age. His dark hair in an unkempt cloud around his eager face; the way he still smiled at her. She knew him so well and yet here she was, learning him for the first time.

There was a subject they needed to clear away, though, before – before whatever was to happen next.

'Do you see much of Ollie?'

'Yes. He's my best friend, after all.' He grimaced at the innocence of the phrase – best friend – and then added, 'Apart from you. And that's different.'

'What happened between the three of us . . .'

'What happened happened, and we all behaved foolishly in our different ways.'

'When you ran away . . .' she said, then asked what she had never before dared because she had dreaded the answer '. . . did you ever think, I mean, ever let yourself imagine . . .' she took a deep breath '. . . killing yourself?'

'No. Yes. I mean, no, I didn't think of it but, yes, of course I imagined it. Sometimes you just want the hurt to stop. That's all you can think of. But you have to hold on to the knowledge that this will pass, even when everything in you tells you it'll go on hurting for ever.'

Marnie heard George's voice: 'Don't hurt him.' Terror rose in her, like dark water. 'Do you still get like that?' she managed to ask.

Ralph gave her a little smile. 'People don't change, not really,' he said. 'At best, I think they learn – if they're the lucky ones, that is – to manage who they are. So, yes and no. Of course I do sometimes – that Ralph-the-boy you were talking about is still there and always will be, I guess. He won't go away. But now I know what to do.'

'What's that?'

'I know how to hold on.'

The waiter arrived, muttered at the sight of their barely

touched plates and picked them up. 'Was everything all right?' he asked them, with bitter politeness.

'Everything was lovely,' said Marnie.

'It was,' said Ralph. 'It is.'

They looked at the pudding menu and decided they only wanted coffee, which came with little almond biscuits on a side plate and the bill. The restaurant had emptied and they were alone in their corner. Outside, it was now quite dark. Ralph shivered.

'What?' asked Marnie.

'I'm happy.'

'Oh, Ralph.'

He put out a hand and covered hers. She let it rest there. They looked at each other for a long moment and Marnie could feel her heart knocking against her chest. Very slowly, she put her other hand flat against his cheek. He gave a sigh and didn't move. She leant forward across the table, sliding her hand to cup the back of his head under the soft clean curls.

'Marnie,' he said. He looked stupefied with bliss and she had a clear sense of her power over him.

'Hello,' she said softly, and kissed his mouth.

'Marnie, I want to ask you.'

'Yes?' She smiled at him and lifted his hand to her lips. She already knew what lay ahead. The walk home (where, though? He lived in Cambridge and her grotty little room was miles away), hands plaited, leaning in to one another, the night together, the way he would look at her.

'I asked you once before, long ago when I was still a kid. Will you marry me?'

Marnie felt as if someone had punched her hard in the

stomach. Ralph's shining face blurred before her eyes and she heard herself gasp in shock. 'Oh,' she whispered. For now she understood – and how could she have been so blind, so stupid and so monumentally cruel? Ever since their days in Normandy, when he had turned up like a soggy knight to rescue her, he had been planning this. That was why he had ended his relationship with the beautiful linguist; that was why he had invited her here this evening and looked so solemn and illuminated by joy. And he thought – no, she saw now with horror that he was sure – she would say yes.

'I'll never love anyone as I love you,' he said. His face was blazing with joy. 'You redeem me. You're my home.'

'But this isn't what I meant. I mean – you can't just –' She stopped. Of course he could. This was Ralph, master of the unexpected and the absurd; Ralph, the last true romantic who had made her into his muse.

'Please, Marnie, tell me you will.' Ralph's face had lost its look of suffused tenderness and had become pinched and chalky.

'I thought we would make love,' she said at last. 'And then see what happens.'

'I don't want to spend a night with you, I want to spend a life with you.'

'But, Ralph, darling Ralph.' Marnie wanted to laugh hysterically, weep, run appalled from the restaurant. She put a hand on his arm. 'We don't know each other like that yet. We haven't even kissed properly.'

'I know you.' He wrenched away his arm. 'Through and through.'

'No. No, you don't. Not like that. You know me as

your friend Marnie, the girl you met when we were barely out of childhood. This is different.'

'No. It isn't different. Everything meets. You're my friend and you're my soul-mate. And I'm begging you to marry me.'

'Can't we just . . .' The words died. She couldn't kiss him now, hold him close. The stakes were too high. He had made everything impossibly serious.

He sat up straight in the chair, formal and intensely serious, in despair. 'Marry me, and I'll devote my whole life to loving you and making you happy.'

There was a fleeting moment when Marnie thought she would say yes: because she loved him, liked him, knew him, because he loved her too – had laid his soul at her feet – because she knew that nobody would ever feel for her, as he did, such unconditional adoration. But even as she imagined it, she saw her life quite clearly: she would mother him, care for him, follow him, fight off his hungry ghosts and save him, give him the home he had longed for all his life. And she, imprisoned by his love, would simply disappear.

'If you make me say it, then . . . no, Ralph.'

There was a moment of terrible silence. His figure seemed to dwindle in front of her; his face shrank, his eyes grew darker in his face. The light had gone out. 'No,' he repeated, in a rusty croak. 'No?'

'No, Ralph. Not like this.'

'But I thought . . .' he whispered '. . . I thought . . .'

'You're in love with an idea,' she said helplessly. 'I'm flesh and blood.'

'An idea. You think you're an idea to me?' His eyes

burnt at her. 'How can you say such a thing?' He stood up. 'Is this an idea?' With one swipe of his hand he sent the coffee cups crashing to the floor, where they shattered. 'This?' The biscuits flew like tiny frisbees through the air.

'Stop, Ralph!'

'Sir? Sir?'

Their waiter was hurrying towards them across the empty room, on his face an expression of horror.

'Flesh and blood?' said Ralph. 'Like this?' And he struck himself in the chest, hard.

'Don't, Ralph. Don't do this. Do you hear?'

'I'm going to call the police,' said the waiter. 'Drunk and disorderly.'

'Why? What have I done? Broken your cups? Here's the money.' Ralph took out his wallet, snatched several ten-pound notes and threw them onto the table as another man – the chef, to judge from his apron – joined the waiter. 'And the bill – how much was the meal? Here, take this.' He thrust a wad of notes at them. 'Is that enough? You can have everything I've got. I don't need it any more.'

'Sorry,' said Marnie. 'We're going. I'm really sorry.'

She tried to take Ralph's arm but he jerked away from her as if scalded. 'If you care about me at all,' he said, 'don't try to help me.'

'Where are you going?'

He stared at her blindly. 'Going? I don't know. Does it matter?' And then, all of a sudden, the anger ran out of him and his face softened and crumpled, became harder for Marnie to bear. 'Don't worry,' he said kindly. 'I won't do anything stupid. That would be inexcusable.'

He left the restaurant and Marnie watched him walk by the window, but he didn't look at her. He passed from her view like a figure dissolving into the shadows.

She bent down and picked up shards of china from the floor. The waiter gave her a glass of water and hovered beside her, solicitous and embarrassed, while she drank it thirstily. Then she, too, left. She walked through the empty night streets and at first she thought she was going to go dismally back to her grim little room in Lewisham. But then she found she was walking instead in the direction of Liverpool Street station, past the grand City buildings where lights were still on in the empty offices.

She arrived in time for the slow train home, which stopped at every small station on the way, disgorging passengers as it went. Her carriage seemed full of half-drunk men in frayed suits, eating fried chicken out of paper bags or sleeping with their mouths open and their eyes flickering in dreams. Marnie pressed her forehead against the vibrating window and stared past her own reflection at the darkness as city gave way to country. She could make out rivers and fields under the starlit sky. A canal, a hamlet, a church with a steeple, an old warehouse with broken windows. She saw a fox on a siding: it lifted its muzzle and gave her a yellow glare, then trotted into the undergrowth.

At last she arrived at her station and climbed out. It was late and there were no taxis so she decided to walk. It was only a few miles; she'd walked it dozens of times, though never, she thought, alone in the small hours. She'd walked it with Lucy, with Ralph, with Oliver, with all of them together. She remembered a time coming back from a concert when they'd all held hands in a chain and sung as they went. She remembered a time with Oliver, so wrapped up in his embrace, his lips against her hair, that their feet tangled and they stumbled. Here was the pub she had been to with David and never again because it brought her too many feelings of unresolved guilt. Here was the little café that had bought one of her charcoals. She didn't know if it still hung on the far wall. The second-hand-clothes shop where Ralph had found most of his outlandish moth-eaten garments – that old trench coat, the white drainpipe jeans, the velvet jacket.

Now she was out of the town and on to the smaller road. Lights petered out, but tonight the moon, though only half full, was high in the sky and bright enough to cast a shadow. She walked slowly; there was no hurry, after all. Could she smell the sea yet? Hear its faint steady roar in the distance?

By the time she came to the track leading to the house, it was dawn. A rim of orange light curved along the horizon, casting a dull glow on the water. Birds were already singing. Marnie could see a wren in the hedge beside her. There was dew on the grass and her feet made tracks over the lawn. The hens clucked in the run as she passed. There was an extra car in the drive, which meant Emma had B-and-B guests, but no lights were on behind the closed curtains: everyone was still asleep.

Marnie didn't have her keys with her so she settled on the bench outside the front door and closed her eyes. The birdsong grew louder and even through the lids she could see the light strengthening as the sun rose above the horizon. She opened her eyes and watched as it climbed the sky, large and orange-red, with a wisp of cloud trailing across its centre. It was going to be another glorious day – and she remembered how she used to feel, looking out of her bedroom window at the morning sun on the water.

She felt surprisingly awake, so she stood up and walked down the garden and onto the path that led to the shore. Her feet crunched over the shingle, where a ragged hem of waves foamed. She squatted near the water's edge and searched for a stone with a hole at its centre that would bring her a wish. She found one, irregular and rusty-brown until the water licked it when it turned golden, and held it tightly in her hand. She would wish that Ralph would be all right. She would wish that this had never happened. She would wish the clock to turn back. She would wish.

From here, the house was invisible, but as she came back over the slight hill she noticed that the lights were on in the guest room and the kitchen. Drawing nearer, she saw her mother through the window: she was standing at the stove, turning rashers of bacon in the pan. Marnie could see the familiar frown, the impatient movements, and smiled to herself – Emma had guests she didn't like so she was ruining their breakfast for them.

She rapped her knuckles on the pane and Emma turned, putting her hand to her eyes against the glare of the sun. She didn't appear particularly surprised to see her, but the frown disappeared, and in its place there was a smile that was both warm and anxious. 'Marnie!' she said at the door, wiping her hands on her striped apron, then putting them on her daughter's shoulders. 'This is a lovely surprise.' And she kissed her on both cheeks. 'Is everything all right?'

'Yes,' said Marnie, although the question brought tears to her eyes. 'Except I think your bacon's burning.'

'So it is.'

'Shall I make breakfast? How many are there?'

'Three.'

'You don't like them.'

'You won't either,' said Emma, ominously. She undid her apron and passed it to Marnie. 'Go on, then. It'll keep you in practice. The sausages are already cooked and in the oven.'

Marnie threw away the burnt bacon and laid several more rashers in the frying pan. She cut three tomatoes in half and added them, face down. She ground coffee beans and boiled water. When the bacon was nearly done, she put slices of bread under the grill and cracked eggs into the second pan. 'No mushrooms?' she asked.

'Nope.'

'They're that bad?'

'Wait and see.'

Marnie laid out three plates and slid the food onto them. She put the cafetière on a tray, with the toast and the pots of marmalade and jam.

'Can we go for a walk when they're gone?'

'Of course. How did you get here, by the way?'

'I got the last train and walked from the station.'

'So you've been up all night?'

'Yes.'

'Hmm. I'll take this through. I've laid the little table

next door for them, so we'll have the kitchen to ourselves. You make us another pot of coffee, OK?'

'OK.'

'Do you want anything to eat?'

'Maybe I'll make porridge. It's comforting.'

'Make some for me as well.'

Next door they could hear the guests' voices rise and fall. Marnie raised her eyebrows at Emma, who said in a hissed whisper, 'Rich smarmy couple, spoilt daughter. They treat me with that kind of gushing condescension that makes my skin crawl – as if they're doing a really good thing in treating the servant well. God only knows what they're doing here rather than staying in some hotel with a Jacuzzi.'

'I see.' Marnie sprinkled soft brown sugar on top of her porridge and watched it darken and melt. She took a spoonful, then a sip of coffee, and looked out of the window beyond the garden to where the sea now sparkled, sending off gleams of light. She sighed contentedly: last night felt a long way off, and its vivid remoteness had the quality of a dream.

'Tell me,' said Emma, as they trudged along the shingle.

'I saw Ralph again. He asked me to marry him.'

'Ah,' said Emma.

'I said no, of course.'

'Of course.'

'He was angry, very upset.'

Emma didn't say anything, just nodded.

'I think it was my fault – I think I led him to believe . . . When we were coming back from France it was so

316

nice with him, and then I think he thought – well, to be absolutely honest, maybe I thought too, for a moment, anyway – I let myself think – because he's always been so – oh, God, sorry, I'm not making much sense.'

'I think I can join up the dots.'

'Yes, you probably can. You always do. I feel so muddled.'

'But you know you don't want to marry him?'

'How could I marry him? We're not in a Victorian novel. We haven't gone out together. We haven't had sex, if that's what you're wondering. Or done anything. It was just a glimmer of possibility, that's all, and Ralph turned it into this huge drama. Anyway, it's a perfectly stupid idea. He's *Ralph*. He's like my brother or something. I don't love him. Yes, I do – I do love him, of course, not in that way, though, not the way he loves me. I don't –' She looked away: this wasn't the kind of thing she usually talked about to her mother. 'I don't really desire him.'

'So you were quite right to say no. Were you unequivocal?'

'Don't you think,' said Marnie, bending down and picking up a flat stone, which she sent skimming over the water, 'that being loved almost makes us love them back? Men are put off women who adore them unconditionally, but women are often won over by men's devotion.'

'That's rather a generalization,' said Emma, drily. 'By "them", I take it you mean Ralph, and "us" would be you?'

'OK, then. Sometimes I think he'll wear me down and win me over. And, to be absolutely honest, if he stopped loving me – which is what most of me wants him to do, for his sake and mine – then I also know I'd feel, I don't know, abandoned. As if I'd lost something rare and precious that I'd never find anywhere else. That's wrong of me, isn't it?'

'To feel it isn't wrong, but to act on it in any way would be. To encourage him would be unkind.'

'I think I encouraged him,' said Marnie, in a low voice.

Emma linked her arm through her daughter's. 'You and Ralph,' she said, with a sigh, 'it just goes on, doesn't it?'

Marnie saw how much older Emma looked, how her hair was turning grey and her face had new lines in it. What did she do, evening after evening alone in the house, with everyone gone from her – even Marnie, even Eric? 'I'm sorry,' she said. 'I know how you feel about Ralph. He's a bit like your son, isn't he? Or, at least, you're like his mother.' There was a silence, thick and heavy, between them. Marnie swallowed hard, staring out across the water.

Emma stopped and looked intently at her. 'It's time for you to leave us behind,' she said.

Lucy comforted me. She had always been waiting to comfort me. I shouldn't have, I shouldn't have, I knew all along, but I didn't seem to have much strength left and she was always so strong. Small and sour as a crisp green apple, straight and true as an arrow.

I can't remember how I got there. Big student house, tiles sliding off the roof, overgrown front garden, ripped curtains, noise. Someone playing the piano, jazz, I think. Notes floating through the rooms. Faces looking at me. I sat on the sofa. And then Lucy came down the stairs, in control. She sat beside me to hold me in her arms.

Thin, wiry arms. She was wearing a white towelling robe that came down almost to her ankles. I put my head on her chest, against the soft folds. She smelt clean and good. She had slender fingers, short nails, small white feet, and a firm chin that rested on my head. She didn't say anything and I felt I could fold up in her embrace for ever. I was in safe hands.

She took me in. She took me out of the dark night and held me. She looked after me. Button nose, ironic mouth, sharp tongue, truthful eyes. I should never have. I was lonely. I knew she was glad. She was too glad.

From her bedroom at the top of the house I could see rooftops and lights spread out to the smudged horizon. I think I cried.

Unhappiness withdrew, stood to one side, still there but no longer eating into me, taking up the space where my heart and lungs and kidneys should have been. Weak and peaceful with weariness. Defeated. Sometimes it's right to admit defeat.

Other people. Lisa-May, round blue eyes and a giggle like a bell pealing in some English village churchyard; I looked her up the other day and she's one of the few female brain surgeons in the country. Fred — yes, Fred was in that house too. Burly, taciturn, clever. Pianist's fingers — it was he who was playing the jazz that night. I liked him but he didn't like me — or didn't trust me. Quite right. He already loved Lucy.

A mess. Fred loved Lucy, Lucy loved me. I loved you. Who did you love, Marnie Still, and who do you love now?

I should never have. Tell her I'm sorry; I liked her more than I could ever say, ever show, ever know.

Chapter Twenty-one

In the middle of the night, Ralph started to cry. Marnie, jerking awake from fitful dreams, sat upright. Tiny sounds were escaping him; his whole body was trembling. But his eyes were still shut and she thought at first that he was asleep and racked by morphine nightmares. Leaning towards him, she put her hand on his shoulder. He opened his eyes and saw her and he was trying to smile, trying to speak, but no words would come.

'Don't cry,' she said. 'It's all right.'

Looking round, she saw that Oliver was stretched out on the sofa, fast asleep. His fists were curled into tight balls and held up to his face, as if he was ready to defend himself. She wouldn't wake him. She took tissues out of her pocket and dabbed at the tears on Ralph's cheeks, but more came. His whole face was wet. He made hardly a sound, just looked helplessly at her out of his streaming eyes.

'Oh, my darling,' she said, her voice cracking with tenderness. 'What can I do for you? Are you in pain?'

He was trying to speak: his face was screwed up with the effort; spittle ran down his chin. His hands clawed towards her. Marnie almost drew back from him; she was frightened, though she couldn't have said of what exactly. He barely seemed human any more and she found it hard to recognize this creature as Ralph. But she made herself look into his eyes, deep in their sockets, red-rimmed, with yellowing irises, but still greeny-blue, still his. The same eyes that had looked at her so longingly all those years ago.

Through shallow, tearing breaths, he managed a sound. Was he trying to tell her something? Trying to say her name? She grasped both flailing hands between hers and pressed them to her lips. She bent over him and tried to cradle him, but he was all sharp bones, flapping skin and matted hair. 'I'm here,' she whispered. 'We're both here. Tell me what to do.'

'Hold me.' Was that what he said? He repeated the words, more clearly this time. Hold me, yes.

She climbed onto the bed and lay beside him, putting both arms around his shuddering form, pressing her lips to his sticky cheek, feeling his breath on her skin. Bit by bit, he became still. His breathing was calmer. Marnie sat up and wriggled out of her long skirt, she took off her pale grey jersey and thick tights. She untied her long hair and shook it loose. Then she climbed under the covers and pressed her body, no longer young and firm, against Ralph's disintegrating one. She spooned him to her, her breasts pressed against his zip-sharp spine, her toes against his quivering calves. She could feel every string and knot of his terrifying body, every artery and bubbled vein.

'I've hugged you like this once before,' she said, to the back of his head. She felt, rather than saw, that Oliver was awake and listening to her. 'In a tent in the rain. Do you remember, Ralph? I know you do. It could have been yesterday, couldn't it? Time doesn't matter any more.

We're here and we're there as well. Adults and children all at the same time, past and present and future all meeting. Let these seconds last for ever.' Nonsense words spooling out in the darkness, but she could tell that Ralph was listening. His body was quiet. She put a hand against his chest and felt his heart still beating there against his fragile ribcage. The impossible preciousness of life. Her voice spilled out like a river to wash over him. 'If you asked me to marry you now, I'd say yes. Yes, Ralph. Don't cry any more – I can't bear it if you cry. Don't be sad. Sorrow has gone. We're here and we love you, and we're not going to leave you, never again. Yes,' she repeated. 'Dry your eyes, dearest friend. Don't be downhearted.'

It seemed to her that she was speaking with Emma's voice as well as her own; that she had become her mother and was cuddling her son and keeping him from harm.

I wish you all the things that I won't have. Have them for me, enjoy them for me. Early-spring sunshine on the back of your neck, a beloved face to wake to, seagulls screeching, long grass moving when the wind blows, scrambled eggs and crosswords on Sunday mornings, though you were never very good at crosswords, were you? Journeys to strange hotel rooms and to empty beaches where sea anemones stir in hidden rock pools, green seas bucking, a horse breathing warmth into your open hand, seasons coming round and round again. Dawn choruses, full moons and new moons and white clouds and high winds, cuckoos in May and owls that call across the woods, storms, people who recognize you, secrets, giggles, eyes across a crowded room. I wish you old age. I wish you love.

Hold me now. If you hold me, surely I can't go.

*

They must have fallen asleep together, because when she opened her eyes dawn was just breaking. Through the open curtains, she could see an eerie pink light on the snow and the pine trees looked as though they were tipped with flames. The smell of coffee filled the room and a fresh fire crackled in the hearth; logs were piled up to one side and the old ash had been removed. Marnie felt stiff, sore. One arm was trapped under Ralph and she had to wriggle it gently free before she slithered out of bed, making sure not to pull the covers off him. She stood on the floor in her T-shirt and knickers, feeling middle-aged, foolish and cold.

'Here,' said Oliver, crossing the room and putting a mug of hot coffee into her hands. 'Why don't you go and have a bath while I make us some porridge? We're running out of milk so it will have to be mostly water. I'll get Dot to bring some more over this morning. I made sure the immersion heater was on so there's enough hot water.'

'Yes,' said Marnie, bemused. She couldn't work out what day it was, or how long she'd been there. She picked up her clothes and rubbed her gritty eyes with the back of her hand. 'All right. Thanks. I could do with a proper wash. I've lost all track of time. How long did I sleep?'

'I'm not sure. Three hours, maybe.'

'And Ralph?'

'The same. He's been very peaceful – no distressing dreams as far as I could tell.'

'That's good.' She hesitated. 'I was afraid I'd wake up and find him dead.'

'I don't think it'll be long now. I'm going to call the doctor and see if he'll come round today.'

'What for?'

Oliver shrugged.

Marnie made her way up the stairs with her coffee. The unheated bathroom was icy, the tiles almost too cold to stand on with bare feet, but the water, for once, was scalding. She lay in the tub, surrounded by clouds of steam, and looked at the icicles that hung from the guttering above the window, a row of glistening, dripping stalactites. She let herself sink beneath the water and now the sounds of the house were reverberating through her: footsteps, drawers opening, Oliver's voice saying something reassuring to Ralph. She surfaced and shook the water out of her hair, planning how she would break the day up into moments: making more custard; changing Ralph's clothes and washing his sweat-stained T-shirt; reading to him, Gerard Manley Hopkins today, she thought, his soaring nature poems, not his sonnets of desolation, which, now she came to think of it, expressed something of Ralph's worst moments of lacerating depression; pots of coffee and tea; a quick walk when Colette came, down to the loch to watch the ice thicken and the light fade; a phone call home to Eva, to Lucy.

She washed her hair and rinsed it, then climbed out of the bath onto the freezing tiles. Soon she was dressed in clean clothes, her hair towelled dry and tied back, her teeth brushed. Ready for what the day might bring.

Chapter Twenty-two

Marnie came home from Italy at Christmas, but only for a few days. They baked ginger biscuits in the shape of hearts and stars, as they had every year that Marnie could remember. Emma, in accordance with carefully preserved tradition, hung an orange spiked with cloves from the beams in the kitchen to fill the air with its pungency; Marnie made snowflakes out of sheets of white paper and stuck them to the windows with dabs of honey. They put out the little cherubs they had made together from ping-pong balls and stiff red card when Marnie was seven. She remembered how she had drawn their faces and hair with a black felt tip; she could smell the glue they had used, feel its plasticky skin on the tips of her fingers.

They bought the tree on Christmas Eve, as they always had, and from the same farm. Emma dragged the box of decorations down from the attic: the same old tin reindeers and glass stars and shiny balls in red and green; the saved fistfuls of silver tinsel to drape over the branches; the rope of coloured lights they had used year after year, replacing its dud bulbs and untwisting its knots, mysteriously acquired over the past year in storage. Emma put the shabby angel on top and they stood back to look at the effect, then carefully tilted the tree in its iron stand so that it stood straight. Everything was the same; everything had changed.

Marnie's room, with the accordion gathering dust in the corner, the empty easel by the window, waited for her; the bedcovers were turned back and Emma had put a miniature cyclamen on the sill. But the air smelt different and the spaces seemed unfamiliar. Her clothes, when she pulled open the chest's drawers or opened her wardrobe, belonged to another age. Giddy with nostalgia, she ran a hand through the dresses and tops hanging in the cupboard; since she almost never threw anything away, it seemed as though her teenage years were captured among their worn folds, memories in the creases of her coat, in the faded cotton shirt.

On an impulse, she went up the stairs to Seth's – and more lately Ralph's – old room and sat on the bed beside the folded covers. It was so clean and bare in here; everything breathed absence and was white with loss. Marnie had a sudden sharp sense of this house, this home, being no longer her centre, the hub from which her life spun out, but something that lay in her past, growing more distant and unreal with each week that passed. Even while she stood at the window looking out at the choppy grey sea, she felt she was observing the distant landscape of her childhood, one that she had left without realizing it.

On Christmas morning they exchanged presents. Marnie had bought Emma a silk scarf in vibrant blues and greens and a pair of gloves in thin, soft leather; she had wrapped them in tissue paper and tied them with thick gold ribbon, and her mother took a long time to open them. Her hands looked as though they were trembling. She draped the scarf round her shoulders and held the gloves against her cheek. 'This is too extravagant,' she said. 'You should be saving your money, not wasting it on me.'

'I wanted to buy you something beautiful, not just practical.'

'Well, you have.'

'Because – well, you're beautiful.'

Emma closed her eyes briefly, then opened them and smiled. 'You're a very kind liar. I'm middle-aged and grey and suffering from the pull of gravity. But thank you.'

'You're welcome.'

They both felt awkward; they weren't accustomed to speaking emotionally to each other.

'Here – this is your present.' Emma handed Marnie a large, square parcel.

'I know what it is – a football!' One or other of them had made the same feeble joke every year for the past fifteen or so.

'That's right. How did you guess? Go on, open it.'

'I don't want to tear the paper.'

'It's something I've been working on,' said Emma, trying to sound casual.

'Hang on. Oh. But . . .'

It was a photo album, with a thick cloth cover. Marnie opened it to the first page, on which Emma had written in her bold calligraphy: 'To my beloved daughter Marnie, who makes me so proud.'

Tears stung her eyes.

'Turn the pages,' said Emma. 'You have to look inside.'

'Oh, goodness,' said Marnie. 'But this is . . .'

'Your father, when we first met. Isn't he handsome?'

'I've never seen these before.'

'No. I'm sorry.'

'And this is you. But you're – you're lovely.'

'I'm young, that's all.'

'Where were they all this time? I used to look in your room for pictures, you know.'

'I know,' said Emma, with a hint of her old dryness. 'I put them all away after the accident. I thought I'd never be able to look at them again. But after you left for Italy, I got them down. I should have shown them to you before. It wasn't fair.'

'Where was this?' She was looking at a photo of Paolo and Emma in yellow oilskins, the hoods up so that only their grinning faces could be seen.

'That? We went walking in Wales the year we met. It rained constantly.'

'I don't know anything,' said Marnie. 'You never said.'

'I was wrong.'

Marnie turned the next page. 'Seth,' she said.

'He's a day old in that one. I thought I'd never seen anything so tiny and breakable. I got home from the hospital and took about three hours to put a vest on him. I thought I'd snap off one of his arms if I wasn't careful. Look, he has a stork mark on his forehead. It never quite disappeared. It was still there when . . .' She stopped for a moment. 'And his hair is slightly red. I don't know where he got that from – not from either of us. I remember his smell. Even his shit smelt clean. I'd never had anything to do with babies so it was all completely new. I used to sit for hours feeling the way his fist closed round my finger. Or watching those involuntary twitches, and the way his eyelids pulsed with dreams. Like a miracle.'

'I didn't know,' Marnie said again.

'There, that's him with your father.'

Marnie looked at the photo of her brother in her parents' bed, bunched up and naked against Paolo's bare chest. On Paolo's face there was an expression of peace.

'And us three together,' said Emma. 'I might have got the order a bit wrong for some of them. You think you'll never forget, but you do. Bit by bit you do.'

'Do you?'

'Not everything, of course.'

Seth learning to crawl, to walk, to ride a tricycle, then a bike with stabilizers; Seth with Paolo, with Emma, with the two of them.

'I'm pregnant in that one,' said Emma, laying a finger on the picture.

'With me?'

'Well, of course, you chump. Who else? And here you are in person.'

'I look like a prune.'

'And there's Seth holding you for the first time.' Indeed, there he was, on his face an expression of outrageous pride.

'Did he like me?'

'What do you mean, did he like you? He adored you.'

'Really?'

'What did you think?'

'I don't know.' She turned the pages, watching herself grow. 'God, I used to scowl a lot.'

'You still do.'

'Do I scowl?'

'Of course.'

Then the pictures stopped. There was a gap of several years before there were any more, and even then they were much sparser, and were almost always of Marnie on days of special importance: first days at school, final assemblies; formal images to mark her official progress through life. 'Why are you giving me this?' she asked at last, closing the book, and tying it shut with the blue ribbon.

'What do you mean?'

'Don't you want these photos yourself?'

'I want you to have them.'

'But what about you?'

'I've kept a few.'

'Of the four of us together?'

'Of course.'

'I don't know what to say.'

'Best not to say anything, then.'

'I don't know if I'm happy or sad.'

'Perhaps you're both.'

'Do you mind me not being here?'

'Mind? No.' Emma's voice was very firm. 'Of course I love seeing you, but you needed to leave.'

'You think?'

'All children need to leave, one way or another. You were always such a homebody, I used to worry that you wouldn't make the separation.'

'What do you do?'

'You mean – do without you?' Emma laughed. 'I'm not completely at a loose end, if that's what you're worried about. Come on, let's go for our walk.'

*

They went for their Christmas Day walk along the shore, in the teeth of a cold easterly wind. Stinging cheeks and watering eyes and the salty spray stiffening their hair. Crunching across shingle, past the old boat that was now a skeleton, its bones sinking into the pebbles and grit, along the ragged hem of the surf. Remember, remember. But the memories weren't so sharp now: they didn't sink their hooks into Marnie's heart.

And later, sitting over their dinner (duck breast with juniper berries followed by an Italian apple and cinnamon ice cream), each wearing a paper crown from their pulled crackers, Marnie said, 'Have you seen Ralph or Lucy recently?'

'He came to see me a week or so ago.'

'Are they still together?'

'Yes. Although . . .'

'Although?'

'Although nothing. He was very frenetic. Talking nineteen to the dozen, as if something terrible would happen the moment he stopped. You know how he can be.'

'I certainly do. Was he all right, do you think?'

Emma hesitated. 'I don't know. Bright and electric with unhappiness, I'd say. Thrilling with it.'

'Oh. I see. D'you think –'

'What I think is that it's not for you to concern yourself with any more. That's over.'

'I know. It's just –'

'That's over,' repeated Emma. 'Let him go. Give him a chance . . . and yourself.'

'You're right.'

'In this case I am, yes.'

Later, over coffee and their game of patience before bed, Marnie took one of her mother's hands and held it.

'You're really OK?'

And Emma replied: 'You're not to worry about me for a single second. I'm really, really fine.'

She wasn't OK, of course; she wasn't really fine. Why hadn't Marnie understood? There were enough clues – the photo album, the newly gaunt face, the tiredness, the insistence with which Emma had sent her back to her life in Italy, her determination that Marnie should strike out on her own, the brief hard hug she had given her at the airport, the cheerful, unwavering smile as she raised her hand in farewell, then turned and walked away.

Chapter Twenty-three

Emma's funeral was the last time that Marnie had seen Ralph – until now, of course, as he lay dying himself.

She came home a few days before Emma died; in Florence all the blossom was out on the trees and the heady glory of an Italian spring had unfurled in the surrounding countryside. Young lovers lay in fields and walked hand in hand along the slow river, feeling the sun beat down on them. But in East Anglia it was still cold, the last sharp nip of winter in the air.

'At least I was there at the end,' she said to Ralph's immobile form.

She couldn't tell if he heard any of the words she spoke any more, or felt her hand holding his. His breath rustled like dry grass in his throat. 'At least she didn't die alone.'

People say that all the arrangements that have to be made after a death help the bereaved. They give them something to do, see them through the first few days of loss. But Marnie moved through the myriad tasks – the bureaucracy of registration and form-filling, the phone calls to distant family and to friends, the meeting with lawyers and organization of the funeral, the cremation – in a state of numb sadness. She couldn't comprehend that Emma had left her, that she no longer had a mother and was alone. It wasn't possible and couldn't be true that she would never speak to her again, never sit in their kitchen peeling potatoes with her, or walk along the beach, or work alongside her in her shed, not needing to speak. Who else could hear Marnie when she didn't speak? Who else understood her when she didn't even understand herself? When she was sad, who would she turn to? When she was glad, who would she tell? If she did well, who would be proud of her, and if she failed, who would still believe in her? Who would comfort her? Who would ever smile like that at her again, understanding her and loving her and seeing right into the heart of her? Nobody would. Her mother was dead. She was no longer a daughter.

She sat by the body in the undertaker's parlour. The body. It wore Emma's clothes – Marnie had chosen an old skirt and a soft woollen jumper because they looked comfortable, and they reminded her of all the times she'd seen her mother in them; she had wrapped the Italian scarf in blues and greens round her neck – but it wasn't Emma. Emma had gone from her.

She put one finger out and touched the cheek and it was cold and unyielding. 'Mummy,' she said. 'Mummy?'

When she had been in Italy, she had relished her aloneness – the way she was finally unencumbered and free. She had felt blithe with the sense of her discon- nectedness from people and from the past; it had made her feel light-headed, light-footed, almost as if she could fly. But now it dazed her with terror. She had no father or mother, she had no son or daughter, no lover who would stay, no family at all. Nothing held her in place; she was a link with no chain, no before and after; a floating speck of humanity in a vast and lonely world.

She picked up her mother's stone hand and fiddled with the gold ring on the fourth finger. She had thought of taking it off and keeping it for herself but it didn't seem right somehow. It was Emma's; Paolo had put it there.

'Lucy? Lucy, Emma died.'

They had spoken since Lucy and Ralph had become a couple, but briefly. Lucy had written her a letter about it, which Marnie had got before she went to Italy. It was long, rather formal, as if Lucy was asking for her blessing, or even her permission. Marnie had sat for a long time with it on her lap, staring at the words, 'so happy . . . you know how I've always felt . . . my dearest friend . . . no awkwardness between us . . .' and then she had phoned Lucy and told her, with formal enthusiasm, how glad she was for both of them. No, of course she didn't mind; yes, of course she wished them well; and, yes, she firmly believed it was the right thing and that they could bring each other joy and contentment. And between the lines, as they both well knew, she was promising, I won't ruin this for you; I won't get in the way of your happiness.

'No! Oh, Marnie. I'm sorry.'

'Yes. It was quite quick at the end. At least I got back in time.'

'That's good.'

'I wanted you to know. She was so fond of you.'

'She was like a second mother to me,' Lucy said simply. Then: 'Are you all right?'

'Me? I don't know. I can't answer that question. I don't think it's quite sunk in yet.'

'Of course not. You were so close to each other.'

'Yes. We were.' The past tense brought tears to her eyes and she wiped them away.

'Is there anything I can do? Do you want me to come and be with you?'

'I don't know. I don't know what I want. I feel a bit – I don't know. At sea.'

'If you want me to come, I'd feel honoured.'

'Thank you. Can I think about it? If it were to be anyone, it would be you.'

'When's the funeral?'

'Next Monday. Just a few days' time. I wanted to get it over with quickly. Will you be there?'

'Of course! How could I not?'

'There won't be many people. But Ralph,' said Marnie, 'I'd like him to be here as well. It would feel all wrong if he wasn't. Will you tell him for me?'

'Yes. He's in Cambridge and I won't see him until tomorrow.

'Maybe I should tell him myself. He and Emma – you know how he felt about her.'

'I do,' said Lucy. 'But you're not to worry about Ralph, do you hear me? I'll break it to him.' Her voice was stern. That's my job now, she seemed to be saying, and Marnie understood with fresh clarity how everything had changed. In the past, with the three of them and then the four, it was she who had kept the group together, the one to whom everyone turned. But the old allegiances had shifted and broken. Oliver had gone, keeping in touch only with Ralph, and Ralph was involved with Lucy. She was on the edge of their world when she had once been at its centre – and now, hearing the involuntary note of warning in Lucy's voice, she felt a spasm of pure panic: even with her closest friend and her once most uncon- ditional lover, she did not come first. She was no one's dearest, then. Self-pity sluiced through her, before she gave herself a mental shake, nodding at the phone. 'You're absolutely right, Lucy,' she said.

'I tell you what.' Lucy reverted to her tone of warm affection. 'Unless I hear otherwise, I'm going to get the train down first thing on Saturday and stay until the funeral's over. I can't bear to think of you going through this alone. We can do it together. OK?'

'OK,' said Marnie, both relieved and resistant. She wanted to ask if Ralph would be there as well, so that they would make up the familiar trio one more time, fill the house with their old intimacy – an impossibility that she desired and dreaded – but she found herself unable to. Her relationship with Ralph was no longer direct: Lucy stood between them, mediating everything. 'Thank you,' she added.

Lucy told Ralph and Ralph apparently contacted Oliver, who was in America, and also Oliver's parents, who promised to come; his mother sent a sympathetic letter and said that Ollie sent his sympathy and heartfelt best wishes, an old-fashioned phrase that made Marnie wince. Marnie rang Eric and held the phone to her ear while he wept. She phoned Diane, her mother's oldest friend, who lived in France now but who had obviously been waiting for the news and promised to fly over. She went through Emma's address book – the same battered moleskin one she'd had all of Marnie's life, full of crossings-out and doodles – and invited a few people, but only those she knew Emma had still been in touch with. She didn't want the funeral to be large and dutiful, but neither did she want there to be just a handful of people barely filling the front row at the crematorium while taped music played and the queue for the next dearly-beloved waited outside, stamping their feet in the unseasonable chill.

The life had gone out of the house; it was like ash after the fire had burnt down. Marnie paced from room to room, sitting on each bed and folding her hands in her lap, waiting, although she didn't know what for. She spent hours in her mother's bedroom, hardly daring to breathe and feeling as if she was invading her secret space. Does a person have a right to privacy after they have died? She took out each item of clothing and held it, feeling the material, putting her face into it and sniffing her mother's smell, which was clean and sharp, like lemons and bergamot, absolutely distinct. She held up dresses, remembering the time when she'd done so before, and imagined her mother wearing each one. She was trying to see Emma as a solid, separate person from herself – not just her mother, flesh of her flesh, but as a woman who had lived and who had died. She slid her hands into each of Emma's shoes. She even opened the drawer containing her underwear – all white or black, some a bit faded; she sat on the floor with a bra in her lap and stared at it for several minutes.

She sat in the kitchen by the empty grate, and listened to the sea in the distance and the wind in the trees, the sounds of her childhood. Sometimes, she forgot and, seeing the albino blackbird that had returned to their bird table, or watching the way a certain shaft of light penetrated the thick cloud, she would turn to speak to her mother.

She opened the fridge and examined the contents. There was almost nothing in it, of course, and what there was was long past its eat-by date: soured milk and fermenting yoghurt, half a melon in cling-film, coffee beans. Everything neat and attended to. She pictured her mother's life after she had left home: she wouldn't have pined; she would have kept herself busy and made herself proper meals, evening after evening, sitting at the table to eat. She pulled open the drawers of the filing cabinet and saw that everything was filed under subject and date. She thought there might be a letter for her, but found nothing. And, anyway, what was she expecting? Some kind of last blessing, some revelation that would make final sense of her mother's life and her own? No, it was just that she didn't want Emma's words to stop; couldn't bring herself to believe that she had heard the last of them and her mother's story was over.

She wandered into the garden and looked at the neat vegetable patch, where Emma had already planted the broad beans and the onions; at the coiled hose and the pruned roses, the grass that would soon need its first mow of the year.

She made her way to the work-shed, unbolting the heavy door and pulling it back with a slow creak; stopping dead on the threshold, almost unable to bear the baked and clean smell of the kiln, the clay, the paint and varnish. So familiar that she could close her eyes and feel her mother standing at the bench in her thick grey apron, her hair tied back, her feet slightly apart and her capable hands pushing into the doughy clay, opening it out into a bowl, drawing it up into a vase, folding it into shapes. She could hear her asking her to lift down this teapot, open that door, stand back a little. Emma had tidied everything up. Pots ready for painting stood on one shelf, others that she had finished on another. A beautiful set of glazed plates was stacked on the table. Marnie picked one up and ran her fingers over its silky surface, traced its asymmetrical outline, examining it as if she might find a secret there.

It was better when Lucy came. They did things together. They bought food for after the funeral and made lemon cake, smoked-salmon sandwiches, salads. They talked – but they didn't really talk about the things that were in their hearts, but chose to remember incidents from their shared past instead, which were all carefully chosen, cheerfully undisturbing, and usually reaching back to the years before Ralph had appeared on the scene. Only on the evening before the funeral did Marnie break their unspoken pact.

'Is everything OK with you?' she asked.

'Fine.'

'Lucy! You know what I mean – OK with Ralph?'

'It's fine,' Lucy repeated. 'You'll see him tomorrow, anyway.'

'How did he react to the news of Emma's death?'

'I don't know. He went very quiet. He didn't say anything at all. And then I came here.'

'Oh. Have you called him since then?'

'No. Well – yes, I called but there wasn't an answer.' Lucy hesitated, biting her lip, then said in a rush, 'Tomorrow, Marnie, when you see him –' She stopped, her face red.

'Yes?'

'I mean, he's quite volatile at the moment, and I'm worried about him going off the rails – oh, never mind. I shouldn't have said anything.'

'You haven't yet. What do you mean? Tell me, now you've started.'

Lucy lifted her head and met Marnie's eyes. Her face took on a cool expression and she said, in a clipped, pedantic voice, 'If you really want to know, I'm always scared that he hasn't got over you. That I'm a poor second best.'

'Oh, Lucy, I'm sure that's not true!'

'You don't know that. It's always been true in the past. And he only came to me because he was so sad about you. I got him when he had no resistance.'

'But he stayed with you.'

'Ye-es. Or, at least, he hasn't left.'

So what are you asking me to do?'

'Just don't be too – too warm and intimate with him. Don't encourage him or lead him on.'

'Oh,' said Marnie. She felt as though Lucy had thrown a bucket of cold water over her. 'I see. Well, don't worry, of course I won't *lead him on*.'

'I knew I shouldn't say it. Certainly not now, when you need to be supported. I can't believe I did. Sorry. Sorry.'

'Oh, God. Listen, Lucy, Ralph is my friend, you're my

friend. I want you to be happy together, I really do – but do you honestly think that if you're right, which I'm sure you're not, that the best way to deal with it is by keeping me at a distance, out of his way? What – for ever? I mean, is that really the way of –'

'I know, I know, I know. You're right. It was stupid. I'm stupid.'

'You've never been stupid in your life.'

'Yes! About this I am. I'm scared of losing him. He's going to leave me, I know he is.'

'You have to have more confidence in yourself.'

'Easy to say.'

'No, you do. You can't keep someone by hanging on to them. He's with you because he wants to be.'

'You make me sound abject.'

'I hope you believe that I'd never do anything to harm you.'

'You don't have to *do* anything,' said Lucy, soberly.

He arrived after the service had already started, pushing a grinning, drooling Grace, the wheels of her chair clattering over the floor. Everyone turned to look. Marnie saw his red-rimmed eyes and hollow cheeks; his black suit. For a moment, the years rolled away and she was back at that other funeral, looking at him in his ill-fitting black suit, with his stricken face. Then she faced the front again: she didn't want to have to think about Ralph today.

But he surprised her and was on his best behaviour. He didn't cry at all during the service – not that Marnie had anything against anyone crying, but she had half expected him to hog the grief, and force her attention away from Emma and towards him. The opposite was true. He sat with his arm round Grace, silent and attentive; he waited for everyone to file out before he left the building, then stood awhile talking quietly with Oliver's parents.

When Lucy approached him, he kissed her lips, then both cheeks, and let her lead him by the hand to Marnie. He told her very simply that he was sorry for her great loss and that he knew how very sad she must be feeling. He said that they were all lucky to have known Emma. He stood quite still and his voice was quiet, but nothing about him seemed at rest. His dark eyes burnt like coals as he looked at her. His thin shoulders twitched under the jacket. Marnie could see a vein pulsing in his temple. When he put a hand on her forearm and leant forward to kiss her, very quickly, on the cheek, she could feel him quivering – it was as if his entire body was vibrating, like a tuning fork. His lips were hot and dry.

'Thank you, Ralph,' she said, conscious of Lucy beside them, watchful as a cat. 'And I'm so very glad you're here. She loved you a great deal, you know.' For a moment their eyes shone with tears. There was nothing she wanted so much as to put her arms round him and be held; only his loss understood hers. No one else's came close.

'I loved her too.' His voice was barely more than a whisper. 'I can't . . .' Then he stopped. She could see him tightening his resolve, pulling himself back into firmer shape.

'And I'm glad you brought Grace.'

'It made me late. I'm sorry.'

'Emma would have been pleased.'

'She was always very kind to her.'

'Yes. I ought to go and speak to Eric. I'll see you back at the house, won't I?'

'Of course.' Lucy spoke for both of them, her voice clipped, her mouth pinched with anxiety.

Later, at the house, she saw how he stared around him, taking in Emma's striped mugs hanging from their hooks, the old fireplace, the table he'd sat at so many times, the hob where he'd cooked fried breakfasts for Emma's B-and-B guests, Marnie's charcoals hanging from the walls. She noticed how he ran his finger over the top of the chair by the fire that Emma used to sit in with her book, as if he was doubting its reality. His gaze lingered on the photograph of Emma and Marnie together in the garden: Eric had taken it several summers ago and the two of them, standing arm in arm, their dark hair tied back and smiles slightly self-conscious, looked ridiculously similar.

She turned away from him abruptly. There were too many sandwiches left and the lettuce was wilting in the salad bowl. Guests were loitering and she just wanted them gone, but at the same time she dreaded the evening that lay ahead. She went outside to the garden, where Grace was sitting alone in a patch of cool sunlight, her thin legs hanging limply and her head lolling. She was crooning softly to herself.

'You're the only person I can talk to,' said Marnie, sitting on the grass at her feet, smiling up into her vacant face. 'Because you won't understand. Or maybe you do. Maybe you understand and just can't tell anyone. What a terrifying thought. Anyway, I don't really know what it is that I want to say. Nothing. There's nothing to say. Emma was good like that. She knew when not to speak. When Eric wrote to me about her death, he said she always reminded him of a boulder in a flooding stream – as if she could withstand anything. Maybe he thought that to make himself feel better about leaving her. She must have suffered so much in her life but she never complained. She didn't even talk about it to me. Probably that was her way of surviving: to keep everything battened down. Some people say that's a form of repression but I don't think so. I think it's more like being unselfish. She was determined not to let her sadness spill over me. She carried herself very carefully, as if there were feelings inside her that might ignite, explode, if they were shaken. Do you understand that? It's the opposite of Ralph, isn't it? He shakes everything up – he's like a walking flare. Tell me, Grace, how is your brother? How's Ralph? Is he OK? I don't think so. And how do I feel about him? What do you think? Would you call it love? Don't worry, there isn't a right answer. Anyway, he's with Lucy. Occasionally I wish I'd never met him – that's a terrible thing to say, I know. Are you cold? Your hands are cold but your hands are always cold, aren't they? We'll go inside soon. I'm talking nonsense anyway. Ignore me. I'm very tired. I keep thinking Emma will walk out of the door carrying a tray of lemonade or something. Or I'll see her standing in the kitchen, at the window, washing the dishes.

'I'm happy you're with us, Grace. It feels right. Ollie's not here. Probably that's a good thing. No, it's definitely a good thing. I could make a fool of myself today. I haven't really thought about him all the time I've been in Italy, but now I'm back, so is he, in my mind, anyway. So are we all. Do you reckon he thinks of me? No, of course he doesn't. I'll return to Italy when things are sorted here. I don't want to stay. I suppose I'll have to sell the house – what an unimaginable thing, not to have this house as home. I always believed I'd have it to return to – I used to imagine arriving with a clutch of children and Emma would be there to greet us. I had it all sorted in my mind. I pictured us on the rug in the garden. Three children, maybe. That would be nice. A baby with chubby legs. I've no idea where the father is in this quaint idyll of mine – he doesn't seem to be anywhere at all. God, I haven't even drunk anything, not a drop. So if this isn't home any longer – and even if I kept it, which I can't, it wouldn't be home anyway – then where will be home? Enough. I'm going to go and be a proper host. Say goodbye to them all. Then, when everyone's gone, I'll go for a walk by the sea and say goodbye to Emma. I'm so full of tears, yet somehow I haven't been able to cry properly. I've never been very good at crying. Like Emma – when did I ever see her cry? Maybe she cried alone, when no one was there to hear her. I hate to think of that. I hate to think I never comforted her.

'I'd better go in now. You wait there – all right? – and someone will come and fetch you in a minute. Ralph and Lucy will take you back.'

All of the mourners had left and she was alone at last. Lucy had asked if Marnie wanted her to stay, rather than going with Ralph to her parents' house, and Marnie, ruefully noting that Lucy said 'me' not 'us', thanked her but insisted she would rather be alone. And, no, she could clear up on her own; she had always rather liked clearing up mess. It was satisfying, somehow, restoring order to chaos.

So she had hurried them out of the house, pretending not to notice Ralph's anguished look and drawing back slightly when he kissed her cheek. It was all too intense; her heart bumped painfully in her chest and her eyes hurt. She stood at the door, watching them as they pushed Grace up the bumpy track towards the main road where Lucy had left her car. At the corner, Ralph stopped and turned, but she gave him a determinedly cheery wave. Then they disappeared from sight, and for a while Marnie remained, staring at the place they had been.

Did she know that he would come back? For the remainder of the day, as she washed plates and glasses, wrapped up sandwiches and put them in the small freezer that she would have to empty and defrost, swept floors and wiped surfaces, she was heavy with a sense of fore-boding and anticipation. She went out for her walk along the sea-front, but every so often she would cast a look back towards the house, as if she might see a figure there, or would strain her eyes into the twilight distance, thinking that perhaps Ralph would suddenly appear, running towards her as he used to with his gangling, lopsided gait, a look of urgency on his face and the wind knotting his wild hair.

He did not come until it was quite dark outside and the owl was shrieking from the beech tree. Marnie had had a bath and was in Emma's ancient dressing-gown; it hadn't been washed and smelt of soap and deodorant and, very faintly, of Emma's sweat. Her hair was wet and twisted on top of her head. Fatigue throbbed behind her eyes, but she was buzzing with a restless energy.

At the frantic hammering on the door, she had no doubt that it was Ralph and, sure enough, when she opened it, he was standing there, still dressed in his dark suit and white shirt. Yet she tried for a note of surprise. 'Ralph! Is everything all right?'

'Marnie, Marnie. Oh, thank God. Oh, Marnie. Please.' She felt his fingers on the hem of her sleeve, then clutching at her hand. He collapsed over the threshold and half fell, then was kneeling on the floor, burying his face in the folds of the dressing-gown.

'What?' But she let him embrace her, running her hands through the tangle of his hair, murmuring words of comfort, finally crouching beside him and holding his thin body, feeling his breath hot against her neck, letting his arms pull her fiercely against him, letting his thumb wipe the tears from her cheek. She hadn't even known she was crying until then.

'I'm so sorry,' he was gabbling. 'So sorry about Emma. Can't believe. When I heard. You poor thing. You poor darling. I just want to help you. I always promised you'd never be alone. You'll never be alone, my lovely love.'

'Ralph, get up now, seriously.'

'Oh, Marnie. I've come to be with you.'

'Please, don't,' she said, half sobbing and at the same time almost laughing at his hysterical intensity. 'This isn't right. Listen, Ralph. If you love me, don't.'

'If I love you. If I love you. Ah!'

348

'Here, come and sit down.'

She put her hand in his and tugged. He scrambled to his feet, swaying, gazing at her.

'I've left,' he said. 'I couldn't. It was wrong. I was wrong. I always knew.'

'What? What are you saying?'

'I've left.'

'Left Lucy?'

'This was my home, the only place. Where you are. I can't – I just can't.'

'Oh, no. No, Ralph.'

'Don't worry. It's not your fault. Nothing's your fault. It's mine.'

'Look, sit down.' She steered him to Emma's old chair by the hearth and he subsided into it, keeping a grip on her hand, holding her beside him. 'What have you done?'

'I've left,' he repeated, then lifted her hand to his face, pressing it against his feverish cheek and giving a small, blissful groan.

'No. This is – it's dreadful. It's all wrong. You must see. You're upset because of Emma. You're not seeing things clearly.'

He lifted his head. 'I'm seeing things very clearly at last. I was trying to persuade myself I could be happy but it was a sham. I couldn't do it. I love her, but not like that – not the way she loves me, not the way I love you. Don't look at me like that, as if I'm mad or monstrous. I don't expect anything.'

'But Lucy,' said Marnie. She could see her friend's small, stubborn face, her wry twist of a smile. 'What about Lucy?'

'Lucy's better without me,' said Ralph, dreamily. All of

a sudden, the urgency seemed to have run out of him and he was left calm and passive, smiling up at Marnie. 'She doesn't know that yet, but she will. I'm no good. Not for anyone. I'm a wrecker.'

'Oh, don't say stupid things like that!' Marnie snatched her hand out of his grip and paced the room. 'Have you told her?'

'Told her?'

'Yes – told her, for God's sake.'

'I left a letter.'

'I see.'

'You think I don't know the damage I've done? But I do. I do. I know. Of course I know. Sometimes I think I'll go mad with knowing, Marnie.'

'She trusted me,' said Marnie, drearily.

'You haven't done anything wrong. It's not you, it's me.' She turned to face him. 'You have to go now.'

'Can't I stay in my old room, just for what's left of the night? I'll leave first thing in the morning.'

'No!' said Marnie, wildly. 'That's no good at all. Don't you see? You can't run from her to me. You can't be here – it's the one place in the whole world you shouldn't be right now. She's my friend, my oldest and most loyal friend – it'd be like a kind of treachery.'

'Treachery? I'm your friend too.'

'You're my – Oh, shit, Ralph. I can't do this. I've just lost Emma. You shouldn't be making me go through all this as well.'

'You're right,' he said, springing to his feet. 'You're right. Of course. Forgive me, Marnie. I wanted to help you. I'm sorry. I'm so sorry.' He lifted his hands in front of him, palms upwards, as if he was offering her something. 'Tell me what to do and I'll do it. Anything.'

'Go,' said Marnie.

'Go? That's what you want?'

'Yes.'

'Now?'

She steeled herself, clenching her fists and digging her nails into her palms. 'Yes, Ralph. Now.'

For a moment, he looked absolutely lost – as lost as he had seemed on that cold night many years ago when she had opened the door and found him standing there, like an abandoned mongrel.

'All right,' he said. 'I'm going. If you ever need me – well, you just –'

'I know.' She tried to smile at him. 'Just call.'

'Yes.'

'Goodbye.'

He took a step forward and so did she. They met in the middle of the room and kissed, hard and mouth to mouth, like two drowning people saving each other. And then he turned and went out of the door, striding into the night. She thought she heard a single howl of pain.

'And that,' said Marnie to Ralph's motionless form, 'was the very last time I saw you. Until now. You simply disappeared out of my life. Later, I tried to track you down, but I didn't try hard enough. I was too scared of what I would find.' She stood up, stretching. 'I'm going to make a really strong pot of coffee now,' she said. 'I'll be back in a few minutes. You just rest.'

Suddenly Ralph's eyes snapped open, like those of a

porcelain doll that has been lifted upright. He stared at her fixedly.

'Ralph?' she whispered. 'Ralph, it's OK. Here I am.'

'Emma?'

'No, it's –'

'Emma,' he repeated, his face softening and his eyes half closing. 'You've come.'

It's you at last. You've been away, but now you're back. I knew you would be. But I can't see your face properly. Everything's going dark. Shadows falling and night coming across the fields.

'He doesn't recognize me. I think he thinks I'm Emma,' said Marnie to Oliver, tears standing in her eyes.

Oliver laid a hand on her shoulder. 'If he does, that's OK, isn't it?'

'I suppose so.'

'You look like her.'

'So people say.'

Grace? Don't go. I wanted to say – I wanted to say. I wanted to tell you. You were always so kind. Not a nasty bone in your poor body. I've missed you since you've been gone.

'What's he saying? I think he's trying to speak but I can't make it out.'

'I don't know. Maybe it's a dream.'

'No. Look, I'm sure he's trying to say something.'

Everyone's here. My mother; I recognize her, she has a disappointed face. No words, though. Even David, flickering into sight for a moment. So young, not a monster, just a boy hiding his shames and fears. I never knew. I never knew. I never knew. I can see faces, like shifting shapes in a fog. Everything changes into something else. Nothing holds its shape. Melting and re-forming, fading, returning and dissolving away. You are you and you're someone else as well. No boundaries, no borders. Everything giving way, walls falling in and ground oozing away under my feet. Ollie, mate? Ollie, is that you? I can't see.

Thoughts dissipate to smoke in my brain, dirty grey wisps that float away and I can't stop them and I can't hold on to them. Slow drift. I want to say — I want to say — my dear friends — can you still hear me or are my words silent now and are my eyes closing and if you touch me will I feel you and am I here still, am I here or am I going, and please, please . . .

Chapter Twenty-four

'Come on,' said Oliver, gently, taking her hand and leading her towards the kitchen area. 'I'll get you that coffee and then we can have something to eat.'

'Eat?' Marnie whispered.

'We've got to eat. I'll heat up the remains of that soup and there's the remains of the loaf of bread Dot brought.'

'You look exhausted.'

'You too. But it's OK.'

'Is it?'

'Of course. He's quite peaceful. He's just slipping away.'

'I know.'

'I couldn't have gone through this without you, Marnie.'

'Really?'

He pushed her hair behind her ears and kissed her forehead, drawing her close to him so that for a moment she stood in the solid warmth of his embrace. 'Really.'

'I'm glad I'm here.'

Where had he gone after he'd left her that night? Probably he'd walked through the night, empty-handed and sore-hearted. She would never know. And where had he gone for all those years? She only had a patchwork impression of his life from then, gathered from Oliver over the past days. She knew that he'd left Cambridge abruptly, in the middle of the term, and never gone back. His book – which had made him a minor celebrity, a maverick young man who stammered endearingly on TV shows or spoke in sudden eloquent bursts, becoming an unlikely and dangerous heart-throb for intense teenagers in search of life's meaning – slowly slipped down and then off the charts. Off the radar. His family didn't know where he'd gone, nor had they ever tried to find out – by then his father, violently alcoholic and violently unhappy, had left his mother, and Grace was in a home, so the very word 'family' had lost its notional significance. Oliver had searched for Ralph but failed to track him down; he had had to wait for Ralph to make contact with him, a year or so later. So she only knew he had become a kind of perpetual wanderer – from country to country, job to job, home to home.

And now there were things she would never find out. Had he found happiness? Peace? Love? Had his life been a disappointment to him? She could almost hear his answer, the one he had given her in different forms throughout their teenage years: that happiness was not what was important. Life was a journey, he used to say. It was about being open to experience, about passion and discovery. She could see his eyes glinting at her, his thin hands waving exuberantly in the air. It was about holding on to what you believe, following your heart, not letting the walls close in on you, not becoming a person you don't like. But Marnie had never entirely believed him. She knew how much he longed for roots, love, a home. When he had sat at their table and let her and Emma tend him, he was a soul in bliss. He was the neediest, hungriest, loneliest creature she had ever encountered.

Marnie had not searched for him, though much later she had looked him up on the Internet, and even tried ringing his old number, which no longer existed. She had got as far as leafing through telephone directories, to see if there was a Tinsley, R., but that was all – she told herself there was no point. The past had gone.

She had asked Lucy, many years later, but Lucy had heard nothing of Ralph after he had left her parents' home, leaving her a letter that said goodbye. Marnie still felt an after-tremor of pain when she remembered how Lucy had been then. She had turned up on Marnie's doorstep at dawn, wearing an old green waterproof belonging to her father that came down below her knees, and her face, which seemed to have shrunk into a tight circle, was white, her eyes like buttons. She looked thin and childlike but when Marnie stepped forward and tried to hug her, she pushed her away and stood back, her face puckered with hostility.

'He's gone,' she said. 'But, then, you probably know that.'

'Yes,' said Marnie. She didn't want to defend herself: she felt that Lucy was right to blame her.

'Is he here?'

'No.'

'But he was?'

'Yes.'

'I knew. He left me and came to you.'

'Yes. But –'

'Did you fuck him?'

'No!'

'He doesn't love me, he loves you.'

'I don't think it's –'

'Shut up, Marnie. Shut up and don't try and tell me it's not simple like that, or that he loves me as a friend, or that you didn't encourage him or anything. I saw him. He was all right and then he took one look at you feeling sad and lonely and that was it. *One look*. I rescue him, take him into my bed and my home, devote myself to his happiness, try to build up his self-belief, make him feel better about himself, make sure my friends are his friends – and it takes one fucking look and I've lost him. How do you think that makes me feel? No! Don't say anything, I'm going to tell you – it makes me hate you. And *don't* tell me you understand that because you don't – you've never in all your life been in the position that I've been in for practically half of mine. And don't you dare tell me it's not your fault because I'm not stupid and I know it's not your fault, not really, and that makes it worse, makes me all the more pathetic and pitiable and humiliated and stupid, and now I'm going and I don't want to see you and I don't want to hear from you.'

'Lucy.'

'No. Don't you see?' Her voice wobbled; her face screwed up tighter. 'I was *happy*. I thought – I thought – don't touch me! – I thought it might be OK. Oh, shit, of course I knew it wouldn't be OK. It was just a foolish dream. What am I going to do now, Marnie? What am I going to *do* without him?'

'I'm so sorry,' Marnie said numbly. 'Really, Lucy, I'm so, so sorry. If there's anything I can do . . .'

'I think you've done enough for now, don't you?'

'Nothing happened.'

'Everything happened. I've lost him.'

'Don't just stand on the doorstep, Lucy. Please come inside.'

'I don't want to.'

'You're my closest friend. Whatever's happened, it mustn't get in the way of that.'

'It already has.' Lucy gave a sharp sniff, then added, 'I'm going now.'

'Will we see each other soon?'

'I don't know.'

'But, Lucy –'

'I said I don't know. I don't know, Marnie. I don't know. All right? Leave it for a while.'

When Marnie returned to Italy, several weeks later, she felt as though she had pulled up her last, deepest roots: Emma, Ralph and Lucy had all vanished from her life and only memories remained. She had cleared the house, sorting Emma's few possessions into those to be thrown away, those to be sold, those to be stored for her future use (Emma and Paolo's double bed, the heavy-bottomed pots and pans, the wooden chair that had always stood in front of the fire, her charcoal and pastel artworks, the plates and bowls that Emma had made) and those she wanted to keep with her now (the two striped mugs, the moonstone ring, the grey jumper that she always pictured her mother in, the old belted mac, the few photos and letters). She worked her way through the shed, folding pottery in bubble-wrap and putting it into boxes, contacting customers who might want spares, packing tools up. She collected her mother's ashes and, alone, scattered them on the graves of her father and brother, then sat for a long time, watching how petals of ash lifted in the breeze. She pressed her hand flat on the grass and imagined she could feel three hearts still beating there. She listened as Emma said, quite clearly and matter-of-factly, 'Come on, Marnie, time to get back to your own life now.'

And timing was crucial. Marnie always knew why she had fallen in love with Fabio. When she had found herself back in Italy, she was alone and unanchored. She had friends and, not often, she had lovers, but was always aware that both were temporary and contingent. Becoming involved with Fabio – wry, dry, mocking, charming, clever Fabio – was a different matter entirely, because he was a decade older than her and, above all, because he had two motherless girls. He came as a package. When people told Marnie how brave she was to take them all on, and in a country not her own, she winced and protested: didn't they understand that they were the ones taking her on, making room for her in their ready-made family, giving her the home she craved? Never mind that Eva resisted her and that Fabio, much later, serially betrayed her. She was needed; she was valued. When she was there, she was maybe taken for granted, but when she was gone, she was missed. To be missed is not nothing. Never mind that Fabio's first wife was the ghost in the house, mythologized by her daughters and by her husband, whose infidelities it appeared she had known about and overlooked: Marnie was for ever grateful for the years she had spent with them all. When she thought of Eva and Luisa, a tender affection and pride would flood over her: she was not their mother, yet her love for them was unconditional.

She thought of them now. Had Luisa arrived yet, inserting herself into the undoubted squalor of her once-immaculate flat? Was Eva managing at the museum? And would she, Marnie, be back in time for Christmas? She turned towards Ralph: it seemed barely possible that he would survive another hour, let alone several days. There was nothing left of him – skin over bones and organs, a distended stomach and a caved-in head, huge, sunken eyes. Yet still his gallant heart went on beating and his ardent breath rattled in and out.

'Coffee,' said Oliver, handing her a mug. 'And a stale oat biscuit to keep you going.'

'I don't –'

'Eat it up.'

She raised her eyebrows at him but took an obedient bite.

'Colette will be here soon and I think the doctor's coming as well. Do you want to go for a walk down to the loch then?'

'That'd be good.'

So it was that, at beautiful dusk, a mysterious light falling across the snow, they stood by the water's edge hand in hand. Snow had settled on the ice, so that it was a sparkling disc of white. The moon rose in the sky. A few stars came out one by one. Silence hung over everything, broken only by the occasional soft thump and flurry of snow falling from a branch above them. Neither Marnie nor Oliver said anything.

She didn't know what made her turn round, but when she did she saw a figure coming over the hill towards them. It was Colette and she lifted her hand and beckoned.

'Oliver, look!'

They started running up the slope, their booted feet creaking in the snow, their breath clouding. Marnie felt her heart jolt in her chest. Flakes of snow caught in her lashes so that it was hard to see.

'Dr Gray thinks you should come,' said Colette, as they reached her.

'Is he –' There was no point in finishing the question.

They hastened towards the house. Dr Gray was bending over Ralph and his face, when he lifted it, was gravely sympathetic.

'Is he still alive?' Marnie whispered.

'Yes. But I think it won't be long at all. His breathing has changed.'

Dr Gray and Colette withdrew to the small side room while Marnie and Oliver sat on either side of Ralph. They held his hands and each other's. Marnie felt the warmth of Oliver's strong fingers and the coldness of Ralph's thin, limp ones. She pressed them between her own, trying to pass some of her own heat into him. The three formed a circuit: the electricity of life was pulsing through their linked hands, and as long as they didn't break apart, as long as she and Oliver held on, Ralph couldn't die.

'Ralph, my old friend,' said Oliver. 'We're both here.'

'We're not going to leave you,' added Marnie, listening to the slow, irregular breathing. Sometimes the gap between breaths was so long that she thought he might have gone, but then a scraping rustle of air escaped him again.

'Never,' said Oliver, with an infinite tenderness. His eyes brimmed with tears and he leant towards Ralph.

It's all right. It's all right. In the end, we have to go alone.

'Do you remember . . .' Oliver's voice cracked and Marnie thought he might cry, but he pulled himself together '. . . the midnight swim we had when we were at Emma's? Do you? The four of us skinny-dipping in the sea.'

I remember. We lay on our backs and laughed at the stars. I've always remembered. Everything was so simple then.

Marnie picked up Oliver's cue. 'Do you remember climbing trees with me, just after we first met? You went right up to the branches at the top and hung there like a monkey, swaying and giggling.'

I can see the ground and I can see the blue sky and I can feel the wind in my face. If I close my eyes the whole earth tips and soon I'll fall.

'Bike rides,' said Oliver. 'Going downhill with no hands. Remember?'

Faster and faster. When will I stop?

'Picnics,' said Marnie. 'Outside the house or down on the beach. You used to throw seaweed at me, and do headstands, jump waves, fall over in the surf.'

'You were mad,' said Oliver.

I was always a bit mad. Mad with fear and mad with hope.

'I remember how I taught you to bake a chocolate cake,' said Marnie. 'Me and Lucy. You always used to love licking out the bowl. I can see you now with chocolate all round your mouth – like a little kid.'

Memories. Do they just disappear with me? Melt away? Nothing left of me. Is this it? Is this all? When I'm gone, will there be nothing left?

'Playing chess,' said Oliver. 'You always beat me. You were the champion.'

Endgames now, checkmate.

'Reading to me by the fire. Poems, whole novels. Helping me with my homework. You were so lovely to me, Ralph. Do you hear me? You were a good friend, never a better friend. I've never had a better friend. I'm so glad I've found you again.'

Waves inside my head. Surging against my skull. Hard to find pictures any more in the darkness. Faces I once knew.

'Here we are.'

Ralph's eyes opened and he looked at Marnie. She saw her reflected face. She smiled at him and pressed his fingers tighter. If they didn't let go of him, she knew he couldn't die.

Waves beat against the shore. Darkness gathers and heaves, and the lights on the far-off horizon glimmer like stars in the swelling ocean of the night. I am tossed in a place of water and air, in a vast swirling world of darkness and light, and there is nothing to hold me, nothing to keep me, no ground beneath me or trees above me, no song of bird or breath of wind or word of human comfort, just the slow, invincible pull of my extinction.

'Ralph?'

'He's endured enough. Let him go.'

Marnie took a deep breath and spoke: 'Yes. You can let go now. You can go.'

Chapter Twenty-five

In the dark corners of the museum, the droll wooden faces smiled; the gusts of wind from the open door made their limbs stir slightly, as if at any moment they might come alive for her. A life-sized marionette near the stair-well spun, very slow and stately, on its wires. She could hear small creaks and groans coming from the old rooms; the house was breathing.

Marnie moved from figure to figure, standing in front of each one for a moment. Her feet tapped quietly over the wooden boards. Her long skirt rustled. She ran her fingers along the shelves, collecting soft grey dust. She inspected small tears in the costumes, rearranged puppets that stood crookedly, rubbed a cloth over the tin armour of the warriors. It was New Year's Eve and the streets outside the museum were icy and almost empty. Every so often she could see, through the windows facing the front, figures pass by in the thickening light, holding bulging bags of last-minute shopping or huddled deep in their coats, shoulders hunched and head down as if they had withdrawn into themselves. Everything was sus-pended; outside it felt as hushed and unreal as it did within this cramped and dimly lit house of puppets.

Snow had fallen during the night, and although it had already turned to a muddy slush on the roads and pave-ment, at the back of the museum it still lay thick and white, the tracks of birds stitched across its surface. Marnie took the key that hung from a hook above the back door and let herself out into the enclosed yard. Her feet in their boots sank into the snow. She bent down and pushed her fingers into its granular cold, then cupped some in her palm and held it there, watching how it glittered in the dusk. A few flakes blew off the treetops and floated slowly down towards her; a wedge of snow slid very slowly off the roof and landed at her feet. She tipped her head and looked up at the darkening sky, the scattering of stars shining above the orange street-lamps. London lay all around her, dirty and vibrant and vast, but here she was in a still and mysterious place that felt remote, like a dream of winter and of loneliness.

She had only been back a few days, but it might have been weeks, months even. The time with Oliver and Ralph, the vigil she had kept through the darkest nights of the year and the shortest days, felt far away and long ago. Sometimes she wondered if it had really happened or if she had imagined it, summoning her lost past and redeeming it, letting herself remember and be forgiven at last.

But of course it had happened. If nothing else could convince her, the terrible chaos of her flat when she returned from Stansted was witness to her absence. She had opened the door and walked in a daze into the kitchen, over dried pasta and shards of crisps that crunched underfoot, waded across drifts of dirty clothes, stepped over ashtrays brimming with stubs, knocked into empty and half-empty bottles. Someone had brought in a Christmas tree and hung any manner of objects on it –

ribbons, mistletoe, socks, Marnie's favourite silk scarf and several of her long bead necklaces; a pewter mug dangled precariously from one branch. Her cupboards had been raided too – the jars of marinated artichokes, the bags of pine nuts, the tins of olives and packets of cheese crackers, all had vanished. Even the limoncello from Naples had gone, with the undrinkable Chinese brandy. Dishes were piled on every surface, pans with the dried-on remains of tomato sauce or congealed egg. There were scummy tidemarks in the bath, no lavatory paper. No shampoo. Her wardrobe held suspicious spaces where clothes had once hung. Her drawers were open and clothes trailed over their edges. There was a nasty stain on her carpet and fingerprints dotting the walls. A young man was fast asleep in her bed. He had milky skin and green-grey eyes and looked young, dirty, hungry and pitiful. There were flea bites on his legs and his hair needed washing.

His name was Josef, he was Polish, and he played his flute in the Covent Garden Underground station, collecting the coins tossed to him to buy food that reminded him of home. With a jolt, Marnie thought of Ralph so she let him stay on, although she banished him to the sofa, ripped off all the bedclothes and washed them twice.

Even now, after days of work, the flat still held surprises: someone had put several tiny plastic soldiers into the honey; they were suspended in it, heads down and guns pointing; apparently a 'friend' had done it for a joke one night. There were others, said Eva, but she didn't know where – certainly Marnie had already found several in her shoes and on the shelves of the fridge, which, when she had arrived, had been empty but sticky with dirt. How was it possible for so much mess to be created in such a short time? How could people be so careless with others' possessions?

In truth, Marnie didn't mind so much. It gave her something to do in those strange and dislocated days after her return. She scrubbed, vacuumed, polished, bleached, mended. She replaced broken glasses and stuck one of her mugs back together with superglue so you could barely see the join. She filled the fridge with yoghurt, smoked salmon, Parma ham and goat's cheese, made a rich fruit cake and ginger biscuits for Christmas, and baked savoury pies, which Josef decorated with pastry leaves. The large bowl that Emma had made shortly before she died, with its green-blue glaze and slightly asymmetrical rim, overflowed with loose-skinned satsumas. She ordered a turkey and made chestnut stuffing.

In memory of her mother, she pierced an orange with cloves and hung it from the kitchen ceiling; she and Luisa cut out paper snowflakes and stuck them with honey to the windows. The five of them – Josef seemed to have moved in – decorated the tree with carefully hoarded baubles from Marnie's childhood. She lit candles on the window-sills, remembering how Emma always used to do the same – how, coming home in the darkness, she would see the small flame and feel welcomed and safe. She got out her watercolours again. She showed Gregor how to play the accordion. She listened to the teenagers laugh raucously when she lay in bed at night, the moon shining through her open curtains, the soft stars close. She held Luisa's hand when she cried because Marnie had left them, because Fabio was with someone else, because she was a teenager and filled with the surge of hormones and exquisite melancholy. She sat at the head of her table, ladling food, and smiled upon this ramshackle, makeshift family of hers.

During the day, she restored the museum to its previous state, rubbing smears off the tin armour of the dangling Italian knights and sweeping dustballs and crumbs off the floor, ordering the receipts, writing down purchases in the old-fashioned ledger Elaine insisted on in her careful, clumsy hand. She would climb the stairs and stand in front of sad princesses with painted cheeks, bellicose warriors and harmless dragons, stare into their unblinking eyes and sometimes feel them staring back at her.

Christmas had come and gone. Crackers pulled and gifts exchanged. Her two girls hung themselves round her neck, kissed her forehead and smiled anxiously at her, to make her smile back. The new year was nearly there and she tried to wrench her mind to the future, which lay blank and bare in front of her: everyone would leave and she would still be here. And yet all the time she was wandering in the cathedrals of forests, in the still white world where owls called in the darkness and a friend lay dying. Or she was walking slowly along the shingle beach in the golden evening sun, while the waves curled at her feet, and saw that someone was waiting for her by the rotting boat. It was Emma; it was Ralph, Lucy, Oliver. Sometimes they were all there together, her dear ones, smiling at her as she moved towards them along the ragged hem of the sea. How was it possible that she would never be with them all again? How could it be true that those bright days would not come again? If she had known then what she knew now, would it have made any difference? Would she have held precious things closer? 'Let go,' said a voice, and it was her voice, those final words to Ralph as he lay between her and Oliver, the last thread waiting to be snapped: 'You can let go now. You can go.'

Her eyes filled with tears as she stood in the yard, in the snow. She had never been good at letting go, at saying goodbye and leaving things behind. Then the doorbell rang, rang again, and she went to answer it, her cheeks still burning from the cold.

'Marnie,' he said, and she drew him inside and closed the door on the street. There, among the puppets, he held her close; she laid her head against his chest, looked at by hundreds of blind eyes. For a long time they didn't speak, but he pressed his lips against her hair and she wrapped her arms tight round him, under his thick coat and his shirt, feeling his skin move over his ribs and his heart beating strongly. Sometimes they drew apart and looked at each other, smiling and foolish with gladness. Then they clutched each other again, pressing against each other. How she'd missed him, all these years.

'Let me take you home,' she said.

At last, oh, at last. Come home with me, my dear heart, my love. I can be your home.

Much later, lying in her narrow bed, he said, 'I've got something for you.' He leant down and tugged his bag along the floor towards him, pulled out a battered hard-backed notebook, kept shut with a thick elastic band.

'What is it?'

'Ralph wanted me to give it to you.'

Taking it, Marnie swung her legs out of bed and put on her dressing-gown. She could hear Eva, Luisa and their friends laughing downstairs. She went over to the window and opened the curtains. There were fireworks going off in all directions, hissing into the night sky in fountains of stars. She took off the band, but for a moment, she didn't open the book, just held it. Its spine was frayed and some of the pages were coming loose.

On the inside cover he'd written his name in full – Ralph Raymond Tinsley – and his address, with unaccustomed neatness. After that his writing returned to its customary slapdash urgency, letters leaning forward and piled up against each other as if he couldn't keep up with his thoughts.

Several photographs slid out. Marnie looked at them one by one. Herself, very young, hair in plaits and a crooked, self-cut fringe, a scowl on her face, wearing denim shorts and a shapeless red T-shirt. Herself and Emma outside the house, arm in arm and squinting into the sun. She could remember Ralph taking that with a bulky camera he had picked up in a second-hand shop. Grace, laughing and waving a man's black shoe at the camera. A young woman with silky blonde hair and a shy smile, looking over her shoulder.

She turned the page.

You painted a bird on my window.
You cut a door in my soul.
The bird opened its wings and it flew
Into my heart.
Oh, my dear heart,
Do you know

And there it stopped.

She turned the next page to a single couplet, with a line slashed viciously through it.

I dreamt I saw you smile at me.
I woke but I was dreaming still . . .

And then, a few pages later, after doodles and gibberish and the repetition of her name in different styles, she found:

Among the long grass, I held you;
By the churned sea, I found you;
In your grey eyes, I drowned
But your smile rescues me
And your voice reminds me
That I am saved.
My shining girl,
The face in all my dreams.

She slid the photos back inside the book, closed it and replaced the rubber band. Then she climbed back into bed where she lay in the circle of Oliver's arms. She closed her eyes. In the darkness, voices from downstairs floated up to her, and although she couldn't catch what they were saying to each other, the rise and fall of their conversation cradled her. A memory slid into her mind of lying in bed as a tiny child, listening to her parents' voices from another room and feeling absolutely safe. Was it real, this sudden image from the past she had thought irretrievably lost in darkness? Some recollection buried deep that had finally worked its way to the surface and broken out at last? She didn't know, but the sense of the past and the present weaving together in her head, of the voices of the dead and those of the living overlapping like waves that rippled across each other on the shingle beach of home, stayed with her like a blessing as she sank towards sleep.

This is what it means to die, Marnie. Darkness lies across the face of the earth. But listen. There are still sounds; there are still voices in the air. Listen now.

THE WINTER HOUSE

A reading group guide

Section 1

Themes for further discussion

- Marnie feels excited as she heads to Scotland. Why do you think this is?

- What effect does the isolated setting of the house have on Marnie, Oliver and Ralph?

- Do you think Oliver is the love of Marnie's life?

- Did Marnie ever love Ralph in the way she loved Oliver?

- Marnie and Ralph both lose members of their family – what impact do David and Emma's deaths have on them both?

- Had Ralph not been ill, do you think Oliver and Marnie would have found each other again?

Section 2

Nicci Gerrard in conversation

What inspired the story behind *The Winter House*?

That's a hard question because *The Winter House* had a long, slow gestation; it lay curled up at the bottom of my consciousness for a while, occasionally stirring. I knew that I wanted to write something about the way that the past breaks through into the present. There's often a way in which things that have happened can haunt us, people we've left behind can be like ghosts, and sometimes we need to move back into the past before we can properly move forward into the future. So I decided to have a structure that would allow me to switch between two time structures. I liked the idea of having Marnie tell Ralph their joint stories, without even knowing that he could hear her. I wanted to fill the novel with different voices – her voice, his, the lost voices of her mother and her brother. In part, *The Winter House* is about things that are lost and can't be recovered but I also wanted it to be about things that are hurt and can in part be healed. It sounds strange to say that a novel which is so much about death and absence is happy, but I did set out to write a happy book.

Marnie came first as a character – someone who isn't beautiful, glamorous, successful or articulate, but who is kind (the older I get, the more I think that real kindness is a very underrated virtue) and who is often invisible to others. I wanted to make her visible. Then it was always important to me that there are several pairs in the novel. Sometimes the story between Marnie and Ralph was central, but sometimes it was the one between her and Oliver, or her and her mother. Also – sorry that this is turning out to be such a long answer – I always wanted to write about the meaning of home and homesickness. Marnie is a home-maker all her life, and Ralph is homesick all of his.

Much of the novel is set in Scotland – why did you decide to place it there?

Because in winter it's cold and remote and beautiful, and you can feel like you've stepped off the edge of the world. I wanted the days that the three of them spend in the little house to have the quality of a dream in which a story is told by the fireside. Actually, when I wrote it, I was thinking as much of winter in Sweden, where we spend each New Year, as much as Scotland – the extraordinary cold and quiet there, the way the world of the summer is transformed.

Who is your favourite character in the novel?

Oh dear – I was about to say Marnie, because she's the kind of person we overlook but who is, in her own practical and unshowy way, making the world a better place. But then I feel incredibly protective towards Ralph: the book is a kind of attempt to save him, to make him all right and ease his anguish.

You capture the voice of each character so well – was it difficult to switch from Marnie's story to Ralph's first-person reminiscences?

I did it with great care. I wanted to make Ralph's unspoken memories, the ones we know are inside his head but Marnie doesn't hear, much more suggestive and lyrical than Marnie's. It became less hard the further into the book I went, because I came to know the sound of their voices.

Do you think incidents that happen in our teenage years shape who we become?

Oh, I do – sometimes I think that things that happened years and years ago feel sharper and more intense than things that happen now. I have four children and they are all teenagers now, or older, and it makes me remember with extraordinary vividness, more like being there again than like a memory, how it felt to be that age – not just the big things like friendships and falling in love for the first time, but little details. I can recall the smell of our kitchen; I can tell you what clothes hung in my wardrobe; I can take you along our drive full of potholes, under the beech trees, down to the road where I took the bus; I can give you a word-for-word account of certain conversations; I can remember a look on a face . . .

Are you still in contact with your friends from school?

Recently, I have re-made contact with several friends to whom I used to be extremely close. When I left school, I think I fled from everything, I couldn't wait for a new life to begin, a new me; I wasn't terribly fond of the old me. And we all went in such different directions. Now I think I regret this. There are ways in which your childhood friends know you that is quite distinct from how people know you as an adult. Perhaps that is what I was fleeing and that is what I have returned to.

You write thrillers with your husband – how different is it writing solo, and also writing in a different genre from crime?

Well, in some ways it is very different. It's lonelier, especially at the planning stage when Sean and I spend weeks and months together, working out the new book. It's scarier – when I write as Nicci French, there's a strange way in which I can hide behind her. And thrillers have a more obvious structure that can carry you along when you write. There were times writing *The Winter House* when I felt suddenly stranded. Indeed, halfway through I stopped for several months; I needed to know exactly what Marnie would have done and felt·before I continued writing and for a while she resisted me. With a thriller there's a kind of irresistible momentum that can be immensely comforting. On the other hand, the actual act of writing remains the same. Sean and I never write together. We need to be private and to sink down into that mysterious internal space, the same space I go to when writing alone.

NICCI GERRARD

THINGS WE KNEW WERE TRUE

At sixteen Edie knows things. She knows that her mother is charming and beautiful, that her older sister Stella is the golden girl of the family, and that her father – clumsy, quiet Vic – is loving, gentle, sometimes detached. And she knows she loves Ricky, even if her parents don't approve.

But one autumn evening when Vic fails to return home from work, Edie's world is suddenly turned upside down. Her life is changed forever, the certainties of her childhood destroyed in one terrible moment.

For twenty years Edie wonders about the truth. What really happened to her father? What became of her lost teenage love? When she reunites with her sisters in their mother's house to sift through their childhood belongings, not only is Edie forced to face her unresolved past, she makes a passionate and dangerous attempt to return to it. And, it looks as though the truth of what happened all those years ago will finally be revealed.

NICCI GERRARD

SOLACE

Irene's husband has chosen another lover.

And over time, Adrian nurtures his deceit and with his new lover, Frankie, he finds the courage to leave Irene and their three children.

Irene is, at first, hurt, angry, broken. If it wasn't for the children, she believes her life would come apart. Their agony, and hers, seems almost too much to bear. But as she battles through the daily routine, the promise of a new life gradually emerges.

She discovers a different Irene – not the endlessly selfless, chore-laden wife and mother – but a woman with the possibility of love. And a future that only she can dictate. Would she really want Adrian back, even if he were to leave Frankie and return to her?

'Beguiling, poignant, wonderful' *Sunday Express*

NICCI GERRARD

THE MOMENT YOU WERE GONE

Gaby and Nancy were inseparable when they were young. They had no secrets and believed nothing would break up their friendship, even when each found love – Gaby with Connor, and Nancy with Gaby's brother, Stefan.

Then one day Nancy left Stefan and walked out of all their lives. Gaby has not seen her now for nearly twenty years, and in all that time she has never know where Nancy went or why.

Now long married to Connor, Gaby is preparing to take their only sun Ethan to university for his first term when, quite by chance, she spots Nancy on a television report about a flood in a tiny village in Cornwall. And in a recklessly impulsive moment, she turns up on Nancy's doorstep, unannounced.

Nancy's secret explodes into all their lives, wreaking havoc on long-held assumptions and beliefs, and Gaby is forced to examine her own past in order to try to save what is most precious to her.

'Subtle, poignant and tremendously skilful' *Observer*

NICCI FRENCH

UNTIL IT'S OVER

DEAD. UNLUCKY.

London cycle courier Astrid Bell is bad luck – for other people. First, Astrid's neighbour Peggy Farrell accidentally knocks her off her bike – and not long after is found bludgeoned to death in an alley. Then, a few days later, Astrid is asked to pick up a package – only to find the client slashed to pieces in the hallway.

For the police, it's more than coincidence. For Astrid and her six housemates, it's the beginning of a nightmare: suspicious glances, bitter accusations, fallings out and a growing fear that the worst is yet to come.

Because if it's true that bad luck comes in threes, who will be next to die?

'Reads like lightning' *Observer*

'Another nail-biting thriller' *Daily Express*

NICCI FRENCH

LOSING YOU

Nina Landry has given up city life for the isolated community of Sandling Island, lying off the bleak east coast of England. At night the wind howls. Sometimes they are cut off by the incoming tide. For Nina though it is home. It is safe.

But when Nina's teenage daughter Charlie fails to return from a sleepover on the day they're due to go on holiday, the island becomes a different place altogether. A place of secrets and suspicions. Where no one – friends, neighbours or the police – believes Nina's instinctive fear that her daughter is in terrible danger. Alone, she undergoes a frantic search for Charlie. And as day turns to night, she begins to doubt not just whether they'll leave the island for their holiday – but whether they will ever leave it again.

'You live through every nail-biting minute' *Guardian*

NICCI FRENCH

CATCH ME WHEN I FALL

You're a whirlwind. You're a success.

You're living life on the edge.

But who'll catch you when you fall?

Holly Krauss is a city girl burning the candle at both ends. Despite a comfortable home life, a tough job and friends who admire her, she secretly enjoys taking reckless, dangerous walks on the wild side.

But Holly can't keep those worlds separate forever. Soon enough her secret life bleeds into her safe one and everything spirals out of control. She's making mistakes at home and at work, owes money to the wrong people – and now it seems that someone's stalking her. Could it just be paranoia or is she in very real danger?

And who can you trust when you can no longer trust yourself?

'Highly persuasive ... dextrous and edgy' *Independent*

'Terrific storytelling, I read the book in one sitting' *Herald*

NICCI FRENCH

SECRET SMILE

You have an affair.
You finish it.
You think it's over.
You're dead wrong . . .

Miranda Cotton thinks she's put boyfriend Brendan out of her life for good.
But two weeks later, he's intimately involved with her sister. Soon what began
as an embarrassment becomes threatening – then even more terrifying than a
girl's worst nightmare. Because this time Brendan will stop at nothing to be
part of Miranda's life – even if it means taking it from her . . .

'Creepy, genuinely gripping' *Heat*

'A must read' *Cosmopolitan*

'Nicci French at the top of her game' *Woman & Home*

He just wanted a decent book to read ...

Not too much to ask, is it? It was in 1935 when Allen Lane, Managing Director of Bodley Head Publishers, stood on a platform at Exeter railway station looking for something good to read on his journey back to London. His choice was limited to popular magazines and poor-quality paperbacks – the same choice faced every day by the vast majority of readers, few of whom could afford hardbacks. Lane's disappointment and subsequent anger at the range of books generally available led him to found a company – and change the world.

'We believed in the existence in this country of a vast reading public for intelligent books at a low price, and staked everything on it'
Sir Allen Lane, 1902–1970, founder of Penguin Books

The quality paperback had arrived – and not just in bookshops. Lane was adamant that his Penguins should appear in chain stores and tobacconists, and should cost no more than a packet of cigarettes.

Reading habits (and cigarette prices) have changed since 1935, but Penguin still believes in publishing the best books for everybody to enjoy. We still believe that good design costs no more than bad design, and we still believe that quality books published passionately and responsibly make the world a better place.

So wherever you see the little bird – whether it's on a piece of prize-winning literary fiction or a celebrity autobiography, political tour de force or historical masterpiece, a serial-killer thriller, reference book, world classic or a piece of pure escapism – you can bet that it represents the very best that the genre has to offer.

Whatever you like to read – trust Penguin.

read more
www.penguin.co.uk